The stories contained in *Novel Ideas*
were later expanded into some very special
novels:

Anne McCaffrey's *The Rowan*
"In this sensitive portrayal (expanded from the author's first published story, 'Lady in the Tower') McCaffrey draws a warm and vivid picture of a struggling frontier society." —*Publishers Weekly*

John Varley's *Millennium*
"Powerhouse entertainment." —*Publishers Weekly*

Orson Scott Card's *Ender's Game*
Winner of both the Hugo and Nebula Awards
"*Intense* is the word for *Ender's Game*."
—*The New York Times*

David Brin's *The Postman*
"*The Postman* will keep you engrossed until you've finished the last page." —*Chicago Tribune*

Connie Willis' *Doomsday Book*
Winner of both the Hugo and Nebula Awards
"A stunning novel that encompasses both suffering and hope . . . the best work yet from one of science fiction's best writers." —*The Denver Post*

Nancy Kress' *Beggars in Spain*
Winner of both the Hugo and Nebula Awards
"Superb . . . an exquisite saga of biological advantages."
—*The Denver Post*

NOVEL IDEAS
—SCIENCE FICTION

EDITED BY
Brian M. Thomsen

DAW BOOKS, INC.
DONALD A. WOLLHEIM, FOUNDER
375 Hudson Street, New York, NY 10014

ELIZABETH R. WOLLHEIM
SHEILA E. GILBERT
PUBLISHERS
http://www.dawbooks.com

First Printing, April 2006
1 2 3 4 5 6 7 8 9

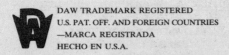

DAW TRADEMARK REGISTERED
U.S. PAT. OFF. AND FOREIGN COUNTRIES
—MARCA REGISTRADA
HECHO EN U.S.A.

PRINTED IN THE U.S.A.

ACKNOWLEDGMENTS

Introduction copyright © 2005 by Brian M. Thomsen.

"Ender's Game" by Orson Scott Card. Copyright © 1977 by Orson Scott Card. First published in *Analog Science Fiction*, August 1977. Reprinted by permission of the author.

"Fire Watch" by Connie Willis. Copyright © 1982 by Connie Willis. First published in *Isaac Asimov's Science Fiction Magazine*, February 1982. Reprinted by permission of the author.

"Air Raid" by John Varley. Copyright © 1977 by John Varley. First published in *Isaac Asimov's Science Fiction Magazine*, Spring 1977. Reprinted by permission of the author.

"Lady in the Tower" by Anne McCaffrey. Copyright © 1959 by Anne McCaffrey. First published in *The Magazine of Fantasy and Science Fiction*, April 1959. Reprinted by permission of the author and her agent, Diana Tyler, MBA Literary Agency.

"The Postman" by David Brin. Copyright © 1982 by David Brin. First published in *Isaac Asimov's Science Fiction Magazine*, November 1982. Reprinted by permission of the author.

"Blood Music" by Greg Bear. Copyright © 1983 by Greg Bear. First published in *Analog Science Fiction*, June 1983. Reprinted by permission of the author.

"Beggars in Spain" by Nancy Kress. Copyright © 1991 by Nancy Kress. First published in *Isaac Asimov's Science Fiction Magazine*, April 1991. Reprinted by permission of the author.

Contents

NOVEL IDEAS
—SCIENCE FICTION

INTRODUCTION

by Brian M. Thomsen

WHERE DO BOOKS come from?
Do authors just spin them on looms of pen, ink, and paper from ideas thread-pulled from the flax of their minds?

Do they spring forth fully grown in chapters and climaxes as Athena did from the head of Zeus?

Perhaps stories function as a tryout for something better, the literary equivalent of the one-act workshop of the play eventually on its way to Broadway or perhaps the first chapter in an ongoing serial whose major plot elements are meant to be resolved later.

Maybe the books evolve in the process of the story production, an idea that needs further elucidation, a character who might want to hang around in the author's domain of creativity for a while longer, or perhaps even a second chance if not to get right, then to do it better.

All of the stories herein are instances where the authors definitely got them right the first time . . . and the second time as well.

They were great SF stories.

They became great SF novels.

'Nuff said.

The stories included herewith, however, gestated into novels in a variety of different manners.

"The Postman" by David Brin reads like a very successful pilot episode for a TV series. It provides the necessary setup of the world situation, introduces us to our hero, and provides him with his signatory handle. It works as a wonderfully self-contained story/episode but also obviously sets the stage for more adventures, the next of which followed shortly thereafter, then leading to the novel that expanded on the previously published materials.

The novel succeeded commercially and garnered numerous critical accolades.

The film based on the book . . . well, the less said the better.

Decades abounded between McCaffrey's "Lady in the Towers" and her novel *The Rowan*. The sheer resilience of the character and the scenario around her demanded that the author revisit her at a later date to allow her a larger stage upon which to shine. This led to several other novels continuing the story, and establishing for McCaffrey yet another world in her literary dynasty, which already included the likes of Pern, Doona, and the Dinosaur Planet.

Likewise the potential of the history-saving objectives of the time travel team/students of Connie Willis' award-winning story "Fire Watch" demanded another journey back for a different mission/objective set at another date, this time in a more fully fleshed-out novel form that begat *Doomsday Book* and *To Say Nothing of the Dog*. Once again, critical accolades to rival those afforded the initial story were repeated for the novels.

John Varley's "Air Raid" and Orson Scott Card's "Ender's Game" demanded more fully fleshed-out versions of the matters initially encapsulated so succinctly in the authors' short-form presentations before each was able to move on with their work. For Varley, the story worked its way through a screenplay treatment before its return to prose fiction in the marvelous novel *Millennium,* while *Ender's Game* the novel occurred as newly discovered prerequisite for the author who first tried to write its sequel *(Speaker for the Dead)* only to find that the initial story itself deserved a fuller treatment. This resulted in the opening of an entire "Ender universe" of stories that included prequel background stories as well as side stories that filled in gaps in the larger stories and shed more light on the importance of the supporting cast and their roles in the universe as newly wrought by Ender's actions.

"Beggars in Spain" by Nancy Kress and "Blood Music" by Greg Bear, when expanded into their eponymous novel forms, allowed the authors to more fully examine the repercussions of the evolutionary acts that provided the thematic inspirations for their award-winning short stories (repercussions which Kress further illuminated over three novels). Indeed, the initial short stories functioned as the setting of the premise and the placement of the tipping point; the novels provided the resultant second act.

Sometimes good things come in small packages.

Sometimes they serve as harbingers of greater things to come.

These stories succeed as both.

ENDER'S GAME

by *Orson Scott Card*

The seeds of the story "Ender's Game" were first planted
when I was sixteen. My brother Bill was in the army, and
I remembered clearly his tales of basic training and officers
candidate school—and why he dropped out of the latter to
remain a noncom throughout his military service. To him,
it made no sense that they would break down a soldier's
initiative and reduce him to blind obedience—as part of the
training that was supposed to make him an effective leader.

That same brother and his then-fiancée (now wife) Laura
Dene Low gave me, as a gift for my sixteenth birthday,
Isaac Asimov's *Foundation* trilogy. I devoured the books and
determined, then and there, that I wanted to write a science
fiction story.

For that, I would need a science fictional idea—which to
me meant something futuristic. My brother's military training came to mind, and I thought: How would they train
young men to be effective as officers and soldiers in space-
based warfare? More specifically, how would they train
them for zero-gravity combat without running the risk of
losing half their trainees to deep-space accidents?

The answer: An enclosed space, a hundred meters cubed,
in which the trainees would dodge obstacles and practice
the kind of close combat that might be required of them in
space. The walls would keep them from drifting off; the use
of laser-activated body armor that would lock as if frozen,

4

simulating injury or death, would allow them to get the experience of combat without casualties.

It was a good idea, that battle room, but it remained as nothing more for several years. When I finally wrote it, a lot more went into the mix than that original idea. But it was the first sci-fi story idea I ever had, and I'm still extrapolating from it even now.

When I did get around to writing "Ender's Game" in 1975, and *Analog* got around to publishing it in 1977, I thought I was done with it. The story did well—it came in second for the Hugo Award and, because of it, I won the John W. Campbell Award for best new writer of science fiction or fantasy. And it continued to be my best-known, most-anthologized, most *popular* story for the next few years.

I was working on an unrelated project, called *Speaker for the Dead*, when it dawned on me that the story would work very powerfully if the hero—who was merely an observer in the first, failed attempts at outlining the book—were Ender Wiggins, many years after the events in the story "Ender's Game." My publisher, Tom Doherty, agreed. And when I found it impossible to write an interesting enough prologue to *Speaker* to account for Ender's passage from the story to the novel, Tom shook hands on the deal that substantially made my career: I would rewrite the story "Ender's Game" into a novel of the same name, and add to it the ending that would bridge the gap between the two books.

But how do you turn a successful short story into a novel? The standard approach, I knew, did not work. You can't start with a story that has a powerful ending, and then glue another hundred thousand words onto the end. With my revision of the story "Mikal's Songbird" into the novel *Songmaster*, I had learned that it is far more effective to start *earlier* than the short story and write most or all of the new material as events leading up to the same climax that the short story had.

Ender's Game thus required that I go back before the beginning of the story, to the time when Ender was picked for Battle School. I gave him a family and siblings who became important to him; I showed something of what was going on in the world, as his left-behind brother and sister became influential in the political conversation on the nets. And I was able to show how Ender learned from good and (mostly) bad commanders before he ever got to be commander of Dragon Army.

Yet the core of the book is still the events that took place in the short story. And the climax is still the same one that the short story records.

"WHATEVER YOUR GRAVITY is when you get to the door, remember—the enemy's gate is *down*. If you step through your own door like you're out for a stroll, you're a big target and you deserve to get hit. With more than a flasher." Ender Wiggins paused and looked over the group. Most were just watching him nervously. A few understanding. A few sullen and resisting.

First day with this army, all fresh from the teacher squads, and Ender had forgotten how young new kids could be. He'd been in it for three years, they'd had six months—nobody over nine years old in the whole bunch. But they were his. At eleven, he was half a year early to be a commander. He'd had a toon of his own and knew a few tricks, but there were forty in his new army. Green. All marksmen with a flasher, all in top shape, or they wouldn't be here—but they were all just as likely as not to get wiped out first time into battle.

"Remember," he went on, "they can't see you till you get through that door. But the second you're out, they'll be on you. So hit that door the way you want to be when they shoot at you. Legs go under you, going straight *down*." He pointed at a sullen kid who looked like he was only seven, the smallest of them all. "Which way is down, greenoh!"

"Toward the enemy door." The answer was quick. It was also surly, as if to say, Yeah, yeah, now get on with the important stuff.

"Name, kid?"

"Bean."

"Get that for size or for brains?"

Bean didn't answer. The rest laughed a little. Ender had chosen right. The kid *was* younger than the rest, must have been advanced because he was sharp. The others didn't like him much, they were happy to see him taken down a little. Like Ender's first commander had taken him down.

"Well, Bean, you're right onto things. Now I tell you this, nobody's gonna get through that door without a good chance of getting hit. A lot of you are going to be turned into cement somewhere. Make sure it's your legs. Right? If only your legs get hit, then only your legs get frozen, and in nullo that's no sweat." Ender turned to one of the dazed ones. "What're legs for? Hmmm?"

Blank stare. Confusion. Stammer.

"Forget it. Guess I'll have to ask Bean here."

"Legs are for pushing off walls." Still bored.

"Thanks, Bean. Get that, everybody?" They all got it, and didn't like getting it from Bean. "Right. You can't *see* with legs, you can't *shoot* with legs, and most of the time they just get in the way. If they get frozen sticking straight out you've turned yourself into a blimp. No way to hide. So how do legs go?"

A few answered this time, to prove that Bean wasn't the only one who knew anything. "Under you. Tucked up under."

"Right. A shield. You're kneeling on a shield, and the shield is your own legs. And there's a trick to the suits. Even when your legs are flashed you can *still* kick off. I've never seen anybody do it but me—but you're all gonna learn it."

Ender Wiggins turned on his flasher. It glowed faintly green in his hand. Then he let himself rise in the weightless workout room, pulled his legs under him as though he were kneeling, and flashed both of them. Immediately his suit stiffened at the knees and ankles, so that he couldn't bend at all.

"Okay, I'm frozen, see?"

He was floating a meter above them. They all looked up at him, puzzled. He leaned back and caught one of the handholds on the wall behind him, and pulled himself flush against the wall.

"I'm stuck at a wall. If I had legs, I'd use legs, and string myself out like a string *bean,* right?"

They laughed.

"But I don't have legs, and that's *better,* got it? Because of this." Ender jackknifed at the waist, then straightened out violently. He was across the workout room in only a moment. From the other side he called to them. "Got that? I didn't use hands, so I still had use of my flasher. *And* I didn't have my legs floating five feet behind me. Now watch it again."

He repeated the jackknife, and caught a handhold on the wall near them. "Now, I don't just want you to do that when they've flashed your legs. I want you to do that when you've still got legs, because it's better. And because they'll never be expecting it. All right now, everybody up in the air and kneeling."

Most were up in a few seconds. Ender flashed the stragglers, and they dangled, helplessly frozen, while the others laughed. "When I give an order, you move. Got it? When we're at a door and they clear it, I'll be giving you orders in two seconds, as soon as I see the setup. And when I give the order you better be out there, because whoever's out there first is going to win, unless he's a fool. I'm not. And you better not be, or I'll have you back in the teacher squads." He saw more than a few of them gulp, and the frozen ones looked at him with fear. "You guys who are hanging there. You watch. You'll thaw out in about fifteen minutes, and let's see if you can catch up to the others."

For the next half hour Ender had them jackknifing off walls. He called a stop when he saw that they all had the basic idea. They were a good group, maybe. They'd get better.

"Now you're warmed up," he said to them, "we'll start working."

Ender was the last one out after practice, since he stayed to help some of the slower ones improve on technique. They'd had good teachers, but like all armies they were uneven, and some of them could be a real drawback in battle. Their first battle might be weeks away. It might be tomorrow. A schedule was never printed. The commander just woke up and found a note by his bunk, giving him the time of his battle and the name of his opponent. So for the first while he was going to drive his boys until they were in top shape—all of them. Ready for anything, at any time. Strategy was nice, but it was worth nothing if the soldiers couldn't hold up under the strain.

He turned the corner into the residence wing and found himself face to face with Bean, the seven-year-old he had picked on all through practice that day. Problems. Ender didn't want problems right now.

"Ho, Bean."

"Ho, Ender."

Pause.

"Sir," Ender said softly.

"We're not on duty."

"In my army, Bean, we're always on duty." Ender brushed past him.

Bean's high voice piped up behind him. "I know what you're doing, Ender, sir, and I'm warning you."

Ender turned slowly and looked at him. "Warning me?"

"I'm the best man you've got. But I'd better be treated like it."

"Or what?" Ender smiled menacingly.

"Or I'll be the worst man you've got. One or the other."

"And what do you want? Love and kisses?" Ender was getting angry now.

Bean was unworried. "I want a toon."

Ender walked back to him and stood looking down into his eyes. "I'll give a toon," he said, "to the boys who prove they're worth something. They've got to be good soldiers, they've got to know how to take orders, they've got to be able to think for themselves in a pinch, and they've got to be able to keep respect. That's how

I got to be a commander. That's how you'll get to be a toon leader. Got it?"

Bean smiled. "That's fair. *If* you actually work that way, I'll be a toon leader in a month."

Ender reached down and grabbed the front of his uniform and shoved him into the wall. "When I say I work a certain way, Bean, then that's the way I work."

Bean just smiled. Ender let go of him and walked away, and didn't look back. He was sure, without looking, that Bean was still watching, still smiling, still just a little contemptuous. He might make a good toon leader at that. Ender would keep an eye on him.

Captain Graff, six foot two and a little chubby, stroked his belly as he leaned back in his chair. Across his desk sat Lieutenant Anderson, who was earnestly pointing out high points on a chart.

"Here it is, Captain," Anderson said. "Ender's already got them doing a tactic that's going to throw off everyone who meets it. Doubled their speed."

Graff nodded.

"And you know his test scores. He thinks well, too."

Graff smiled. "All true, all true, Anderson, he's a fine student, shows real promise."

They waited.

Graff sighed. "So what do you want me to do?"

"Ender's the one. He's got to be."

"He'll never be ready in time, Lieutenant. He's eleven, for heaven's sake, man, what do you want, a miracle?"

"I want him into battles, every day starting tomorrow. I want him to have a year's worth of battles in a month."

Graff shook his head. "That would have his army in the hospital."

"No, sir. He's getting them into form. And we need Ender."

"Correction, Lieutenant. We need somebody. You think it's Ender."

"All right, I think it's Ender. Which of the commanders if it isn't him?"

"I don't know, Lieutenant." Graff ran his hands over

his slightly fuzzy bald head. "These are children, Anderson. Do you realize that? Ender's army is nine years old. Are we going to put them against the older kids? Are we going to put them through hell for a month like that?"

Lieutenant Anderson leaned even farther over Graff's desk.

"Ender's test scores, Captain!"

"I've seen his bloody test scores! I've watched him in battle, I've listened to tapes of his training sessions. I've watched his sleep patterns, I've heard tapes of his conversations in the corridors and in the bathrooms, I'm more aware of Ender Wiggins than you could possibly imagine! And against all the arguments, against his obvious qualities, I'm weighing one thing. I have this picture of Ender a year from now, if you have your way. I see him completely useless, worn down, a failure, because he was pushed farther than he or any living person could go. But it doesn't weigh enough, does it, Lieutenant, because there's a war on, and our best talent is gone, and the biggest battles are ahead. So give Ender a battle every day this week. And then bring me a report."

Anderson stood and saluted. "Thank you, sir."

He had almost reached the door when Graff called his name. He turned and faced the captain.

"Anderson," Captain Graff said. "Have you been outside, lately I mean?"

"Not since last leave, six months ago."

"I didn't think so. Not that it makes any difference. But have you ever been to Beaman Park, there in the city? Hmm? Beautiful park. Trees. Grass. No nullo, no battles, no worries. Do you know what else there is in Beaman Park?"

"What, sir?" Lieutenant Anderson asked.

"Children," Graff answered.

"Of course, children," said Anderson.

"I mean children. I mean kids who get up in the morning when their mothers call them and they go to school and then in the afternoons they go to Beaman Park and play. They're happy, they smile a lot, they laugh, they have fun. Hmmm?"

"I'm sure they do, sir."

"Is that all you can say, Anderson?"

Anderson cleared his throat. "It's good for children to have fun, I think, sir. I know I did when I was a boy. But right now the world needs soldiers. And this is the way to get them."

Graff nodded and closed his eyes. "Oh, indeed, you're right, by statistical proof and by all the important theories, and dammit they work and the system is right but all the same Ender's older than I am. He's not a child. He's barely a person."

"If that's true, sir, then at least we all know that Ender is making it possible for the others of his age to be playing in the park."

"And Jesus died to save all men, of course." Graff sat up and looked at Anderson almost sadly. "But we're the ones," Graff said, "we're the ones who are driving in the nails."

Ender Wiggins lay on his bed staring at the ceiling. He never slept more than five hours a night—but the lights went off at 2200 and didn't come on again until 0600. So he stared at the ceiling and thought.

He'd had his army for three and a half weeks. Dragon Army. The name was assigned, and it wasn't a lucky one. Oh, the charts said that about nine years ago a Dragon Army had done fairly well. But for the next six years the name had been attached to inferior armies, and finally, because of the superstition that was beginning to play about the name, Dragon Army was retired. Until now. And now, Ender thought, smiling, Dragon Army was going to take them by surprise.

The door opened quietly. Ender did not turn his head. Someone stepped softly into his room, then left with the sound of the door shutting. When soft steps died away Ender rolled over and saw a white slip of paper lying on the floor. He reached down and picked it up.

"Dragon Army against Rabbit Army, Ender Wiggins and Carn Carby, 0700."

The first battle. Ender got out of bed and quickly dressed. He went rapidly to the rooms of each of his toon leaders and told them to rouse their boys. In five minutes they were all gathered in the corridor, sleepy and slow. Ender spoke softly.

"First battle, 0700 against Rabbit Army. I've fought them twice before but they've got a new commander. Never heard of him. They're an older group, though, and I know a few of their old tricks. Now wake up. Run, doublefast, warmup in workroom three."

For an hour and a half they worked out, with three mock battles and calisthenics in the corridor out of the nullo. Then for fifteen minutes they all lay up in the air, totally relaxing in the weightlessness. At 0650 Ender roused them and they hurried into the corridor. Ender led them down the corridor, running again, and occasionally leaping to touch a light panel on the ceiling. The boys all touched the same light panel. And at 0658 they reached their gate to the battleroom.

The members of toons C and D grabbed the first eight handholds in the ceiling of the corridor. Toons A, B, and E crouched on the floor. Ender hooked his feet into two handholds in the middle of the ceiling, so he was out of everyone's way.

"Which way is the enemy's door?" he hissed.

"Down! they whispered back, and laughed.

"Flashers on." The boxes in their hands glowed green. They waited for a few seconds more, and then the gray wall in front of them disappeared and the battleroom was visible.

Ender sized it up immediately. The familiar open grid of most early games, like the monkey bars at the park, with seven or eight boxes scattered through the grid. They called the boxes *stars*. There were enough of them, and in forward enough positions, that they were worth going for. Ender decided this in a second, and he hissed, "Spread to near stars. E hold!"

The four groups in the corners plunged through the forcefield at the doorway and fell down into the battleroom. Before the enemy even appeared through the opposite gate Ender's army had spread from the door to the nearest stars.

Then the enemy soldiers came through the door. From their stance Ender knew they had been in a different gravity, and didn't know enough to disorient themselves from it. They came through standing up, their entire bodies spread and defenseless.

"Kill 'em, E!" Ender hissed, and threw himself out the door knees first, with his flasher between his legs and firing. While Ender's group flew across the room the rest of Dragon Army lay down a protecting fire, so that E group reached a forward position with only one boy frozen completely, though they had all lost the use of their legs—which didn't impair them in the least. There was a lull as Ender and his opponent, Carn Carnby, assessed their positions. Aside from Rabbit Army's losses at the gate, there had been few casualties, and both armies were near full strength. But Carn had no originality—he was in a four-corner spread that any five-year-old in the teacher squads might have thought of. And Ender knew how to defeat it.

He called out, loudly, "E covers A, C down. B, D angle east wall." Under E toon's cover, B and D toons lunged away from their stars. While they were still exposed, A and C toons left their stars and drifted toward the near wall. They reached it together, and together jackknifed off the wall. At double the normal speed they appeared behind the enemy's stars, and opened fire. In a few seconds the battle was over, with the enemy almost entirely frozen, including the commander, and the rest scattered to the corners. For the next five minutes, in squads of four, Dragon Army cleaned out the dark corners of the battleroom and shepherded the enemy into the center, where their bodies, frozen at impossible angles, jostled each other. Then Ender took three of his boys to the enemy gate and went through the formality of reversing the one-way field by simultaneously touching a Dragon Army helmet at each corner. Then Ender as-

sembled his army in vertical files near the knot of frozen
Rabbit Army soldiers.

Only three of Dragon Army's soldiers were immobile.
Their victory margin—38 to 0—was ridiculously high,
and Ender began to laugh. Dragon Army joined him,
laughing long and loud. They were still laughing when
Lieutenant Anderson and Lieutenant Morris came in
from the teachergate at the south end of the battleroom.

Lieutenant Anderson kept his face stiff and unsmiling,
but Ender saw him wink as he held out his hand and
offered the stiff, formal congratulations that were ritually
given to the victor in the game.

Morris found Carn Carby and unfroze him, and the
thirteen-year-old came and presented himself to Ender, who
laughed without malice and held out his hand. Carn graciously took Ender's hand and bowed his head over it.
It was that or be flashed again.

Lieutenant Anderson dismissed Dragon Army, and
they silently left the battleroom through the enemy's
door—again part of the ritual. A light was blinking on
the north side of the square door, indicating where the
gravity was in that corridor. Ender, leading his soldiers,
changed his orientation and went through the forcefield
and into gravity on his feet. His army followed him at a
brisk run back to the workroom. When they got there
they formed up into squads, and Ender hung in the air,
watching them.

"Good first battle," he said, which was excuse enough
for a cheer, which he quieted. "Dragon Army did all
right against Rabbits. But the enemy isn't always going
to be that bad. And if that had been a good army we
would have been smashed. We still would have won, but
we would have been smashed. Now let me see B and D
toons out here. Your takeoff from the stars was way too
slow. If Rabbit Army knew how to aim a flasher, you all
would have been frozen solid before A and C even got
to the wall."

They worked out for the rest of the day.

That night Ender went for the first time to the commanders' mess hall. No one was allowed there until he had won at least one battle, and Ender was the youngest commander ever to make it. There was no great stir when he came in. But when some of the other boys saw the Dragon on his breast pocket, they stared at him openly, and by the time he got his tray and sat at an empty table, the entire room was silent, with the other commanders watching him. Intensely self-conscious, Ender wondered how they all knew, and why they all looked so hostile.

Then he looked above the door he had just come through. There was a huge scoreboard across the entire wall. It showed the win/loss record for the commander of every army; that day's battles were lit in red. Only four of them. The other three winners had barely made it—the best of them had only two men whole and eleven mobile at the end of the game. Dragon Army's score of thirty-eight mobile was embarrassingly better.

Other new commanders had been admitted to the commanders' mess hall with cheers and congratulations. Other new commanders hadn't won thirty-eight to zero.

Ender looked for Rabbit Army on the scoreboard. He was surprised to find that Carn Carby's score to date was eight wins and three losses. Was he that good? Or had he only fought against inferior armies? Whichever, there was still a zero in Carn's mobile and whole columns, and Ender looked down from the scoreboard grinning. No one smiled back, and Ender knew that they were afraid of him, which meant that they would hate him, which meant that anyone who went into battle against Dragon Army would be scared and angry and less competent. Ender looked for Carn Carby in the crowd, and found him not too far away. He stared at Carby until one of the other boys nudged the Rabbit commander and pointed to Ender. Ender smiled again and waved slightly. Carby turned red, and Ender, satisfied, leaned over his dinner and began to eat.

At the end of the week Dragon Army had fought seven battles in seven days. The score stood 7 wins and

0 losses. Ender had never had more than five boys frozen in any game. It was no longer possible for the other commanders to ignore Ender. A few of them sat with him and quietly conversed about game strategies that Ender's opponents had used. Other much larger groups were talking with the commanders that Ender had defeated, trying to find out what Ender had done to beat them.

In the middle of the meal the teacher door opened and the groups fell silent as Lieutenant Anderson stepped in and looked over the group. When he located Ender he strode quickly across the room and whispered in Ender's ear. Ender nodded, finished his glass of water, and left with the lieutenant. On the way out, Anderson handed a slip of paper to one of the older boys. The room became very noisy with conversation as Anderson and Ender left.

Ender was escorted down corridors he had never seen before. They didn't have the blue glow of the soldier corridors. Most were wood paneled, and the floors were carpeted. The doors were wood, with nameplates on them, and they stopped at one that said "Captain Graff, supervisor." Anderson knocked softly, and a low voice said, "Come in."

They went in. Captain Graff was seated behind a desk, his hands folded across his pot belly. He nodded, and Anderson sat. Ender also sat down. Graff cleared his throat and spoke.

"Seven days since your first battle, Ender."

Ender did not reply.

"Won seven battles, one every day."

Ender nodded.

"Scores unusually high, too."

Ender blinked.

"Why?" Graff asked him.

Ender glanced at Anderson, and then spoke to the captain behind the desk. "Two new tactics, sir. Legs doubled up as a shield, so that a flash doesn't immobilize. Jackknife takeoffs from the walls. Superior strategy, as Lieutenant Anderson taught, think places, not spaces.

Five toons of eight instead of four of ten. Incompetent
opponents. Excellent toon leaders, good soldiers."

Graff looked at Ender without expression. Waiting for
what, Ender wondered. Lieutenant Anderson spoke up.

"Ender, what's the condition of your army?"

Do they want me to ask for relief? Not a chance, he
decided. "A little tired, in peak condition, morale high,
learning fast. Anxious for the next battle."

Anderson looked at Graff. Graff shrugged slightly and
turned to Ender.

"Is there anything you want to know?"

Ender held his hands loosely in his lap. "When are
you going to put us up against a good army?"

Graff's laughter rang in the room, and when it stopped,
Graff handed a piece of paper to Ender.

"Now," the captain said, and Ender read the paper:
"Dragon Army against Leopard Army, Ender Wiggins
and Pol Slattery, 2000."

Ender looked up at Captain Graff. "That's ten minutes
from now, sir."

Graff smiled. "Better hurry, then, boy."

As Ender left he realized Pol Slattery was the boy who
had been handed his orders as Ender left the mess hall.

He got to his army five minutes later. Three toon leaders were already undressed and lying naked on their
beds. He sent them all flying down the corridors to rouse
their toons, and gathered up their suits himself. When
all his boys were assembled in the corridor, most of them
still getting dressed, Ender spoke to them.

"This one's hot and there's no time. We'll be late to
the door, and the enemy'll be deployed right outside our
gate. Ambush, and I've never heard of it happening before. So we'll take our time at the door. A and B toons,
keep your belts loose, and give your flashers to the leaders and seconds of the other toons."

Puzzled, his soldiers complied. By then all were
dressed, and Ender led them at a trot to the gate. When
they reached it the forcefield was already on one-way,
and some of his soldiers were panting. They had had one
battle that day and a full workout. They were tired.

Ender stopped at the entrance and looked at the placement of the enemy soldiers. Some of them were grouped not more than twenty feet out from the gate. There was no grid, there were no stars. A big empty space. Where were most of the enemy soldiers? There should have been thirty more.

"They're flat against this wall," Ender said, "where we can't see them."

He took A and B toons and made them kneel, their hands on their hips. Then he flashed them, so that their bodies were frozen rigid.

"You're shields," Ender said, and then had boys from C and D kneel on their legs and hook both arms under the frozen boys' belts. Each boy was holding two flashers. Then Ender and the members of E toon picked up the duos, three at a time, and threw them out the door.

Of course, the enemy opened fire immediately. But they mainly hit the boys who were already flashed, and in a few moments pandemonium broke out in the battleroom. All the soldiers of Leopard Army were easy targets as they lay pressed flat against the wall or floated, unprotected, in the middle of the battleroom; and Ender's soldiers, armed with two flashers each, carved them up easily. Pol Slattery reacted quickly, ordering his men away from the wall, but not quickly enough—only a few were able to move, and they were flashed before they could get a quarter of the way across the battleroom.

When the battle was over Dragon Army had only twelve boys whole, the lowest score they had ever had. But Ender was satisfied. And during the ritual of surrender Pol Slattery broke form by shaking hands and asking, "Why did you wait so long getting out of the gate?"

Ender glanced at Anderson, who was floating nearby. "I was informed late," he said. "It was an ambush."

Slattery grinned, and gripped Ender's hand again. "Good game."

Ender didn't smile at Anderson this time. He knew that now the games would be arranged against him, to even up the odds. He didn't like it.

* * *

It was 2150, nearly time for lights out, when Ender knocked at the door of the room shared by Bean and three other soldiers. One of the others opened the door, then stepped back and held it wide. Ender stood for a moment, then asked if he could come in. They answered, of course, of course, come in, and he walked to the upper bunk, where Bean had set down his book and was leaning on one elbow to look at Ender.

"Bean, can you give me twenty minutes?"

"Near lights out," Bean answered.

"My room," Ender answered. "I'll cover for you."

Bean sat up and slid off his bed. Together he and Ender padded silently down the corridor to Ender's room. Bean entered first, and Ender closed the door behind them.

"Sit down," Ender said, and they both sat on the edge of the bed, looking at each other.

"Remember four weeks ago, Bean? When you told me to make you a toon leader?"

"Yeah."

"I've made five toon leaders since then, haven't I? And none of them was you."

Bean looked at him calmly.

"Was I right?" Ender asked.

"Yes, sir," Bean answered.

Ender nodded. "How have you done in these battles?"

Bean cocked his head to one side. "I've never been immobilized, sir, and I've immobilized forty-three of the enemy. I've obeyed orders quickly, and I've commanded a squad in mop-up and never lost a soldier."

"Then you'll understand this." Ender paused, then decided to back up and say something else first.

"You know you're early, Bean, by a good half year. I was, too, and I've been made a commander six months early. Now they've put me into battles after only three weeks of training with my army. They've given me eight battles in seven days. I've already had more battles than boys who were made commander four months ago. I've won more battles than many who've been commanders for a year. And then tonight. You know what happened tonight."

Bean nodded. "They told you late."

"I don't know what the teachers are doing. But my army is getting tired, and I'm getting tired, and now they're changing the rules of the game. You see, Bean, I've looked in the old charts. No one has ever destroyed so many enemies and kept so many of his own soldiers whole in the history of the game. I'm unique—and I'm getting unique treatment."

Bean smiled. "You're the best, Ender."

Ender shook his head. "Maybe. But it was no accident that I got the soldiers I got. My worst soldier could be a toon leader in another army. I've got the best. They've loaded things my way—but now they're loading it all against me. I don't know why. But I know I have to be ready for it. I need your help."

"Why mine?"

"Because even though there are some better soldiers than you in Dragon Army—not many, but some—there's nobody who can think better and faster than you." Bean said nothing. They both knew it was true.

Ender continued, "I need to be ready, but I can't re-train the whole army. So I'm going to cut every toon down by one, including you. With four others you'll be a special squad under me. And you'll learn to do some new things. Most of the time you'll be in the regular toons just like you are now. But when I need you. See?"

Bean smiled and nodded. "That's right, that's good, can I pick them myself?"

"One from each toon except your own, and you can't take any toon leaders."

"What do you want us to do?"

"Bean, I don't know. I don't know what they'll throw at us. What would you do if suddenly our flashers didn't work, and the enemy's did? What would you do if we had to face two armies at once? The only thing I know is—there may be a game where we don't even try for score. Where we just go for the enemy's gate. That's when the battle is technically won—four helmets at the corners of the gate. I want you ready to do that any time I call for it. Got it? You take them for two hours a day during regular workout. Then you and I and your soldiers, we'll work at night after dinner."

"We'll get tired."

"I have a feeling we don't know what tired is." Ender reached out and took Bean's hand, and gripped it. "Even when it's rigged against us, Bean. We'll win."

Bean left in silence and padded down the corridor.

Dragon Army wasn't the only army working out after hours now. The other commanders had finally realized they had some catching up to do. From early morning to lights out soldiers all over Training and Command Center, none of them over fourteen years old, were learning to jackknife off walls and use each other as living shields.

But while other commanders mastered the techniques that Ender had used to defeat them, Ender and Bean worked on solutions to problems that had never come up.

There were still battles every day, but for a while they were normal, with grids and stars and sudden plunges through the gate. And after the battles, Ender and Bean and four other soldiers would leave the main group and practice strange maneuvers. Attacks without flashers, using feet to physically disarm or disorient an enemy. Using four frozen soldiers to reverse the enemy's gate in less than two seconds. And one day Bean came to workout with a 300-meter cord.

"What's that for?"

"I don't know yet." Absently Bean spun one end of the cord. It wasn't more than an eighth of an inch thick, but it could have lifted ten adults without breaking.

"Where did you get it?"

"Commissary. They asked what for. I said to practice tying knots."

Bean tied a loop in the end of the rope and slid it over his shoulders.

"Here, you two, hang on to the wall here. Now don't

let go of the rope. Give me about fifty yards of slack."
They complied, and Bean moved about ten feet from
them along the wall. As soon as he was sure they were
ready, he jackknifed off the wall and flew straight out,
fifty yards. Then the rope snapped taut. It was so fine
that it was virtually invisible, but it was strong enough
to force Bean to veer off at almost a right angle. It happened so suddenly that he had inscribed a perfect arc
and hit the wall hard before most of the other soldiers
knew what had happened. Bean did a perfect rebound
and drifted quickly back to where Ender and the others
waited for him.

Many of the soldiers in the five regular squads hadn't
noticed the rope, and were demanding to know how it
was done. It was impossible to change direction that
abruptly in nullo. Bean just laughed.

"Wait till the next game without a grid! They'll never
know what hit them."

They never did. The next game was only two hours
later, but Bean and two others had become pretty good
at aiming and shooting while they flew at ridiculous
speeds at the end of the rope. The slip of paper was
delivered, and Dragon Army trotted off to the gate, to
battle with Griffin Army. Bean coiled the rope all the
way.

When the gate opened, all they could see was a large
brown star only fifteen feet away, completely blocking
their view of the enemy's gate.

Ender didn't pause. "Bean, give yourself fifty feet of
rope and go around the star." Bean and his four soldiers
dropped through the gate and in a moment Bean was
launched sideways away from the star. The rope snapped
taut, and Bean flew forward. As the rope was stopped
by each edge of the star in turn, his arc became tighter
and his speed greater, until when he hit the wall only a
few feet away from the gate, he was barely able to control his rebound to end up behind the star. But he immediately moved all his arms and legs so that those waiting
inside the gate would know that the enemy hadn't flashed
him anywhere.

Ender dropped through the gate, and Bean quickly told him how Griffin Army was situated. "They've got two squares of stars, all the way around the gate. All their soldiers are under cover, and there's no way to hit any of them until we're clear to the bottom wall. Even with shields, we'd get there at half strength and we wouldn't have a chance."

"They moving?" Ender asked.

"Do they need to?"

"I would." Ender thought for a moment. "This one's tough. We'll go for the gate, Bean."

Griffin Army began to call out to them.

"Hey, is anybody there!"

"Wake up, there's a war on!"

"We wanna join the picnic!"

They were still calling when Ender's army came out from behind their star with a shield of fourteen frozen soldiers. William Bee, Griffin Army's commander, waited patiently as the screen approached, his men waiting at the fringes of their stars for the moment when whatever was behind the screen became visible. About ten yards away the screen suddenly exploded as the soldiers behind it shoved the screen north. The momentum carried them south twice as fast, and at the same moment the rest of Dragon Army burst from behind their star at the opposite end of the room, firing rapidly.

William Bee's boys joined battle immediately, of course, but William Bee was far more interested in what had been left behind when the shield disappeared. A formation of four frozen Dragon Army soldiers was moving headfirst toward the Griffin Army gate, held together by another frozen soldier whose feet and hands were hooked through their belts. A sixth soldier hung to his waist and trailed like the tail of a kite. Griffin Army was winning the battle easily, and William Bee concentrated on the formation as it approached the gate. Suddenly the soldier trailing in back moved—he wasn't frozen at all! And even though William Bee flashed him immediately, the damage was done. The formation drifted to the Griffin Army gate, and their helmets touched all four corners simultaneously. A buzzer sounded, the gate reversed, and the frozen soldier in the middle was carried by momentum right through the gate. All the flashers stopped working, and the game was over.

The teachergate opened and Lieutenant Anderson came in. Anderson stopped himself with a slight movement on his hands when he reached the center of the battleroom. "Ender," he called, breaking protocol. One of the frozen Dragon soldiers near the south wall tried to call through jaws that were clamped shut by the suit. Anderson drifted to him and unfroze him.

Ender was smiling.

"I beat you again, sir," Ender said.

Anderson didn't smile. "That's nonsense, Ender," Anderson said softly. "Your battle was with William Bee of Griffin Army."

Ender raised an eyebrow.

"After that maneuver," Anderson said, "the rules are being revised to require that all of the enemy's soldiers must be immobilized before the gate can be reversed."

"That's all right," Ender said. "It could only work once, anyway." Anderson nodded, and was turning away when Ender added, "Is there going to be a new rule that armies be given equal positions to fight from?"

Anderson turned back around. "If you're in one of the positions, Ender, you can hardly call them equal, whatever they are."

William Bee counted carefully and wondered how in the world he had lost when not one of his soldiers had been flashed and only four of Ender's soldiers were even mobile.

And that night as Ender came into the commanders' mess hall, he was greeted with applause and cheers, and his table was crowded with respectful commanders, many of them two or three years older than he was. He was friendly, but while he ate he wondered what the teachers would do to him in his next battle. He didn't need to worry. His next two battles were easy victories, and after that he never saw the battleroom again.

*   *   *

It was 2100 and Ender was a little irritated to hear someone knock at his door. His army was exhausted, and he had ordered them all to be in bed after 2030. The last two days had been regular battles, and Ender was expecting the worst in the morning.

It was Bean. He came in sheepishly, and saluted.

Ender returned his salute and snapped, "Bean, I wanted everybody in bed."

Bean nodded but didn't leave. Ender considered ordering him out. But as he looked at Bean it occurred to him for the first time in weeks just how young Bean was. He had turned eight a week before, and he was still small and—no, Ender thought, he wasn't young. Nobody was young. Bean had been in battle, and with a whole army depending on him he had come through and won. And even though he was small, Ender could never think of him as young again.

Ender shrugged and Bean came over and sat on the edge of the bed. The younger boy looked at his hands for a while, and finally Ender grew impatient and asked, "Well, what is it?"

"I'm transferred. Got orders just a few minutes ago."

Ender closed his eyes for a moment. "I knew they'd pull something new. Now they're taking—where are you going?"

"Rabbit Army."

"How can they put you under an idiot like Carn Carby!"

"Carn was graduated. Support squads."

Ender looked up. "Well, who's commanding Rabbit then?"

Bean held his hands out helplessly.

"Me," he said.

Ender nodded, and then smiled. "Of course. After all, you're only four years younger than the regular age."

"It isn't funny," Bean said. "I don't know what's going on here. First all the changes in the game. And now this. I wasn't the only one transferred, either, Ender. Ren, Peder, Brian, Wins, Younger. All commanders now."

Ender stood up angrily and strode to the wall. "Every

damn toon leader I've got!" he said, and whirled to face Bean. "If they're going to break up my army, Bean, why did they bother making me a commander at all?"

Bean shook his head. "I don't know. You're the best, Ender. Nobody's ever done what you've done. Nineteen battles in fifteen days, sir, and you won every one of them, no matter what they did to you."

"And now you and the others are commanders. You know every trick I've got, I trained you, and who am I supposed to replace you with? Are they going to stick me with six greenohs?"

"It stinks, Ender, but you know that if they gave you five crippled midgets and armed you with a roll of toilet paper you'd win."

They both laughed, and then they noticed that the door was open.

Lieutenant Anderson stepped in. He was followed by Captain Graff.

"Ender Wiggins," Graff said, holding his hands across his stomach.

"Yes, sir," Ender answered.

"Orders."

Anderson extended a slip of paper. Ender read it quickly, then crumpled it, still looking at the air where the paper had been. After a few moments he asked, "Can I tell my army?"

"They'll find out," Graff answered. "It's better not to talk to them after orders. It makes it easier."

"For you or for me?" Ender asked. He didn't wait for an answer. He turned quickly to Bean, took his hand for a moment, and then headed for the door.

"Wait," Bean said. "Where are you going? Tactical or Support School?"

"Command School," Ender answered, and then he was gone and Anderson closed the door.

Command School, Bean thought. Nobody went to Command School until they had gone through three years of Tactical. But then, nobody went to Tactical until they had been through at least five years of Battle School. Ender had only had three.

The system was breaking up. No doubt about it, Bean thought. Either somebody at the top was going crazy, or something was going wrong with the war—the real war, the one they were training to fight in. Why else would they break down the training system, advance somebody—even somebody as good as Ender—straight to Command School? Why else would they ever have an eight-year-old greenoh like Bean command an army?

Bean wondered about it for a long time, and then he finally lay down on Ender's bed and realized that he'd never see Ender again, probably. For some reason that made him want to cry. But he didn't cry, of course. Training in the preschools had taught him how to force down emotions like that. He remembered how his first teacher, when he was three, would have been upset to see his lip quivering and his eyes full of tears.

Bean went through the relaxing routine until he didn't feel like crying anymore. Then he drifted off to sleep. His hand was near his mouth. It lay on his pillow hesitantly, as if Bean couldn't decide whether to bite his nails or suck on his fingertips. His forehead was creased and furrowed. His breathing was quick and light. He was a soldier, and if anyone had asked him what he wanted to be when he grew up, he wouldn't have known what they meant.

There's a war on, they said, and that was excuse enough for all the hurry in the world. They said it like a password and flashed a little card at every ticket counter and customs check and guard station. It got them to the head of every line.

Ender Wiggins was rushed from place to place so quickly he had no time to examine anything. But he did see trees for the first time. He saw men who were not in uniform. He saw women. He saw strange animals that didn't speak, but that followed docilely behind women and small children. He saw suitcases and conveyor belts and signs that said words he had never heard of. He would have asked someone what the words meant, except that purpose and authority surrounded him in the persons of four very high officers who never spoke to each other and never spoke to him.

Ender Wiggins was a stranger to the world he was being trained to save. He did not remember ever leaving Battle School before. His earliest memories were of childish war games under the direction of a teacher, of meals with other boys in the gray and green uniforms of the armed forces of his world. He did not know that the gray represented the sky and the green represented the great forests of his planet. All he knew of the world was from vague references to "outside."

And before he could make any sense of the strange world he was seeing for the first time, they enclosed him again within the shell of the military, where nobody had to say There's a war on anymore because no one within the shell of the military forgot it for a single instant of a single day.

They put him in a spaceship and launched him to a large artificial satellite that circled the world.

This space station was called Command School. It held the ansible.

On his first day Ender Wiggins was taught about the ansible and what it meant to warfare. It meant that even though the starships of today's battles were launched a hundred years ago, the commanders of the starships were men of today, who used the ansible to send messages to the computers and the few men on each ship. The ansible sent words as they were spoken, orders as they were made. Battleplans as they were fought. Light was a pedestrian.

For two months Ender Wiggins didn't meet a single person. They came to him namelessly, taught him what they knew, and left him to other teachers. He had no time to miss his friends at Battle School. He only had time to learn how to operate the simulator, which flashed battle patterns around him as if he were in a starship at the center of the battle. How to command mock ships in mock battle by manipulating the keys on the simulator and speaking words into the ansible. How to recognize instantly every enemy ship and the weapons it carried by the pattern that the simulator showed. How to transfer all that he learned in the nullo battles at Battle School to the starship battles at Command School.

He had thought the game was taken seriously before. Here they hurried him through every step, were angry and worried beyond reason every time he forgot something or made a mistake. But he worked as he had always worked, and learned as he had always learned. After a while he didn't make any more mistakes. He used the simulator as if it were a part of himself. Then they stopped being worried and gave him a teacher.

Maezr Rackham was sitting cross-legged on the floor when Ender awoke. He said nothing as Ender got up and showered and dressed, and Ender did not bother to ask him anything. He had long since learned that when something unusual was going on, he would often find out more information faster by waiting than by asking.

Maezr still hadn't spoken when Ender was ready and went to the door to leave the room. The door didn't open. Ender turned to face the man sitting on the floor. Maezr was at least forty, which made him the oldest man Ender had ever seen close up. He had a day's growth of black and white whiskers that grizzled his face only slightly less than his close-cut hair. His face sagged a little and his eyes were surrounded by creases and lines. He looked at Ender without interest.

Ender turned back to the door and tried again to open it.

"All right," he said, giving up. "Why's the door locked?"

Maezr continued to look at him blankly.

Ender became impatient. "I'm going to be late. If I'm not supposed to be there until later, then tell me so I can go back to bed." No answer. "Is it a guessing game?" Ender asked. No answer. Ender decided that maybe the man was trying to make him angry, so he went through a relaxing exercise as he leaned on the door, and soon he was calm again. Maezr didn't take his eyes off Ender.

For the next two hours the silence endured, Maezr watching Ender constantly, Ender trying to pretend he didn't notice the old man. The boy became more and more nervous, and finally ended up walking from one end of the room to the other in a sporadic pattern.

He walked by Maezr as he had several times before, and Maezr's hand shot out and pushed Ender's left leg into his right in the middle of a step. Ender fell flat on the floor.

He leaped to his feet immediately, furious. He found Maezr sitting calmly, cross-legged, as if he had never moved. Ender stood poised to fight. But the other's immobility made it impossible for Ender to attack, and he found himself wondering if he had only imagined the old man's hand tripping him up.

The pacing continued for another hour, with Ender Wiggins trying the door every now and then. At last he gave up and took off his uniform and walked to his bed.

As he leaned over to pull the covers back, he felt a hand jab roughly between his thighs and another hand grab his hair. In a moment he had been turned upside down. His face and shoulders were being pressed into the floor by the old man's knee, while his back was excruciatingly bent and his legs were pinioned by Maezr's arm. Ender was helpless to use his arms, and he couldn't bend his back to gain slack so he could use his legs. In less than two seconds the old man had completely defeated Ender Wiggins.

"All right," Ender gasped. "You win."

Maezr's knee thrust painfully downward.

"Since when," Maezr asked in a soft, rasping voice, "do you have to tell the enemy when he has won?"

Ender remained silent.

"I surprised you once, Ender Wiggins. Why didn't you destroy me immediately afterward? Just because I looked peaceful? You turned your back on me. Stupid. You have learned nothing. You have never had a teacher."

Ender was angry now. "I've had too many damned teachers, how was I supposed to know you'd turn out to be a—" Ender hunted for a word. Maezr supplied one.

"An enemy, Ender Wiggins," Maezr whispered. "I am your enemy, the first one you've ever had who was smarter than you. There is no teacher but the enemy, Ender Wiggins. No one but the enemy will ever tell you what the enemy is going to do. No one but the enemy will ever teach you how to destroy and conquer. I am your enemy, from now on. From now on I am your teacher."

Then Maezr let Ender's legs fall to the floor. Because the old man still held Ender's head to the floor, the boy couldn't use his arms to compensate, and his legs hit the plastic surface with a loud crack and a sickening pain that made Ender wince. Then Maezr stood and let Ender rise.

Slowly the boy pulled his legs under him, with a faint groan of pain, and he knelt on all fours for a moment, recovering. Then his right arm flashed out. Maezr quickly danced back and Ender's hand closed on air as his teacher's foot shot forward to catch Ender on the chin.

Ender's chin wasn't there. He was lying flat on his back, spinning on the floor, and during the moment that Maezr was off balance from his kick Ender's feet smashed into Maezr's other leg. The old man fell on the ground in a heap.

What seemed to be a heap was really a hornet's nest. Ender couldn't find an arm or a leg that held still long enough to be grabbed, and in the meantime blows were landing on his back and arms. Ender was smaller—he couldn't reach past the old man's flailing limbs.

So he leaped back out of the way and stood poised near the door.

The old man stopped thrashing about and sat up, cross-legged again, laughing. "Better, this time, boy. But slow. You will have to be better with a fleet than you are with your body or no one will be safe with you in command. Lesson learned?"

Ender nodded slowly.

Maezr smiled. "Good. Then we'll never have such a battle again. All the rest with the simulator. I will program your battles, I will devise the strategy of your enemy, and you will learn to be quick and discover what tricks the enemy has for you. Remember, boy. From now on the enemy is more clever than you. From now on the enemy is stronger than you. From now on you are always about to lose."

Then Maezr's face became serious again. "You will be about to lose, Ender, but you will win. You will learn to defeat the enemy. He will teach you how."

Maezr got up and walked toward the door. Ender stepped back out of the way. As the old man touched the handle of the door, Ender leaped into the air and kicked Maezr in the small of the back with both feet. He hit hard enough that he rebounded onto his feet, as Maezr cried out and collapsed on the floor.

Maezr got up slowly, holding on to the door handle, his face contorted with pain. He seemed disabled, but Ender didn't trust him. He waited warily. And yet in spite of his suspicion he was caught off guard by Maezr's speed. In a moment he found himself on the floor near the opposite wall, his nose and lip bleeding where his face had hit the bed. He was able to turn enough to see Maezr open the door and leave. The old man was limping and walking slowly.

Ender smiled in spite of the pain, then rolled over onto his back and laughed until his mouth filled with blood and he started to gag. Then he got up and painfully made his way to the bed. He lay down and in a few minutes a medic came and took care of his injuries.

As the drug had its effect and Ender drifted off to sleep he remembered the way Maezr limped out of his room and laughed again. He was still laughing softly as his mind went blank and the medic pulled the blanket over him and snapped off the light. He slept until the pain woke him in the morning. He dreamed of defeating Maezr.

The next day Ender went to the simulator room with his nose bandaged and his lip still puffy. Maezr was not there. Instead, a captain who had worked with him before showed him an addition that had been made. The captain pointed to a tube with a loop at one end. "Radio. Primitive, I know, but it loops over your ear and we tuck the other end into your mouth like this."

"Watch it," Ender said as the captain pushed the end of the tube into his swollen lip.

"Sorry. Now you just talk."

"Good. Who to?"

The captain smiled. "Ask and see."

Ender shrugged and turned to the simulator. As he did a voice reverberated through his skull. It was too loud for him to understand, and he ripped the radio off his ear.

"What are you trying to do, make me deaf?"

The captain shook his head and turned a dial on a small box on a nearby table. Ender put the radio back on.

"Commander," the radio said in a familiar voice.

Ender answered, "Yes."

"Instructions, sir?"

The voice was definitely familiar. "Bean?" Ender asked.

"Yes, sir."

"Bean, this is Ender."

Silence. And then a burst of laughter from the other side. Then six or seven more voices laughing, and Ender waited for silence to return. When it did, he asked, "Who else?"

A few voices spoke at once, but Bean drowned them out. "Me, I'm Bean, and Peder, Wins, Younger, Lee, and Vlad."

Ender thought for a moment. Then he asked what the hell was going on. They laughed again.

"They can't break up the group," Bean said. "We were commanders for maybe two weeks, and here we are at Command School, training with the simulator, and all of a sudden they told us we were going to form a fleet with a new commander. And that's you."

Ender smiled. "Are you boys any good?"

"If we aren't, you'll let us know."

Ender chuckled a little. "Might work out. A fleet."

For the next ten days Ender trained his toon leaders until they could maneuver their ships like precision dancers. It was like being back in the battleroom again, except that now Ender could always see everything, and could speak to his toon leaders and change their orders at any time.

One day as Ender sat down at the control board and switched on the simulator, harsh green lights appeared in the space—the enemy.

"This is it," Ender said. "X, Y, bullet, C, D, reserve screen, E, south loop, Bean, angle north."

The enemy was grouped in a globe, and outnumbered Ender two to one. Half of Ender's force was grouped in a tight, bulletlike formation, with the rest in a flat circular screen—except for a tiny force under Bean that moved off the simulator, heading behind the enemy's formation. Ender quickly learned the enemy's strategy: whenever Ender's bullet formation came close, the enemy would give way, hoping to draw Ender inside the globe where he would be surrounded. So Ender obligingly fell into the trap, bringing his bullet to the center of the globe.

The enemy began to contract slowly, not wanting to come within range until all their weapons could be brought to bear at once. Then Ender began to work in earnest. His reserve screen approached the outside of the globe, and the enemy began to concentrate his forces there. Then Bean's force appeared on the opposite side, and the enemy again deployed ships on that side.

Which left most of the globe only thinly defended. Ender's bullet attacked, and since at the point of attack it outnumbered the enemy overwhelmingly, he tore a hole in the formation. The enemy reacted to try to plug the gap, but in the confusion the reserve force and Bean's small force attacked simultaneously, with the bullet moved to another part of the globe. In a few more minutes the formation was shattered, most of the enemy ships destroyed, and the few survivors rushing away as fast as they could go.

Ender switched the simulator off. All the lights faded. Maezr was standing beside Ender, his hands in his pockets, his body tense. Ender looked up at him.

"I thought you said the enemy would be smart," Ender said.

Maezr's face remained expressionless. "What did you learn?"

"I learned that a sphere only works if your enemy's a fool. He had his forces so spread out that I outnumbered him whenever I engaged him."

"And?"

"And," Ender said, "you can't stay committed to one pattern. It makes you too easy to predict."

"Is that all?" Maezr asked quietly.

Ender took off his radio. "The enemy could have defeated me by breaking the sphere earlier."

Maezr nodded. "You had an unfair advantage."

Ender looked up at him coldly. "I was outnumbered two to one."

Maezr shook his head. "You have the ansible. The enemy doesn't. We include that in the mock battles. Their messages travel at the speed of light."

Ender glanced toward the simulator. "Is there enough space to make a difference?"

"Don't you know?" Maezr asked. "None of the ships was ever closer than thirty thousand kilometers to any other."

Ender tried to figure the size of the enemy's sphere. Astronomy was beyond him. But now his curiosity was stirred.

"What kind of weapons are on those ships? To be able to strike so fast?"

Maezr shook his head. "The science is too much for you. You'd have to study many more years than you've lived to understand even the basics. All you need to know is that the weapons work."

"Why do we have to come so close to be in range?"

"The ships are all protected by forcefields. A certain distance away the weapons are weaker and can't get through. Closer in the weapons are stronger than the shields. But the computers take care of all that. They're constantly firing in any direction that won't hurt one of our ships. The computers pick targets, aim; they do all the detail work. You just tell them when and get them in a position to win. All right?"

"No." Ender twisted the tube of the radio around his fingers. "I have to know how the weapons work."

"I told you, it would take—"

"I can't command a fleet—not even on the simulator—unless I know." Ender waited a moment, then added, "Just the rough idea."

Maezr stood up and walked a few steps away. "All right, Ender. It won't make any sense, but I'll try. As simply as I can." He shoved his hands into his pockets. "It's this way, Ender. Everything is made up of atoms, little particles so small you can't see them with your eyes. These atoms, there are only a few different types, and they're all made up of even smaller particles that are pretty much the same. These atoms can be broken, so that they stop being atoms. So that this metal doesn't hold together anymore. Or the plastic floor. Or your body. Or even the air. They just seem to disappear, if you break the atoms. All that's left is the pieces. And they fly around and break more atoms. The weapons on the ships set up an area where it's impossible for atoms of anything to stay together. They all break down. So things in that area—they disappear."

Ender nodded. "You're right, I don't understand it. Can it be blocked?"

"No. But it gets wider and weaker the farther it goes from the ship, so that after a while a forcefield will block it. OK? And to make it strong at all, it has to be focused, so that a ship can only fire effectively in maybe three or four directions at once."

Ender nodded again, but he didn't really understand, not well enough. "If the pieces of the broken atoms go breaking more atoms, why doesn't it just make everything disappear?"

"Space. Those thousands of kilometers between the ships, they're empty. Almost no atoms. The pieces don't hit anything, and when they finally do hit something, they're so spread out they can't do any harm." Maezr cocked his head quizzically. "Anything else you need to know?"

"Do the weapons on the ships—do they work against anything besides ships?"

Maezr moved in close to Ender and said firmly, "We

only use them against ships. Never anything else. If we used them against anything else, the enemy would use them against us. Got it?"

Maezr walked away, and was nearly out the door when Ender called to him.

"I don't know your name yet," Ender said blandly.

"Maezr Rackham."

"Maezr Rackham," Ender said, "I defeated you."

Maezr laughed.

"Ender, you weren't fighting me today," he said. "You were fighting the stupidest computer in the Command School, set on a ten-year-old program. You don't think I'd use a sphere, do you?" He shook his head. "Ender, my dear little fellow, when you fight me you'll know it. Because you'll lose." And Maezr left the room.

Ender still practiced ten hours a day with his toon leaders. He never saw them, though, only heard their voices on the radio. Battles came every two or three days. The enemy had something new every time, something harder—but Ender coped with it. And won every time. And after every battle Maezr would point out mistakes and show Ender that he had really lost. Maezr only let Ender finish so that he would learn to handle the end of the game.

Until finally Maezr came in and solemnly shook Ender's hand and said, "That, boy, was a good battle."

Because the praise was so long in coming, it pleased Ender more than praise had ever pleased him before. And because it was so condescending, he resented it.

"So from now on," Maezr said, "we can give you hard ones."

From then on Ender's life was a slow nervous breakdown.

He began fighting two battles a day, with problems that steadily grew more difficult. He had been trained in nothing but the game all his life, but now the game began to consume him. He woke in the morning with new strategies for the simulator and went fitfully to sleep at night with the mistakes of the day preying on him. Sometimes he would wake up in the middle of the night crying for a reason he didn't remember. Sometimes he woke with his knuckles bloody from biting them. But every day he went impassively to the simulator and drilled his toon leaders until the battles, and drilled his toon leaders after the battles, and endured and studied the harsh criticism that Maezr Rackham piled on him. He noted that Rackham perversely criticized him more after his hardest battles. He noted that every time he thought of a new strategy the enemy was using it within a few days. And he noted that while his fleet always stayed the same size, the enemy increased in numbers every day.

He asked his teacher.

"We are showing you what it will be like when you really command. The ratios of enemy to us."

"Why does the enemy always outnumber us?"

Maezr bowed his gray head for a moment, as if deciding whether to answer. Finally he looked up and reached out his hand and touched Ender on the shoulder. "I will tell you, even though the information is secret. You see, the enemy attacked us first. He had good reason to attack us, but that is a matter for politicians, and whether the fault was ours or his, we could not let him win. So when the enemy came to our worlds, we fought back, hard, and spent the finest of our young men in the fleets. But we won, and the enemy retreated."

Maezr smiled ruefully. "But the enemy was not through, boy. The enemy would never be through. They came again, with more numbers, and it was harder to beat them. And another generation of young men was spent. Only a few survived. So we came up with a plan—the big men came up with the plan. We knew that we had to destroy the enemy once and for all, totally, eliminate his ability to make war against us. To do that we had to go to his home worlds—his home world, really, since the enemy's empire is all tied to his capital world."

"And so?" Ender asked.

"And so we made a fleet. We made more ships than

the enemy ever had. We made a hundred ships for every ship he had sent against us. And we launched them against his twenty-eight worlds. They started leaving a hundred years ago. And they carried on them the ansible, and only a few men. So that someday a commander could sit on a planet somewhere far from the battle and command the fleet. So that our best minds would not be destroyed by the enemy."

Ender's question had still not been answered. "Why do they outnumber us?"

Maezr laughed. "Because it took a hundred years for our ships to get there. They've had a hundred years to prepare for us. They'd be fools, don't you think, boy, if they waited in old tugboats to defend their harbors. They have new ships, great ships, hundreds of ships. All we have is the ansible, that and the fact that they have to put a commander with every fleet, and when they lose—and they will lose—they lose one of their best minds every time."

Ender started to ask another question.

"No more, Ender Wiggins. I've told you more than you ought to know as it is."

Ender stood angrily and turned away. "I have a right to know. Do you think this can go on forever, pushing me through one school and another and never telling me what my life is for? You use me and the others as a tool, someday we'll command your ships, someday maybe we'll save your lives, but I'm not a computer, and I have to *know*!"

"Ask me a question, then, boy," Maezr said, "and if I can answer, I will."

"If you use your best minds to command the fleets, and you never lose any, then what do you need me for? Who am I replacing, if they're all still there?"

Maezr shook his head. "I can't tell you the answer to that, Ender. Be content that we will need you, soon. It's late. Go to bed. You have a battle in the morning."

Ender walked out of the simulator room. But when

Maezr left by the same door a few moments later, the boy was waiting in the hall.

"All right, boy," Maezr said impatiently, "what is it? I don't have all night and you need to sleep."

Ender wasn't sure what his question was, but Maezr waited. Finally Ender asked softly, "Do they live?"

"Does who live?"

"The other commanders. The ones now. And before me."

Maezr snorted. "Live. Of course they live. He wonders if they live." Still chuckling, the old man walked off down the hall. Ender stood in the corridor for a while, but at last he was tired and he went off to bed. They live, he thought. They live, but he can't tell me what happens to them.

That night Ender didn't wake up crying. But he did wake up with blood on his hands.

Months wore on with battles every day, until at last Ender settled into the routine of the destruction of himself. He slept less every night, dreamed more, and he began to have terrible pains in his stomach. They put him on a very bland diet, but soon he didn't even have an appetite for that. "Eat," Maezr said, and Ender would mechanically put food in his mouth. But if nobody told him to eat he didn't eat.

One day as he was drilling his toon leaders the room went black and he woke up on the floor with his face bloody where he had hit the controls.

They put him to bed then, and for three days he was very ill. He remembered seeing faces in his dreams, but they weren't real faces, and he knew it even while he thought he saw them. He thought he saw Bean sometimes, and sometimes he thought he saw Lieutenant Anderson and Captain Graff. And then he woke up and it was only his enemy Maezr Rackham.

"I'm awake," he said to Maezr.

"So I see," Maezr answered. "Took you long enough. You have a battle today."

So Ender got up and fought the battle and he won it. But there was no second battle that day, and they let him go to bed earlier. His hands were shaking as he undressed.

During the night he thought he felt hands touching him gently, and he dreamed he heard voices saying, "How long can he go on?"

"Long enough."

"So soon?"

"In a few days, then he's through."

"How will he do?"

"Fine. Even today, he was better than ever."

Ender recognized the last voice as Maezr Rackham's. He resented Rackham's intruding even in his sleep.

He woke up and fought another battle and won.

Then he went to bed.

He woke up and won again.

And the next day was his last day in Command School, though he didn't know it. He got up and went to the simulator for the battle.

Maezr was waiting for him. Ender walked slowly into the simulator room. He step was slightly shuffling, and he seemed tired and dull. Maezr frowned.

"Are you awake, boy?" If Ender had been alert, he would have cared more about the concern in his teacher's voice. Instead, he simply went to the controls and sat down. Maezr spoke to him.

"Today's game needs a little explanation, Ender Wiggins. Please turn around and pay strict attention."

Ender turned around, and for the first time he noticed that there were people at the back of the room. He recognized Graff and Anderson from Battle School, and vaguely remembered a few of the men from Command School—teachers for a few hours at some time or another. But most of the people he didn't know at all.

"Who are they?"

Maezr shook his head and answered, "Observers. Every now and then we let observers come in to watch the battle. If you don't want them, we'll send them out."

Ender shrugged. Maezr began his explanation. "Today's game, boy, has a new element. We're staging this battle around a planet. This will complicate things in two ways. The planet isn't large, on the scale we're using, but the ansible can't detect anything on the other side of it— so there's a blind spot. Also, it's against the rules to use weapons against the planet itself. All right?"

"Why, don't the weapons work against planets?"

Maezr answered coldly, "There are rules of war, Ender, that apply even in training games."

Ender shook his head slowly. "Can the planet attack?"

Maezr looked nonplussed for a moment, then smiled. "I guess you'll have to find that one out, boy. And one more thing. Today, Ender, your opponent isn't the computer. I am your enemy today, and today I won't be letting you off so easily. Today is a battle to the end. And I'll use any means I can to defeat you."

Then Maezr was gone, and Ender expressionlessly led his toon leaders through maneuvers. Ender was doing well, of course, but several of the observers shook their heads, and Graff kept clasping and unclasping his hands, crossing and uncrossing his legs. Ender would be slow today, and today Ender couldn't afford to be slow.

A warning buzzer sounded, and Ender cleared the simulator board, waiting for today's game to appear. He felt muddled today, and wondered why people were there watching. Were they going to judge him today? Decide if he was good enough for something else? For another two years of grueling training, another two years of struggling to exceed his best? Ender was twelve. He felt very old. And as he waited for the game to appear, he wished he could simply lose it, lose the battle badly and completely so that they would remove him from the program, punish him however they wanted, he didn't care, just so he could sleep.

Then the enemy formation appeared, and Ender's weariness turned to desperation.

The enemy outnumbered him a thousand to one, the simulator glowed green with them, and Ender knew that he couldn't win.

And the enemy was not stupid. There was no formation that Ender could study and attack. Instead the vast swarms of ships were constantly moving, constantly shifting from one momentary formation to another, so that a space that for one moment was empty was immediately filled with formidable enemy force. And even though Ender's fleet was the largest he had ever had, there was no place he could deploy it where he would outnumber the enemy long enough to accomplish anything.

And behind the enemy was the planet. The planet, which Maezr had warned him about. What difference did a planet make, when Ender couldn't hope to get near it? Ender waited, waited for the flash of insight that would tell him what to do, how to destroy the enemy. And as he waited, he heard the observers behind him begin to shift in their seats, wondering what Ender was doing, what plan he would follow. And finally it was obvious to everyone that Ender didn't know what to do, that there was nothing to do, and a few of the men at the back of the room made quiet little sounds in their throats.

Then Ender heard Bean's voice in his ear. Bean chuckled and said, "Remember, the enemy's gate is *down*." A few of the other toon leaders laughed and Ender thought back to the simple games he had played and won in Battle School. They had put him against hopeless odds there, too. And he had beaten them. And he'd be damned if he'd let Maezr Rackham beat him with a cheap trick like outnumbering him a thousand to one. He had won a game in Battle School by going for something against the rules—he had won by going against the enemy's gate.

And the enemy's gate was down.

Ender smiled, and realized that if he broke this rule they'd probably kick him out of school, and that way he'd win for sure: He would never have to play a game again.

He whispered into the microphone. His six commanders each took a part of the fleet and launched themselves against the enemy. They pursued erratic courses, darting off in one direction and then another. The enemy immediately stopped his aimless maneuvering and began to group around Ender's six fleets.

Ender took off his microphone, leaned back in his chair, and watched. The observers murmured out loud, now. Ender was doing nothing—he had thrown the game away.

But a pattern began to emerge from the quick confrontations with the enemy. Ender's six groups lost ships constantly as they brushed with each enemy force—but they never stopped for a fight, even when for a moment they could have won a small tactical victory. Instead they continued on their erratic course that led, eventually, down. Toward the enemy planet.

And because of their seemingly random course the enemy didn't realize it until the same time that the observers did. By then it was too late, just as it had been too late for William Bee to stop Ender's soldiers from activating the gate. More of Ender's ships could be hit and destroyed, so that of the six fleets only two were able to get to the planet, and those were decimated. But those tiny groups *did* get through, and they opened fire on the planet.

Ender leaned forward now, anxious to see if his guess would pay off. He half expected a buzzer to sound and the game to be stopped, because he had broken the rule. But he was betting on the accuracy of the simulator. If it could simulate a planet, it could simulate what would happen to a planet under attack.

It did.

The weapons that blew up little ships didn't blow up the entire planet at first. But they did cause terrible explosions. And on the planet there was no space to dissipate the chain reaction. On the planet the chain reaction found more and more fuel to feed it.

The planet's surface seemed to be moving back and forth, but soon the surface gave way in an immense explosion that sent light flashing in all directions. It swallowed up Ender's entire fleet. And then it reached the enemy ships.

The first simply vanished in the explosion. Then, as

the explosion spread and became less bright, it was clear what happened to each ship. As the light reached them they flashed brightly for a moment and disappeared. They were all fuel for the fire of the planet.

It took more than three minutes for the explosion to reach the limits of the simulator, and by then it was much fainter. All the ships were gone, and if any had escaped before the explosion reached them, they were few and not worth worrying about. Where the planet had been there was nothing. The simulator was empty.

Ender had destroyed the enemy by sacrificing his entire fleet and breaking the rule against destroying the enemy planet. He wasn't sure whether to feel triumphant at his victory or defiant at the rebuke he was certain would come. So instead he felt nothing. He was tired. He wanted to go to bed and sleep.

He switched off the simulator, and finally heard the noise behind him.

There were no longer two rows of dignified military observers. Instead there was chaos. Some of them were slapping each other on the back; some of them were bowed, head in hands; others were openly weeping. Captain Graff detached himself from the group and came to Ender. Tears streamed down his face, but he was smiling. He reached out his arms, and to Ender's surprise he embraced the boy, held him tightly, and whispered, "Thank you, thank you, thank you, Ender."

Soon all the observers were gathered around the bewildered child, thanking him and cheering him and patting him on the shoulder and shaking his hand. Ender tried to make sense of what they were saying. Had he passed the test after all? Why did it matter so much to them?

Then the crowd parted and Maezr Rackham walked through. He came straight up to Ender Wiggins and held out his hand.

"You made the hard choice, boy. But heaven knows there was no other way you could have done it. Congratulations. You beat them, and it's all over."

All over. Beat them. "I beat *you*, Maezr Rackham."

Maezr laughed, a loud laugh that filled the room.

"Ender Wiggins, you never played me. You never played a *game* since I was your teacher."

Ender didn't get the joke. He had played a great many games, at a terrible cost to himself. He began to get angry.

Maezr reached out and touched his shoulder. Ender shrugged him off. Maezr then grew serious and said, "Ender Wiggins, for the last months you have been the commander of our fleets. There were no games. The battles were real. Your only enemy was *the* enemy. You won every battle. And finally today you fought them at their home world, and you destroyed their world, their fleet, you destroyed them completely, and they'll never come against us again. You did it. You."

Real. Not a game. Ender's mind was too tired to cope with it all. He walked away from Maezr, walked silently through the crowd that still whispered thanks and congratulations to the boy, walked out of the simulator room and finally arrived in his bedroom and closed the door.

He was asleep when Graff and Maezr Rackham found him. They came in quietly and roused him. He awoke slowly, and when he recognized them he turned away to go back to sleep.

"Ender," Graff said. "We need to talk to you."

Ender rolled back to face them. He said nothing.

Graff smiled. "It was a shock to you yesterday, I know. But it must make you feel good to know you won the war."

Ender nodded slowly.

"Maezr Rackham here, he never played against you. He only analyzed your battles to find out your weak spots, to help you improve. It worked, didn't it?"

Ender closed his eyes tightly. They waited. He said, "Why didn't you tell me?"

Maezr smiled. "A hundred years ago, Ender, we found out some things. That when a commander's life is in danger he becomes afraid, and fear slows down his thinking. When a commander knows that he's killing people, he becomes cautious or insane, and neither of those help him do well. And when he's mature, when he has responsibilities and an understanding of the world, he becomes cautious and sluggish and can't do his job. So we trained children, who didn't know anything but the game, and never knew when it would become real. That was the theory, and you proved that the theory worked."

Graff reached out and touched Ender's shoulder. "We launched the ships so that they would all arrive at their destination during these few months. We knew that we'd probably have only one good commander, if we were lucky. In history it's been very rare to have more than one genius in a war. So we planned on having a genius. We were gambling. And you came along and we won."

Ender opened his eyes again and they realized that he was angry. "Yes, you won."

Graff and Maezr Rackham looked at each other. "He doesn't understand," Graff whispered.

"I understand," Ender said. "You needed a weapon, and you got it, and it was me."

"That's right," Maezr answered.

"So tell me," Ender went on, "how many people lived on that planet that I destroyed."

They didn't answer him. They waited awhile in silence, and then Graff spoke. "Weapons don't need to understand what they're pointed at, Ender. We did the pointing, and so we're responsible. You just did your job."

Maezr smiled. "Of course, Ender, you'll be taken care of. The government will never forget you. You served us all very well."

Ender rolled over and faced the wall, and even though they tried to talk to him, he didn't answer them. Finally they left.

Ender lay in his bed for a long time before anyone disturbed him again. The door opened softly. Ender didn't turn to see who it was. Then a hand touched him softly.

"Ender, it's me, Bean."

Ender turned over and looked at the little boy who was standing by his bed.

"Sit down," Ender said.

Bean sat. "That last battle, Ender. I didn't know how you'd get us out of it."

Ender smiled. "I didn't. I cheated. I thought they'd kick me out."

"Can you believe it! We won the war. The whole war's over, and we thought we'd have to wait till we grew up to fight in it, and it was us fighting it all the time. I mean, Ender, we're little kids. I'm a little kid, anyway." Bean laughed and Ender smiled. Then they were silent for a little while, Bean sitting on the edge of the bed, Ender watching him out of half-closed eyes.

Finally Bean thought of something else to say.

"What will we do now that the war's over?" he said.

Ender closed his eyes and said, "I need some sleep, Bean."

Bean got up and left and Ender slept.

Graff and Anderson walked through the gates into the park. There was a breeze, but the sun was hot on their shoulders.

"Abba Technics? In the capital?" Graff asked.

"No, in Biggock County. Training division," Anderson replied. "They think my work with children is good preparation. And you?"

Graff smiled and shook his head. "No plans. I'll be here for a few more months. Reports, winding down. I've had offers. Personnel development for DCIA, executive vice-president for U and P, but I said no. Publisher wants me to do memoirs of the war. I don't know."

They sat on a bench and watched leaves shivering in the breeze. Children on the monkey bars were laughing and yelling, but the wind and the distance swallowed their words. "Look," Graff said, pointing. A little boy jumped from the bars and ran near the bench where the two men sat. Another boy followed him, and holding his hands like a gun he made an explosive sound. The child he was shooting at didn't stop. He fired again.

"I got you! Come back here!"

The other little boy ran on out of sight.

"Don't you know when you're dead?" The boy shoved

his hands in his pockets and kicked a rock back to the monkey bars. Anderson smiled and shook his head. "Kids," he said. Then he and Graff stood up and walked on out of the park.

FIRE WATCH

by Connie Willis

My obsession with history, time travel, Oxford, and St. Paul's Cathedral officially began on my first trip to England in 1977, although it probably actually began much earlier, with a teenage-hood steeped in Dorothy Sayers' *Gaudy Night*, Robert A. Heinlein's *The Door into Summer*, and innumerable Dickens, Austen, Trollope, and Agatha Christie novels.

I wanted to see St. Paul's because I'd read about its priests and vergers forming the famous "fire watch" which spent every night of the London Blitz on St. Paul's roofs, putting out incendiary bombs (twenty-nine on the night of December twenty-ninth, when half the City of London burned down) and who, during the day, slept down in the crypt. I had a vague idea of writing a poem about the irony of their sleeping among the tombs of the heroes of other wars while a new war raged over their heads.

St. Paul's was beautiful—wide, echoing spaces and massive Portland stone arches and golden ceilings. We did the usual tour, Lord Nelson's tomb, William Holman Hunt's painting of *The Light of the World*, the Whispering Gallery, and then climbed up into the dome and went outside to look at the view of London.

I'd been expecting some sort of Mary Poppins chimney pots and Victorian rooftops scene. Instead, below us on all sides lay hideous modern cement-block buildings and carparks. Well, that was hardly worth climbing all these steps for, I thought, and then, Oh, my God, this was all built in the fifties. Because it all burned down.

Everything. On all sides of the cathedral for as far as the eye could see. St. Paul's can't have survived, I thought, it should have burned down. Until that moment, in spite of everything I'd read, in spite of the fire watch stone in front of St. Paul's great west doors, dedicated to "St. Paul's fire watch, who by the grace of God saved this church," and that famous photo of St. Paul's dome rising out of a sea of cloud and flame on the night of the twenty-ninth, I hadn't understood how close that beautiful, beautiful façade had come to being destroyed.

And I knew instantly what I wanted to write—not a poem, but a story, a time travel story about the fire watch "which by the grace of God saved St. Paul's Cathedral," and the fire watch stone and the Whispering Gallery and *The Light of the World*.

"Fire Watch" took me two years and lots of research to write, and in the process I invented the net and Mr. Dunworthy and Oxford's time-traveling historians and became fascinated with World War II and history, which have held me in thrall ever since.

In "Fire Watch," the hero John Bartholomew had a roommate named Kivrin. She appeared only briefly and then mostly as a source of irritation for John—he didn't think it was fair that he'd drawn the dangerous and deadly Blitz for his practicum while she'd gone to the quiet, idyllic Middle Ages. At the end of the story he found out, among many other hard lessons, that her sojourn in the 1300s had been anything but idyllic, that it had been even more dangerous and deadly than his, and that he knew almost nothing about Kivrin.

Neither did I, and as time went by, I began to think more and more about the whys and wherefores of her presence there (nobody in their right mind would *choose* to go where she'd gone) and about what her sojourn there might have been like. Which led me to write *Doomsday Book*.

I expected it to end there. I had always said I would never write a series because of their sameness and because in a series nothing lasting or important or transforming can happen to the main characters because they need to remain the same for the next book. And the next. *The Further Adventures of Kivrin* was the last thing I wanted to write.

But I loved writing about Oxford and its historians, and I hadn't said nearly all I wanted to say about the nature of history. After the tragic grimness of "Fire Watch," I especially wanted to show the other side of history, its humor, its hopefulness. So I wrote *To Say Nothing of the Dog*, which was set in the same world as "Fire Watch" and *Doomsday Book*, but which took place in a different time and place (the Thames in 1889) and was about an entirely different set of characters, except for Mr. Dunworthy, who appeared as a minor character, and his secretary Finch.

It was also a very different sort of book, a comedy, heavily influenced by P.G. Wodehouse and Jerome K. Jerome and involving bulldogs, boating on the Thames, seances, butlers, jumble sales, eccentric Oxford dons, and a hideous (and elusive) piece of ghastly Victorian statuary known as the bishop's bird stump. And the Blitz, in this case the bombing of Coventry and the burning of Coventry Cathedral.

I also wrote about the Blitz in two novellas—"Jack" and "The Winds of Marble Arch," and it became increasingly clear to me that I was not done with the Blitz, that I was going to have to write a novel about it and about the war and the Underground station shelters and the V-1s and the ARP wardens and ambulance drivers and rescue workers and the Battle of Britain and Ultra. And St. Paul's.

That novel is *All Clear*, which I have been working on for the past three years. It's about several Oxford historians who are studying different parts of World War II—one's with the evacuated children in northern England in 1939, one's observing the rescue of the British army from Dunkirk in May of 1940, one's in the Blitz, and one's in the midst of the war of deception against Hitler in the months leading up to D-Day. St. Paul's is in it, too, and Mr. Dunworthy. And John Bartholomew.

I've written *All Clear* partly in the hope that it will finally get the Blitz and St. Paul's and history out of my system once and for all. But I doubt it. At this writing, I love St. Paul's and the Blitz and history as much or more than that first day, standing on the gallery of the dome.

> *History hath triumphed over time, which besides it*
> *nothing but eternity hath triumphed over.*
> —Sir Walter Raleigh

SEPTEMBER 20—Of course the first thing I looked for was the fire watch stone. And of course it wasn't there yet. It wasn't dedicated until 1951, accompanying a speech by the Very Reverend Dean Walter Matthews, and this is only 1940. I knew that. I went to see the fire watch stone only yesterday, with some kind of misplaced notion that seeing the scene of the crime would somehow help. It didn't.

The only things that would have helped were a crash course in London during the Blitz and a little more time. I had not gotten either.

"Traveling in time is not like taking the tube, Mr. Bartholomew," the esteemed Dunworthy had said, blinking at me through those antique spectacles of his. "Either you report on the twentieth or you don't go at all."

"But I'm not ready," I'd said. "Look, it took me four years to get ready to travel with St. Paul. *St. Paul.* Not St. Paul's. You can't expect me to get ready for London in the Blitz in two days."

"Yes," Dunworthy had said. "We can." End of conversation.

"Two days!" I had shouted at my roommate Kivrin. "All because some computer adds an *'s.* And the esteemed Dunworthy doesn't even bat an eye when I tell him. 'Time travel is not like taking the tube, young man,' he says. 'I'd suggest you get ready. You're leaving day after tomorrow.' The man's a total incompetent."

"No," she said. "He isn't. He's the best there is. He wrote the book on St. Paul's. Maybe you should listen to what he says."

I had expected Kivrin to be at least a little sympathetic. She had been practically hysterical when she got her practicum changed from fifteenth- to fourteenth-century England, and how did either century qualify as a practicum? Even counting infectious diseases they couldn't have been more than a five. The Blitz is an eight, and St. Paul's itself is, with my luck, a ten.

"You think I should go see Dunworthy again?" I said.

"Yes."

"And then what? I've got two days. I don't know the money, the language, the history. Nothing."

"He's a good man," Kivrin said. "I think you'd better listen to him while you can." Good old Kivrin. Always the sympathetic ear.

The good man was responsible for my standing just inside the propped-open west doors, gawking like the country boy I was supposed to be, looking for a stone that wasn't there. Thanks to the good man, I was about as unprepared for my practicum as it was possible for him to make me.

I couldn't see more than a few feet into the church. I could see a candle gleaming feebly a long way off and a closer blur of white moving toward me. A verger, or possibly the Very Reverend Dean himself. I pulled out the letter from my clergyman uncle in Wales that was supposed to gain me access to the dean, and patted my back pocket to make sure I hadn't lost the microfiche *Oxford English Dictionary, Revised, with Historical Supplements* I'd smuggled out of the Bodleian. I couldn't pull it out in the middle of the conversation, but with luck I could muddle through the first encounter by context and look up the words I didn't know later.

"Are you from the ayarpee?" he said. He was no older than I am, a head shorter and much thinner. Almost ascetic looking. He reminded me of Kivrin. He was not wearing white, but clutching it to his chest. In other circumstances I would have thought it was a pillow. In other circumstances I would know what was being said to me, but there had been no time to unlearn sub-Mediterranean Latin and Jewish law and learn Cockney and air raid procedures. Two days, and the esteemed Dunworthy, who wanted to talk about the sacred burdens of the historian instead of telling me what the ayarpee was.

"Are you?" he demanded again.

I considered whipping out the OED after all on the grounds that Wales was a foreign country, but I didn't think they had microfilm in 1940. Ayarpee. It could be anything, including a nickname for the fire watch, in which case the impulse to say no was not safe at all. "No," I said.

He lunged suddenly toward and past me and peered out the open doors. "Damn," he said, coming back to me. "Where are they then? Bunch of lazy bourgeois tarts!" And so much for getting by on context.

He looked at me closely, suspiciously, as if he thought I was only pretending not to be with the ayarpee. "The church is closed," he said finally.

I held up the envelope and said, "My name's Bartholomew. Is Dean Matthews in?"

He looked out the door a moment longer as if he expected the lazy bourgeois tarts at any moment and intended to attack them with the white bundle; then he turned and said, as if he were guiding a tour, "This way, please," and took off into the gloom.

He led me to the right and down the south aisle of the nave. Thank God I had memorized the floor plan or at that moment, heading into total darkness, led by a raving verger, the whole bizarre metaphor of my situation would have been enough to send me out the west doors and back to St. John's Wood. It helped a little to know where I was. We should have been passing number twenty-six: Hunt's painting of *The Light of the World*— Jesus with his lantern—but it was too dark to see it. We could have used the lantern ourselves.

He stopped abruptly ahead of me, still raving. "We weren't asking for the bloody Savoy, just a few cots. Nelson's better off than we are—at least he's got a pillow provided." He brandished the white bundle like a torch in the darkness. It was a pillow after all. "We asked for them over a fortnight ago, and here we still are, sleeping on the bleeding generals from Trafalgar because those bitches want to play tea and crumpets with the Tommies at Victoria and the hell with us!"

He didn't seem to expect me to answer his outburst, which was good, because I had understood perhaps one key word in three. He stomped on ahead, moving out of sight of the one pathetic altar candle and stopping again at a black hole. Number twenty-five: stairs to the Whispering Gallery, the Dome, the library (not open to the public). Up the stairs, down a hall, stop again at a medieval door and knock. "I've got to go wait for them," he said. "If I'm not there they'll likely take them over to the Abbey. Tell the Dean to ring them up again, will you?" and he took off down the stone steps, still holding his pillow like a shield against him.

He had knocked, but the door was at least a foot of solid oak, and it was obvious the Very Reverend Dean had not heard. I was going to have to knock again. Yes, well, and the man holding the pinpoint had to let go of it, too, but even knowing it will all be over in a moment and you won't feel a thing doesn't make it any easier to say, "Now!" So I stood in front of the door, cursing the history department and the esteemed Dunworthy and the computer that had made the mistake and brought me here to this dark door with only a letter from a fictitious uncle that I trusted no more than I trusted the rest of them.

Even the old reliable Bodleian had let me down. The batch of research stuff I cross-ordered through Balliol and the main terminal is probably sitting in my room right now, a century out of reach. And Kivrin, who had already done her practicum and should have been bursting with advice, walked around as silent as a saint until I begged her to help me.

"Did you go to see Dunworthy?" she said.

"Yes. You want to know what priceless bit of information he had for me? 'Silence and humility are the sacred burdens of the historian.' He also told me I would love St. Paul's. Golden gems from the Master. Unfortunately, what I need to know are the times and places of the bombs so one doesn't fall on me." I flopped down on the bed. "Any suggestions?"

"How good are you at memory retrieval?" she said.

I sat up. "I'm pretty good. You think I should assimilate?"

"There isn't time for that," she said. "I think you should put everything you can directly into long-term."

"You mean endorphins?" I said.

The biggest problem with using memory-assistance drugs to put information into your long-term memory is that it never sits, even for a microsecond, in your short-term memory, and that makes retrieval complicated, not to mention unnerving. It gives you the most unsettling sense of déjà vu to suddenly know something you're positive you've never seen or heard before.

The main problem, though, is not eerie sensations but retrieval. Nobody knows exactly how the brain gets what it wants out of storage, but short-term is definitely involved. That brief, sometimes microscopic, time information spends in short-term is apparently used for something besides tip-of-the-tongue availability. The whole complex sort-and-file process of retrieval is apparently centered in short-term, and without it, and without the help of the drugs that put it there or artificial substitutes, information can be impossible to retrieve. I'd used endorphins for examinations and never had any difficulty with retrieval, and it looked like it was the only way to store all the information I needed in anything approaching the time I had left, but it also meant that I would *never* have known any of the things I needed to know, even for long enough to have forgotten them. If and when I could retrieve the information, I would know it. Till then I was as ignorant of it as if it were not stored in some cob-webbed corner of my mind at all.

"You can retrieve without artificials, can't you?" Kivrin said, looking skeptical.

"I guess I'll have to."

"Under stress? Without sleep? Low body endorphin levels?" What exactly had her practicum been? She had never said a word about it, and undergraduates are not supposed to ask. Stress factors in the Middle Ages? I thought everybody slept through them.

"I hope so," I said. "Anyway, I'm willing to try this idea if you think it will help."

She looked at me with that martyred expression and said, "Nothing will help." Thank you, St. Kivrin of Balliol.

But I tried it anyway. It was better than sitting in Dunworthy's rooms having him blink at me through his historically accurate eyeglasses and tell me I was going to love St. Paul's. When my Bodleian requests didn't come, I overloaded my credit and bought out Blackwell's. Tapes on World War II, Celtic literature, history of mass transit, tourist guidebooks, everything I could think of. Then I rented a high-speed recorder and shot up. When I came out of it, I was so panicked by the feeling of not knowing any more than I had when I started that I took the tube to London and raced up Ludgate Hill to see if the fire watch stone would trigger any memories. It didn't.

"Your endorphin levels aren't back to normal yet," I told myself and tried to relax, but that was impossible with the prospect of the practicum looming up before me. And those are real bullets, kid. Just because you're a history major doing his practicum doesn't mean you can't get killed. I read history books all the way home on the tube and right up until Dunworthy's flunkies came to take me to St. John's Wood this morning.

Then I jammed the microfiche OED in my back pocket and went off feeling as if I would have to survive by my native wit and hoping I could get hold of artificials in 1940. Surely I could get through the first day without mishap, I thought, and now here I was, stopped cold by almost the first word that was spoken to me.

Well, not quite. In spite of Kivrin's advice that I not put anything in short-term, I'd memorized the British money, a map of the tube system, a map of my own Oxford. It had gotten me this far. Surely I would be able to deal with the Dean.

Just as I had almost gotten up the courage to knock,

he opened the door, and as with the pinpoint, it really was over quickly and without pain. I handed him my letter and he shook my hand and said something understandable like, "Glad to have another man, Bartholomew." He looked strained and tired and as if he might collapse if I told him the Blitz had just started. I know, I know: Keep your mouth shut. The sacred silence, etc.

He said, "We'll get Langby to show you round, shall we?" I assumed that was my Verger of the Pillow, and I was right. He met us at the foot of the stairs, puffing a little but jubilant.

"The cots came," he said to Dean Matthews. "You'd have thought they were doing us a favor. All high heels and hoity-toity. 'You made us miss our tea, luv,' one of them said to me. 'Yes, well, and a good thing, too,' I said. 'You look as if you could stand to lose a stone or two.'"

Even Dean Matthews looked as though he did not completely understand him. He said, "Did you set them up in the crypt?" and then introduced us. "Mr. Bartholomew's just got in from Wales," he said. "He's come to join our volunteers." Volunteers, not fire watch.

Langby showed me around, pointing out various dimnesses in the general gloom and then dragged me down to see the ten folding canvas cots set up among the tombs in the crypt, and also, in passing, Lord Nelson's black marble sarcophagus. He told me I don't have to stand a watch the first night and suggested I go to bed, since sleep is the most precious commodity in the raids. I could well believe it. He was clutching that silly pillow to his breast like his beloved.

"Do you hear the sirens down here?" I asked, wondering if he buried his head in it.

He looked around at the low stone ceilings. "Some do, some don't. Brinton has to have his Horlich's. Bence-Jones would sleep if the roof fell in on him. I have to have a pillow. The important thing is to get your eight in no matter what. If you don't, you turn into one of the walking dead. And then you get killed."

On that cheering note he went off to post the watches for tonight, leaving his pillow on one of the cots with orders for me to let nobody touch it. So here I sit, waiting for my first air raid siren and trying to get all this down before I turn into one of the walking or nonwalking dead.

I've used the stolen OED to decipher a little Langby. Middling success. A tart is either a pastry or a prostitute (I assume the latter, although I was wrong about the pillow). Bourgeois is a catchall term for all the faults of the middle class. A Tommy's a soldier. Ayarpee I could not find under any spelling and I had nearly given up when something in long-term about the use of acronyms and abbreviations in wartime popped forward (bless you, St. Kivrin) and I realized it must be an abbreviation. ARP. Air Raid Precautions. Of course. Where else would you get the bleeding cots from?

September 21—Now that I'm past the first shock of being here, I realize that the history department neglected to tell me what I'm suppose to do in the three-odd months of this practicum. They handed me this journal, the letter from my uncle, and ten pounds in pre-war money and sent me packing into the past. The ten pounds (already depleted by train and tube fares) is supposed to last me until the end of December and get me back to St. John's Wood for pickup when the second letter calling me back to Wales to sick uncle's bedside comes. Till then I live here in the crypt with Nelson, who, Langby tells me, is pickled in alcohol inside his coffin. If we take a direct hit, will he burn like a torch or simply trickle out in a decaying stream onto the crypt floor, I wonder. Board is provided by a gas ring, over which are cooked wretched tea and indescribable kippers. To pay for all this luxury I am to stand on the roofs of St. Paul's and put out incendiaries.

I must also accomplish the purpose of this practicum, whatever it may be. Right now the only purpose I care about is staying alive until the second letter from uncle arrives and I can go home.

I am doing make-work until Langby has time to "show me the ropes." I've cleaned the skillet they cook the foul little fishes in, stacked wooden folding chairs at the altar end of the crypt (flat instead of standing because they tend to collapse like bombs in the middle of the night), and tried to sleep.

I am apparently not one of the lucky ones who can sleep through the raids. I spent most of the night wondering what St. Paul's risk rating is. Practica have to be at least a six. Last night I was convinced this was a ten, with the crypt as ground zero, and that I might as well have applied for Denver.

The most interesting thing that's happened so far is that I've seen a cat. I am fascinated, but trying not to appear so, since they seem commonplace here.

September 22—Still in the crypt. Langby comes dashing through periodically cursing various government agencies (all abbreviated) and promising to take me up on the roofs. In the meantime I've run out of make-work and taught myself to work a stirrup pump. Kivrin was overly concerned about my memory retrieval abilities. I have not had any trouble so far. Quite the opposite. I called up fire-fighting information and got the whole manual with pictures, including instructions on the use of the stirrup pump. If the kippers set Lord Nelson on fire, I shall be a hero.

Excitement last night. The sirens went early and some of the chars who clean offices in the City sheltered in the crypt with us. One of them woke me out of a sound sleep, going like an air raid siren. Seems she'd seen a mouse. We had to go whacking at tombs and under the cots with a rubber boot to persuade her it was gone. Obviously what the history department had in mind: murdering mice.

September 24—Langby took me on rounds. Into the choir, where I had to learn the stirrup pump all over again, assigned rubber boots and a tin helmet. Langby says Commander Allen is getting us asbestos firemen's coats, but hasn't yet, so it's my own wool coat and muffler and very cold on the roofs even in September. It feels like November and looks it, too, bleak and cheerless with no sun. Up to the dome and onto the roofs, which should be flat but in fact are littered with towers, pinnacles, gutters, statues, all designed expressly to catch and hold incendiaries out of reach. Shown how to smother an incendiary with sand before it burns through the roof and sets the church on fire. Shown the ropes (literally) lying in a heap at the base of the dome in case somebody has to go up one of the west towers or over the top of the dome. Back inside and down to the Whispering Gallery.

Langby kept up a running commentary through the whole tour, part practical instruction, part church history. Before we went up into the Gallery he dragged me over to the south door to tell me how Christopher Wren stood in the smoking rubble of Old St. Paul's and asked a workman to bring him a stone from the graveyard to mark the cornerstone. On the stone was written in Latin, "I shall rise again," and Wren was so impressed by the irony that he had the word inscribed above the door. Langby looked as smug as if he had not told me a story every first-year history student knows, but I suppose without the impact of the fire watch stone, the other is just a nice story.

Langby raced me up the steps and onto the narrow balcony circling the Whispering Gallery. He was already halfway around to the other side, shouting dimensions and acoustics at me. He stopped facing the wall opposite and said softly, "You can hear me whispering because of the shape of the dome. The sound waves are reinforced around the perimeter of the dome. It sounds like the very crack of doom up here during a raid. The dome is one hundred and seven feet across. It is eighty feet above the nave."

I looked down. The railing went out from under me and the black-and-white marble floor came up with dizzying speed. I hung on to something in front of me and dropped to my knees, staggered and sick at heart. The sun had come out, and all of St. Paul's seemed drenched in gold. Even the carved wood of the choir, the white stone pillars, the leaden pipes of the organ, all of it golden, golden.

Langby was beside me, trying to pull me free. "Bartholomew," he shouted, "what's wrong? For God's sake, man."

I knew I must tell him that if I let go, St. Paul's and all the past would fall in on me, and that I must not let that happen because I was an historian. I said something, but it was not what I intended because Langby merely tightened his grip. He hauled me violently free of the railing and back onto the stairway, then let me collapse limply on the steps and stood back from me, not speaking.

"I don't know what happened in there," I said. "I've never been afraid of heights before."

"You're shaking," he said sharply. "You'd better lie down." He led me back to the crypt.

September 25—Memory retrieval: ARP manual. Symptoms of bombing victims. Stage one—shock; stupefaction; unawareness of injuries; words may not make sense except to victim. Stage two—shivering; nausea; injuries, losses felt; return to reality. Stage three—talkativeness that cannot be controlled; desire to explain shock behavior to rescuers.

Langby must surely recognize the symptoms, but how does he account for the fact there was no bomb? I can hardly explain my shock behavior to him, and it isn't just the sacred silence of the historian that stops me.

He has not said anything, in fact assigned me my first watches for tomorrow night as if nothing had happened, and he seems no more preoccupied than anyone else. Everyone I've met so far is jittery (one thing I had in short-term was how calm everyone was during the raids) and the raids have not come near us since I got here. They've been mostly over the East End and the docks.

There was a reference tonight to a UXB, and I have been thinking about the Dean's manner and the church being closed when I'm almost sure I remember reading it was open through the entire Blitz. As soon as I get a chance, I'll try to retrieve the events of September. As to retrieving anything else, I don't see how I can hope to remember the right information until I know what it is I am supposed to do here, if anything.

There are no guidelines for historians, and no restrictions either. I could tell everyone I'm from the future if I thought they would believe me. I could murder Hitler if I could get to Germany. Or could I? Time paradox talk abounds in the history department, and the graduate students back from their practica don't say a word one way or the other. Is there a tough, immutable past? Or is there a new past every day and do we, the historians, make it? And what are the consequences of what we do, if there are consequences? And how do we dare do anything without knowing them? Must we interfere boldly, hoping we do not bring about all our downfalls? Or must we do nothing at all, not interfere, stand by and watch St. Paul's burn to the ground if need be so that we don't change the future?

All those are fine questions for a late-night study session. They do not matter here. I could no more let St. Paul's burn down than I could kill Hitler. No, that is not true. I found that out yesterday in the Whispering Gallery. I could kill Hitler if I caught him setting fire to St. Paul's.

September 26—I met a young woman today. Dean Matthews has opened the church, so the watch have been doing duties as chars and people have started coming in again. The young woman reminded me of Kivrin, though Kivrin is a good deal taller and would never frizz her hair like that. She looked as if she had been crying. Kivrin has looked like that since she got back from her practicum. The Middle Ages were too much for her. I wonder how she would have coped with this. By pouring out her fears to the local priest, no doubt, as I sincerely hoped her look-alike was not going to do.

"May I help you?" I said, not wanting in the least to help. "I'm a volunteer."

She looked distressed. "You're not paid?" she said, and wiped at her reddened nose with a handkerchief. "I read about St. Paul's and the fire watch and all, and I thought perhaps there's a position there for me. In the canteen, like, or something. A paying position." There were tears in her red-rimmed eyes.

"I'm afraid we don't have a canteen," I said as kindly as I could, considering how impatient Kivrin always makes me, "and it's not actually a real shelter. Some of the watch sleep in the crypt. I'm afraid we're all volunteers, though."

"That won't do, then," she said. She dabbed at her eyes with the handkerchief. "I love St. Paul's, but I can't take on volunteer work, not with my little brother Tom back from the country." I was not reading this situation properly. For all the outward signs of distress she sounded quite cheerful and no closer to tears than when she had come in. "I've got to get us a proper place to stay. With Tom back, we can't go on sleeping in the tubes."

A sudden feeling of dread, the kind of sharp pain you get sometimes from involuntary retrieval, went over me. "The tubes?" I said, trying to get at the memory.

"Marble Arch, usually," she went on. "My brother Tom saves us a place early and I go . . ." She stopped, held the handkerchief close to her nose, and exploded into it. "I'm sorry," she said, "this awful cold!"

Red nose, watering eyes, sneezing. Respiratory infection. It was a wonder I hadn't told her not to cry. It's only by luck that I haven't made some unforgivable mistake so far, and this is not because I can't get at the long-term memory. I don't have half the information I need even stored: cats and colds and the way St. Paul's looks in full sun. It's only a matter of time before I am stopped cold by something I do not know. Nevertheless, I am going to try for retrieval tonight after I come off watch. At least I can find out whether and when something is going to fall on me.

I have seen the cat once or twice. He is coal-black with a white patch on his throat that looks as if it were painted on for the blackout.

September 27—I have just come down from the roofs. I am still shaking.

Early in the raid the bombing was mostly over the East End. The view was incredible. Searchlights everywhere, the sky pink from the fires and reflecting in the Thames, the exploding shells sparkling like fireworks. There was a constant, deafening thunder broken by the occasional droning of the planes high overhead, then the repeating stutter of the ack-ack guns.

About midnight the bombs began falling quite near with a horrible sound like a train running over me. It took every bit of will I had to keep from flinging myself flat on the roof, but Langby was watching. I didn't want to give him the satisfaction of watching a repeat performance of my behavior in the dome. I kept my head up and my sand bucket firmly in hand and felt quite proud of myself.

The bombs stopped roaring past about three, and there was a lull of about half an hour, and then a clatter like hail on the roofs. Everybody except Langby dived for shovels and stirrup pumps. He was watching me. And I was watching the incendiary.

It had fallen only a few meters from me, behind the clock tower. It was much smaller than I had imagined, only about thirty centimeters long. It was sputtering violently, throwing greenish-white fire almost to where I was standing. In a minute it would simmer down into a molten mass and begin to burn through the roof. Flames and the frantic shouts of firemen, and then the white rubble stretching for miles, and nothing, nothing left, not even the fire watch stone.

It was the Whispering Gallery all over again. I felt that I had said something, and when I looked at Langby's face he was smiling crookedly.

"St. Paul's will burn down," I said. "There won't be anything left."

"Yes," Langby said. "That's the idea, isn't it? Burn St. Paul's to the ground? Isn't that the plan?"

"Whose plan?" I said stupidly.

"Hitler's, of course," Langby said. "Who did you think I meant?" and, almost casually, picked up his stirrup pump.

The page of the ARP manual flashed suddenly before me. I poured the bucket of sand around the still-sputtering bomb, snatched up another bucket and dumped that on top of it. Black smoke billowed up in such a cloud that I could hardly find my shovel. I felt for the smothered bomb with the tip of it and scooped it into the empty bucket, then shoveled the sand in on top of it. Tears were streaming down my face from the acrid smoke. I turned to wipe them on my sleeve and saw Langby.

He had not made a move to help me. He smiled. "It's not a bad plan, actually. But of course we won't let it happen. That's what the fire watch is here for. To see that it doesn't happen. Right, Bartholomew?"

I know now what the purpose of my practicum is. I must stop Langby from burning down St. Paul's.

September 28—I try to tell myself I was mistaken about Langby last night, that I misunderstood what he said. Why would he want to burn down St. Paul's unless he is a Nazi spy? How can a Nazi spy have gotten on the fire watch? I think about my faked letter of introduction and shudder.

How can I find out? If I set him some test, some fatal thing that only a loyal Englishman in 1940 would know, I fear I am the one who would be caught out. I *must* get my retrieval working properly.

Until then, I shall watch Langby. For the time being at least that should be easy. Langby has just posted the watches for the next two weeks. We stand every one together.

September 30—I know what happened in September. Langby told me.

Last night in the choir, putting on our coats and boots, he said, "They've already tried once, you know."

I had no idea what he meant. I felt as helpless as that first day when he asked me if I was from the ayarpee.

"The plan to destroy St. Paul's. They've already tried once. The tenth of September. A high explosive bomb. But of course you didn't know about that. You were in Wales."

I was not even listening. The minute he had said "high explosive bomb" I had remembered it all. It had burrowed in under the road and lodged on the foundations. The bomb squad had tried to defuse it, but there was a leaking gas main. They decided to evacuate St. Paul's, but Dean Matthews refused to leave, and they got it out after all and exploded it in Barking Marshes. Instant and complete retrieval.

"The bomb squad saved her that time," Langby was saying. "It seems there's always somebody about."

"Yes," I said, "there is," and walked away from him.

October 1—I thought last night's retrieval of the events of September tenth meant some sort of breakthrough, but I have been lying here on my cot most of the night trying for Nazi spies in St. Paul's and getting nothing. Do I have to know exactly what I'm looking for before I can remember it? What good does that do me?

Maybe Langby is not a Nazi spy. Then what is he? An arsonist? A madman? The crypt is hardly conducive to thought, being not at all as silent as a tomb. The chars talk most of the night and the sound of the bombs is muffled, which somehow makes it worse. I find myself straining to hear them. When I did get to sleep this morning, I dreamed about one of the tube shelters being hit, broken mains, drowning people.

October 4—I tried to catch the cat today. I had some idea of persuading it to dispatch the mouse that has been terrifying the chars. I also wanted to see one up close. I took the water bucket I had used with the stirrup pump last night to put out some burning shrapnel from one of the antiaircraft guns. It still had a bit of water in it, but not enough to drown the cat, and my plan was to clamp the bucket over him, reach under, and pick him up, then carry him down to the crypt and point him at the mouse. I did not even come close to him.

I swung the bucket, and as I did so, perhaps an inch of water splashed out. I thought I remembered that the cat was a domesticated animal, but I must have been wrong about that. The cat's wide complacent face pulled back into a skull-like mask that was absolutely terrifying, vicious claws extended from what I had thought were harmless paws, and the cat let out a sound to top the chars.

In my surprise I dropped the bucket and it rolled against one of the pillars. The cat disappeared. Behind me, Langby said, "That's no way to catch a cat."

"Obviously," I said, and bent to retrieve the bucket.

"Cats hate water," he said, still in that expressionless voice.

"Oh," I said, and started in front of him to take the bucket back to the choir. "I didn't know that."

"Everybody knows it. Even the stupid Welsh."

October 8—We have been standing double watches for a week—bomber's moon. Langby didn't show up on the roofs, so I went looking for him in the church. I found him standing by the west doors talking to an old man. The man had a newspaper tucked under his arm and he handed it to Langby, but Langby gave it back to him. When the man saw me, he ducked out. Langby said, "Tourist. Wanted to know where the Windmill Theatre is. Read in the paper the girls are starkers."

I know I looked as if I didn't believe him because he said, "You look rotten, old man. Not getting enough sleep, are you? I'll get somebody to take the first watch for you tonight."

"No," I said coldly. "I'll stand my own watch. I like being on the roofs," and added silently, where I can watch you.

He shrugged and said, "I suppose it's better than being

down in the crypt. At least on the roofs you can hear the one that gets you."

October 10—I thought the double watches might be good for me, take my mind off my inability to retrieve. The watched-pot idea. Actually, it sometimes works. A few hours of thinking about something else, or a good night's sleep, and the fact pops forward without any prompting, without any artificials.

The good night's sleep is out of the question. Not only do the chars talk constantly, but the cat has moved into the crypt and sidles up to everyone, making siren noises and begging for kippers. I am moving my cot out of the transept and over by Nelson before I go on watch. He may be pickled, but he keeps his mouth shut.

October 11—I dreamed Trafalgar, ships' guns and smoke and falling plaster and Langby shouting my name. My first waking thought was that the folding chairs had gone off. I could not see for all the smoke.

"I'm coming," I said, limping toward Langby and pulling on my boots. There was a heap of plaster and tangled folding chairs in the transept. Langby was digging in it. "Bartholomew!" he shouted, flinging a chunk of plaster aside. "Bartholomew!"

I still had the idea it was smoke. I ran back for the stirrup pump and then knelt beside him and began pulling on a splintered chair back. It resisted, and it came to me suddenly. There is a body under here. I will reach for a piece of the ceiling and find it is a hand. I leaned back on my heels, determined not to be sick, then went at the pile again.

Langby was going far too fast, jabbing with a chair leg. I grabbed his hand to stop him, and he struggled against me as if I were a piece of rubble to be thrown aside. He picked up a large flat square of plaster, and under it was the floor. I turned and looked behind me. Both chars huddled in the recess by the altar. "Who are you looking for?" I said, keeping hold of Langby's arm.

"Bartholomew," he said, and swept the rubble aside, his hands bleeding through the coating of smoky dust.

"I'm here," I said. "I'm all right." I choked on the white dust. "I moved my cot out of the transept."

He turned sharply to the chars and then said quite calmly, "What's under here?"

"Only the gas ring," one of them said timidly from the shadowed recess, "and Mrs. Galbraith's pocketbook." He dug through the mess until he had found them both. The gas ring was leaking at a merry rate, though the flame had gone out.

"You've saved St. Paul's and me after all," I said, standing there in my underwear and boots, holding the useless stirrup pump. "We might all have been asphyxiated."

He stood up. "I shouldn't have saved you," he said.

Stage one: shock, stupefaction, unawareness of injuries, words may not make sense except to victim. He would not know his hand was bleeding yet. He would not remember what he had said. He had said he shouldn't have saved my life.

"I shouldn't have saved you," he repeated. "I have my duty to think of."

"You're bleeding," I said sharply. "You'd better lie down." I sounded just like Langby in the gallery.

October 13—It was a high-explosive bomb. It blew a hole in the Choir, and some of the marble statuary is broken, but the ceiling of the crypt did not collapse, which is what I thought at first. It only jarred some plaster loose.

I do not think Langby has any idea what he said. That should give me some sort of advantage, now that I am sure where the danger lies, now that I am sure it will not come crashing down from some other direction. But what good is all this knowing, when I do not know what he will do? Or when?

Surely I have the facts of yesterday's bomb in long-term, but even falling plaster did not jar them loose this time. I am not even trying for retrieval, now. I lie in the darkness waiting for the roof to fall in on me. And remembering how Langby saved my life.

October 15—The girl came in again today. She still has the cold, but she has gotten her paying position. It was a joy to see her. She was wearing a smart uniform and open-toed shoes, and her hair was in an elaborate frizz around her face. We are still cleaning up the mess from the bomb, and Langby was out with Allen getting wood to board up the Choir, so I let the girl chatter at me while I swept. The dust made her sneeze, but at least this time I knew what she was doing.

She told me her name is Enola and that she's working for the WVS, running one of the mobile canteens that are sent to the fires. She came, of all things, to thank me for the job. She said that after she told the WVS that there was no proper shelter with a canteen for St. Paul's, they gave her a run in the City. "So I'll just pop in when I'm close and let you know how I'm making out, won't I just?"

She and her brother Tom are still sleeping in the tubes. I asked her if that was safe and she said probably not, but at least down there you couldn't hear the one that got you and that was a blessing.

October 18—I am so tired I can hardly write this. Nine incendiaries tonight and a land mine that looked as though it was going to catch on the dome till the wind drifted its parachute away from the church. I put out two of the incendiaries. I have done that at least twenty times since I got here and helped with dozens of others, and still it is not enough. One incendiary, one moment of not watching Langby, could undo it all.

I know that is partly why I feel so tired. I wear myself out every night trying to do my job and watch Langby, making sure none of the incendiaries falls without my seeing it. Then I go back to the crypt and wear myself out trying to retrieve something, anything, about spies, fires, St. Paul's in the fall of 1940, anything. It haunts me that I am not doing enough, but I do not know what else to do. Without the retrieval, I am as helpless as these poor people here, with no idea what will happen tomorrow.

If I have to, I will go on doing this till I am called home. He cannot burn down St. Paul's so long as I am here to put out the incendiaries. "I have my duty," Langby said in the crypt.

And I have mine.

October 21—It's been nearly two weeks since the blast and I just now realized we haven't seen the cat since. He wasn't in the mess in the crypt. Even after Langby and I were sure there was no one in there, we sifted through the stuff twice more. He could have been in the Choir, though.

Old Bence-Jones says not to worry. "He's all right," he said. "The Jerries could bomb London right down to the ground and the cats would waltz out to greet them. You know why? They don't love anybody. That's what gets half of us killed. Old lady out in Stepney got killed the other night trying to save her cat. Bloody cat was in the Anderson."

"Then where is he?"

"Someplace safe, you can bet on that. If he's not around St. Paul's, it means we're for it. That old saw about the rats deserting a sinking ship, that's a mistake, that is. It's cats, not rats."

October 25—Langby's tourist showed up again. He cannot still be looking for the Windmill Theatre. He had a newspaper under his arm again today, and he asked for Langby, but Langby was across town with Allen, trying to get the asbestos firemen's coats. I saw the name of the paper. It was *The Worker*. A Nazi newspaper?

November 2—I've been up on the roofs for a week straight, helping some incompetent workmen patch the hole the bomb made. They're doing a terrible job. There's still a great gap on one side a man could fall into, but they insist it'll be all right because, after all, you wouldn't fall clear through but only as far as the ceiling, and "the fall can't kill you." They don't seem to understand it's a perfect hiding place for an incendiary.

And that is all Langby needs. He does not even have to set a fire to destroy St. Paul's. All he needs to do is let one burn uncaught until it is too late.

I could not get anywhere with the workmen. I went down into the church to complain to Matthews, and saw Langby and his tourist behind a pillar, close to one of the windows. Langby was holding a newspaper and talking to the man. When I came down from the library an hour later, they were still there. So is the gap. Matthews says we'll put planks across it and hope for the best.

November 5—I have given up trying to retrieve. I am so far behind on my sleep I can't even retrieve information on a newspaper whose name I already know. Double watches the permanent thing now. Our chars have abandoned us altogether (like the cat), so the crypt is quiet, but I cannot sleep.

If I do manage to doze off, I dream. Yesterday I dreamed Kivrin was on the roofs, dressed like a saint. "What was the secret of your practicum?" I said. "What were you supposed to find out?"

She wiped her nose with a handkerchief and said, "Two things. One, that silence and humility are the sacred burdens of the historian. Two"—she stopped and sneezed into the handkerchief—"don't sleep in the tubes."

My only hope is to get hold of an artificial and induce a trance. That's a problem. I'm positive it's too early for chemical endorphins and probably hallucinogens. Alcohol is definitely available, but I need something more concentrated than ale, the only alcohol I know by name. I do not dare ask the watch. Langby is suspicious enough of me already. It's back to the OED, to look up a word I don't know.

November 11—The cat's back. Langby was out with Allen again, still trying for the asbestos coats, so I thought it was safe to leave St. Paul's. I went to the grocer's for supplies, and hopefully an artificial. It was late, and the sirens sounded before I had even gotten to Cheapside, but the raids do not usually start until after dark. It took a while to get all the groceries and to get up my courage to ask whether he had any alcohol—he told me to go to a pub—and when I came out of the shop, it was as if I had pitched suddenly into a hole.

I had no idea where St. Paul's lay, or the street, or the shop I had just come from. I stood on what was no longer the sidewalk, clutching my brown-paper parcel of kippers and bread with a hand I could not have seen if I held it up before my face. I reached up to wrap my muffler closer about my neck and prayed for my eyes to adjust, but there was no reduced light to adjust to. I would have been glad of the moon, for all St. Paul's watch cursed it and called it a fifth columnist. Or a bus, with its shuttered headlights giving just enough light to orient myself by. Or a searchlight. Or the kickback flare of an ack-ack gun. Anything.

Just then I did see a bus, two narrow yellow slits a long way off. I started toward it and nearly pitched off the curb. Which meant the bus was sideways in the street, which meant it was not a bus. A cat meowed, quite near, and rubbed against my leg. I looked down into the yellow lights I had thought belonged to the bus. His eyes were picking up light from somewhere, though I would have sworn there was not a light for miles, and reflecting it flatly up at me.

"A warden'll get you for those lights, old Tom," I said, and then as a plane droned overhead, "Or a Jerry."

The world exploded suddenly into light, the searchlights and a glow along the Thames seeming to happen almost simultaneously, lighting my way home.

"Come to fetch me, did you, old Tom?" I said gaily. "Where've you been? Knew we were out of kippers, didn't you? I call that loyalty." I talked to him all the way home and gave him half a tin of the kippers for saving my life. Bence-Jones said he smelled the milk at the grocer's.

November 13—I dreamed I was lost in the blackout. I could not see my hands in front of my face, and Dunworthy came and shone a pocket torch at me, but I could only see where I had come from and not where I was going.

"What good is that to them?" I said. "They need a light to show them where they're going."

"Even the light from the Thames? Even the light from the fires and the ack-ack guns?" Dunworthy said.

"Yes. Anything is better than this awful darkness." So he came closer to give me the pocket torch. It was not a pocket torch, after all, but Christ's lantern from the Hunt picture in the south nave. I shone it on the curb before me so I could find my way home, but it shone instead on the fire watch stone and I hastily put the light out.

November 20—I tried to talk to Langby today. "I've seen you talking to the old gentleman," I said. It sounded like an accusation. I meant it to. I wanted him to think it was and stop whatever he was planning.

"Reading," he said. "Not talking." He was putting things in order in the choir, piling up sandbags.

"I've seen you reading then," I said belligerently, and he dropped a sandbag and straightened.

"What of it?" he said. "It's a free country. I can read to an old man if I want, same as you can talk to that little WVS tart."

"What do you read?" I said.

"Whatever he wants. He's an old man. He used to come home from his job, have a bit of brandy and listen to his wife read the papers to him. She got killed in one of the raids. Now I read to him. I don't see what business it is of yours."

It sounded true. It didn't have the careful casualness of a lie, and I almost believed him, except that I had heard the tone of truth from him before. In the crypt. After the bomb.

"I thought he was a tourist looking for the Windmill," I said.

He looked blank only a second, and then he said, "Oh, yes, that. He came in with the paper and asked me to tell him where it was. I looked it up to find the address. Clever, that. I didn't guess he couldn't read it for himself." But it was enough. I knew that he was lying.

He heaved a sandbag almost at my feet. "Of course you wouldn't understand a thing like that, would you? A simple act of human kindness?"

"No," I said coldly. "I wouldn't."

None of this proves anything. He gave away nothing, except perhaps the name of an artificial, and I can hardly go to Dean Matthews and accuse Langby of reading aloud.

I waited till he had finished in the choir and gone down to the crypt. Then I lugged one of the sandbags up to the roof and over to the chasm. The planking has held so far, but everyone walks gingerly around it, as if it were a grave. I cut the sandbag open and spilled the loose sand into the bottom. If it has occurred to Langby that this is the perfect spot for an incendiary, perhaps the sand will smother it.

November 21—I gave Enola some of "uncle's" money today and asked her to get me the brandy. She was more reluctant than I thought she'd be, so there must be societal complications I am not aware of, but she agreed.

I don't know what she came for. She started to tell me about her brother and some prank he'd pulled in the tubes that got him in trouble with the guard, but after I asked her about the brandy, she left without finishing the story.

November 25—Enola came today, but without bringing the brandy. She is going to Bath for the holidays to see her aunt. At least she will be away from the raids for a while. I will not have to worry about her. She finished the story of her brother and told me she hopes to persuade this aunt to take Tom for the duration of the Blitz but is not at all sure the aunt will be willing.

Young Tom is apparently not so much an engaging scapegrace as a near criminal. He has been caught twice picking pockets in the Bank tube shelter, and they have had to go back to Marble Arch. I comforted her as best I could, told her all boys were bad at one time or another. What I really wanted to say was that she needn't worry at all, that young Tom strikes me as a true survivor type, like my own tom, like Langby, totally unconcerned with anybody but himself, well equipped to survive the Blitz and rise to prominence in the future.

Then I asked her whether she had gotten the brandy. She looked down at her open-toed shoes and muttered unhappily, "I thought you'd forgotten all about that."

I made up some story about the watch taking turns buying a bottle, and she seemed less unhappy, but I am not convinced she will not use this trip to Bath as an excuse to do nothing. I will have to leave St. Paul's and buy it myself, and I don't dare leave Langby alone in the church. I made her promise to bring the brandy today before she leaves. But she is still not back, and the sirens have already gone.

November 26—No Enola, and she said their train left at noon. I suppose I should be grateful that at least she is safely out of London. Maybe in Bath she will be able to get over her cold.

Tonight one of the ARP girls breezed in to borrow half our cots and tell us about a mess over in the East End where a surface shelter was hit. Four dead, twelve wounded. "At least it wasn't one of the tube shelters!" she said. "Then you'd see a real mess, wouldn't you?"

November 30—I dreamed I took the cat to St. John's Wood.

"Is this a rescue mission?" Dunworthy said.

"No, sir," I said proudly. "I know what I was supposed to find in my practicum. The perfect survivor. Tough and resourceful and selfish. This is the only one I could find. I had to kill Langby, you know, to keep him from burning down St. Paul's. Enola's brother has gone to Bath, and the others will never make it. Enola wears open-toed shoes in the winter and sleeps in the tubes and puts her hair up on metal pins so it will curl. She cannot possibly survive the Blitz."

Dunworthy said, "Perhaps you should have rescued her instead. What did you say her name was?"

"Kivrin," I said, and woke up cold and shivering.

December 5—I dreamed Langby had the pinpoint bomb. He carried it under his arm like a brown paper parcel, coming out of St. Paul's Station and around Ludgate Hill to the west doors.

"This is not fair," I said, barring his way with my arm. "There is no fire watch on duty."

He clutched the bomb to his chest like a pillow. "That is your fault," he said, and before I could get to my stirrup pump and bucket, he tossed it in the door.

The pinpoint was not even invented until the end of the twentieth century, and it was another ten years before the dispossessed communists got hold of it and turned it into something that could be carried under your arm. A parcel that could blow a quarter mile of the City into oblivion. Thank God that is one dream that cannot come true.

It was a sunlit morning in the dream, and this morning when I came off watch the sun was shining for the first time in weeks. I went down to the crypt and then came up again, making the rounds of the roofs twice more, then the steps and the grounds and all the treacherous alleyways between where an incendiary could be missed. I felt better after that, but when I got to sleep I dreamed again, this time of fire and Langby watching it, smiling.

December 15—I found the cat this morning. Heavy raids last night, but most of them over toward Canning Town and nothing on the roofs to speak of. Nevertheless the cat was quite dead. I found him lying on the steps this morning when I made my own, private rounds. Concussion. There was not a mark on him anywhere except the white blackout patch on his throat, but when I picked him up, he was all jelly under the skin.

I could not think what to do with him. I thought for one mad moment of asking Matthews if I could bury him in the crypt. Honorable death in war or something. Trafalgar, Waterloo, London, died in battle. I ended by wrapping him in my muffler and taking him down Ludgate Hill to a building that had been bombed out and burying him in the rubble. It will do no good. The rubble will be no protection from dogs or rats, and I shall never get another muffler. I have gone through nearly all of uncle's money.

I should not be sitting here. I haven't checked the alleyways or the rest of the steps, and there might be a dud or a delayed incendiary or something that I missed.

When I came here, I thought of myself as the noble rescuer, the savior of the past. I am not doing very well at the job. At least Enola is out of it. I wish there were some way I could send St. Paul's to Bath for safekeeping. There were hardly any raids last night. Bence-Jones said cats can survive anything. What if he was coming to get me, to show me the way home? All the bombs were over Canning Town.

December 16—Enola has been back a week. Seeing her, standing on the west steps where I found the cat, sleeping in Marble Arch and not safe at all, was more than I could absorb. "I thought you were in Bath," I said stupidly.

"My aunt said she'd take Tom but not me as well. She's got a houseful of evacuation children, and what a noisy lot. Where is your muffler?" she said. "It's dreadful cold up here on the hill."

"I . . ." I said, unable to answer. "I lost it."

"You'll never get another one," she said. "They're going to start rationing clothes. And wool, too. You'll never get another one like that."

"I know," I said, blinking at her.

"Good things just thrown away," she said. "It's absolutely criminal, that's what it is."

I don't think I said anything to that, just turned and walked away with my head down, looking for bombs and dead animals.

December 20—Langby isn't a Nazi. He's a communist. I can hardly write this. A communist.

One of the chars found *The Worker* wedged behind a pillar and brought it down to the crypt as we were coming off the first watch.

"Bloody communists," Bence-Jones said. "Helping Hitler, they are. Talking against the king, stirring up trouble in the shelters. Traitors, that's what they are."

"They love England same as you," the char said.

"They don't love nobody but themselves, bloody selfish lot. I wouldn't be surprised to hear they were ringing Hitler up on the telephone," Bence-Jones said. " 'Ello, Adolf, here's where to drop the bombs.' "

The kettle on the gas ring whistled. The char stood up and poured the hot water into a chipped teapot, then sat back down. "Just because they speak their minds don't mean they'd burn down old St. Paul's, does it now?"

"Of course not," Langby said, coming down the stairs. He sat down and pulled off his boots, stretching his feet in their wool socks. "Who wouldn't burn down St. Paul's?"

"The communists," Bence-Jones said, looking straight at him, and I wondered if he suspected Langby too.

Langby never batted an eye. "I wouldn't worry about them if I were you," he said. "It's the Jerries that are doing their bloody best to burn her down tonight. Six incendiaries so far, and one almost went into that great hole over the choir." He held out his cup to the char, and she poured him a cup of tea.

I wanted to kill him, smashing him to dust and rubble on the floor of the crypt while Bence-Jones and the char looked on in helpless surprise, shouting warnings to them and the rest of the watch. "Do you know what the communists did?" I wanted to shout. "Do you? We have to stop him." I even stood up and started toward him as he sat with his feet stretched out before him and his asbestos coat still over his shoulders.

And then the thought of the Gallery drenched in gold, the communist coming out of the tube station with the package so casually under his arm, made me sick with the same staggering vertigo of guilt and helplessness, and I sat back down on the edge of my cot and tried to think what to do.

They do not realize the danger. Even Bence-Jones, for all his talk of traitors, thinks they are capable only of talking against the king. They do not know, cannot know, what the communists will become. Stalin is an ally. Communists mean Russia. They have never heard of Karinsky or the New Russia or any of the things that will make "communist" into a synonym for "monster." They will never know it. By the time the communists become what they became, there will be no fire watch. Only I know what it means to hear the name "communist" uttered here, so carelessly, in St. Paul's.

A communist. I should have known. I should have known.

December 22—Double watches again. I have not had any sleep and I am getting very unsteady on my feet. I nearly pitched into the chasm this morning, only saved myself by dropping to my knees. My endorphin levels are fluctuating wildly, and I know I must get some sleep soon or I will become one of Langby's walking dead, but I am afraid to leave him alone on the roofs, alone in the church with his communist party leader, alone anywhere. I have taken to watching him when he sleeps.

If I could just get hold of an artificial, I think I could induce a trance, in spite of my poor condition. But I cannot even go out to a pub. Langby is on the roofs constantly, waiting for his chance. When Enola comes again I must convince her to get the brandy for me. There are only a few days left.

December 28—Enola came this morning while I was on the west porch, picking up the Christmas tree. It has been knocked over three nights running by concussion. I righted the tree and was bending down to pick up the scattered tinsel when Enola appeared suddenly out of the fog like some cheerful saint. She stooped quickly and kissed me on the cheek. Then she straightened up, her nose red from her perennial cold, and handed me a box wrapped in colored paper.

"Merry Christmas," she said. "Go on then, open it. It's a gift."

My reflexes are almost totally gone. I knew the box was far too shallow for a bottle of brandy. Nevertheless, I believed she had remembered, had brought me my salvation. "You darling," I said, and tore it open.

It was a muffler. Gray wool. I stared at it for fully half a minute without realizing what it was. "Where's the brandy?" I said.

She looked shocked. Her nose got redder and her eyes started to blur. "You need this more. You haven't any clothing coupons and you have to be outside all the time. It's been so dreadful cold."

"I *needed* the brandy," I said angrily.

"I was only trying to be kind," she started, and I cut her off.

"Kind?" I said. "I asked you for brandy. I don't recall ever saying I needed a muffler." I shoved it back at her and began untangling a string of colored lights that had shattered when the tree fell.

She got that same holy martyr look Kivrin is so wonderful at. "I worry about you all the time up here," she said in a rush. "They're *trying* for St. Paul's, you know. And it's so close to the river. I didn't think you should be drinking. I—it's a crime when they're trying so hard to kill us all that you won't take care of yourself. It's like you're in it with them. I worry someday I'll come up to St. Paul's and you won't be here."

"Well, and what exactly am I supposed to do with a muffler? Hold it over my head when they drop the bombs?"

She turned and ran, disappearing into the gray fog before she had gone down two steps. I started after her, still holding the string of broken lights, tripped over it, and fell almost all the way to the bottom of the steps.

Langby picked me up. "You're off watches," he said grimly.

"You can't do that," I said.

"Oh, yes, I can. I don't want any walking dead on the roofs with me."

I let him lead me down here to the crypt, make me a cup of tea, put me to bed, all very solicitous. No indication that this is what he has been waiting for. I will lie here till the sirens go. Once I am on the roofs he will not be able to send me back without seeming suspicious. Do you know what he said before he left, asbestos coat and rubber boots, the dedicated fire watcher? "I want you to get some sleep." As if I could sleep with Langby on the roofs. I would be burned alive.

December 30—The sirens woke me, and old Bence-Jones said, "That should have done you some good. You've slept the clock round."

"What day is it?" I said, going for my boots.

"The twenty-ninth," he said, and as I dived for the door, "no need to hurry. They're late tonight. Maybe they won't come at all. That'd be a blessing, that would. The tide's out."

I stopped by the door to the stairs, holding on to the cool stone. "Is St. Paul's all right?"

"She's still standing," he said. "Have a bad dream?"

"Yes," I said, remembering the bad dreams of all the past weeks—the dead cat in my arms in St. John's Wood, Langby with his parcel and his *Worker* under his arm, the fire watch stone garishly lit by Christ's lantern. Then I remembered I had not dreamed at all. I had slept the kind of sleep I had prayed for, the kind of sleep that would help me remember.

Then I remembered. Not St. Paul's, burned to the ground by communists. A headline from the dailies. "Marble Arch hit. Eighteen killed by blast." The date was not clear except for the year. Nineteen forty. There were exactly two more days left in 1940. I grabbed my

coat and muffler and ran up the stairs and across the
marble floor.

"Where the hell do you think you're going?" Langby
shouted to me. I couldn't see him.

"I have to save Enola," I said, and my voice echoed
in the dark sanctuary. "They're going to bomb Marble
Arch."

"You can't leave now," he shouted after me, standing
where the fire watch stone would be. "The tide's out.
You dirty—"

I didn't hear the rest of it. I had already flung myself
down the steps and into a taxi. It took almost all the
money I had, the money I had so carefully hoarded for
the trip back to St. John's Wood. Shelling started while
we were still in Oxford Street, and the driver refused to
go any further. He let me out into pitch blackness, and
I saw I would never make it in time.

Blast. Enola crumpled on the stairway down to the
tube, her open-toed shoes still on her feet, not a mark
on her. And when I try to lift her, jelly under the skin.
I would have to wrap her in the muffler she gave me,
because I was too late. I had gone back a hundred years
to be too late to save her.

I ran the last blocks, guided by the gun emplacement
that had to be in Hyde Park, and skidded down the steps
into Marble Arch. The woman in the ticket booth took
my last shilling for a ticket to St. Paul's Station. I stuck
it in my pocket and raced toward the stairs.

"No running," she said placidly. "To your left, please."
The door to the right was blocked off by wooden barricades, the metal gates beyond pulled to and chained. The
board with names on it for the stations was x-ed with
tape, and a new sign that read ALL TRAINS was nailed to
the barricade, pointing left.

Enola was not on the stopped escalators or sitting
against the wall in the hallway. I came to the first stairway and could not get through. A family had set out,
just where I wanted to step, a communal tea of bread
and butter, a little pot of jam sealed with waxed paper,
and a kettle on a ring like the one Langby and I had

rescued out of the rubble, all of it spread on a cloth embroidered at the corners with flowers. I stood staring down at the layered tea, spread like a waterfall down the steps.

"I—Marble Arch—" I said. Another twenty killed by flying tiles. "You shouldn't be here."

"We've as much right as anyone," the man said belligerently, "and who are you to tell us to move on?"

A woman lifting saucers out of a cardboard box looked up at me, frightened. The kettle began to whistle.

"It's you that should move on," the man said. "Go on then." He stood off to one side so I could pass. I edged past the embroidered cloth apologetically.

"I'm sorry," I said. "I'm looking for someone. On the platform."

"You'll never find her in there, mate, it's hell in there," the man said, thumbing in that direction. I hurried past him, nearly stepping on the tea cloth, and rounded the corner into hell.

It was not hell. Shop girls folded coats and leaned back against them, cheerful or sullen or disagreeable, but certainly not damned. Two boys scuffled for a shilling and lost it on the tracks. They bent over the edge, debating whether to go after it, and the station guard yelled to them to back away. A train rumbled through, full of people. A mosquito landed on the guard's hand and he reached out to slap it and missed. The boys laughed. And behind and before them, stretching in all directions down the deadly tile curves of the tunnel like casualties, back into the entranceways and onto the stairs, were people. Hundreds and hundreds of people.

I stumbled back onto the stairs, knocking over a teacup. It spilled like a flood across the cloth.

"I told you, mate," the man said cheerfully. "It's hell in there, ain't it? And worse below."

"Hell," I said. "Yes." I would never find her. I would never save her. I looked at the woman mopping up the tea, and it came to me that I could not save her either. Enola or the cat or any of them, lost here in the endless stairways and cul-de-sacs of time. They were already dead a hundred years, past saving. The past is beyond saving. Surely that was the lesson the history department sent me all this way to learn. Well, fine, I've learned it. Can I go home now?

Of course not, dear boy. You have foolishly spent all your money on taxicabs and brandy, and tonight is the night the Germans burn the City. (Now it is too late, I remember it all. Twenty-eight incendiaries on the roofs.) Langby must have his chance, and you must learn the hardest lesson of all and the one you should have known from the beginning. You cannot save St. Paul's.

I went back out onto the platform and stood behind the yellow line until a train pulled up. I took my ticket out and held it in my hand all the way to St. Paul's Station. When I got there, smoke billowed toward me like an easy spray of water. I could not see St. Paul's.

"The tide's out," a woman said in a voice devoid of hope, and I went down in a snake pit of limp cloth hoses. My hands came up covered with rank-smelling mud, and I understood finally (and too late) the significance of the tide. There was no water to fight the fires.

A policeman barred my way and I stood helplessly before him with no idea what to say. "No civilians allowed here," he said. "St. Paul's is for it." The smoke billowed like a thundercloud, alive with sparks, and the dome rose golden above it.

"I'm fire watch," I said, and his arm fell away, and then I was on the roofs.

My endorphin levels must have been going up and down like an air raid siren. I do not have any short-term from then on, just moments that do not fit together: the people in the church when we brought Langby down, huddled in a corner playing cards, the whirlwind of burning scraps of wood in the dome, the ambulance driver who wore open-toed shoes like Enola and smeared salve on my burned hands. And in the center, the one clear moment when I went after Langby on a rope and saved his life.

I stood by the dome, blinking against the smoke. The

City was on fire and it seemed as if St. Paul's would ignite from the heat, would crumble from the noise alone. Bence-Jones was by the northwest tower, hitting at an incendiary with a spade. Langby was too close to the patched place where the bomb had gone through, looking toward me. An incendiary clattered behind him. I turned to grab a shovel, and when I turned back, he was gone.

"Langby!" I shouted, and could not hear my own voice. He had fallen into the chasm and nobody saw him or the incendiary. Except me. I do not remember how I got across the roof. I think I called for a rope. I got a rope. I tied it around my waist, gave the ends of it into the hands of the fire watch, and went over the side. The fires lit the walls of the hole almost all the way to the bottom. Below me I could see a pile of whitish rubble. He's under there, I thought, and jumped free of the wall. The space was so narrow there was nowhere to throw the rubble. I was afraid I would inadvertently stone him, and I tried to toss the pieces of planking and plaster over my shoulder, but there was barely room to turn. For one awful moment I thought he might not be there at all, that the pieces of splintered wood would brush away to reveal empty pavement, as they had in the crypt.

I was numbed by the indignity of crawling over him. If he was dead I did not think I could bear the shame of stepping on his helpless body. Then his hand came up like a ghost's and grabbed my ankle, and within seconds I had whirled and had his head free.

He was the ghastly white that no longer frightens me. "I put the bomb out," he said. I stared at him, so overwhelmed with relief I could not speak. For one hysterical moment I thought I would even laugh, I was so glad to see him. I finally realized what it was I was supposed to say.

"Are you all right? I said.

"Yes," he said, and tried to raise himself on one elbow. "So much the worse for you."

He could not get up. He grunted with pain when he tried to shift his weight to his right side and lay back, the uneven rubble crunching sickeningly under him. I tried to lift him gently so I could see where he was hurt. He must have fallen on something.

"It's no use," he said, breathing hard. "I put it out."

I spared him a startled glance, afraid that he was delirious and went back to rolling him onto his side.

"I know you were counting on this one," he went on, not resisting me at all. "It was bound to happen sooner or later with all these roofs. Only I went after it. What'll you tell your friends?"

His asbestos coat was torn down the back in a long gash. Under it his back was charred and smoking. He had fallen on the incendiary. "Oh, my God," I said, trying frantically to see how badly he was burned without touching him. I had no way of knowing how deep the burns went, but they seemed to extend only in the narrow space where the coat had torn. I tried to pull the bomb out from under him, but the casing was as hot as a stove. It was not melting, though. My sand and Langby's body had smothered it. I had no idea if it would start up again when it was exposed to the air. I looked around, a little wildly, for the bucket and stirrup pump Langby must have dropped when he fell.

"Looking for a weapon?" Langby said, so clearly it was hard to believe he was hurt at all. "Why not just leave me here? A bit of overexposure and I'd be done for by morning. Or would you rather do your dirty work in private?"

I stood up and yelled to the men on the roof above us. One of them shone a pocket torch down at us, but its light didn't reach.

"Is he dead?" somebody shouted down to me.

"Send for an ambulance," I said. "He's been burned."

I helped Langby up, trying to support his back without touching the burn. He staggered a little and then leaned against the wall, watching me as I tried to bury the incendiary, using a piece of the planking as a scoop. The rope came down and I tied Langby to it. He had not spoken since I helped him up. He let me tie the rope around his waist, still looking steadily at me. "I should have let you smother in the crypt," he said.

He stood leaning easily, almost relaxed against the wooden supports, his hands holding him up. I put his hands on the slack rope and wrapped it once around them for the grip I knew he didn't have. "I've been on to you since that day in the Gallery. I knew you weren't afraid of heights. You came down here without any fear of heights when you thought I'd ruined your precious plans. What was it? An attack of conscience? Kneeling there like a baby, whining. 'What have we done? What have we done?' You made me sick. But you know what gave you away first? The cat. Everybody knows cats hate water. Everybody but a dirty Nazi spy."

There was a tug on the rope. "Come ahead," I said, and the rope tautened.

"That WVS tart? Was she a spy, too? Supposed to meet you in Marble Arch? Telling me it was going to be bombed. You're a rotten spy, Bartholomew. Your friends already blew it up in September. It's open again."

The rope jerked suddenly and began to lift Langby. He twisted his hands to get a better grip. His right shoulder scraped the wall. I put up my hands and pushed him gently so that his left side was to the wall. "You're making a big mistake, you know," he said. "You should have killed me. I'll tell."

I stood in the darkness, waiting for the rope. Langby was unconscious when he reached the roof. I walked past the fire watch to the dome and down to the crypt.

This morning the letter from my uncle came and with it a five-pound note.

December 31—Two of Dunworthy's flunkies met me in St. John's Wood to tell me I was late for my exams. I did not even protest. I shuffled obediently after them without even considering how unfair it was to give an exam to one of the walking dead. I had not slept in— how long? Since yesterday when I went to find Enola. I had not slept in a hundred years.

Dunworthy was in the Examination Buildings, blinking at me. One of the flunkies handed me a test paper and the other one called time. I turned the paper over and left an oily smudge from the ointment on my burns. I stared uncomprehendingly at them. I had grabbed at the incendiary when I turned Langby over, but these burns were on the backs of my hands. The answer came to me suddenly in Langby's unyielding voice. "They're rope burns, you fool. Don't they teach you Nazi spies the proper way to come up a rope?"

I looked down at the test. I read, "Number of incendiaries that fell on St. Paul's——— Number of land mines——— Number of high explosive bombs———Method most commonly used for extinguishing incendiaries———land mines———high explosive bombs———Number of volunteers on first watch———second watch———Casualties——— Fatalities———" The questions made no sense. There was only a short space, long enough for the writing of a number, after any of the questions. Method most commonly used for extinguishing incendiaries. How would I ever fit what I knew into that narrow space? Where were the questions about Enola and Langby and the cat?

I went up to Dunworthy's desk. "St. Paul's almost burned down last night," I said. "What kind of questions are these?"

"You should be answering questions, Mr. Bartholomew, not asking them."

"There aren't any questions about the people," I said. The outer casing of my anger began to melt.

"Of course there are," Dunworthy said, flipping to the second page of the test. "Number of casualties, 1940. Blast, shrapnel, other."

"Other?" I said. At any moment the roof would collapse on me in a shower of plaster dust and fury. "Other? Langby put out a fire with his own body. Enola has a cold that keeps getting worse. The cat . . ." I snatched the paper back from him and scrawled "one cat" in the narrow space next to "blast." "Don't you care about them at all?"

"They're important from a statistical point of view,"

he said, "but as individuals they are hardly relevant to the course of history."

My reflexes were shot. It was amazing to me that Dunworthy's were almost as slow. I grazed the side of his jaw and knocked his glasses off. "Of course they're relevant!" I shouted. "They *are* the history, not all these bloody numbers!"

The reflexes of the flunkies were very fast. They did not let me start another swing at him before they had me by both arms and were hauling me out of the room.

"They're back there in the past with nobody to save them. They can't see their hands in front of their faces and there are bombs falling down on them and you tell me they aren't important? You call that being an historian?"

The flunkies dragged me out the door and down the hall. "Langby saved St. Paul's. How much more important can a person get? You're no historian! You're nothing but a—" I wanted to call him a terrible name, but the only curses I could summon up were Langby's. "You're nothing but a dirty Nazi spy!" I bellowed. "You're nothing but a lazy bourgeois tart!"

They dumped me on my hands and knees outside the door and slammed it in my face. "I wouldn't be an historian if you paid me!" I shouted, and went to see the fire watch stone.

I am having to write this in bits and pieces. My hands are in pretty bad shape, and Dunworthy's boys didn't help matters much. Kivrin comes in periodically, wearing her St. Joan look, and smears so much salve on my hands that I can't hold a pencil.

St. Paul's Station is not there, of course, so I got out at Holborn and walked, thinking about my last meeting with Dean Matthews on the morning after the burning of the city. This morning.

"I understand you saved Langby's life," he said. "I also understand that between you, you saved St. Paul's last night."

I showed him the letter from my uncle and he stared

at it as if he could not think what it was. "Nothing stays saved forever," he said, and for a terrible moment I thought he was going to tell me Langby had died. "We shall have to keep on saving St. Paul's until Hitler decides to bomb something else."

The raids on London are almost over, I wanted to tell him. He'll start bombing the countryside in a matter of weeks. Canterbury, Bath, aiming always at the cathedrals. You and St. Paul's will both outlast the war and live to dedicate the fire watch stone.

"I am hopeful, though," he said. "I think the worst is over."

"Yes, sir," I thought of the stone, its letters still readable after all this time. No, sir, the worst is not over.

I managed to keep my bearings almost to the top of Ludgate Hill. Then I lost my way completely, wandering about like a man in a graveyard. I had not remembered that the rubble looked so much like the white plaster dust Langby had tried to dig me out of. I could not find the stone anywhere. In the end I nearly fell over it, jumping back as if I had stepped on a body.

It is all that's left. Hiroshima is supposed to have had a handful of untouched trees at ground zero. Denver the capitol steps. Neither of them says, "Remember men and women of St. Paul's Watch who by the grace of God saved this cathedral." The grace of God.

Part of the stone is sheared off. Historians argue there was another line that said, "for all time," but I do not believe that, not if Dean Matthews had anything to do with it. And none of the watch it was dedicated to would have believed it for a minute. We saved St. Paul's every time we put out an incendiary, and only until the next one fell. Keeping watch on the danger spots, putting out the little fires with sand and stirrup pumps, the big ones with our bodies, in order to keep the whole vast complex structure from burning down. Which sounds to me like a course description for History Practicum 401. What a fine time to discover what historians are for when I have tossed my chance for being one out the windows as easily as they tossed the pinpoint bomb in! No, sir, the worst is not over.

There are flash burns on the stone, where legend says the Dean of St. Paul's was kneeling when the bomb went off. Totally apocryphal, of course, since the front door is hardly an appropriate place for prayers. It is more likely the shadow of a tourist who wandered in to ask the whereabouts of the Windmill Theatre, or the imprint of a girl bringing a volunteer his muffler. Or a cat.

Nothing is saved forever, Dean Matthews, and I knew that when I walked in the west doors that first day, blinking into the gloom, but it is pretty bad nevertheless. Standing here knee-deep in rubble out of which I will not be able to dig any folding chairs or friends, knowing that Langby died thinking I was a Nazi spy, knowing that Enola came one day and I wasn't there. It's pretty bad.

But it is not as bad as it could be. They are both dead, and Dean Matthews too, but they died without knowing what I knew all along, what sent me to my knees in the Whispering Gallery, sick with grief and guilt: that in the end none of us saved St. Paul's. And Langby cannot turn to me, stunned and sick at heart, and say, "Who did this? Your friends the Nazis?" And I would have to say, "No, the communists." That would be the worst.

I have come back to the room and let Kivrin smear more salve on my hands. She wants me to get some sleep. I know I should pack and get gone. It will be humiliating to have them come and throw me out, but I do not have the strength to fight her. She looks so much like Enola.

January 1—I have apparently slept not only through the night, but through the morning mail drop as well. When I woke up just now, I found Kivrin sitting on the end of the bed holding an envelope. "Your grades came," she said.

I put my arm over my eyes. "They can be marvelously efficient when they want to, can't they?"

"Yes," Kivrin said.

"Well, let's see it," I said, sitting up. "How long do I have before they come and throw me out?"

She handed the flimsy computer envelope to me. I tore it along the perforation. "Wait," she said. "Before you open it, I want to say something." She put her hand gently on my burns. "You're wrong about the history department. They're very good."

It was not exactly what I expected her to say. "Good is not the word I'd use to describe Dunworthy," I said and yanked the inside slip free.

Kivrin's look did not change, not even when I sat there with the printout on my knees where she could surely see it.

"Well," I said.

The slip was hand-signed by the esteemed Dunworthy. I have taken a first. With honors.

January 2—Two things came in the mail today. One was Kivrin's assignment. The history department thinks of everything—even to keeping her here long enough to nursemaid me, even to coming up with a prefabricated trial by fire to send their history majors through.

I think I wanted to believe that was what they had done. Enola and Langby only hired actors, the cat a clever android with its clockwork innards taken out for the final effect, not so much because I wanted to believe Dunworthy was not good at all, but because then I would not have this nagging pain at not knowing what had happened to them.

"You said your practicum was England in 1400?" I said, watching her as suspiciously as I had watched Langby.

"Thirteen forty-nine," she said, and her face went slack with memory. "The plague year."

"My God," I said. "How could they do that? The plague's a ten."

"I have a natural immunity," she said, and looked at her hands.

Because I could not think of anything to say, I opened the other piece of mail. It was a report on Enola.

Computer-printed, facts and dates and statistics, all the numbers the history department so dearly loves, but it told me what I thought I would have to go without knowing: that she had gotten over her cold and survived the Blitz. Young Tom had been killed in the Baedaker raids on Bath, but Enola had lived until 2006, the year before they blew up St. Paul's.

I don't know whether I believe the report or not, but it does not matter. It is, like Langby's reading aloud to the old man, a simple act of human kindness. They think of everything.

Not quite. They did not tell me what happened to Langby. But I find as I write this that I already know: I saved his life. It does not seem to matter that he might have died in the hospital the next day, and I find, in spite of all the hard lessons the history department has tried to teach me, I do not quite believe this one: that nothing is saved forever. It seems to me that perhaps Langby is.

January 3—I went to see Dunworthy today. I don't know what I intended to say—some pompous drivel about my willingness to serve in the fire watch of history, standing guard against the falling incendiaries of the human heart, silent and saintly.

But he blinked at me nearsightedly across his desk, and it seemed to me that he was blinking at that last bright image of St. Paul's in sunlight before it was gone forever and that he knew better than anyone that the past cannot be saved, and I said instead, "I'm sorry that I broke your glasses, sir."

"How did you like St. Paul's?" he said, and like my first meeting with Enola, I felt I must be somehow reading the signals all wrong, that he was not feeling loss, but something quite different.

"I loved it, sir," I said.

"Yes," he said. "So do I."

Dean Matthews is wrong. I have fought with memory my whole practicum only to find that it is not the enemy at all, and being an historian is not some saintly burden after all. Because Dunworthy is not blinking against the fatal sunlight of the last morning, but into the gloom of that first afternoon, looking in the great west doors of St. Paul's at what is, like Langby, like all of it, every moment, in us, saved forever.

AIR RAID

by John Varley

The saga of "Air Raid"/*Millennium* is the stuff of comic opera, as the development process so often is in Hollywood.

"Air Raid" was conceived one sleepy afternoon at the Milford Conference at the home of Damon Knight and Kate Wilhelm in Eugene, Oregon. It came to me in about thirty seconds, and I went right home and wrote it in one night. I had no way of knowing it, but that story would eventually earn me more money than any of my novels, probably more than any three put together.

The movie rights were optioned by MGM and a production company consisting of John Foreman, a long-time friend of and producer for Paul Newman; Freddie Fields, who used to be Judy Garland's agent; and David Begelman, who had just been convicted of forging checks in Cliff Robertson's name. The director was to be Doug Trumbull, who needs no introduction.

I had no screenwriting experience, but I was hired to write a treatment outlining how to turn the story into a movie while someone else wrote the script. I was also contracted to write a novelization of sorts, though the novel would be independent of the screenplay and in fact would be written long before the screenplay was finalized. This didn't make a lot of sense to me, but the money was good, and I had a free hand.

When the original screenwriter laid an egg, I was hired

to write a script myself. I was hired, eventually, to write *eight* scripts. Six directors and ten years later, after all the life had been squeezed out of the project and I had pretty much lost interest, the resultant movie began filming in Toronto, and I was there from beginning to end, along with no less than seven producers. I'll leave it to the reader to figure out why the end result was less than satisfactory. I take full responsibility.

But I had a lot of fun along the way.

I WAS JERKED awake by the silent alarm vibrating my skull. It won't shut down until you sit up, so I did. All around me in the darkened bunkroom the Snatch Team members were sleeping singly and in pairs. I yawned, scratched my ribs, and patted Gene's hairy flank. He turned over. So much for a romantic send-off.

Rubbing sleep from my eyes, I reached to the floor for my leg, strapped it on, and plugged it in. Then I was running down the rows of bunks toward Ops.

The situation board glowed in the gloom. Sun-Belt Airlines Flight 128, Miami to New York, September 15, 1979. We'd been looking for that one for three years. I should have been happy, but who can afford it when you wake up?

Liza Boston muttered past me on the way to Prep. I muttered back and followed. The lights came on around the mirrors, and I groped my way to one of them. Behind us, three more people staggered in. I sat down, plugged in, and at last I could lean back and close my eyes.

They didn't stay closed for long. Rush! I sat up straight as the sludge I use for blood was replaced with supercharged go-juice. I looked around me and got a series of idiot grins. There was Liza, and Pinky, and Dave. Against the far wall Cristabel was already turning slowly in front of the airbrush, getting a Caucasian paint job. It looked like a good team.

I opened the drawer and started preliminary work on my face. It's a bigger job every time. Transfusion or no,

I looked like death. The right ear was completely gone now. I could no longer close my lips; the gums were permanently bared. A week earlier, a finger had fallen off in my sleep. And what's it to you, bugger?

While I worked, one of the screens around the mirror glowed. A smiling young woman, blonde, high brow, round face. Close enough. The crawl line read *Mary Katrina Sondergard, born Trenton, New Jersey, age in 1979: 25*. Baby, this is your lucky day.

The computer melted the skin away from her face to show me the bone structure, rotated it, gave me cross sections. I studied the similarities with my own skull, noted the differences. Not bad, and better than some I'd been given.

I assembled a set of dentures that included the slight gap in the upper incisors. Putty filled out my cheeks. Contact lenses fell from the dispenser and I popped them in. Nose plugs widened my nostrils. No need for ears; they'd be covered by the wig. I pulled a blank plastiflesh mask over my face and had to pause while it melted in. It took only a minute to mold it to perfection. I smiled at myself. How nice to have lips.

The delivery slot clunked and dropped a blonde wig and a pink outfit into my lap. The wig was hot from the styler. I put it on, then the pantyhose.

"Mandy? Did you get the profile on Sondergard?" I didn't look up; I recognized the voice.

"Roger."

"We've located her near the airport. We can slip you in before takeoff, so you'll be the joker."

I groaned and looked up at the face on the screen. Elfreda Baltimore-Louisville, Director of Operational Teams: lifeless face and tiny slits for eyes. What can you do when all the muscles are dead?

"Okay." You take what you get.

She switched off, and I spent the next two minutes trying to get dressed while keeping my eyes on the screens. I memorized names and faces of crew members plus the few facts known about them. Then I hurried out and caught up with the others. Elapsed time from first alarm: twelve minutes and seven seconds. We'd better get moving.

"Goddam Sun-Belt," Cristabel groused, hitching at her bra.

"At least they got rid of the high heels," Dave pointed out. A year earlier we would have been teetering down the aisles on three-inch platforms. We all wore short pink shifts with blue and white diagonal stripes across the front, and carried matching shoulder bags. I fussed trying to get the ridiculous pillbox cap pinned on.

We jogged into the dark Operations Control Room and lined up at the gate. Things were out of our hands now. Until the gate was ready, we could only wait.

I was first, a few feet away from the portal. I turned away from it; it gives me vertigo. I focused instead on the gnomes sitting at their consoles, bathed in yellow lights from their screens. None of them looked back at me. They don't like us much. I don't like them, either. Withered, emaciated, all of them. Our fat legs and butts and breasts are a reproach to them, a reminder that Snatchers eat five times their ration to stay presentable for the masquerade. Meantime, we continue to rot. One day I'll be sitting at a console. One day I'll be *built in* to a console, with all my guts on the outside and nothing left of my body but stink. The hell with them.

I buried my gun under a clutter of tissues and lipsticks in my purse. Elfreda was looking at me.

"Where is she?" I asked.

"Motel room. She was alone from ten P.M. to noon on flight day."

Departure time was one-fifteen. She had cut it close and would be in a hurry. Good.

"Can you catch her in the bathroom? Best of all, in the tub?"

"We're working on it." She sketched a smile with a fingertip drawn over lifeless lips. She knew how I liked to operate, but she was telling me I'd take what I got. It never hurts to ask. People are at their most defenseless stretched out and up to their necks in water.

"Go!" Elfreda shouted. I stepped through, and things started to go wrong.

I was facing the wrong way, stepping *out* of the bathroom door and facing the bedroom. I turned and spotted Mary Katrina Sondergard through the haze of the gate. There was no way I could reach her without stepping back through. I couldn't even shoot without hitting someone on the other side.

Sondergard was at the mirror, the worst possible place. Few people recognize themselves quickly, but she'd been looking right at herself. She saw me and her eyes widened. I stepped to the side, out of her sight.

"What the hell is . . . hey? Who the hell—" I noted the voice, which can be the trickiest thing to get right.

I figured she'd be more curious than afraid. My guess was right. She came out of the bathroom, passing through the gate as if it wasn't there, which it wasn't, since it only has one side. She had a towel wrapped around her.

"Jesus Christ! What are you doing in my—" Words fail you at a time like that. She knew she ought to say something, but what? *Excuse me, haven't I seen you in the mirror?*

I put on my best stew smile and held out my hand.

"Pardon the intrusion. I can explain everything. You see, I'm—" I hit her on the side of the head and she staggered and went down hard. Her towel fell to the floor. "—working my way through college." She started to get up, so I caught her under the chin with my artificial knee. She stayed down.

"Standard fuggin' *Oil!*" I hissed, rubbing my injured knuckles. But there was no time. I knelt beside her, checked her pulse. She'd be okay, but I think I loosened some front teeth. I paused a moment. Lord, to look like that with no makeup, no prosthetics! She nearly broke my heart.

I grabbed her under the knees and wrestled her to the gate. She was a sack of limp noodles. Somebody reached through, grabbed her feet, and pulled. *So long, love! How would you like to go on a long voyage?*

I sat on her rented bed to get my breath. There were

car keys and cigarettes in her purse, genuine tobacco, worth its weight in blood. I lit six of them, figuring I had five minutes of my very own. The room filled with sweet smoke. They don't make 'em like that anymore.

The Hertz sedan was in the motel parking lot. I got in and headed for the airport. I breathed deeply of the air, rich in hydrocarbons. I could see for hundreds of yards into the distance. The perspective nearly made me dizzy, but I live for those moments. There's no way to explain what it's like in the pre-meck world. The sun was a fierce yellow ball through the haze.

The other stews were boarding. Some of them knew Sondergard so I didn't say much, pleading a hangover. That went over well, with a lot of knowing laughs and sly remarks. Evidently it wasn't out of character. We boarded the 707 and got ready for the goats to arrive.

It looked good. The four commandos on the other side were identical twins for the women I was working with. There was nothing to do but be a stewardess until departure time. I hoped there would be no more glitches. Inverting a gate for a joker run into a motel room was one thing, but in a 707 at twenty thousand feet . . .

The plane was nearly full when the woman Pinky would impersonate sealed the forward door. We taxied to the end of the runway, then we were airborne. I started taking orders for drinks in first.

The goats were the usual lot, for 1979. Fat and sassy, all of them, and as unaware of living in a paradise as a fish is of the sea. *What would you think, ladies and gents, of a trip to the future? No? I can't say I'm surprised. What if I told you this plane is going to—*

My alarm beeped as we reached cruising altitude. I consulted the indicator under my Lady Bulova and glanced at one of the restroom doors. I felt a vibration pass through the plane. *Damn it, not so soon.*

The gate was in there. I came out quickly, and motioned for Diana Gleason—Dave's pigeon—to come to the front.

"Take a look at this," I said, with a disgusted look. She started to enter the restroom, stopped when she saw the green glow. I planted a boot on her fanny and shoved. Perfect. Dave would have a chance to hear her voice before popping in. Though she'd be doing little but screaming when she got a look around. . . .

Dave came through the gate, adjusting his silly little hat. Diana must have struggled.

"Be disgusted," I whispered.

"What a mess," he said as he came out of the rest-room. It was a fair imitation of Diana's tone though he'd missed the accent. It wouldn't matter much longer.

"What is it?" It was one of the stews from tourist. We stepped aside so she could get a look, and Dave shoved her through. Pinky popped out very quickly.

"We're minus on minutes," Pinky said. "We lost five on the other side."

"Five?" Dave-Diana squeaked. I felt the same way. We had a hundred and three passengers to process.

"Yeah. They lost contact after you pushed my pigeon through. It took that long to realign."

You get used to that. Time runs at different rates on each side of the gate, though it's always sequential, past to future. Once we'd started the Snatch with me entering Sondergard's room, there was no way to go back any earlier on either side. Here, in 1979, we had a rigid ninety-four minutes to get everything done. On the other side, the gate could never be maintained longer than three hours.

"When you left, how long was it since the alarm went in?"

"Twenty-eight minutes."

It didn't sound good. It would take at least two hours just customizing the wimps. Assuming there was no more slippage on 79-time, we might just make it. But there's *always* slippage. I shuddered, thinking about riding it in.

"No time for any more games, then," I said. "Pink, you go back to tourist and call both of the other girls up here. Tell 'em to come one at a time, and tell 'em we've got a problem. You know the bit."

"Biting back the tears. Got you." She hurried aft. In no time the first one showed up. Her friendly Sun-Belt

Airlines smile was stamped on her face, but her stomach would be churning. *Oh God, this is it!*

I took her by the elbow and pulled her behind the curtains in front. She was breathing hard.

"Welcome to the twilight zone," I said, and put the gun to her head. She slumped, and I caught her. Pinky and Dave helped me shove her through the gate.

"Fug! The rotting thing's flickering."

Pinky was right. A very ominous sign. But the green glow stabilized as we watched, with who knows how much slippage on the other side. Cristabel ducked through.

"We're plus thirty-three," she said. There was no sense talking about what we were all thinking: things were going badly.

"Back to tourist," I said. "Be brave, smile at everyone, but make it just a little bit too good, got it?"

"Check," Cristabel said.

We processed the other quickly, with no incident. Then there was no time to talk about anything. In eighty-nine minutes Flight 128 was going to be spread all over a mountain whether we were finished or not.

Dave went into the cockpit to keep the flight crew out of our hair. Me and Pinky were supposed to take care of first class, then back up Cristabel and Liza in tourist. We used the standard "coffee, tea, or milk" gambit, relying on our speed and their inertia.

I leaned over the first two seats on the left.

"Are you enjoying your flight?" Pop, pop. Two squeezes on the trigger, close to the heads and out of sight of the rest of the goats.

"Hi, folks. I'm Mandy. Fly me." Pop, pop.

Halfway to the galley, a few people were watching us curiously. But people don't make a fuss until they have a lot more to go on. One goat in the back row stood up, and I let him have it. By now there were only eight left awake. I abandoned the smile and squeezed off four quick shots. Pinky took care of the rest. We hurried through the curtains, just in time.

There was an uproar building in the back of tourist,

with about sixty percent of the goats already processed. Cristabel glanced at me, and I nodded.

"Okay, folks," she bawled. "I want you to be quiet. Calm down and listen up. *You*, fathead, *pipe down* before I cram my foot up your ass sideways."

The shock of hearing her talk like that was enough to buy us a little time, anyway. We had formed a skirmish line across the width of the plane, guns out, steadied on seat backs, aimed at the milling, befuddled group of thirty goats.

The guns are enough to awe all but the most foolhardy. In essence, a standard-issue stunner is just a plastic rod with two grids about six inches apart. There's not enough metal in it to set off a hijack alarm. And to people from the Stone Age to about 2190 it doesn't look any more like a weapon than a ballpoint pen. So Equipment Section jazzes them up in a plastic shell to real Buck Rogers blasters, with a dozen knobs and lights that flash and a barrel like the snout of a hog. Hardly anyone ever walks into one.

"We are in great danger, and time is short. You must all do exactly as I tell you, and you will be safe."

You can't give them time to think, you have to rely on your status as the Voice of Authority. The situation is just *not* going to make sense to them, no matter how you explain it.

"Just a minute, I think you owe us—"

An airborne lawyer. I made a snap decision, thumbed the fireworks switch on my gun, and shot him.

The gun made a sound like a flying saucer with hemorrhoids, spit sparks and little jets of flame, and extended a green laser finger to his forehead. He dropped.

All pure kark, of course. But it sure is impressive.

And it's damn risky, too. I had to choose between a panic if the fathead got them to thinking, and a possible panic from the flash of the gun. But when a 20th gets to talking about his "rights" and what he is "owed," things can get out of hand. It's infectious.

It worked. There was a lot of shouting, people ducking

behind seats, but no rush. We could have handled it, but we needed some of them conscious if we were ever going to finish the Snatch.

"Get up. Get *up,* you *slugs!*" Cristabel yelled. "He's stunned, nothing worse. But I'll *kill* the next one who gets out of line. Now *get to your feet* and do what I tell you. *Children first! Hurry,* as fast as you can, to the front of the plane. Do what the stewardess tells you. Come on, kids, *move!*"

I ran back into first class just ahead of the kids, turned at the open restroom door, and got on my knees.

They were petrified. There were five of them—crying, some of them, which always chokes me up—looking left and right at dead people in the first class seats, stumbling, near panic.

"Come on, kids," I called to them, giving my special smile. "Your parents will be along in just a minute. Everything's going to be all right, I promise you. Come on."

I got three of them through. The fourth balked. She was determined not to go through that door. She spread her legs and arms and I couldn't push her through. I will *not* hit a child, never. She raked her nails over my face. My wig came off, and she gaped at my bare head. I shoved her through.

Number five was sitting in the aisle, bawling. He was maybe seven. I ran back and picked him up, hugged him and kissed him, and tossed him through. God, I needed a rest, but I was needed in tourist.

"You, you, you, and you. Okay, you too. Help him, will you?" Pinky had a practiced eye for the ones that wouldn't be any use to anyone, even themselves. We herded them toward the front of the plane, then deployed ourselves along the left side where we could cover the workers. It didn't take long to prod them into action. We had them dragging the limp bodies forward as fast as they could go. Me and Cristabel were in tourist, with the others up front.

Adrenaline was being catabolized in my body now; the rush of action left me and I started to feel very tired. There's an unavoidable feeling of sympathy for the poor dumb goats that starts to get me about this stage of the game. Sure, they were better off; sure, they were going to die if we didn't get them off the plane. But when they saw the other side they were going to have a hard time believing it.

The first ones were returning for a second load, stunned at what they'd just seen: dozens of people being put into a cubicle that was crowded when it was empty. One college student looked like he'd been hit in the stomach. He stopped by me and his eyes pleaded.

"Look, I want to *help* you people, just . . . what's going *on?* Is this some new kind of rescue? I mean, are we going to crash—"

I switched my gun to prod and brushed it across his check. He gasped and fell back.

"Shut your fuggin' mouth and get moving, or I'll kill you." It would be hours before his jaw was in shape to ask any more stupid questions.

We cleared tourist and moved up. A couple of the work gang were pretty damn pooped by then. Muscles like horses, all of them, but they can hardly run up a flight of stairs. We let some of them go through, including a couple that were at least fifty years old. *Je*-zus. Fifty! We got down to a core of four men and two women who seemed strong, and worked them until they nearly dropped. But we processed everyone in twenty-five minutes.

The portapak came through as we were stripping off our clothes. Cristabel knocked on the door to the cockpit and Dave came out, already naked. A bad sign.

"I had to work 'em," he said. "Bleeding captain just *had* to make his grand march through the plane. I tried *every*thing."

Sometimes you have to do it. The plane was on autopilot, as it normally would be at this time. But if any of us did anything detrimental to the craft, changed the fixed course of events in any way, that would be it. All that work for nothing, and Flight 128 inaccessible to us for all Time. I don't know sludge about time theory, but I know the practical angles. We can do things in the past only at times and in places where it won't make any difference. We have to cover our tracks. There's flexibility; once a Snatcher left her gun behind and it went in with the plane. Nobody found it, or if they did, they didn't have the smoggiest idea of what it was, so we were okay.

Flight 128 was mechanical failure. That's the best kind; it means we don't have to keep the pilot unaware of the situation in the cabin right down to ground level. We can cork him and fly the plane, since there's nothing he could have done to save the flight anyway. A pilot-error smash is almost impossible to Snatch. We mostly work midairs, bombs, and structural failures. If there's even one survivor, we can't touch it. It would not fit the fabric of space-time, which is immutable (though it can stretch a little), and we'd all just fade away and appear back in the ready room.

My head was hurting. I wanted that portapak very badly.

"Who has the most hours on a 707?" Pinky did, so I sent her to the cabin, along with Dave, who could do the pilot's voice for air traffic control. You have to have a believable record in the flight recorder, too. They trailed two long tubes from the portapak, and the rest of us hooked in up close. We stood there, each of us smoking a fistful of cigarettes, wanting to finish them but hoping there wouldn't be time. The gate had vanished as soon as we tossed our clothes and the flight crew through.

But we didn't worry long. There's other nice things about Snatching, but nothing to compare with the rush of plugging into a portapak. The wake-up transfusion is nothing but fresh blood, rich in oxygen and sugars. What we were getting now was an insane brew of concentrated adrenaline, supersaturated hemoglobin, methedrine, white lightning, TNT, and Kickapoo joyjuice. It was like a firecracker in your heart; a boot in the box that rattled your sox.

"I'm growing hair on my chest," Cristabel said solemnly. Everyone giggled.

"Would someone hand me my eyeballs?"

"The blue ones, or the red ones?"

"I think my ass just fell off."

We'd heard them all before, but we howled anyway. We were strong, *strong,* and for one golden moment we had no worries. Everything was hilarious. I could have torn sheet metal with my eyelashes.

But you get hyper on that mix. When the gate didn't show, and didn't show, and *didn't sweetjeez show* we all started milling. This bird wasn't going to fly all that much longer.

Then it did show, and we turned on. The first of the wimps came through, dressed in the clothes taken from a passenger it had been picked to resemble.

"Two thirty-five elapsed upside time," Cristabel announced.

"Je-zuz."

It is a deadening routine. You grab the harness around the wimp's shoulders and drag it along the aisle, after consulting the seat number painted on its forehead. The paint would last three minutes. You seat it, strap it in, break open the harness and carry it back to toss through the gate as you grab the next one. You have to take it for granted they've done the work right on the other side: fillings in the teeth, fingerprints, the right match in height and weight and hair color. Most of those things don't matter much, especially on Flight 128 which was a crash-and-burn. There would be bits and pieces, and burned to a crisp at that. But you can't take chances. Those rescue workers are pretty thorough on the parts they do find; the dental work and fingerprints especially are important.

I hate wimps. I really hate 'em. Every time I grab the harness of one of them, if it's a child, I wonder if it's Alice. *Are you my kid, you vegetable, you slug, you slimy worm?* I joined the Snatchers right after the brain bugs ate the life out of my baby's head. I couldn't stand to think she was the last generation, that the last humans there would ever be would live with nothing in their heads, medically dead by standards that prevailed even in 1979, with computers working their muscles to keep them in tone. You grow up, reach puberty still fertile—one in a thousand—rush to get pregnant in your first heat. Then you find out your mom or pop passed on a chronic disease bound right into the genes, and none of your kids will be immune. I *knew* about the paraleprosy; I grew up with my toes rotting away. But this was too much. What do you do?

Only one in ten of the wimps had a customized face. It takes times and a lot of skill to build a new face that will stand up to a doctor's autopsy. The rest came pre-mutilated. We've got millions of them; it's not hard to find a good match in the body. Most of them would stay breathing, too dumb to stop, until they went in with the plane.

The plane jerked, hard. I glanced at my watch. Five minutes to impact. We should have time. I was on my last wimp. I could hear Dave frantically calling the ground. A bomb came through the gate, and I tossed it into the cockpit. Pinky turned on the pressure sensor on the bomb and came running out, followed by Dave. Liza was already through. I grabbed the limp dolls in stewardess costume and tossed them to the floor. The engine fell off and a piece of it came through the cabin. We started to depressurize. The bomb blew away part of the cockpit (the ground crash crew would read it—we hoped—that part of the engine came through and killed the crew: no more words from the pilot on the flight recorder) and we turned, slowly, left and down. I was lifted toward the hole in the side of the plane, but I managed to hold onto a seat. Cristabel wasn't so lucky. She was blown backward.

We started to rise slightly, losing speed. Suddenly it was uphill from where Cristabel was lying in the aisle. Blood oozed from her temple. I glanced back; everyone was gone, and three pink-suited wimps were piled on the floor. The plane began to stall, to nose down, and my feet left the floor.

"Come on, Bel!" I screamed. That gate was only three feet away from me, but I began pulling myself along to where she floated. The plane bumped, and she hit the floor. Incredibly, it seemed to wake her up. She started to swim toward me, and I grabbed her hand as the floor came up to slam us again. We crawled as the plane went through its final death agony, and we came to the door. The gate was gone.

There wasn't anything to say. We were going in. It's hard enough to keep the gate in place on a plane that's moving in a straight line. When a bird gets to corkscrewing and coming apart, the math is fearsome. So I've been told.

I embraced Cristabel and held her bloodied head. She was groggy, but managed to smile and shrug. You take what you get. I hurried into the restroom and got both of us down on the floor. Back to the forward bulkhead, Cristabel between my legs, back to front. Just like in training. We pressed our feet against the other wall. I hugged her tightly and cried on her shoulder.

And it was there. A green glow to my left. I threw myself toward it, dragging Cristabel, keeping low as two wimps were thrown headfirst through the gate above our heads. Hands grabbed and pulled us through. I clawed my way a good five yards along the floor. You can leave a leg on the other side and I didn't have one to spare.

I sat up as they were carrying Cristabel to Medical. I patted her arm as she went by on the stretcher, but she was passed out. I wouldn't have minded passing out myself.

For a while, you can't believe it all really happened. Sometimes it turns out it *didn't* happen. You come back and find out all the goats in the holding pen have softly and suddenly vanished away because the continuum won't tolerate the changes and paradoxes you've put into it. The people you've worked so hard to rescue are spread like tomato surprise all over some goddam hillside in Carolina and all you've got left is a bunch of ruined wimps and an exhausted Snatch Team. But not this time. I could see the goats milling around in the holding pen, naked and more bewildered than ever. And just starting to be *really* afraid.

Elfreda touched me as I passed her. She nodded, which meant well done in her limited repertoire of gestures. I shrugged, wondering if I cared, but the surplus adrenaline was still in my veins and I found myself grinning at her. I nodded back.

Gene was standing by the holding pen. I went to him, hugged him. I felt the juices start to flow. *Damn it, let's squander a little ration and have us a good time.*

Someone was beating on the sterile glass wall of the pen. She shouted, mouthing angry words at us. *Why? What have you done to us?* It was Mary Sondergard. She implored her bald, one-legged twin to make her understand. She thought she had problems. God, was she pretty. I hated her guts.

Gene pulled me away from the wall. My hands hurt, and I'd broken off all my fake nails without scratching the glass. She was sitting on the floor now, sobbing. I heard the voice of the briefing officer on the outside speaker.

". . . Centauri Three is hospitable, with an Earthlike climate. By that, I mean *your* Earth, not what it has become. You'll see more of that later. The trip will take five years, shiptime. Upon landfall, you will be entitled to one horse, a plow, three axes, two hundred kilos of seed grain . . ."

I leaned against Gene's shoulder. At their lowest ebb, this very moment, they were so much better than us. I had maybe ten years, half of that as a basket case. They are our best, our very brightest hope. Everything is up to them.

". . . that no one will be forced to go. We wish to point out again, not for the last time, that you would all be dead without our intervention. There are things you should know, however. You cannot breathe our air. If you remain on Earth, you can never leave this building. We are not like you. We are the result of a genetic winnowing, a mutation process. We are the survivors, but our enemies have evolved along with us. They are winning. You, however, are immune to the diseases that afflict us. . . ."

I winced and turned away.

". . . the other hand, if you emigrate you will be given a chance at a new life. It won't be easy, but as Americans you should be proud of your pioneer heritage. Your ancestors survived, and so will you. It can be a rewarding experience, and I urge you . . ."

Sure. Gene and I looked at each other and laughed. *Listen to this, folks. Five percent of you will suffer nervous breakdowns in the next few days, and never leave. About the same number will commit suicide, here and on the way. When you get there, sixty to seventy percent will die in the first three years. You will die in childbirth, be eaten by animals, bury two out of three of your babies, starve slowly when the rains don't come. If you live, it will be to break your back behind a plow, sunup to dusk. New Earth is Heaven, folks!*

God, how I wish I could go with them.

LADY IN THE TOWER

by Anne McCaffrey

I was always dabbling in romantic and emotional themes in my early SF writings . . . mainly because I felt the genre could use such treatments. The Lady in isolation who is attracted by a male of mysterious origin . . . and then falls in love with this irresistible force. The Tower, of course, is on one of the Moons, Callisto. Well, old as the world, but I added telepathy and agoraphobia to the mix and voila, a good love story, told with an SF kick.

It was Susan Allison who asked me to take the original story and extend it into a novel as she wanted something quite romantic to appeal to readers. Well, it worked out there was enough meat in the yarn to do a five-book series. I had to go back to the Rowan's early years, her training in which her mentor inadvertently imbued her with her own agoraphobia (aka the Curse of Talent). And how the Rowan, with the help of her fascinating and multitalented lover and husband, managed to overcome this phobia. They have kids, and the kids grow up in their Talent without their mother's limiting agoraphobia and prosper. Then we deal with an alien menace, muddy the waters a bit more, and then save the worlds. I did have fun with it, and the kids, and a space navy of considerable size.

Along the way, I had to confer with experts in phero-mones and to discover what I could about identifying and quantifying "smells." Such a portable device was essential to the workings of the plot of *The Tower and the Hive*. Searching the Web, I contacted a firm in Cambridge Massachusetts, which actually constructed such instrumentation. A pair of their scientists agreed to help me . . . despite the fact that a chromatograph is a big, unwieldy affair. I did suggest that, by the time of my novel, surely smaller hand units would be available, considering the need for such items in space exploration. However, they were as amused as I was when a few months after *The Tower and the Hive* was published, they sent me an announcement that a portable gas chromatograph had been created. (I honestly doubt if the inventors read sf, but you never know, do you?) [I found out from my friend Colonel Pamela Melroy of NASA that a great many of the astronauts do read SF. She has never said if they laugh at the mistakes or misconceptions, but she has taken some of my books on her shuttle trips into space to read. I have a copy of *White Dragon* which did 177 orbits of earth at 244 miles above the surface.]

WHEN THE ROWAN CAME storming toward the station, its personnel mentally and literally ducked. Mentally, because she was apt to forget to shield. Literally, because the Rowan was prone to slamming around desks and filing cabinets when she got upset. Today, however, she was in fair command of herself and merely stamped up the stairs into the tower. A vague rumble of noisy thoughts tossed around the first floor of the station for a few minutes, but the computer and analogue men ignored the depressing effects with the gratitude of those saved from greater disaster.

From the residue of her passage, Brian Ackerman, the stationmaster, caught the impression of intense purple frustration. He was basically only a T-9, but constant association with the Rowan had widened his area of perception. Ackerman appreciated this side effect of his position—when he was anywhere else but at the station.

He had been trying to quit Callisto for more than five years, with no success. Federal Telepathers and Teleporters, Inc., had established a routine regarding his continuous applications for transfer. The first one handed in each quarter was ignored; the second brought an adroitly worded reply on how sensitive and crucial a position he held at Callisto Prime Station; his third—often a violently worded demand—always got him a special shipment of scotch and tobacco; his fourth—a piteous wail—brought the Section Supervisor out for a face-to-face chat and, only then, a few discreet words to the Rowan.

Ackerman was positive she always knew the full story before the Supervisor finally approached her. It pleased her to be difficult, but the one time Ackerman discarded protocol and snarled back at her, she had mended her ways for a whole quarter. It had reluctantly dawned on Ackerman that she must like him and he had since used this knowledge to advantage. He had lasted eight years, as against five stationmasters in three months before his appointment.

Each of the twenty-three station staff members had gone through a similar shuffling until the Rowan had accepted them. It took a very delicate balance of mental talent, personality, and intelligence to achieve the proper *gestalt* needed to move giant liners and tons of freight. Federal Tel and Tel had only five complete Primes—five T-1's—each strategically placed in a station near the five major and most central stars to effect the best possible transmission of commerce and communications throughout the sprawling Nine-Star League. The lesser staff positions at each Prime Station were filled by personnel who could only teleport, or telepath. It was FT & T's dream someday to provide instantaneous transmission of anything, anywhere, anytime. Until that day, FT & T exercised patient diplomacy with its five T-1's, putting up with their vagaries like the doting owners of so many golden geese. If keeping the Rowan happy had meant changing the entire lesser personnel twice daily, it would probably have been done. As it happened, the present staff had been intact for over two years and only minor soothing had been necessary.

Ackerman hoped that only minor soothing would be

needed today. The Rowan had been peevish for a week, and he was beginning to smart under the backlash. So far no one knew why the Rowan was upset.

Ready for the liner! Her thought lashed out so piercingly that Ackerman was sure everyone in the ship waiting outside had heard her. But he switched the intercom in to the ship's captain.

"I heard," the captain said wryly. "Give me a five-count and them set us off."

Ackerman didn't bother to relay the message to the Rowan. In her mood, she'd be hearing straight to Capella and back. The generator men were hopping between switches, bringing the booster field up to peak, while she impatiently revved up the launching units to push-off strength. She was well ahead of the standard timing, and the pent-up power seemed to keen through the station. The countdown came fast as the singing power note increased past endurable limits.

ROWAN, NO TRICKS, Ackerman said.

He caught her mental laugh, and barked a warning to the captain. He hoped the man had heard it, because the Rowan was on zero before he could finish and the ship was gone beyond radio transmission distance in seconds.

The keening dynamos lost only a minute edge of sharpness before they sang at peak again. The lots on the launchers snapped out into space as fast as they could be set up. Then the loads rocketed into receiving area from other Prime Stations, and the ground crews hustled rerouting and hold orders. The power note settled to a bearable hum as the Rowan worked out her mood without losing the efficient and accurate thrust that made her FT & T's best Prime.

One of the ground crew signaled a frantic yellow across the board, then red as ten tons of cargo from Earth settled on the Priority Receiving cradle. The waybill said Deneb VIII, which was at the Rowan's limit. But the shipment was marked "Rush/Emergency, priority medicine for a virulent plague on the colony planet." And the waybill specified direct transmission.

Well, where're my coordinates and my placement photo? snapped the Rowan. *I can't thrust blind, you know, and we've always rerouted for Deneb VIII.*

Bill Powers was flipping through the indexed catalogue, but the Rowan reached out and grabbed the photo.

Zowie! Do I have to land all that mass there myself?

No, Lazybones, I'll pick it up at 24.578.82—that nice little convenient black dwarf midway. You won't have to strain a single convolution. The lazy masculine voice drawled in every mind.

The silence was deafening.

Well, I'll be . . . came from the Rowan.

Of course, you are, sweetheart—just push that nice little package out my way. Or is it too much for you? The lazy voice was solicitous rather than insulting.

You'll get your package! replied the Rowan, and the dynamos keened piercingly just once as the ten tons disappeared out of the cradle.

Why, you little minx . . . slow it down or I'll burn your ears back!

Come out and catch it! The Rowan's laugh broke off in a gasp of surprise and Ackerman could feel her slamming up her mental shields.

I want that stuff in one piece, not smeared a millimeter thin on the surface, my dear, the voice said sternly. *Okay, I've got it. Thanks! We need this.*

Hey, who the blazes are you? What's your placement?

Deneb Sender, my dear, and a busy little boy right now. Ta ta.

The silence was broken only by the whine of the dynamos dying to an idle burr.

Not a hint of what the Rowan was thinking came through now, but Ackerman could pick up the aura of incredulity, shock, speculation, and satisfaction that pervaded the thoughts of everyone else in the station. The Rowan had met her match. No one except a T-1 could have projected that far. There'd been no mention of another T-1 at FT & T, and, as far as Ackerman knew,

FT & T had all of the five known T-1s. However, Deneb was now in its third generation and colonial peculiarities had produced the Rowan in two.

"Hey, people," Ackerman said, "sock up your shields. She's not going to like your drift."

Dutifully the aura was dampened, but the grins did not fade and Powers started to whistle cheerfully.

Another yellow flag came up from a ground man on the Altair hurdle and the waybill designated *Live shipment to Betelgeuse*. The dynamos whined noisily and then the launcher was empty. Whatever might be going through her mind at the moment, the Rowan was doing her work.

All told, it was an odd day, and Ackerman didn't know whether to be thankful or not. He had no precedents to go on and the Rowan wasn't leaking any clues. She spun the day's lot in and out with careless ease. By the time Jupiter's bulk had moved around to blanket out-system traffic, Callisto's day was over, and the Rowan wasn't off-power as much as decibel one. Once the in-Sun traffic was finished with, Ackerman signed off for the day. The computer banks and dynamos were slapped off . . . but the Rowan did not come down.

Ray Loftus and Afra, the Capellan T-4, came over to sit on the edge of Ackerman's desk. They took out cigarettes. As usual, Afra's yellow eyes began to water from the smoke.

"I was going to ask her Highness to give me a lift home," Loftus said, "but I dunno now. Got a date with—"

He disappeared. A moment later, Ackerman could see him near a personnel carrier. Not only had he been set gently down, but various small necessities, among them a shaving kit, floated out of nowhere onto a neat pile in the carrier. Ray was given time to settle himself before the hatch sealed and he was whisked off.

Powers joined Afra and Ackerman.

"She's sure in a funny mood," he said.

When the Rowan got peevish, few of the men at the station asked her to transport them to Earth. She was

psychologically held planetbound, and resented the fact
that lesser talents could be moved about through space
without suffering traumatic shock.

Anyone else?

Adler and Toglia spoke up and promptly disappeared
together. Ackerman and Powers exchanged looks which
they hastily suppressed as the Rowan appeared before
them, smiling. It was the first time that welcome and
totally unexpected expression had crossed her face for
two weeks.

She smiled but said nothing. She took a drag of Ackerman's cigarette and handed it back with a thank-you. For
all her temperament, the Rowan acted with propriety
face to face. She had grown up with her skill, carefully
taught by the old and original T-1, Siglen, the Altairian.
She'd had certain courtesies drilled into her: the less
gifted could be alienated by inappropriate use of talent.
She was perfectly justified in "reaching" things during
business hours, but she employed the usual methods at
other times.

"The big boys mention our Denebian friend before?"
she asked, all too casually.

Ackerman shook his head. "Those planets are three
generations colonized, and you came out of Altair in
two."

"That could explain it, but there isn't even an FT & T
station. And you know they advertise continuously for
anyone with Talent."

"He's a wild talent?" Powers helpfully suggested.

"Too far off the beaten track." She shook her head.
"I checked it. All I can get from Center is that they
received an urgent call about a virus, were given a run-
down on the syndrome and symptoms. Lab came up with
a serum, batched and packed it. They were assured that
there was someone capable of picking it up and taking
it the rest of the way past 24.578.82 if a Prime would get
it that far. And that's all anybody knows." Then she
added thoughtfully, "Deneb VIII isn't a very big colony."

Oh, we're big enough, sweetheart, interrupted the
drawling voice. *Sorry to get you after hours, my dear, but*

I can't seem to get in to Terra and I heard you coloring the atmosphere.

What's wrong? the Rowan asked. *Did you smear your serum after all that proud talk?*

Smear it, hell! I've been drinking it. We've got some ET visitors. They think they're exterminators. Thirty UFO's are perched four thousand miles above us. That batch of serum you wafted out to me this morning was for the sixth virus we've been socked with in the last two weeks. Soon as our boys whip up something to knock out one, another takes its place. It's always worse than the one before. We've lost 25 percent of our population already and this last virus is a beaut. I want two top germdogs out here on the double and about three patrol squadrons. We're flat on our backs now. I doubt our friends will hover around, dousing us with nasty bugs much longer. They're going to start blowing holes in us any minute now. So sort of push the word along to Earth, will you, sweetheart? And get us some heavy support!

I'll relay, naturally. But why don't you send direct?

To whom? You're the only one I can hear.

Your isolation won't last much longer if I know my bosses.

You may know your bosses, but you don't know me.

That can always be arranged.

This is no time for flirting. Get that message through for me like a good girl.

Which message?

The one I just gave you.

That old one? They say you can have two germdogs in the morning as soon as we clear Jupiter. But Earth says no squadrons. No armed attack.

You can double-talk too, huh? You're talented. But the morning does us no good. Now is when we need them. Can't you sling them . . . no, they might leave a few important atoms or something in Jupiter's mass. But I've got to have some pretty potent help, and if six viruses don't constitute armed attack, what does?

Missiles constitute armed attack, the Rowan said primly.

I'll notify my friends up there. Missiles would be preferable. Them I can see. I need those germdogs now. Can't you turn your sweet little mind to a solution?

As you mentioned, it's after hours.

But the Horsehead, woman! the drawl was replaced by a cutting mental roar. *My friends are dying!*

Look, after hours here means we're behind Jupiter . . . But . . . Wait! How deep is your range?

I don't honestly know. And doubt crept into the bodiless voice in their minds.

"Ackerman." The Rowan turned to her stationmaster. "I've been listening."

Hang on, Deneb, I've got an idea. I'll deliver your germdogs. Open to me in half an hour.

The Rowan whirled on Ackerman. "I want my shell." Her brilliant eyes were flashing and her face was alight. "Afra!"

The station's T-4, a handsome yellow-eyed Capellan, raised himself from the chair in which he'd been quietly watching her. Afra was second in command of the station.

"Yes, Rowan?"

Abruptly she realized that her mental conversation with the Denebian had been heard by all the others. Her fleeting frown was replaced by the miraculous smile that always disconcerted Ackerman with its hint of suppressed passion. She looked at each of the men, bathing them in that smile.

"I want to be launched, slowly, over Jupiter's curve," she said to Afra. Ackerman switched up the dynamos, Bill Powers punched for her special shell to be deposited on the launching rack. "Real slow, Afra. Then I'll want to draw heavy." She took a deep breath. Like all Primes, she was unable to launch herself through space. Her initial trip from Altair to Callisto had almost driven her mad with agoraphobia. Only by the exercise of severe self-discipline was she able to take her specially opaque shell a short way off Callisto.

She took another deep breath and disappeared from

the station. Then she was beside the launcher. She settled daintily into the shock couch of the shell. The moment the lock whistle shut off, she could feel the shell moving gently, gently away from Callisto. She could sense Afra's reassuring mental touch. Only when the shell had swung into position over Jupiter's great curve did she reply to the priority call coming from Earth Central.

Now what the Billy blue blazes are you doing, Rowan? The voice of Reidinger, the FT & T Central Prime, cracked across the void. *Have you lost what's left of your precious mind?*

She's doing me a favor, Deneb said, unexpectedly joining them.

Who'n hell're you? demanded Reidinger. Then, in shocked surprise, *Deneb! How'd you get out there?*

Wishful thinking. Hey, push those germdogs to my pretty friend here, huh?

Now, wait a minute! You're going a little too far, Deneb. You can't burn out my best prime with an unbased send like this.

Oh, I'll pick up midway. Like those antibiotics this morning.

Deneb, what's this business with antibiotics and germdogs? What're you cooking up out there in that heathenish hole?

Oh, we're merely fighting a few plagues with one hand and keeping thirty bogey ET's upstairs. Deneb gave them a look with his vision at an enormous hospital, a continuous stream of airborne ambulances coming in: at crowded wards, grim-faced nurses and doctors, and uncomfortable high piles of sheeted still figures.

Well, I didn't realize. All right, you can have anything you want—within reason. But I want a full report, said Reidinger.

And patrol squadrons?

Reidinger's tone changed to impatience. *You've obviously got an exaggerated idea of our capabilities. I can't mobilize patrol squadrons like that!* There was a mental snap of fingers.

Would you perhaps drop a little word in the C.O.C.'s ear? Those ET's may gobble Deneb tonight and go after Terra tomorrow.

I'll do what I can, of course, but you colonists agreed to the risks when you signed up. The ET's were probably hoping for a soft touch. You're showing them different. They'll give up and get—

You're all heart, said Deneb.

Reidinger was silent for a moment. Then he said, *Germdogs sealed, Rowan; pick 'em up and throw 'em out,* and signed off.

Rowan—that's a pretty name, said Deneb.

Thanks, she said absently. She had followed along Reidinger's initial push, and picked up the two personnel carriers as they materialized beside her shell. She pressed into the station dynamos and gathered strength. The generators whined and she pushed out. The carriers disappeared.

They're coming in, Rowan. Thanks a lot.

A passionate and tender kiss was blown to her across eighteen light-years of space. She tried to follow after the carriers and pick up his touch again, but he was no longer receiving.

She sank back in her couch. Deneb's sudden appearance had disconcerted her completely. All of the Primes were isolated in their high talents, but the Rowan was more alone than any of the others.

Siglen, the Altairian Prime who had discovered the Rowan as a child and carefully nursed her talent into its tremendous potential, was the oldest Prime of all. The Rowan, a scant twenty-three now, had never gotten anything from Siglen to comfort her except old-fashioned platitudes. Betelgeuse Prime David was madly in love with his T-2 wife and occupied with raising a brood of high-potential brats. Although Reidinger was always open to the Rowan, he also had to keep open every single minute to all the vast problems of the FT & T system. Capella was available but so mixed up herself that her touch aggravated the Rowan to the point of fury.

Reidinger had tried to ease her devastating loneliness

by sending up T-3's and T-4's like Afra, but she had never taken to any of them. The only male T-2 ever discovered in the Nine-Star League had been a confirmed homosexual. Ackerman was a nice, barely talented guy, devoted to his wife. And now, on Deneb, a T-1 had emerged, out of nowhere—and so very, very far away.

Afra, take me home now, she said, very tired.

Afra brought the shell down with infinite care.

After the others had left the station, the Rowan lay for a long while on her couch in the personnel carrier. In her unsleeping consciousness, she was aware that the station was closing down, that Ackerman and the others had left for their homes until Callisto once more came out from behind Jupiter's titan bulk. Everyone had some place to go, except the Rowan who made it all possible. The bitter, screaming loneliness that overcame her during her off hours welled up—the frustration of being unable to go off-planet past Afra's sharply limited range—alone, alone with her two-edged talent. Murky green and black swamped her mind until she remembered the blown kiss. Suddenly, completely, she fell into her first restful sleep in two weeks.

Rowan. It was Deneb's touch that roused her. *Rowan, please wake up.*

Hmmmmm? Her sleepy response was reluctant.

Our guests are getting rougher . . . since the germdogs . . . whipped up a broad spectrum antibiotic . . . that phase . . . of their attack failed . . . so now they're . . . pounding us . . . with missiles . . . give my regards to your space-lawyer friend . . . Reidinger.

You're playing pitch with missiles? The Rowan came awake hurriedly. She could feel Deneb's contact cutting in and out as he interrupted himself to catch incoming missiles and fling them back.

I need backup help, sweetheart, like you and . . . any twin sisters . . . you happen . . . to have . . . handy. Buzz over . . . here, will you?

Buzz? What? I can't go there!

Why not?

I can't! I can't! The Rowan moaned, twisting against the web of the couch.

But I've got . . . to . . . have . . . help, he said and faded away.

Reidinger! The Rowan's call was a scream.

Rowan, I don't care if you are a T-1. There are certain limits to my patience and you've stretched every blasted one of them, you little white-haired ape!

His answer scorched her. She blocked automatically but clung to his touch. *Someone has got to help Deneb!* she cried, transmitting the Mayday.

What? He's joking!

How could he, about a thing like that!

Did you see the missiles? Did he show you what he was actually doing?

No, but I felt him thrusting. And since when does one of us distrust another when he asks for help.

Since when? Reidinger's reply crackled across space. *Since Eve handed Adam a rosy round fruit and said "eat." And exactly since Deneb's never been integrated into the prime network. We can't be sure who or what he is—or exactly where he is. I don't like this taking everything at his word. Try and get him back for me to hear.*

I can't reach him! He's too busy lobbing missiles spaceward.

That's a hot one! Look, he can tap any other potentials on his own planet. That's all the help he needs.

But . . .

But me no buts and leave me alone. I'll play cupid only so far. Meanwhile I've got a company—a league—to hold together. Reidinger signed off with a backlash that stung. The Rowan lay in her couch, bewildered by Reidinger's response. He was always busy, always gruff. But he had never been stupidly unreasonable. While out there, Deneb was growing weaker . . .

Callisto was clear of Jupiter and the station was operating again. Incoming cargoes were piling up on the launchers. But there was no outgoing traffic. Tension and worry hung over the station.

"There must be something we can do for him . . . something," the Rowan said, choked with tears.

Afra looked down at her sadly and compassionately, and patted her frail shoulder.

"What? Not even you can reach all the way out to him. Patrol Squadrons are needed by what you've said, but we can't send them. Did you ask him if he's tried to find help on his own planet?"

"He needs Prime help and—"

"You're all tied to your little worlds with the unbilical cord of space-fear," Afra finished for her, a blunt summation of the problem that made her wince for her devastating inability.

Kerrist! The radar warning! Ackerman's mental shout startled both of them.

Instantly the Rowan linked her mind to his as Ackerman plunged toward the little-used radar screen. As she probed into space, she found the intruder, a highly powered projectile, arrowing in from behind Uranus. Guiltily she flushed, for she ought to have detected it away beyond the radar's range.

There was no time to run up the idling dynamos. The projectile was coming in too fast.

I want a wide-open mind from everyone on this moon! The Rowan's broadcast was inescapable. She felt the surge of power as forty-eight talents on Callisto, including Ackerman's ten-year-old son, lowered their shields. She picked up their power—from the least 12 to Afra's sturdy 4—sent her touch racing out beyond Jupiter, and reached the alien bomb. She had to wrestle for a moment with the totally unfamiliar molecular structure of its constituents. Then, with her augmented energy, it was easy enough to deactivate the trigger and then scatter the fissionables from the warhead into Jupiter's seething mass.

She released the others who had joined her and fell back into the couch.

"How in hell did that thing find us?" Afra asked from the chair in which he had slumped.

She released the others who had joined her and fell back into the couch.

"How in hell did that thing find us?" Afra asked from the chair in which he had slumped.

She shook her head wearily. Without the dynamos, there had been no surge of power to act as the initial carrier wave for her touch. Even with the help of the others—and all of them put together didn't add up to one-third the strength of another Prime—it had been a wearying exercise. She thought of Deneb—alone, without an FT & T Station to assist him—doing this again, and again, and again—and her heart twisted.

Warm up the dynamos, Brian—there'll be more of those missiles.

Afra looked up, startled.

Prime Rowan of Callisto Station alerting Earth Prime Reidinger and all other primes! Prepare for possible attack by fissionable projectiles of alien origin. Alert all radar watch stations and patrol forces. She lost her official calm and added angrily, *We've got to help Deneb now—we've got to! It's no longer an isolated aggression against an outlying colony. It's a concerted attack on our heart world. It's an attack on every Prime in the nine-star league.*

Rowan! Before Reidinger got more than her name into her mind, she opened to him and showed the five new projectiles driving toward Callisto. *For the love of little apples!* Reidinger's mind radiated incredulity. *What has our little man been stirring up?*

Shall we find out? Rowan asked with deadly sweetness.

Reidinger transmitted impatience, fury, misery and then shock as he gathered her intention.

Your plan won't work. It's impossible. We can't merge minds to fight. All of us are too egocentric. Too unstable. We'd burn out, fighting each other.

You, me, Altair, Betelgeuse and Capella. We can do it. If I can deactivate one of those hell missiles with only forty-eight minor talents and no power for help, five Primes plus full power ought to be able to turn the trick. We can knock the missiles off. Then we can merge with

Deneb to help him, that'll make six of us. Show me the ET who could stand up to such a counterassault!

Look girl, Reidinger replied, almost pleading, *We don't have his measure. We can't just merge—He could split us apart, or we could burn him up. We don't know him. We can't gauge a telepath of unknown ability.*

You'd better catch that missile coming at you, she said calmly. *I can't handle more than ten at a time and keep up a sensible conversation.*

She felt Reidinger's resistance to her plan weakening. She pushed the advantage. *If Deneb's been handling a planet-wide barrage, that's a pretty good indication of his strength. I'll handle the ego-merge because I damned well want to. Besides, there isn't any other course open to us now, is there?*

We could launch patrol squadrons.

We should have done that *the first time he asked. It's too late now.*

Their conversation was taking the briefest possible time and yet more missiles were coming in. All the Prime stations were under bombardment.

All right, Reidinger said in angry resignation, and contacted the other Primes.

No, no, no! You'll burn her out—burn her out, poor thing! Old Siglen from Altair babbled. *Let us stick to our last—we dare not expose ourselves, no, no, no! The ET's would attack us then.*

Shut up, Ironpants, David said.

Shoulder to the wheel, you old wart, Capella chimed in waspishly. *Hit hard first, that's safest.*

Look, Rowan, Reidinger said. *Siglen's right. He could burn you out.*

I'll take the chance.

Damn Deneb for starting all this! Reidinger didn't quite shield his aggravation.

We've got to do it. And now!

Tentatively at the outset, and then with stunningly increased force, the unleashed power of the other FT & T Primes, augmented by the mechanical surge of the five stations' generators, was forced through the Rowan. She grew, grew and only dimly saw the puny ET bombardment swept aside like so many mayflies. She grew, grew until she felt herself a colossus, larger than ominous Jupiter, Slowly, carefully, tentatively, because the massive power was braked only by her slender conscious control, she reached out to Deneb.

She spun on, in grandeur, astounded by the limitless force she had become. She passed the small black dwarf that was the midway point. Then she felt the mind she searched for; a tired mind, its periphery wincing with weariness but doggedly persevering its evasive actions.

Oh, Deneb, Deneb, you're still intact! She was so relieved, so grateful to find him fighting his desperate battle that they merged before her ego could offer even a token resistance. She abandoned her most guarded self to him and, with the surrender, the massed power she held flowed into him. The tired mind of the man grew, healed, strengthened and blossomed until she was a mere fraction of the total, lost in the greater part of this immense mental whole. Suddenly she saw with his eyes, heard with his ears and felt with his touch, was immersed in the titanic struggle.

The greenish sky above was pitted with mushroom puffs, and the raw young hills around him were scarred with deflected missiles. Easily now, he was turning aside the warheads aimed at him.

Let's go up there and find out what they are, the Reidinger segment said. *Now!*

Deneb approached the thirty mile-long ships. The mass-mind took indelible note of the intruders. Then, off-handedly, Deneb broke the hulls of twenty-nine of the ET ships, spilling the contents into space. To the occupants of the survivor, he gave a searing impression of the Primes and the indestructability of the worlds in this section of space. With one great heave, he threw the one ship away from his exhausted planet, set it hurtling farther than it had come, into uncharted black immensity.

He thanked the Primes for the incomparable compliment of an ego-merge and explained in a millisecond the tremendous gratitude of his planet, based on all that Denebians had accomplished in three generations which had been so nearly obliterated and emphasized by their hopes for the future.

The Rowan felt the links dissolving as the other Primes, murmuring withdrawal courtesies, left him. Deneb caught her mind fast to his and held on. When they were alone, he opened all his thoughts to her, so that now she knew him as intimately as he knew her.

Sweet Rowan. Look around you. It'll take a while for Deneb to be beautiful again but we'll make it lovelier than ever. Come live with me, my love.

The Rowan's wracked cry of protest reverberated cruelly in both naked minds.

I can't! I can't! She cringed against her own outburst and closed off her inner heart so that he couldn't see the pitiful why. In the moment of his confusion, she retreated back to her frail body, and beat her fists hopelessly against her thighs.

Rowan! came his cry. *Rowan, I love you.*

She deadened the outer fringe of her perception to everything and curled forward in her chair. Afra, who had watched patiently over her while her mind was far away, touched her shoulder.

Oh, Afra! To be so close to love and so far away. Our minds were one. Our bodies are forever separate. Deneb! Deneb!

The Rowan forced her bruised self into sleep. Afra picked her up gently and carried her to a bed in a room off the station's main level. He shut the door and tiptoed away. Then he sat down, on watch in the corridor outside, his handsome face dark with sorrow, his yellow eyes blinking away moisture.

Afra and Ackerman reached the only possible conclusion: the Rowan had burned herself out. They'd have to tell Reidinger. Forty-eight hours had elapsed since they'd had a single contact with her mind. She had not heard, or had ignored, their tentative requests for her assistance. Afra, Ackerman, and the machines could handle some of the routing and freighting, but two liners were due in and that required her. They knew she was alive but that was all: her mind was blank to any touch. At first, Ackerman had assumed that she was recuperating. Afra had known better and, for that forty-eight hours, he'd hoped fervently that she would accept the irreconcilable situation.

"I'll run up the dynamos," Ackerman said to Afra with a reluctant sigh, "and we'll tell Reidinger."

Well, where's Rowan? Reidinger asked. A moment's touch with Afra told him. He, too, sighed. *We'll just have to rouse her some way. She isn't burned out; that's one mercy.*

Is it? replied Ackerman bitterly. *If you'd paid attention to her in the first place . . .*

Yes, I'm sure, Reidinger cut him off brusquely. *If I'd gotten her light of love his patrol squadrons when she wanted me to, she wouldn't have thought of merging with him mentally. I put as much pressure on her as I dared. But when that cocky young rooster on Deneb started lobbing deflected ET missiles at us . . . I hadn't counted on that development. At least we managed to spur her to act. And off-planet at that.* He sighed. *I was hoping that love might make at least one Prime fly.*

Whaaa-at? Afra roared. *You mean that battle was staged?*

Hardly. As I said, we hadn't anticipated the ET. Deneb presumably had only a mutating virus plague to cope with. Not ET.

Then you didn't know about them?

Of course not! Reidinger sounded disgusted. *Oh, the original contact with Deneb for biological assistance was sheer chance. I took it as providential, an opportunity to see if I couldn't break the fear psychosis we all have. Rowan's the youngest of us. If I could get her to go to him—physically—I failed.* Reidinger's resignation saddened Afra, too. One didn't consider the Central Prime as a fallible human. *Love isn't as strong as it's supposed to be. And where I'll get new Primes if I can't breed 'em, I don't know. I'd hoped that Rowan and Deneb . . .*

As a matchmaker . . .

I should resign . . .

Afra cut the contact abruptly as the door opened, admitting the Rowan, a wan, pale, very quiet Rowan.

She smiled apologetically. "I've been asleep a long time."

"You had a tiring day," Ackerman said gently.

She winced and then smiled to ease Ackerman's instant concern. "I still am, a little." Then she frowned. "Did I hear you two talking to Reidinger just now?"

"We got worried," Ackerman replied. "There're two liners coming in, and Afra and I just plain don't care to handle human cargo, you know."

The Rowan gave a rueful smile. "I know. I'm all set." She walked slowly up the stairs to her tower.

Ackerman shook his head sadly. "She sure has taken it hard."

Her chastened attitude wasn't the relief that her staff had once considered it might be. The work that day went on with monotonous efficiency, with none of the byplay and freakish temperament that had previously kept them on their toes. The men moved around automatically, depressed by this gently tragic Rowan. That might have been one reason why no one noticed particularly when, toward the very end of the day, the young man came in. Only when Ackerman rose from his desk for more coffee did he notice him sitting there quietly.

"You new?"

"Well, yes. I was told to see the Rowan. Reidinger signed me on in his office late this morning." He spoke pleasantly, rising to his feet slowly and ending his explanation with a smile. Fleetingly Ackerman was reminded of the miracle of the Rowan's sudden smiles that hinted at some incredible treasure of the spirit. This man's smile was full of uninhibited, magnetic vigor, and the brilliant blue eyes danced with good humor and friendliness.

Ackerman found himself grinning back like a fool, and shaking the man's hand stoutly.

"Mightly glad to know you. What's your name?"

"Jeff Raven. I just got in from—"

"Hey, Afra, want you to meet Jeff Raven. Here, have a coffee. A little raw on the walk up from the freighting station, isn't it? Been on any other Prime stations?"

"As a matter of fact . . ."

Toglia and Loftus had looked around from their computers to the recipient of such unusual cordiality. They found themselves as eager to welcome this magnetic stranger. Raven graciously accepted the coffee from Ackerman, who instantly proffered cigarettes. The stationmaster had the feeling that he must give this wonderful guy something else, it had been such a pleasure to provide him with coffee.

Afra looked quietly at the stranger, his calm yellow eyes a little clouded. "Hello," he said in a rueful murmur.

Jeff Raven's grin altered imperceptibly. "Hello," he replied, and more was exchanged between the two men than a simple greeting.

Before anyone in the station quite realized what was happening, everyone had left his post and gathered around Raven, chattering and grinning, using the simplest excuse to touch his hand or shoulder. He was genuinely interested in everything said to him, and although there were twenty-three people vying anxiously to monopolize his attention, no one felt slighted. His reception seemed to envelop them all.

What the hell is happening down there? asked the Rowan with a tinge of her familiar irritation. *Why . . .*

Contrary to all her previously sacred rules, she appeared suddenly in the middle of the room, looked about wildly. Raven touched her hand gently.

"Reidinger said you needed me," he said.

"Deneb?" Her body arched to project the astounded whisper. *"Deneb? But you're . . . you're here!* You're *here!"*

He smiled tenderly and drew his hand across her shining hair. The Rowan's jaw dropped and she burst out laughing, the laughter of a supremely happy carefree girl. Then her laughter broke off in a gasp of pure terror.

How did you get here?

Just came. You can, too, you know.

No, no, I can't. No T-1 can. The Rowan tried to free herself from his grasp as if he were suddenly repulsive.

I did, though. His gentle insistence was unequivocable. *It's only a question of rearranging atoms. Why should it matter whose they are?*

Oh, no, no . . .

"Did you know," Raven said conversationally, speaking for everyone's benefit "that Siglen of Altair gets sick just going up and down stairs?" He looked straight at the Rowan. "You remember that she lives all on one floor? Ever wondered why all her furniture has short legs, Rowan?"

The girl shook her head, her eyes wonderingly wide.

"No one ever stopped to ask why, did they? I did. Seemed damned silly to me when I met the woman. Siglen's middle ear reacts very badly to free-fall. She was so miserably sick the first time she tried moving herself anywhere, she went into a trauma about it. Of course, it never occurred to *her* to find out why. So she went a little crazy on the subject, and *who* trained all the other Primes?"

"Siglen . . . Oh, Deneb, you mean? . . ."

Raven grinned. "Yes, I do. She passed on the trauma to every one of you. The Curse of Talent! The Great Fear! The great bushwah! But agoraphobia, or a middle-ear imbalance, is not a stigma of Talent! Siglen never trained *me*." He laughed with wicked boyish delight and opened his mind to the Rowan. Warmth and reassurance passed between them. Her careful conditioning began to wither in that warmth. Her eyes shone.

Now come live with me and be my love, Rowan. Reidinger says you can commute from here to Deneb every day.

"Commute?" She said it aloud, conscious of the over-all value of Siglen's training, but already questioning every aspect.

"Certainly," Jeff said, approving her thoughts. "You're still a working T-1 under contract to FT & T. And so, my love, am I."

"I guess I do know my bosses, don't I?" she said with a chuckle.

"Well, the terms were fair. Reidinger didn't haggle for a second after I walked into his private office at eleven this morning."

"Commuting to Callisto?" the Rowan repeated dazedly.

"All finished here for the day?" Raven asked Ackerman, who shook his head after a glance at the launching racks.

"C'mon, gal. Take me to your ivory tower and we'll finish up in a jiffy. Then we'll go home. With two of us working in our spare time, Deneb'll be put to rights in no time . . . *And when we've finished that . . .*

Jeff Raven smiled wickedly at the Rowan and pressed her hand to his lips in the age-old gesture of courtliness. The Rowan's smile answered his with blinding joy.

The others were respectfully silent as the two Talents made their way up the stairs to the once-lonely tower.

Afra broke the tableau by taking the burning cigarette from Ackerman's motionless hand. He took a deep drag that turned his skin a deeper green. It wasn't the cigarette smoke that caused his eyes to water so profusely.

"Not that that pair needs much of our help, people," he said, "but we can add a certain flourish and speed them on their way."

THE POSTMAN

by David Brin

"The Postman" was written as an answer to all those post-apocalyptic books and films that seem to revel in the idea of civilization's fall. It's a story about how much we take for granted—and how desperately we would miss the little, gracious things that connect us today. Little things that we have become so accustomed to that they scarcely come to mind. They all seemed to coalesce—in my mind—around the image of a postman, who quietly delivers mail, and by linking people together helps us to be more than a scattering of fractious cavemen.

Many dramas revolve around the question—*what would I do if* . . . And I suppose that, growing up in the 1950s and 60s, it is only natural that I would—sooner or later—write a tale expressing the fear that we had all known as kids. A stark realization that humanity might end the world with a bang. Your mind worried—like a dog with a bone—over the possibility that civilization might sustain a horrible body blow, and yet still possess the components for recovery.

But would those components find a will and a way to reunite? To reweave the fabric of a decent society?

I suppose it is possible that today the same story would revolve around The Internet Guy, since our latter-day connectivity is even more vibrant and empowering than Ben Franklin's postal system ever was. And yet, somehow, there is something much more palpable and satisfying about this image of a con man who starts delivering letters and then makes a dream come true in spite of himself.

The notion must have resonated with some people. Long before Kevin Costner made that movie version (visually gorgeous and big-hearted, though kind of dumb), this story became the only one ever to come in second for three Hugo Awards in the field of science fiction. Once for the original novella, once for the sequel novella "Cyclops," and finally, in the novel category, when those two stories joined a third to complete the book.

Though centered around the last idealist in a fallen America, "The Postman" has been extraordinarily popular in more than 20 languages around the world. It is about a man who cannot let go of a dream we all once shared. One who sparks restored faith that we can recover, and perhaps even become better than we were.

1

ONCE, LONG AGO, Gordon Krantz had heard somebody contend that there was nothing more dangerous than a desperate man. There was no defeat so total that a determined person could not pull something from the ashes by negotiation . . . by risking all he had left.

Only an hour before Gordon had been well stocked, and as comfortable as a solitary traveler could expect to be these days. Now he was a fugitive, robbed and terrorized, scratched and torn from his frantic escape through the blackberry thicket.

From his hiding place, in a rock cleft surrounded by thick brush, Gordon could hear the sounds of looting taking place a few hundred yards down the mountainside. He tried not to listen to the delighted yells. They signaled the loss of gear he had spent years gathering. The thought was too painful to consider yet.

They had caught him off guard, sipping weak elderberry tea by his late afternoon campfire. It had been clear in that first instant, as they charged up the trail at him, that the raiders would as soon kill him as look at him. He snatched his belt and dove into the nearby brambles before they got close enough to choose.

He had cut his foot during that mad scramble and collected innumerable scrapes.

The fact that he had got away at all was as much a testament to his speed—preventing them from getting within knife range as they chuffed up the narrow path—as to the bandits' stinginess with ammo. They probably thought he had abandoned all of his goods, and his carcass was not worth a bullet.

Gordon allowed himself an ironic smile as he carefully replaced the moccasin on his injured foot. He had not left everything behind. As had been his habit even before the war, when he went on backpacking trips as a boy, he never spent a waking moment without his travel belt strapped on or within reach.

He was thankful for that old precaution as he picked up his revolver from a nearby rock and slid it back into its holster. He clutched a nearby rock outcrop to help himself stand up.

The happy sounds were fading now. The bandits were leaving. He heard a few derisive calls, obviously designed to taunt the victim, who had got away with his life, but little more. Then there was silence.

He had, indeed, got away with very little more than his life. Even that last part was in doubt, since he had no supplies.

Gordon had already decided. He had no choice but to follow the raiders. Something might occur to him. They might abandon some of his goods. Turning away would be turning toward death in the wilderness.

As he picked his way back toward the trail as quietly as he could, Gordon checked his inventory. Besides his holstered pistol, the hip pouches on his belt held his scout knife, a few days' concentrated rations, his compass, first aid packet, space blanket, a miniature fishing kit, and ten spare rounds of ammunition. He silently blessed those small relics of industrial civilization.

Unfortunately, these were still paltry gleanings from a

disaster. All considered, Gordon's chances of survival had easily been halved. Those chances had, of late, seemed quite slim enough.

Gordon moved as quickly and silently as he could through the bone-dry forest. He began to see the outlines of a plan forming—to cut above the main trail and, traversing the east slope of the mountain, to come down upon his opponents while it was still light . . . while they were still gloating over their acquisitions, carelessly contemptuous of the man they had robbed.

The bearded, denim-clad men had taunted him as he escaped through the bramble, calling him "brer rabbit" and promising to eat him if he ever returned. Gordon wasn't entirely sure they had been joking about the last part. He had seen cases of cannibalism in the early days. Some of these mountain men might have acquired a taste for the "long-pork." One thing he thought was pretty certain. The marauders probably thought he was unarmed. That was Gordon's slim advantage.

His own survival depended on his ability to catch up with his robbers and to persuade them that a man with nothing to lose was someone to be reckoned with. If he could show them how far he was willing to go, they might let him have back some of his goods—perhaps enough to keep him alive in the wild mountains of what had once been the state of Oregon.

He had on a shirt, jeans, camp slippers, and socks. The loss of his jacket was a major disaster. As he moved quickly down the trail, Gordon couldn't avoid all of the sharp stones and sticks that covered the trail. His left foot throbbed every time it was poked. Moccasins would get him nowhere. He had to have his boots back, at least!

Gordon cautiously entered the small clearing that had been his campsite. There was next to nothing left.

They had made litter of his tent, ripping it into tiny pieces of nylon and aluminum. Apparently the robbers had no use for it, and had destroyed out of malice whatever they didn't want to carry. The only things of value the robbers had left intact were the slim longbow Gordon had been carving and his experimental line of gut strings.

Although it had been one and a half decades since the fall of industrial civilization, ammunition for firearms had only recently begun to get scarce; there had been so much around before the war. Gordon's enemies were apparently men of little imagination. When they seized everything else at his campsite, they had failed to see the value of the bow and strings.

His shotgun and ammo, boots, jacket, geiger counter, and his slim, crab-written diaries were all gone, along with his food supply, of course. Carefully prepared pemmican . . . some split grains his last appreciative audience had donated . . . his tiny hoard of rock candy, which he had found in an abandoned gas station vending machine.

It was just as well he had lost the candy. His tooth brush was lost, too, trampled in amidst the trash the bandits had left in his campsite.

If he survived this day's disaster, Gordon swore he would find another toothbrush. In his travels he had seen too many once pearly smiles that had been ravaged by neglect. The idea of his own teeth rotting in his mouth was Gordon's personal phobia. He was a fastidious anomaly in a world of ever-growing barbarism and decay.

Even limping, he was able to move silently and quickly. That was the only advantage camp moccasins had over boots. Soon he could hear the raiding party below him, laughing over the morning's escapade.

Gordon carefully considered his recollection of yesterday's hike up this same trail. He thought he could remember the perfect site for a bushwhack. There was a switchback that passed beneath a horseshoe-shaped rocky outcrop. A sniper could easily break brush just above that turn and position himself within point-blank range of anyone hiking along the hairpin.

Gordon kept a close watch on the foliage on the left side of the trail. When he came to a slope that promised a fast shortcut to the south, he broke through the scrub oak, leaving the path and breaking his own trail. If he could get to the ambuscade first, he might be able to pin them down from the start and force a negotiated withdrawal.

That was the advantage of being the one with little to lose. The bandits would probably prefer to live to rob another day. It was easy to believe that they would part with boots, some food and ammo, a blanket and a geiger counter in order to save the lives of one or two of their number.

Gordon was willing to snipe now and live with himself later. In sixteen years, he had yet to kill a man that he knew of—though he had fired at dim figures early on, as a volunteer in the militia. That had been back when there *was* still a militia and a National Guard.

The voices of the party on the trail faded with distance. There was no way he could catch up with them in a straight chase, when they were on a trail and he was breaking ground cross country. Also, there wasn't much time left before nightfall.

Gordon decided to gamble on a shortcut. He concentrated on finding the quickest way southwest, toward the rocky overhang he remembered. Soon he was in a thick undergrowth. The sun was hard to find, through the trees. He had to pause frequently to check his compass.

Grimly, he kept on. He didn't remember the trail very well from yesterday, but it seemed that the switchback came only after a sweep southward along the face of the mountain. It presented him with a quandary. To stand a chance of catching his adversaries, he had to stay above them. Yet if he went too high, he might go right past them.

He chose a direction and persevered.

But soon the game path turned slightly westward, into a pass to the south of the one he had camped in. It appeared to lead to another route upward, toward the Divide, where the Cascade range changed from semi-arid forest to the rain-drenched climate of the coast.

He stopped a moment to catch his breath. The other side of the pass had been Gordon's goal before the robbery. He looked at the slight mist that gathered in the pass above. Once he was over the Divide he need never again worry about scarce or poisoned water, or the desert sun. There might be salmon to fish . . . and there might be a semblance of civilization.

Gordon shook his head, driving out the temptation to abandon the chase. For certain there would be rain and snow over that range, along with predators and the threat of starvation. He *had* to have supplies!

He began angling downslope a bit. Surely by now the main trail was quite a bit below him, if it hadn't already switched back a few times. He surprised a flock of wild turkeys as he entered a small clearing: one more sign that he had come into wetter country. It was also an indication of how far wildlife had recovered from the overhunting of the first postwar years, now that the human population had been thinned. How useful his bow someday might become, should he live long enough to finish and perfect it.

Now the game path was definitely turning west. The switchback had to be below, if not behind him. Gordon drifted downslope when he could, but the path forced him to continue west through the undergrowth.

Suddenly he stopped. His ears picked up something.

Gordon hurried along the path until the steepness of a ravine caused the forest to open up around him. Now he could see the mountain, and the other mountains of the chain, wrapped in a thick summer haze. The sound was coming from below, and to the northeast.

Voices. Gordon peered, then saw the trail. He caught a glimpse of color moving upward, slowly, through the woods.

The bandits! But why were they moving uphill? They wouldn't, unless Gordon was already far south of the trail he had taken the day before. He must have missed the ambush site altogether.

If the vandals had taken a fork he failed to notice

yesterday, they were now climbing back toward . . . Gordon looked up the mountain. Yes, he could see how a small hollow could fit over to the west, on a shoulder near the lesser used pass. It would be defensible and very hard to discover by chance.

Gordon turned west. If he hurried, he might beat the bandits to their base by five minutes or so. Perhaps he could take some women at the hideout hostage. The image struck him as grossly unpalatable, far less pleasing than the plan of ambushing his own ambushers.

Still, what choice had he? There wasn't a decent ambush site. It would be too easy to outflank him on this broad hillside.

He started to run, leaping over the shorter scrub and fallen trees. Gordon felt exuberant as he coursed through the forest. He was committed, and none of his typical introspection or self-doubt would get in the way now. The battle adrenaline made him almost high. Running, he stretched to leap over a decayed trunk into a summer-dry creekbed. But the instant, he landed, a sharp pain lanced through his left foot and streaked up his left leg.

He barely caught himself as he fell. Sudden tears filled his eyes. He grabbed the trunk and lowered himself to the ground. Something had stabbed him in the foot, through the flimsy camp moccasins he wore.

For several minutes he had to sit there, massaging his foot until the cramps slowly subsided. Meanwhile, he could hear the sounds of the bandit party passing below, taking away the head start that had been his only advantage.

Nightfall wasn't many hours away. The "space blanket" in his pouch didn't seem like much protection against the cold. He had little faith in something that, folded in its plastic bag, measured about the size of a cupcake.

As he stood up, carefully, leaning on the bow, Gordon's eye was caught by a sudden flash. Something glinted amidst the trees, across the narrow pass.

He could see the object to the southeast, or rather he could see its reflection. From the folds in the hillsides, Gordon guessed that it could not be seen by anyone standing too far from this very spot, and then only in the late afternoon. The forest was thick over there on the other side of this saddle, and the hillsides gathered closely around. The many forest fires that had seared this dry part of the Cascades since the war seemed to have spared that mountainside.

Above the reflection, along the ridgeline above, Gordon could see the faint outlines of an old road or firebreak. This had been National Forest, before the war. But even then there had been people hereabouts.

So. That had to be the hideout, not the hollow to the west.

The voices of the passing gang fell away into the hazy mountainside. Gordon listened until he was sure they were gone. Then he relaxed enough to begin thinking again. He had to come up with another plan.

Gordon went slowly, nursing his injured foot and listening carefully for an ambush. If he read his enemies right, their pickets would be close to home, if they maintained any at all.

Unfortunately, there were many more side paths than in the other pass. Gordon had to choose among several likely tracks. He couldn't make out footprints in the gravelly soil, especially in the fading light of the dying afternoon. The sun had already passed behind the mountain to the southwest. He visualized his destination, a ravine on the opposite shoulder of the saddle. He chose a trail that began to swing once more to the east.

He climbed into the thick forested hollow where he had seen the reflection earlier. Gordon guessed that he was within a half-mile of his goal, and slightly higher in altitude, when the path failed. It was growing dark fast. Gordon had to push through undergrowth, peering about for hazards to his feet. He regretted the loss of his flashlight. It was probably the last working electric light on this side of the Divide. The handpowered novelty had been a gift from his brother just before the war.

Groping and blundering, Gordon kept his forearms in front to protect his face from the dry brush as he poked about for the quietest approach. He fought down the urge to cough in the floating dust. The evening chill was coming on. Still, Gordon shivered less from the cold than from nervousness. He knew he was nearing his destination. One way or another, Gordon felt he was about to have an encounter with Death—his own or somebody else's, perhaps both. Gordon hadn't wanted his Dharma to come to this.

He had chosen to become a minstrel, a traveling actor and laborer, partly because he wanted to keep moving, to search for a haven where someone was trying to put things back together again, his personal dream. But he also couldn't stay in one place because many of the surviving postwar communities demanded that a new male member prove his skill at killing before being allowed to join. He might have to duel-kill for the right to sit at the communal table, or bring back the scalp of a member of a feuding clan. Many survivor outposts had adopted rituals in which he wanted no part.

Now he found himself counting the bullets he had for his revolver and noting that there were probably enough for all the bandits. It was a grim mental exercise for a man who thought of himself as one of the last Humanists. He told himself this was different, that it was self-defense, but a part of him still protested.

Gordon detoured around another sparse berry patch. What the thicket lacked in fruit, it made up for in thorns. He moved along its edge, careful in the gray twilight.

Gordon thought it a miracle that a man like him had lived this long. Everyone he had known or admired when he was a boy was dead, along with virtually every hope any of them had had. The soft world that had encouraged dreamers broke apart when he was seventeen. Long ago he realized that his brand of persistent optimism had to be a form of hysterical insanity.

Gordon paused at a small blob of color. About a yard into the nearby bramble, a solitary clump of blackberries hung, apparently missed by the local black bear. Ignoring the stabbing thorns, Gordon reached in to pick a few and popped them into his mouth.

He savored the wild, tart sweetness and wished it had not been so long since he had been with a woman.

Twilight was almost gone. Gordon made slow progress in the gathering gloom, even as the chill made him yearn to hurry up and get it over with. He finally rounded the thicket. There, suddenly, he saw the glint of a glass window only a hundred feet away.

Gordon ducked back behind the thorns. Breathing deeply, he pulled his revolver and checked the action to be certain no dirt was caught in the mechanism. He touched his breast pocket to make certain his spare ammo was ready. His hand was shaking.

Am I really going to go through with this?

A hazard to quick or forceful motion, the thicket was soft and yielding to his muscled back as he settled against it. Gordon closed his eyes and meditated for peace, for calm, and for forgiveness. In the chilly darkness, the only accompaniment to his breathing was the rhythmic ratchet of the crickets. A swirl of cold fog blew around him.

He sighed. There's no other way. He raised his weapon and swung around to face death.

The structure looked odd. The distant patch of glass was dark.

That was strange, but stranger still was the silence. He'd have thought the bandits would have a fire going, that they would be celebrating their successful robbery.

The glass reflected silvery highlights of a rolling cloud cover. Then wisps of haze drifted between Gordon and his objective, confusing the image, making it shimmer. Gordon walked forward slowly, giving most of his attention to the ground. If they could afford to feed one, the bandits would surely have a dog, or several. Now was not the time to step on a dry twig or to be stabbed by a sharp stone as he stumbled in the dimness.

He glanced up, and once more the eerie feeling struck him. There was something very odd about the structure. It didn't look right. Its upper section seemed mostly glass. Below, it looked like painted metal. At the corners . . .

The fog grew thicker. Gordon could tell his perspective was wrong. He had been looking for a house or a large cottage. As he neared, he realized that the thing was closer than he had thought. The shape was familiar, somehow.

His foot came down on twig. The "snap!" filled his ears as he crouched, peering into the gloom, desperate to see.

The ragged fog fell open before him. Pupils dilated, Gordon suddenly saw that he was bare meters from the window; he saw his own face reflected upon its surface, wide-eyed and wild haired; and he saw, superimposed on his own image, a vacant, grinning death mask—a hooded skull smiling in welcome.

Gordon crouched, hypnotized, unable to move or make a sound. A superstitious thrill coursed up his spine. The haze slowly swirled as he listened for proof that this was really happening—wishing with all his might that the death's head was an illusion.

"Alas, poor Gordon!" The sepulchral image seemed to shimmer a greeting as it overlay his reflection. Gordon's frozen mind could think of nothing but to attend the figure's bidding.

Finally, he exhaled and he heard it whistle between his teeth. Without willing them to, Gordon felt his eyes turn slightly from the visage of death. A part of him noted that the window was part of a door. The handle lay before him. To the left there was another window. To the right . . . to the right was the hood.

The hood of the Jeep. The hood of the abandoned, rusted Jeep that lay in a faint rut in the forest. The hood of the abandoned, rusted Jeep with ancient US Government markings and the skeleton of a poor dead civil servant within, skull pressed against the passenger-side window, facing Gordon.

The strangled sigh Gordon let out felt almost ectoplasmic, the relief and embarrassment was so palpable. Gordon forced himself to straighten up and felt as if he were unwinding from the fetal position. He moved his arms and legs, then slowly began to pace around the vehicle, obsessively glancing back at its dead occupant. His heartbeat settled, and the adrenaline roar gradually ebbed.

He walked around the vehicle four times, then sat down on the forest floor against the cool door on the left side. Shaking slightly, he put the revolver back on safety and slid it into its holster. Then he pulled his canteen and drank with slow, full swallows. Gordon wished he had something stronger than water.

The night was full upon him. The cold was chilling, but Gordon spent a few moments putting off the obvious. The Jeep was, at minimum, shelter for the night. Finally the cold made him admit that now was the time to use that shelter.

The latch operated after a stubborn moment. He had to pull hard to pry the rusted door open. It let out a screech, but Gordon didn't care. He slid over onto the cracked vinyl of the seat and inspected the interior.

The Jeep was one of those backward, driver on-the-right types the post office had used. The dead mailman— what was left of him—was slumped on the far right. Gordon avoided looking at the skeleton for the moment.

The back was half-full of canvas sacks. The smell of old paper and the musky odor from the mummified remains filled the small cabin. Gordon snatched up a metal flask he found on the floor. It sloshed! To have held liquid for sixteen years it had to be closed tightly. Gordon swore as he twisted and pried at the cap. He pounded it against the door frame. On the verge of tears, he finally felt the cap give slightly. He redoubled his efforts and was rewarded with a slow, rough turning and the heady, distantly familiar odor of whiskey.

Gordon decided that he must have been a good boy

after all and that there was indeed a God. He took a mouthful and almost coughed as the warming fire streamed down his esophagus. He took two more small swallows and fell back against the seat, gasping for breath.

He was unwilling to face the task of removing the jacket the skeleton wore. Let it wait until daylight, he thought. Gordon grabbed sacks from the rear and bundled them about him. They bore the imprint US POSTAL SERVICE on them. He left the door open just an inch to let in the crisp mountain air. Burrowing under the sacks with his bottle, Gordon drifted into a semi-slumber, waking from time to time to take a sip from the bottle.

Gordon finally looked over at his host and contemplated the American flag patch on the arm of the civil servant's jacket. He unscrewed the flask for another swig. This time he raised the container toward the hooded garment.

"Believe it or not, Mr. Postman," he said, "I always thought you folks gave good and honest service. I was proud of you all, even before the war. But this, Mr. Mailman, this is service beyond anything I'd come to expect! I consider my taxes very well spent!"

He brought the flask to his mouth and drank to the postman, then screwed the cap back on and settled deeper into the mail sacks. Gordon felt a sad poignancy come upon him, like home sickness. The Jeep, the symbolic, faithful letter carrier, the flag . . . they reminded him of comfort, innocence, cooperation, and the easy life that had once allowed millions of men and women to relax, to smile, to be tolerant with one another.

Today, Gordon had been ready to kill and be killed. He smiled, glad that that had been averted. They had called him Mr. Rabbit and left him to die. But he would call the bandits "countrymen" and let them have their lives.

Gordon allowed sleep to come, welcoming back the optimism he had thought he'd lost. He lay in a blanket

of his own honor and spent the rest of the night dreaming
of parallel worlds.

2

A camp robber bird, looking for jays to chase, landed
on the hood with a hollow thump. It squawked, once for
territoriality and once for pleasure, then began poking
through the thick detritus with its beak.

Gordon awakened to the tap-tapping sound and
looked about, bleary-eyed. He looked at the bird through
the dust-smeared window and took time to remember
where he was. The glass windshield, the steering wheel,
the smell of metal and paper felt like a continuation of
the dream he had had most of the night, a dream about
the Old Days, before the war. Then memory of the
events of yesterday settled in.

Gordon rubbed his eyes and began to consider his situation. If he hadn't left an elephant's trail on his way into
this hollow last night, he should be perfectly safe right
now. The fact that the whiskey had been here untouched
for sixteen years obviously meant that the bandits were
lazy hunters. They had never even fully explored their
own mountain.

Unaccustomed to eighty-proof liquor, Gordon felt a
little thick-headed. The war had begun when he was seventeen, a young college prodigy, and since then there
had been few opportunities to build up a tolerance to
alcohol. The whiskey had left him cotton-mouthed and
a bit scratchy behind the eyelids.

He regretted his lost comforts. There would be no tea
this morning, no damp washcloth, no hearty breakfast of
venison jerky, and, especially, no toothbrush. Gordon
tried to be philosophical: after all, he was alive.

He had a feeling there would be times when each of
the items stolen from him would fall into the category
"missed most of all." If the gods still favored him, he
would never feel that way about the geiger counter.

Radiation had been one of his main reasons for going ever westward since he left Minnesota, five years before. He had grown tired of walking everywhere with his precious counter, always afraid it would be stolen. Everyone knew the west coast had been spared the worst of the nuclear catastrophe. The seasonal winds had blown true to form, from west to east, that year. While the Conelrad stations were still broadcasting, Gordon and his fellow survivors had learned of the streaks of fallout that speared eastward from Vandenberg, in California, and the Puget Sound Trident pens. But a thoughtful look at a map made it clear that the Pacific coast was still better off than the Midwest. The deadly rains expected from Asia had somehow never come in force.

The war had been fought mostly with death rays and death bugs, anyway. The former eradicated the space stations with surgical effectiveness. The latter destroyed the last semblances of civilization and governmental control. The plagues were well constructed, at least. Gordon gave their designers that much. After a year most of the viruses had passed a built-in time limit and either disappeared or become benign. Still, Gordon had fled several times from villages where strangers were shot at on sight, as potential carriers.

Gordon pushed aside the mail sacks that had been his blankets. He opened his left belt pouch and pulled out a small package. It was wrapped in aluminum foil that had been coated with melted wax.

If there ever had been an emergency, this was one. Gordon would need energy to get through the day. A dozen cubes of boullion and a chunk of rock candy were all he had.

Sucking on a broken-off piece of the hard sugar, Gordon kicked open the door of the Jeep. He dropped several of the mail sacks out onto the ground to get them out of the way.

He got out and circled around to look at the muffled skeleton that had shared the night with him.

"Mr. Postman," he said. "I'm going to give you as close to a decent burial as I can manage. I know that's not much recompense for all you're giving me. But it's all I have to offer."

The rusty door groaned as he pulled it open. Holding an emptied mail sack out to catch the skeleton as it pitched forward, Gordon managed to get the bundle of clothes and bones laid out on the forest floor. Gordon was amazed at the state of preservation. The dry climate had almost mummified the postman's remains. The other contents of the Jeep appeared to have been free from mold for sixteen years.

An inventory was in order before he started digging a grave. First he checked the mailman's apparel. The jacket was a wonderful find. If big enough, it would improve Gordon's chances of survival substantially. The footgear looked old and cracked, but it might fit. They had once been rugged work shoes. Gordon carefully shook out the dry remnants of skin and bone and laid them against his moccasins. They looked just a little large. Too bad the postman's socks were beyond redemption. The shirt and pants seemed all right, though they were stiff and musty. Gordon slid the bones out of the clothing and onto the mail sack with as little violence as he could manage, all the time a little surprised at how easy it was. It seemed that all of his superstition had been used up the night before. All that remained was a mild reverence for and an ironic gratitude to the corpse.

He carried the treasures over to a Jeffrey pine, shook them vigorously, holding his breath against the dust, and hung them on a branch to air out.

On the floor below the driver's seat was a large leather carrier's sack. It too was dry and cracked in spots, but the straps held when he tugged on them, and the flaps looked as if they'd keep out water. Gordon laid it outside, near the precious flask of scotch. He pried open the glove compartment. A brittle map he found replaced the one he had lost.

With a joyful shout, Gordon grabbed a small cube of clear plastic from under a pile of papers. It was a scintillator! Far better than his geiger counter, the little crystal would give off tiny flashes whenever gamma radiation struck it. It needed no power. Gordon cupped it in front of his eye and watched as a sparse set of flickerings told of cosmic ray background flux. Otherwise, the cube was quiescent.

Now what was a prewar mailman doing with a gadget like that? Gordon wondered. He put the scintillator into his pants pocket and returned to the glove compartment.

The flashlight was a dead loss. The emergency flares were crumbling. He tossed two of them over onto his salvage pile. The tool kit had many items that would make good trade somewhere, but the weight of the metal made it unrealistic to carry more than a few pieces, which he carefully selected.

A scattering of small packages spilled from the leather carrier's bag. Gordon decided he might as well empty the bag right now. It wouldn't come close to replacing his lost Kelty, but it would be a vast improvement over nothing at all.

He opened the flaps and upended the bag. Bundles of aged correspondence spilled out, breaking into scattered piles as brittle rubber bands snapped apart. Gordon picked up a few of the nearest pieces.

"From the office of the mayor of Bend, Oregon, to the Chairman of the Department of Veterinary medicine of the University of Oregon, Eugene." Gordon intoned the address as if he were playing Polonius. He flipped through more letters. The addresses sounded pompous and archaic.

"And Dr. Franklin Davis, of the small town of Gilchrist writes—with the word URGENT printed clearly on the envelope—a rather bulky letter to the Director of Regional Disbursement of Medical Supplies . . . no doubt pleading priority for his requisitions."

Gordon's sardonic smile faded into a frown of concentration as he turned over one letter after another. Something was wrong here.

He had expected to be amused by junk mail and personal correspondence, but there didn't seem to be a single advertisement in the bag. And while there were many private letters, most of the envelopes were official stationery.

Well, he really didn't have much time for snooping anyway. He would have to get organized, decide on a plan, and act soon if he wanted to eat. Perhaps now was the time to begin relearning the art of arrow-making.

He would take a dozen or so letters for amusement, and use the backsides of the letters for his new journal. He hadn't allowed himself to feel the loss of sixteen years' tiny scratchings, which was now doubtless being perused by some bandit.

As he selected a few letters to stuff back into the bag, the sense of something unexpected returned to Gordon. The mix of addresses bothered him. Too many were labeled URGENT. It made Gordon wonder.

What was a US Postal Service Jeep doing out here, anyway? And what had killed the postman?

Gordon got up and went around to the back of the vehicle. There were bullet holes in the tailgate window, well grouped midway up toward the right side. Gordon looked over to the Jeffrey pine. Yes, the shirt and jacket each had two holes in the back of the upper-chest area. He hadn't noticed them before because of the number of other stains and rips.

Gordon looked at the skeleton, skewed and jumbled on its mail sack. Logic narrowed the range of possible explanations considerably. The attempted hijacking or robbery could not have been prewar. Mail carriers, if he remembered correctly, had almost never been attacked, even in the late eighties rioting. Besides, a missing carrier would have been searched for until found. So the attack took place *after* the three-day holocaust. But what was a mailman doing driving alone through the countryside after the United States had effectively ceased to exist? How long after had this happened?

The fellow must have driven off from his ambush, then sought the most obscure roads and trails to get away from his assailants. Perhaps he was unaware of the severity of his wounds. Perhaps he had simply panicked. But

Gordon suspected that there was another reason the letter carrier had chosen to weave in and out of blackberry thickets to hide.

"He was protecting his cargo," Gordon thought. "He measured the chance that he'd black out on the road against the possibility of getting help and decided to save the mail rather than try to live."

So, this was a bona fide postwar postman, hero of the flickering twilight of civilization. Gordon thought of the oldtime ode of the mails . . . . "Through rain, snow, sleet . . ." and wondered at the fact that some had tried this hard to keep the light alive.

That explained the official letters and the lack of junk mail. Gordon hadn't realized that even a semblance of normality had remained after the first bombs.

Of course, as a seventeen-year-old recruit with his militia unit, Gordon had been unlikely to see anything normal. The mob rule and general looting in the main disbursement centers kept armed authority busy until the militia finally vanished into the disturbances it had been sent to quell. If men and women elsewhere were behaving more like human beings during those months of horror, Gordon never witnessed it.

The brave story of the postman served only to depress Gordon. This hint of a short-term struggle against chaos, by mayors and university professors and postmen, had a "what if" flavor that was too poignant for him to consider for long.

Gordon found himself touching the bullet holes in the rear window. He forced himself to stop it and instead to pry open the tailgate. It opened reluctantly, but finally Gordon could begin moving mailsacks aside, looking for useful items. He found the letter carrier's hat with its tarnished badge, then an empty lunchbox. He snatched up a valuable pair of sunglasses lying in a thick layer of dust on a wheel well.

Amongst the heavier tools that lay jumbled in the storage compartment above the rear axle, Gordon found a small shovel. Intended to help free the four-wheel drive vehicle from ruts in the road, it would now help to bury the driver.

Just behind the driver's seat, under several heavy sacks, Gordon found a smashed guitar. A large-caliber bullet had snapped its neck. Near it, a large yellowed plastic bag held a pound of desicated herbs that gave off a strong, musky odor. Gordon barely remembered the smell: marijuana.

He had envisioned the postman as a middle aged, balding, conservative type. Gordon now recreated the image and made the fellow look more like himself: a member of a sub-generation that had hardly begun to flower before the war snuffed out it and everything else optimistic, a neo-hippie dying to protect the establishment's mail. It didn't surprise Gordon. He had had friends who were part of the movement, before the Chaos. They had been sincere people, though a little strange. Their motto had been cooperation and selflessness—in rejection of the egotism of the eighties. A neo-hippy would have been susceptible to the mystique of the Post.

Gordon threw the guitar out the tailgate and resumed searching.

The letter carrier hadn't even been armed! Did he really believe he was inviolable? Gordon remembered reading once that the US Mail operated through both sides of the lines for three years into the 1860s Civil War. Perhaps the postman had been a pacifist. Perhaps he had trusted his countrymen to respect tradition.

Post-Chaos America had no tradition but survival. In his travels, Gordon had found that some isolated communities welcomed him in the same way minstrels had been kindly received far and wide in medieval days. In other cases there were wild varieties of paranoia. Gordon had learned to read the subtle clues that told which hamlet would welcome strangers. Fewer than half spoke before shooting.

Even in those rare cases where he had found friendliness, where decent people seemed willing to welcome a stranger with a steady hand and a good heart, Gordon had always, before long, found himself ready to leave. Whenever he stayed in one place for very long, he began to dream of wheels turning and things flying in the sky. After about a year in one place, he generally found himself moving on.

By midmorning he had decided. His gleanings were sufficient to make the chances of survival better without a confrontation with the bandits. The sooner he was over the pass and into a decent watershed, the better off he would be.

Someday, when he was resupplied and confident, he would return to claim his property.

He would bury the postman and take the guitar strings and sunglasses. Nothing else in back of the Jeep would serve him half so well as would a stream, somewhere out of the range of the bandit gang, where he could fish for trout to fill his belly.

3

". . . They said fear not, Macbeth, 'til Birnam Wood comes to Dunsinane; and now a wood comes to Dunsinane!

"Arm, arm, arm yourselves! If this is what the witch spoke of—that thing out there—there'll be no running, or hiding here!"

Gordon clutched his wooden sword, which he had contrived earlier from an old piece of planking and a bit of tin. He motioned to an invisible aide-de-camp.

"I'm getting weary of the sun and wish the world were undone.

"Ring the alarum bell! Blow, wind! come wrack! At least we'll die with harness on our back!"

Gordon squared his shoulders, flourished his sword, and marched Macbeth offstage to his doom.

Out of the glare of the tallow lamps, he swiveled to catch a glimpse of his audience. They had loved his earlier acts. But this bastardized one-man version of *Mac-*

beth might have gone over their heads, in spite of his bowdlerizations and simplified verses.

To be honest, a lot of the "updated" parts had been changed because Gordon couldn't remember the original. He'd most recently seen a copy of the play a decade ago. The last lines of his soliloquy had been canon, at least. The part about "wind and wrack" he would never forget.

Those in the front row began applauding enthusiastically the instant after he made his exit; they were led by Mrs. Adele Thompson, the leader of this clan. The younger citizens clapped awkwardly. Those below twenty years of age slapped their hands together as though they were taking part in this strange rite of group appreciation for the first time in their lives.

Grinning Gordon jumped onto the makeshift stage to take his bows. The stage was a plank-covered garage lift in what had once been the only gas station in the tiny hamlet.

Driven by hunger and isolation, Gordon had gambled on the hospitality of this mountain village, with its fenced fields and stout log wall. The gamble had paid off. His initial welcome had been cordial, with a minimum of suspicion. His offer of a series of performances in exchange for his meals had passed by a fair majority of the voting adults of the village.

"Bravo! Excellent!" Mrs. Thompson stood in the front row, clapping enthusiastically. White-haired and bony but still robust, she turned to encourage the thirty-odd others, including small children, to show their appreciation. Gordon did a flourish with one hand and bowed deeper than before.

His performance had been pure crap, but he was probably the only person within a hundred miles who had once studied drama. There were "peasants" once again in America, and, like his predecessors in the minstrel trade, Gordon had learned to go for the unsubtle.

Timing his final bow for the moment before the applause began to fade, Gordon again left the stage. He removed his crude, slapped-together costume. He had set

firm limits. There would be no encore. His stock was
theater, and he meant to keep them hungry for it until
it was time to leave.

"Marvelous. Just wonderful!" Mrs. Thompson greeted
him as he joined the villagers, now gathering at a buffet
table along the back wall. The people were making a
festival of the event. The older children formed a circle
around him, staring in wonderment.

"Thank you, Mrs. Thompson. I appreciate the kind
words of a perceptive critic, especially when it's so long
between performances."

"No, no seriously," the clan leader insisted, as if Gordon had been trying to be modest. "I haven't been so
delighted in years. Wow! That last bit with Macbeth sent
shivers down my spine! I only wish I'd watched it on TV
back when I had a chance. I didn't know it was so good!

"And that inspiring Abraham Lincoln speech you gave
us . . . well, you know, we tried to start a school here,
in the beginning. But back in the early days it just didn't
work out. We needed every hand, even the kids', and it
seemed no one had the heart. Well, that speech got me
to thinking. We've got some old books someplace.
Maybe . . ."

Gordon nodded politely. He had seen this syndrome
before. It was the best of a half-dozen types of reception
he had experienced over the years, but it was also among
the saddest. It always made him feel a little bit like a
charlatan when his shows brought out grand, submerged
hopes in one of the decent older people who remembered better days, hopes that had always fallen through
before a week or a month had passed. It was as if the
seeds of civilization needed more than good will and the
dreams of aging high-school graduates to water them. He
was no traveling messiah. The symbols he offered would
not give the hopeful the sustenance they needed to overcome the inertia of a dark age.

Gordon was spared hearing more of Mrs. Thompson's
plans. The crowd that surrounded him squeezed out a
small, silver-haired black woman, wiry and leather-

skinned, who seized Gordon's arm with a friendly but viselike grip.

"Now, Adele," she said to the clan matriarch, "Mister Krantz hasn't had a bite since noontime. If we want him well enough to perform tomorrow night, we'd better feed him, hmmm?"

Mrs. Thompson gave the other woman a look of patient indulgence. "Of course, Patricia," she said. "I'll speak with you more about this, later, Mr. Krantz, after Mrs. Howlett has succeeded in fattening you up a bit. She gave Gordon an intelligent, ironic smile. Gordon re-evaluated his initial impression of Adele Thompson. She certainly was no fool.

Mrs. Howlett seized Gordon's arm and propelled him through the crowd. Gordon smiled and nodded as hands came out to touch his sleeve. Wide eyes followed his every movement. One of those watching him was a young woman who stood behind the long buffet table. She had hair blacker than Gordon remembered ever seeing before, and deep almond eyes. She was barely taller than Mrs. Howlett. Twice, she turned to slap the hand of a child who tried to help himself to the banquet before the honored guest. But each time she quickly looked back at Gordon and smiled.

Beside her, a tall, burly red-haired man stroked his short red beard and gave Gordon a strange look of resignation.

"Abby," Mrs. Howlett addressed the pretty brunette. "Let's have a little bit of everything on a plate for Mr. Krantz. Then he can make up his mind what he wants seconds of. I baked the blueberry pie, Mr. Krantz."

Dizzily, Gordon made a diplomatic note to himself to have two helpings of the pie. It was hard to concentrate on politics, though. He hadn't seen or smelled anything like the buffet before him in years! There was a large stuffed turkey. A huge steaming bowl of boiled potatoes, dollied up with beer-soaked jerky, carrots, and onions, was the second course. Down the table Gordon saw apple cobbler and a barrel of dried apple flakes.

He would have to cozzen a supply of those before he left.

Not bothering with further inventory, he eagerly held out his plate. Abby kept her eyes on him as she took it.

The red-haired man suddenly muttered something indecipherable and reached out and grabbed Gordon's right hand with both of his own. Gordon flinched, but the taciturn fellow would not let go until he answered the grip and shook hands. The man then nodded and let go. Blushing slightly he bent down to kiss the brunette quickly and stalked off, eyes downcast. Gordon blinked. Did I just miss something, he wondered as he took back his heaped plate. The girl blushed prettily as he thanked her.

"That was Abby's husband, Michael," Mrs. Howlett said. He stayed to see your show, but now he's got to go and relieve Edward at the trap string, so Edward can bring back what he's caught and dried over the last week. He wanted to stay to see your show, though. I think when he was little, he used to love to watch shows . . ."

Gordon was in a haze as the steam from his plate rose to his face. Mrs. Howlett rattled on beside him as he found a seat on a pile of old tires and proceeded to stuff himself.

"You'll get to talk to Abby later," the black woman went on. "Now, you eat. And when you get a little less hungry, I think we'd all like to hear, one more time, how you got to be a mailman."

Gordon looked up at the eager faces around him. He hurriedly took a swig of beer to chase down a too-hot mouthful of potatoes.

"I'm just a traveler," Gordon said around a full mouth while lifting a turkey drumstick. "It's not much of a story, how I got the bag and clothes." Gordon shrugged. He didn't care whether they stared or touched or talked to him so long as they let him eat!

Mrs. Howlett smiled and watched him for a few moments. Then, unable to hold back, she started in again. "You know, when I was a little girl, we used to give milk and cookies to the mailman. And my father always left a little glass of whiskey for him the day before New Year's. Dad used to tell us that poem—you know, "Through sleet, through mud, through war, through blight, through bandits and through darkest night . . ."

Gordon coughed and looked up from his plate for a moment, astonished and delighted by the old woman's misremembrance. But the impulse faded quickly as he returned to his slab of roast turkey and stuffing. He hadn't the will to try to figure out what the old woman was driving at.

"*Our* mailman used to sing to us!"

The speaker was a dark-haired giant with a silver-streaked beard. His eyes seemed to mist as he remembered. "We could hear him coming, on Saturdays when we were home from school, sometimes when he was over a block away. He was black, blacker than Mrs. Howlett or Jim Horton over there. Man, did he have a nice voice! He brought me all those mail-order coins I used to collect. Ringed the doorbell so he could hand 'em to me personal, with his own hand."

His voice was hushed.

"Our mailman just whistled when I was little," said a middle-aged woman. She sounded a little disappointed. "But he *was* real nice. Later, when I was grown up, I came home from work one day and found out the mailman had saved the life of one of my neighbors—heard him choking and gave him mouth-to-mouth until an ambulance came."

There was a collective sigh from the circle of listeners, as if they were hearing the heroic adventures of a single ancient hero.

"Now," Mrs. Howlett touched Gordon's knee. "Tell us again how you got to be a mailman."

Gordon shrugged again, a little desperately. "I just found the mailman's things."

"Ah." Several of the villagers looked at each other knowingly and nodded, as if Gordon's answer had had some profound significance. Gordon heard his own words repeated to those on the edges of the circle.

"He found the mailman's things . . . so naturally he became . . ."

Gordon shrugged. His answer must have appeased them, somehow. The crowd thinned as each villager took his or her polite turn getting a plateful from the buffet. It wasn't until much later that Gordon, on reflection, saw the significance of the transaction that had taken place while he crammed himself nearly to bursting with good food.

4

". . . we found, then, that our clinic seems to have an abundant supply of disinfectants and pain killers of several varieties. We hear these are in short supply in Bend, and in the relocation centers up north. We are willing to trade some of these—along with a truckload of de-ionizing resin columns that happened to be abandoned here—for one thousand doses of tetracycline, to guard against the bubonic plague outbreak to the east. Also, we are in desperate need of . . ."

The mayor of Gilchrist must have been a strong-willed man to have persuaded his local emergency committee to offer such a trade. Hoarding, however illogical and uncooperative, had been one of the worst contributors to the collapse after the war. He was astonished that there were people with this much good sense, still, during the first two years of the Chaos.

Gordon rubbed his eyes. Reading wasn't easy by the light of a pair of homemade candles. But he found it difficult to get to sleep on the soft mattress. And he'd be damned if he'd sleep on the floor after all these months of dreaming of just such a bed, in just such a room!

He had been a little sick earlier. The home-brewed ale he had consumed had almost taken him over the line from delirious happiness to utter misery. He had teetered along the boundary for several hours before stumbling into the room they had prepared for him.

There had been a toothbrush waiting on his nightstand and an iron tub filled with hot water. There had been soap! In the bath his stomach had settled, and a warm clean glow spread over his skin.

Gordon had smiled when he saw that his postman's uniform had been cleaned and pressed. It lay on a nearby chair; the rips and tears he had crudely patched were now neatly sewn.

He could not fault the people of this tiny hamlet for neglecting his one remaining longing. He was almost in Paradise.

He lay in a sated haze between a pair of elderly but well-maintained sheets, waiting for sleep to come as he read an ancient piece of correspondence between two dead men.

"We are having extreme difficulty with local gangs of 'Survivalists,'" the mayor of Gilchrist went on.

"Fortunately, these tiny infestations of egotists are too paranoid to band together. They're as much trouble to each other as they are to us. Nevertheless, they are becoming a real problem.

"Our deputy is regularly fired on by well-armed men in army surplus camouflage suits when he tries to patrol outlying roads. No doubt the idiots think he's a 'Russian Lackey' or some such nonsense. They've taken to hunting game on a massive scale, killing everything in the forest and doing a typically rotten job of butchering and preserving the meat. Our own hunters frequently come back disgusted over the waste and often having been shot at without provocation.

"I know it's a lot to ask, but when you can spare a platoon from relocation riot duty, could you send them up here to help us root out these self-centered, hoarding, romantic scoundrels from their little filtered armories? Maybe a unit or two of the US Army will convince them that we won the war and have to cooperate with each other from now on . . ."

Gordon put the letter down.

Yes, that's the way it had been. The "last straw" had been this plague of "survivalists." One of Gordon's last duties in the militia had been to help snuff out some of those small gangs of city-bred cutthroats and gun nuts.

The number of fortified caves and cabins his unit had found in the mountains had been staggering, all set up in a rash of paranoia in the decade before the war. Of course, such prizes changed hands a dozen times each in the first months; they were such tempting targets. The battles had raged until every solar collector was shattered, every windmill wrecked, and every cache of valuable medicines scattered.

Only the ranches and villages, those possessing a more sensible brand of paranoia mixed with internal cohesiveness, survived. When the Guard units themselves dissolved into roving gangs of battling survivalists, few of the original population of armed and armored hermits remained alive.

There was a faint sound. Gordon might almost have imagined it. Then, only slightly louder, came a faint knock on his door.

"Come in."

The door opened about halfway. Abby, the petite, vaguely Oriental-looking girl he had seen earlier, smiled timidly from the opening. Gordon refolded the letter and slipped it into its envelope.

"I've come to ask if there is anything else you need," she said, a little quickly. "Did you enjoy your bath?"

"Oh, boy." Gordon sighed. He found himself slipping into MacDuff's brogue. "That I did, lass. And in particular I appreciated the toothbrush."

"You mentioned you'd lost yours." She looked at the floor. "I pointed out that we had at least five or six unused ones in the storage room. I'm glad you were pleased."

"It was your idea? Then I am indeed in your debt."

Abby looked up at him and smiled.

"Was that a letter you were just looking at? Could I look at it? I've never seen a letter before."

Gordon laughed. "Surely you're not that young! What about before the war?"

Abby blushed at his laughter. "I was only four when it all happened. It was so frightening and confusing. I really don't remember much from before."

Had it been that long? Yes. Sixteen years was long enough to have beautiful women in the world who knew nothing but the dark age.

"All right, then." He patted the bed, near his knees. Grinning, she came over and sat beside him.

Gordon reached into the stack and pulled out one of the yellowed envelopes. Carefully, he spread out the letter and handed it to her.

Abby looked at it so intently that he thought she was reading the whole thing. She concentrated, her thin eyebrows almost coming together in a crease on her forehead. But finally she handed the letter back, saying, "I guess I can't really read. I mean, I can read labels on cans and stuff. But I never learned sentences."

She sounded embarrassed but unafraid, trusting, as if Gordon were her confessor.

He smiled. "No matter. I'll tell you what it's about."

He held the letter up to the candlelight.

"It's from one John Briggs, of Fort Rock, Oregon, to his ex-employer in Klamath falls. I'd guess from the lathe and hobby horse letterhead that Briggs was a retired machinist. Hmmm."

Gordon concentrated on the barely legible handwriting. "It seems Mr. Briggs was a pretty nice man. Here he's offering to take in his ex-boss's children until the emergency was over. Also he says he has a good garage machine shop, his own power, and plenty of metal stock. He wants to know if the fellow wants to order any parts made up, especially of things in short supply . . ."

Gordon's voice faded. He was still so thick-headed from his excesses that it had just struck him that a beautiful female was sitting on his bed. He cleared his throat quickly and went back to scanning the letter.

Abby looked at him. Apparently half of what he had said about the letter writer, John Briggs, might as well have been in a foreign language to her. "Metal stock" and "machine shop" could have been ancient, magical words of power.

"Why didn't you bring us any letters here in Pine View?" she asked.

Gordon frowned at the non sequitur. The girl wasn't stupid. One learned how to tell such things. Obviously she was quite bright.

Then why had everything he said, when he arrived here and at the party, been completely misunderstood? She still thought he was a mailman, as, apparently, did all but a few of the others in this small settlement. From whom did she believe they might get mail?

Probably she didn't realize that the letters he carried were from dead men and women to other dead men and women and that he carried them for . . . for his own reasons. The myth that had spontaneously developed here in Pine View depressed Gordon. It was one more sign of the deterioration of civilized minds.

He considered telling her the truth, as brutally and frankly as he could, to stop this fantasy once and for all. He started to.

"There aren't any letters because . . ." He paused. Once more he was aware of her nearness, the scent of her hair, and the gentle curves of her body. Of her trust, as well. He sighed. "There aren't any letters for you folks because . . . because I'm coming west out of Idaho, and nobody back there knows you here in Pine View. From here, I'm going to the coast. There may even be some large towns left, down there. Maybe . . ."

"Maybe someone down there will write to us if we send them a letter first!" Abby suggested. "Then, when you pass this way again, on your way back to Idaho, you could give us the letters they send. By then I'll be able to read sentences, I promise!"

Gordon shook his head and smiled. It was beyond his right to dash such dreams.

"Maybe so, Abby. Maybe so. But you know, you may get to learn to read easier than that. Mrs. Thompson's offered to put it up for a vote to let me stay on here for a while. I guess officially I'd be schoolteacher, though I'd have to prove myself as good a hunter and farmer as anybody. I could give archery lessons . . ."

Abby looked at him with surprise. Then she shook her head vigorously.

"But I thought you'd heard! They voted on it after you went to take your bath. Mrs. Thompson should be ashamed of trying to bribe a man like you that way, with your important work having to be done!"

He sat forward, not believing his ears. "What did you say?" He had begun hope he could stay in Pine View for at least the season, maybe a year. Who could tell? Perhaps here the wanderlust would leave him, and he could find a home.

Gordon fought to stifle his anger. Abby apparently noticed his agitation and hurried on.

"I mean, that wasn't the only reason, of course. There was the problem of there being no woman for you. And then . . ." Her voice trailed off so that Gordon could barely hear her. "Mrs. Howlett thought you'd be ideal for helping me and Michael finally have a baby . . ."

Gordon blinked. "Um," he said, expressing the full contents of his mind.

"We've been trying for five years. We really want children. But Mrs. Horton thinks Michael can't because he had the mumps really bad when he was twelve. You remember the real bad mumps?"

Gordon nodded. It had been the last of the warbugs. The resultant sterility had made for unusual social arrangements everywhere he had travelled.

Abby went on quickly. "Well, it would cause problems if we asked any of the other men here to—to be the body father. I mean, when you live close to people like this, you have to look on the men who aren't your husband as not being really 'men' . . . at least not that way. I don't think I'd like it, and it might cause trouble. Besides, I'll tell you something if you promise to keep a secret. I don't think any of the other men would be able to give Michael the kind of son he deserves. He's really very smart. He's the only one of us youngsters who can *really* read . . ."

The flow of strange logic came on too fast for Gordon to follow.

"But you're different." She smiled at him. "I mean, even Michael saw that! He's not too happy, but he figures you'll only be through once a year or so, and he could stand that. He'd rather do that than never have any kids."

Gordon cleared his throat. "You're sure he feels this way?"

"Oh, yes. Why do you think Mrs. Howlett introduced us in that funny way? It was to make it clear without really saying it out loud. Mrs. Tompson didn't like it much, but I think that's because she wanted you to stay."

Gordon's throat felt very dry. "How do *you* feel about all this?" he asked.

She looked at him as if he were a visiting prophet.

"I'd be honored if you'd say yes," she said quietly. She lowered her eyes.

"And you'd be able to think of me as a man, 'that way'?" Gordon asked.

Abby grinned, then answered Gordon by crawling up on top of him and planting her mouth upon his. The intensity of her assault was testimony enough.

There was a momentary pause as she shimmied out of her clothes. Gordon turned to snuff the candle on the bed stand. Beside it lay the gray letterman's uniform cap. Its brass badge cast multiple reflections of the dancing flame. The figure of a man, hunched forward upon a horse with bulging saddle bags, seemed to move at a flickering gallop.

"This is another one I owe you, Mr. Postman," Gordon thought, as Abby's smooth skin slid along his side. He blew the candle out.

5

For ten days, Gordon's life followed a new pattern. As if to catch up on six months' lack, he slept late. Each morning Abby awoke before dawn. She was gone, like the night's dreams, when he opened his eyes to the sunshine that streamed in through his window.

During the day he conferred with Mrs. Thompson and the other village leaders, gave reading and archery lessons, and prepared for the evening's performance. Each night, by the time he had delivered his last soliloquy and led the adults in a group sing of beloved old commercial jingles, he would come to wonder if Abby had been a dream.

Each night she came to him after he retired. She sat on the edge of his bed and talked of her life. She brought him books to ask their meanings. And then, when her active mind seemed sated, she slid under the covers while he took care of the candle.

On the tenth morning, she did not slip away with the predawn light but instead wakened Gordon with a kiss.

"Hmmmn," he commented, as he reached for her. Abby pulled away. She leaned over for her clothes, brushing her breasts across the soft hairs of his flat stomach; then she sat up and smiled at him.

"I should let you sleep, but I wanted to tell you something," she said. She held her clothing in a ball.

"Mmm, what is it?" Gordon raised his head a little and stuffed the pillow behind it for support.

"You're supposed to be going today, aren't you?"

"Yes, Abby. That would be best. I'd like to stay longer, but since I can't, I'd best be heading west again. Besides, there are circumstances that make it hard to delay any longer, as I'm sure you're aware."

"I know." She nodded seriously. "We'll all miss you here. But . . . well, I'm going to meet Michael out at the trapline this evening. I miss him terribly. That doesn't bother you, does it? I mean, it's been wonderful here with you, but he's my husband and . . ."

Gordon smiled. He touched her cheek. To his amazement, he had little difficulty. He was more envious than jealous of Michael. He had long become accustomed to a self-image of denial.

Abby's and Michael's desire for children and their obvious love for each other made the situation, in retrospect, as obvious as the need for a clean break at the end. He only hoped he had done them the favor they sought, for despite their fantasies, it was unlikely he would ever be this way again.

"I have something for you," Abby said. She reached under the bed and pulled out a small silvery object on a chain, and a paper package.

"It's a whistle. Mrs. Howlett says you should have a whistle. Also, she helped me write this letter. I found some stamps in a drawer in the gas station, but they wouldn't stick on. So I got some money. I think this is fourteen dollars. Will that be enough?

Gordon couldn't help smiling. Yesterday, five or six of the others had privately approached him. He had accepted their small packages and payments for postage. He might have used the opportunity to charge them something he needed, but the community had already supplied him with a month's stock of jerky, dried apples, and twenty straight arrows, newly produced from the assembly line he had shown them how to build.

Some of the older citizens had relatives in Eugene or Portland or towns elsewhere in the Cascades. It was the direction he was heading, so he took the letters. A few were addressed to people who had lived in Oakridge and Blue River. Those he filed deep in the safest part of his sack. The rest he might as well throw into Crater Lake, for all the good they would ever do.

He seriously pretended to count out a few paper bills, then handed her back the rest of the worthless faded currency. "And who are you writing to?" Gordon asked, as he took the letter. He felt as if he was playing Santa Claus, and he enjoyed it.

"I'm writing to the University. You know, at Eugene? I asked a bunch of questions like, are they taking new students again, yet? And do they take married students?" Abby blushed. "I know I'd have to work on my reading real hard to get good enough. And maybe they aren't recovered enough to take many new students. But by the time I hear from them maybe things will be better. I'll for sure be reading by then. Mrs. Thompson promises she'll help me, and her husband has agreed to start a school. I'm going to help with the little kids."

Gordon had thought himself beyond surprise. But this touched him. In spite of Abby's totally unrealistic estimate of the state of the world, Gordon felt warmed by her hope. He found himself dreaming along with her. He saw no harm in wishing.

"Actually," Abby went on. "One of the big reasons I'm writing is to get a . . . a pen pal. That's the word, isn't it? Maybe someone in Eugene will write to me. That way we'll get letters here. Also, that will give you another reason to come back, in a year or two . . . besides maybe wanting to see the baby."

She smiled. "I got the idea from your Sherlock Holmes play. That's an 'ulterior motive,' isn't it?"

She was so delighted with her own cleverness and so eager for his approval that Gordon felt a great, almost painful rush of love and tenderness for her. Tears welled as he reached out and pulled her into an embrace. He held her tightly and rocked slowly, his eyes shut against reality, and breathed in, with her sweet smell, an optimism he had thought gone from the world.

"Well, this is where I turn back." Mrs. Thompson said, shaking hands with Gordon. "Down this road things should be pretty tame until you get to Davis Lake. Our boys cleared out the last of the old survivalists that way some years back, but I'd still be careful."

The straight-backed old woman handed Gordon an old road map.

"I had Jimmie Horton mark the places we know of where homesteaders have set up. I wouldn't bother any of them unless you have to. Mostly they're a suspicious type, likely to shoot first. We've been trading with the nearest only for a short time now."

Gordon nodded. He folded the map carefully and slipped it into its pouch. The alterations he had made to the leather shoulder pack would make it more appropriate for cross-country travel.

He felt rested and ready. He would regret leaving Pine View as much as he had any haven in recent memory. But he was becoming eager to see what had happened in the Columbia Valley.

In the years since he had left the wreckage of Minneapolis, he had found himself moving westward into ever wilder territory, encountering increasingly hostile signs of the dark age. But now he was in a new watershed. Oregon had once been a pleasant place, with well dispersed light industry, productive farms, and an elevated level of culture. Perhaps it was merely Abby's innocence infecting him, but he told himself that the Columbia Valley would be the place to look for civilization, if it existed anywhere.

He held the old woman's hand once again.

"Mrs. Thompson, I'm not sure I could ever repay what you people have done for me."

She shook her head. "No, Gordon, you paid your keep. I would have liked it if you'd been able to stay, and help me get a school going. But now I see maybe it won't be so hard to do myself.

"You know, we've been living in a kind of a daze these last years, since the crops have started coming in well, and the hunting's come back. You can tell how bad things have got when a bunch of grown men and women who once had jobs and filled out their own taxes and read news magazines start treating a battered wandering play-actor as if he was something like the Easter Bunny. Even Jim Horton gave you a couple of letters to deliver, didn't he?"

Gordon gave Mrs. Thompson an embarrassed sidelong glance. Then he burst out laughing. The relief of having the group fantasy lifted off his shoulders made his eyes fill.

Mrs. Thompson chuckled. "But it was harmless, I think. And more than that. You've served as a . . . is catalyst that old word? Anyway, the children are already exploring ruins for miles around, bringing me books they find. I won't have any trouble making school into a privilege. Imagine, *punishing* them by suspending them from class! I hope I handle it right."

"I wish you the best of luck, Mrs. Thompson." Gordon said sincerely. "God, it would be nice to see a light here and there in all this desolation."

She looked thoughtful. "Right, son. That'd be bliss."

Mrs. Thompson sighed. "Now you come back again, hmm? I'd recommend you wait a year, but come on back. You're discreet, and you're kind. You treated my people, especially Abby and Michael, real well." She frowned momentarily. "I *think* I understand what went on back there, and I guess it's for the best. Anyway, you're always welcome back."

Mrs. Thompson turned to go. She walked two paces, then paused and half-turned to look back at Gordon.

"You aren't really a postman, are you?"

Gordon smiled. "If I bring back some letters, you'll know for sure."

She nodded, then waved and set off up the ruined asphalt road.

Gordon watched her until she passed the first turn. Then he came about to face the west, and the long downgrade toward the Pacific.

6

The barricades had been long abandoned. The main baffle on highway 58, at the east end of the town of Oakridge, had weathered into a tumbled mass of concrete debris and curled, rusting steel. The town itself was silent. This end at least was clearly long abandoned.

Gordon looked down the main street. The signs were clear. The town had tried to hold out. Two, possibly three pitched battles had been fought. A storefront with a sign reading "Emergency Services Clinic" was the center of a major circle of devastation.

Three unsmashed panes reflected morning sunlight from the top floor of a hotel. Elsewhere, even where store windows had been boarded, the prismatic sparkle of shattered glass glistened.

Just twenty yards from his vantage point Gordon saw the wreckage of a gas station. The mechanic's tool cabinet lay on its side; its store of wrenches, pliers, and replacement wiring lay scattered on the floor.

Gordon knew Oakridge to be the worst of all possible Oakridges, from his point of view. The things needed by a machine culture would be available everywhere, untouched and rotting, implying there was no such machine culture. At the same time he would have to pick through the wreckage of fifty waves of previous looters to find anything of use to him.

Well, he had done it before. He had even sifted the downtown ruins of Boise once. The gleaners who had come before him had missed a small treasure trove of canned food in a loft behind a shoe store—some hoarder's stash, long untouched. There was a pattern to such things, worked out over the years.

Gordon slipped down off the baffle on the forest side. He entered the overgrowth and zigzagged, just in case he had been watched.

At a place where he could verify three landmarks, at diverse angles, Gordon dropped his leather shoulder bag and cap. He took off the blue carrier's jacket and laid it on top, then cut brush to cover the cache. He carried his bow, .38, and a cloth sack.

He started with houses on the outskirts. Sometimes the first generation of looters were more exuberant than thorough. The wreckage they left discouraged those who came after, but there could be useful items within.

By the time Gordon reached the fourth house, his sack contained a pair of boots almost useless with mildew, a magnifying glass, and two spools of thread. It wasn't much. He had looked in all the usual hoarder's crannies—and some unusual ones—but hadn't found food of any sort. His Pine View jerky wasn't entirely gone, but he had dipped down almost to the level set aside for emergencies.

The pace he had set had not allowed for much hunting or fishing. His archery was better, and he had bagged a pair of birds a few days before. But if he didn't have better luck gleaning, he might have to give up on the Columbia Valley for the season and find a semi-permanent hunting camp.

Gordon stood beside the four-poster bed in what had once been a physician's prosperous two-story home. The attic, a frequent source of useful junk, had been picked clean. It was a maelstrom of scrapbooks and papers, but there wasn't an old shoe or out-of-style coat in sight.

The bedroom appeared empty of all but furniture, but there Gordon thought, for the first time, he might have found something the earlier looters had missed.

The large, heavy area rug that lay upon the hardwood floor seemed out of place. The left two legs of the bed rested upon it. The right pair did not. It was as if the owner had purposely placed the carpet in an awkward position.

Gordon laid down his burdens, grabbed the edge of the rug, and lifted. He crouched to curl the end and started rolling it toward the bed.

Yes! There was a square crack in the floor under the carpet. One leg of the bed pinned the rug over one of two brass hinges.

He stood and heaved against the bedpost. The leg hopped up, then fell back with a boom that echoed through the house. Twice more he pushed, and twice more loud echoes reverberated.

On his fourth heave, the leg bounced aside just far enough, but the bedpost snapped in two. Gordon barely escaped being impaled on the sharp, jagged stub as he fell onto the mattress. The canopy followed him and the aged bed collapsed in a noisy crash.

Gordon cursed as he fought with the canopy. Then he

sneezed violently. The cloud of floating dust made it almost impossible to breathe.

Regaining a bit of sense, Gordon slithered from under the canopy and stumbled out of the room in a fit of sneezing.

The attack subsided slowly. As he stood gripping the upstairs bannister, he heard a distant murmur that sounded something like, "I think I heard it over this way . . ."

Gordon shook his head vigorously. Then wiping his eyes, he reentered the bedroom. The trapdoor was exposed. Gordon had to pry for a few moments before the edge would come up. Finally, the secret panel rose with a high, rusty skreel. Cobwebs greeted Gordon. Simultaneously, he heard a commotion outside. Now the voices could not be denied.

He quickly brushed the webs aside with his bow and peered into the hole.

There was a large metal box inside. Gordon reached in and almost strained his back hauling it out onto the floor. The hinges and hasp were rusted. A stainless steel lock bound the chest shut. Gordon looked back into the hole. The things a prewar doctor might have kept in a locked chest would be of less use than the canned goods and trade items he might have merely hidden in a spree of hoarding.

But there was nothing but the box. Gordon lifted the haft of his knife to smash the small lock. The chest might still hold weapons and ammunition.

He stopped. The voices were perilously close now.

"I think it came from this house!" A man's voice called out. There were footsteps on the wooden porch. More feet shuffled through the dry leaves on the large, overgrown lawn.

Gordon sheathed the knife and snatched up his gear. He hurried out of the room to the stairwell. This was not the best of circumstances to meet other men. In Boise and other mountain ruins there had been almost a code. Gleaners from ranches all around could try their luck in the open city, and though the groups and individuals were wary, they seldom preyed on one another. .

In other places, though, territoriality was the rule. Gordon might be searching in some clan's turf. In any case, a quick departure was definitely in order.

Boots walked noisily downstairs. Going down would be useless, and it was too late to close the trap door or hide the heavy box. Gordon turned as quietly as he could to the narrow attic ladder. He climbed up into one end of the A-framed, gabled garret. He had searched among the useless mementos here earlier. Now he looked for a hiding place for himself.

Gordon walked, stooped over, near the sloping walls to avoid creaks in the floorboards. He chose a large trunk near a small gable window and laid his sack and quiver upon it. Quickly, he strung his bow, then settled behind the trunk.

Would they search? If they did, the strongbox would certainly attract attention! If so, would they take it as an offering and leave him a share of whatever it contained? He had known such things to happen in places where a primitive sort of honor system had developed.

He had the drop on anyone searching the attic. Gordon had mixed feelings about that. He would much rather take a hostage than a corpse, for numerous reasons, not the least of which was the fact that he was cornered in a wooden building, and the vengeful survivors of an ambush undoubtedly would have retained, even in the middle of a dark age, the craft of firemaking.

At least three pairs of booted feet could be heard now. In a rapid, hollow echo, one after another took the first stairs. When everyone was on the second floor, Gordon heard voices.

"Hey! Bob! Looka this!"

"What? You catch a couple of the kids playing doctor in an old bed ag . . . sheeit!"

There was a loud thump, followed by the hammering of metal on metal. A creak told Gordon that the strongbox had been opened.

"Sheeit!"

There were shuffling sounds and muttered conversation. Then, "Sure was nice of that fellow," the first voice spoke. Wish we could thank him. Ought to get to know him so we don't shoot first if we ever see him."

If that was bait, Gordon wasn't biting. He waited.

"Well, he at least deserves a warning," a third voice said, louder. "We got a shoot-first rule in Oakridge. He better scat before someone puts a hole in him bigger than the gap between a Survivalist's ears."

The footsteps echoed down the stairwell, and out onto the wooden porch.

Gordon laid down the bow and snatched up his pistol. He crawled to the gable that overlooked the front entrance. Three men walked away from the house. They carried rifles and wore canvas day packs. They walked with several yards between them, in a stalker's pattern, then disappeared into the woods.

Gordon hurried to the other windows. He saw no other motion.

He thought he had heard three pairs of feet earlier. It wasn't likely only one man would stay in ambush. Still, Gordon moved carefully. He lay down beside the trap-door to the attic, his bow, bag, and quiver next to him. He crawled until his head and shoulders extended out over the opening, slightly above the level of the floor.

He pulled the revolver, held it out in front of him, and allowed gravity to take his head and torso into a sudden downward arc.

His head and his pistol popped through the second-floor ceiling in a fashion an ambusher would be unlikely to expect. As the blood rushed to his head, Gordon was primed to snap off six quick shots at anything that moved.

Nothing moved.

He reached for his canvas bag, never taking his gaze or the pistol bearing from the hallway.

Gordon dropped the bag. If sound was the cue, that should bring an ambusher's head into view.

It didn't.

He dropped the bow and quiver more gently. Then he dropped his feet through the door to land in a crouch. Still nothing moved.

Gordon gathered his gear, made it travel-ready, then began a skirmish exit, examining each potential ambush site.

In the bedroom, the strongbox was empty. Beside it was a scatter of papers.

As he had expected, there were such curiosities as stock certificates, a stamp collection, and the deed to this house. But some of the other trash turned out to be recently torn cardpaper boxes.

The largest box, from which the cellophane had been recently removed, had, until a few minutes before, held an AR-15 collapsible survival rifle. Gordon looked at the lightweight weapon pictured on the box and stifled a strangled cry of agony. Undoubtedly there had also been boxes of ammo.

But the other trash almost drove him wild. Labels were strewn about, saying empirin with codeine, eurythromycin, megavitamin complex, morphine . . .

Carefully handled . . . cached and traded in dribbles . . . these could have bought Gordon admission to any hamlet he chose. He might have won his way into one of the rich Wyoming ranch communities! He remembered a good doctor, in what was left of Butte, whose clinic was a sanctuary, protected by all the surrounding villages and clans. What the sainted gentleman could have done with these!

It was all right, he told himself over and over. He was alive. And if he could get back to his backpack, he would probably *stay* alive.

Gordon peeked out of the room, then resumed his stalking progress toward an exit from the house of false expectations.

A man who spends a long time alone in the wilderness can have one great advantage over a very good hunter who goes home to friends and companions each night.

Gordon sensed something before he could identify it. At first he shrugged his unease off as a remnant of his fear and anger in the house. Then he realized that the forest sounded different somehow.

Gordon had been retracing his steps toward the eastern edge of town, where he had hidden his gear. Now he stopped and considered: this route would help him find his landmarks, but might it not give an antagonist who had found his previous trail an advantage?

Was he overreacting? He was no Jeremiah Johnson, who could read the sounds of the woods like the street signs of a city. He looked around for something to back up his unease. Activity around him had been sparse until he had stopped moving. But when he kept still, an avian ebb and flow slowly returned to this patch of forest. Camp robber birds flitted in conveys from spot to spot, playing guerrilla war with jays for the best of the tiny bug-infested glades. Smaller birds hopped from branch to branch, chirping. Birds in this size range had no great love of man, but they didn't go to great lengths to avoid him if he was quiet.

Then what?

There was a snapping sound to his left, near one of the ubiquitous blackberry thickets, But there, too, there were birds, or rather a bird. A mockingbird. The creature swooped up through the branches and landed in a bundle of twigs Gordon guessed to be its nest. It stood there, like a small lordling, haughty and proud. It squawked once, then dove toward the thicket again. As it passed out of sight, there was another tiny rustle; then the mockingbird swooped into view again.

Gordon froze an expression of nonchalance onto his face and idly picked at the loam with his bow. Meanwhile, he loosened the loop on his revolver. It took an effort to keep from displaying his nervousness.

He began moving diagonally to the thicket, about twenty yards away, moving neither toward it nor away from it, but in the direction of a large Ponderosa pine. The hackles on his neck were as far up as a furless ape could lift them.

Something behind that thicket had stimulated the nest defense response of the mockingbird. Whatever it was behaved most un-animal like, trying to ignore the nuisance attacks—to stay hidden.

Alerted, Gordon recognized a hunting blind.

He slung the bow over his shoulder with exaggerated carelessness, but as he passed behind the pine, he drew his revolver and ran into the forest at a sharp angle, trying to keep the bulk of the tree between himself and the thicket.

He remained in the tree's umbra only a moment. Surprise protected him a moment longer. Then the cracking of three loud shots, all of different caliber, diffracted down the lattice of trees.

Gordon lengthened his stride. There was a fallen log ahead, at the top of a small rise. It would not only provide shelter if he could reach it; it would also conceal his movements. He heard three more bangs as he dove over the decaying trunk. He hit the ground and felt a stabbing pain in his right arm.

Gordon felt a moment's blind panic as the hand holding his revolver cramped. If he had broken his arm . . . Blood soaked the cuff of his US Government Issue tunic. The pain was exaggerated by his imagination as he pulled back on the sleeve. The wound was a shallow gash. Small slivers of wood hung from the laceration. His bow had broken and stabbed him as he had fallen upon it.

His ears picked up sounds of pursuit. Whoops of gleeful chase carried over the tiny hillock.

Gordon threw the bow aside; later he would have time to curse its loss. He hurried uphill and to the right, crouching to take advantage of the creekbed and underbrush. Hunted men often run downstream. Gordon raced upslope, hoping that one of his enemies knew that bit of trivia.

There were shouts behind him. For a few minutes sounds of pursuit came closer. Gordon's own racket seemed loud enough to wake sleeping bears. Twice, he caught his breath behind boulders or clumps of foliage.

Finally the shouts became diminished with distance.

Gordon sighed as he settled back against a large oak and waited. When the noises had receded far enough, he pulled the aid kit from his belt pouch.

His arm would be all right. There was no reason to expect infection from the polished wood of the bow. The tear was far from vessels or tendons. It hurt like hell, though. He bound it, then looked around to get his bearings.

To his surprise, he recognized two landmarks at once . . . the shattered sign of the Oakridge Motel, seen over the treetops, and a cattle grate across a worn asphalt path just to the east.

Gordon moved to the place where he had left his goods. The stuff was exactly as he had left it. Apparently the Fates were not so cruel as to deal him another blow just yet. He knew they didn't operate that way. They always let you hope, for a while, before They let you have it.

It was hard to believe they had missed him. They'd had the drop on him. Were they *so* surprised by his sudden break for it? Gordon wondered. They must have had semi-automatic weapons, yet he remembered only six shots.

At first he thought there were no bullet wounds on the Ponderosa pine, across the clearing. Then he looked a bit higher. Two fresh scars blemished the bark ten feet up.

So. They had not meant to kill him at all. They had aimed high to scare him off.

Gordon's lips curled. Ironically, this made his assailants easier to hate. Unthinking malice he had come to accept, from many former Americans, as he accepted foul weather. But calculated contempt he had to take personally. These men understood the concept of mercy, but they had robbed, injured, and terrorized him.

He picked up their trail a few hundred yards to the west. It was clear and uncovered. They were almost arrogant. Gordon took no chances, however. It was almost dusk before he reached the palisade that surrounded New Oakridge.

It was apparently the most prosperous community he had found since leaving Idaho. An enclosure that had once been a city park was enclosed by a high, wooden fence. From within, Gordon heard the lowing of numerous cattle. A horse whinnied. Gordon could smell hay and the rich scent of livestock.

Nearby, a still higher wall surrounded three blocks of what had been the southwest corner of Oakridge town. A row of two-story buildings a half-block long took up the center of the village. Gordon could see the tops of these, including a watertower with a crow's nest atop it. There was motion in the crow's nest. A guard stood watch.

There was no entrance on this side. He skirted around to the south.

The forest had been cut, years ago, to provide a free fire zone around the village wall. Less care had apparently been taken of late. Undergrowth half as high as a man had encroached on the open area. Gordon crouched when he heard voices; then cautiously he approached from behind a curtain of trees.

A large gate swung open as Gordon reached the south wall. As he settled down to watch, two armed men sauntered out, looked around, then waved to someone within.

With a shout and a snap of reins a wagon pulled by two draft horses sallied through the gate. The driver paused by the two guards. Gordon could barely make out what he said.

"Tell the Mayor we appreciate the loan, Jeff. I know I'm in the hole pretty deep. But we'll pay him back out of the harvest, for sure. He already owns a piece of the farm, so this seed ought to be a good investment for him."

One of the guards nodded. "Sure thing, Sonny. Now you be careful on your way out, okay? Some of the boys spotted a loner down at the east end of old town today. There was some shootin'."

The farmer gasped. "Was anyone hurt? Are you sure it was a loner?"

"Yeah, pretty sure. He ran like a rabbit, according to Bob."

Gordon's heart beat faster. The insults had reached a point almost beyond bearing.

"The fellow did the Mayor a real favor, though," the guard went on. "Found a hidey hole full of drugs before Bob's guys drove him off. Mayor's going to pass some of them around to some of the owners at a party tonight, to find out what they'll do. I sure wish I moved in those circles."

"Me too!" the younger guard agreed. "Hey, Sonny, you think the Mayor might pay you some of your bonus in drugs if you make quota this year? You could have a real party!"

Sonny smiled sheepishly and shrugged. Then, for some reason, his head drooped. The older guard looked at him quizzically.

"What's the matter?" he asked.

Sonny shook his head. "We don't wish for very much anymore, do we, Jeff?"

Jeff frowned. "What do you mean?"

"I mean as long as we're wishing to be cronies of the Mayor, why don't we wish we had a Mayor without cronies at all!"

"I . . ."

"Hell, if pigs had wings! Jeff, remember when we used to talk about the old days? Remember when we dreamed that things could be decent again? Remember when we wished—"

The farmer's voice choked.

Jeff put his hand on the farmer's arm. Sonny nodded acknowledgement, then said, "Yaah!" and snapped the reins. The wagon rolled down the road.

Jeff looked after the wagon for a long moment and chewed on a grass stem. Then he turned to his younger companion.

"Jimmy, did I ever tell you about Portland? Sonny and I used to go there, before the war. We used to . . ."

They passed through the gate, out of Gordon's hearing.

Under other circumstances Gordon might have pondered for hours the information that one small conversation had offered, about the psychology and social structure of Oakridge and its environs. But right now he was too angry. His outrage over the "rabbit" remark met his indignation over the proposed use of the drugs he had found and made him think purple thoughts. He remembered the doctor in Wyoming and thought of the benefit he might make of the drugs. Why, most of the substances wouldn't even make these ignorant savages high!

He imagined himself scaling the walls, finding the storage facilities, and reclaiming his discoveries, along with some added items to make up for the insults, his wound, and his broken bow.

The image wasn't satisfying enough. Gordon embellished. He envisioned dropping in on the Mayor's party and wasting all of the power-hungry cronies who were making a midget empire out of this corner of the dark age. He imagined acquiring power, power to do good . . . power to *force* these yokels to use the education of their younger days, before the educated generation disappeared forever from the world.

Gordon considered his options. Leaving was out of the question. He recognized that his pride would not allow him to go. He would do battle, and that was that. Unfortunately, he was less sure about *how* he would do battle. Gordon stood up and scratched his head, dislodging his cap. He caught it before it fell. He was about to put it back on when he stopped and looked at it. Slowly, he smiled. A plan began to form. It would be audacious, but it had an element of consistency that appealed to Gordon. He supposed he was the last man alive who had the temperament to choose a course of deadly danger for aesthetic reasons. If his scheme failed, it would still be spectacular.

The plan would require a brief foray into the ruins of

old Oakridge—to one of the buildings certain to be among the least looted. He would have to be careful not to be spotted during the remaining daylight.

Two hours later, Gordon stepped along the road in the dusk. He had retraced his steps from town until he came to the road Sonny had used, south of the village wall. Now he approached the gate boldly.

The guard was lax. Gordon came to within thirty feet unchallenged. He saw a sentry near the far end of the palisade, but the idiot was looking the other way.

Gordon placed Abby's whistle between his lips and blew, hard, three times. The shrill cry echoed among the buildings and trees all around.

Hurried footsteps pounded along the parapet. Three men carrying shotguns appeared above the gate to look down upon him in the gathering twilight.

"Who are you, and what do you want?" one voice called out. "We don't welcome strangers here!"

"I must speak with someone in authority," Gordon hailed. "This is official business, and I demand entry to the town of Oakridge!"

There was a long silence. The guards whispered among themselves, and one man hurried off.

"Come again?" The chief guard shouted. "I don't think I heard you properly. Are you feverish? Have you got the Sickness?"

"I am not ill. I am tired and hungry and angry at being shot at. But all of that can wait until I have done my duty here."

"Duty? What the devil are you talking about?"

Footsteps echoed on the parapet. Several more men arrived; then a number of children and women began to string out to the left and right. Apparently, discipline had become lax in Oakridge.

Gordon repeated himself. Slowly and firmly he reiterated his demand to be allowed entry.

A group of figures carrying lanterns appeared on the parapet to the right. Those on that side made way.

"Look, loner," the chief guard said, "you're just asking

for a bullet. We have no 'official business' with anyone
outside this valley since we broke relations with that
commie place down at Blakeville. And I'm not bothering
the Mayor for some crazy—"

He turned in surprise as the party of dignitaries
reached the gate. A new voice spoke.

"I was just nearby. Heard the commotion. What's
going on here?"

"Fellow claims he has official business here, but he's
not from the valley. They all wear those hat things."

"He must be sick, or else he's one of those crazies
that always used to come through. I thought they'd all
be dead by now."

Gordon waited. In the growing darkness he saw the
leading dignitary lean over the parapet to look at him.

"I am the Mayor of Oakridge," the man announced.
"We don't believe in charity here, but if you're that fellow who found the goodies this afternoon and graciously
donated them to my boys, I'll admit we owe you. I'll
have a nice hot meal lowered over the gate. You can
sleep there by the road. Tomorrow, though, you gotta
be gone. We don't want disease here. And from what I
hear, you must be delirious."

Gordon smiled. It would be a pleasure to bluff this
jerk. It wouldn't feel like lying at all.

"Your generosity astounds me, Mr. Mayor, but I have
come too far on official business to turn away now. First,
though, can you tell me if Oakridge has a wireless
facility?"

The silence brought on by his non sequitur was long
and heavy. Gordon could imagine the Mayor's puzzle-
ment. Finally, perhaps out of curiosity, the town boss
answered.

"We haven't had a working radio in ten years. Why?
What has that to do with anything—"

"That's a shame. I'd hoped you had a transmitter. The
airwaves have been a shambles since the war, of course—
all the radioactivity—but I'd hoped I could report back
to my superiors."

He delivered the lines with aplomb. This time they caused

not silence but a buzz of conversation that ran up and down the parapet. Most of the population of Oakridge must be up there by now. Gordon hoped the wall was well built.

"Get that lantern over here!" The Mayor commanded. "No, you idiot! The one with the reflector! Yes! Now shine it on that man! I want a look at him!"

The light speared out at Gordon, but he was expecting it. He didn't cover his eyes, or squint. He turned to bring his "costume" to the best angle. The cap, with its polished crest, lay at a rakish angle on his head.

He shifted the leather bag. The muttering of the crowd grew.

"Mr. Mayor," he called. "My patience is wearing thin. Please don't make me invoke my authority. I already will have to have words with you about the behavior of your 'boys' this afternoon. You are on the verge of losing your privilege of communication with the rest of the nation."

"Communication? Nation? What the are you talking about? There's just the Blakeville commies and savages beyond them! Who the hell are you!"

Gordon touched his cap. "Gordon Krantz, of the United States Postal Service. I am the courier assigned to reestablish a mail route in lower Oregon and general federal inspector for the region."

Gordon hadn't thought of the last part until it was out. Was it inspiration? Or a dare? Well, he might as well be hanged for a sheep as a goat.

The crowd became noisy. Several times Gordon heard the words, *outside,* and *inspector,* and especially *mailman.*

The Mayor shouted for silence. He was obeyed grudingly and slowly. He shouted again. Finally he got order.

"So you're a mailman?" he called down to Gordon sarcastically. "What kind of idiots do you take us for, Krantz? A shiny suit makes you a government official? What government? What proof can you give us? Show us you're not a wild lunatic with radiation fever!"

Gordon pulled out the papers he had prepared only an hour before, using the seal stamp he had found in the ruins of the Oakridge Post Office.

"I have my credentials here," he offered. But he was interrupted.

"We're not letting you come close enough to give any of these people your fever!" the Mayor shouted. "There's no government but what we have right here! You're lucky this isn't like the plague years, and we're willing to let you go without a cremation, to cure you of your bug!"

Rats! If they wouldn't even look at the "credentials" he had forged, the trip into oldtown this afternoon had been wasted. Gordon was down to his last ace. He smiled for the crowd.

He reached into his side pocket and pulled out a small bundle. He made a pretense of shuffling through the items he held and squinting at the labels, but he actually knew the names by heart.

"Is there a Donald Smith here?" he called.

The muttering crowd grew louder. Finally a voice called out, not without an awed tone.

"He died a year after the war, in the last battle of the warehouse!"

Gordon was pleased at the tremor in the speaker's voice. Surprise was not the only emotion at work here. Still, he needed something a lot better.

"Oh, well," he called. "I'll have to confirm that, of course." Before the Mayor could speak, he hurried on.

"Is there either a Mr. or Mrs. Franklin Thompson, in town? Or their son or daughter?"

Now a tide of hushed whispering carried almost a note of superstition. A woman replied.

"Dead! The boy lived until last year. Worked on the Jascowisc stead. His folks were in Portland when it blew."

Damn! Gordon had only one name left. It was all very well to strike their hearts with his knowledge, but what he really needed was somebody alive!

"Right!" he called. "We'll confirm that. Finally, is there a Grace Horton here?"

"No, there ain't no Grace Horton here!" the Mayor shouted sarcastically. "I know everyone in my territory.

Never been no Grace Horton in the ten years since I arrived! You imposter! Can't you all see what he did? He found an old telephone book in town and copied down some names! Buddy, I rule that you are disturbing the peace! You've got five seconds to be gone before I order my men to fire!"

Gordon had no choice. At least he could beat a retreat and nothing would be lost but his pride.

But his body would not turn. His feet would not move. His will to run away had evaporated. Straightening his shoulders, he called the Mayor's bluff.

"Assault on a postal courier is one of the few federal crimes that the pro tem Congress has not suspended for the Recovery Period, Mr. Mayor. The United States has always protected its mailmen."

He looked coldly into the glare. "Always," he emphasized. And for a moment he felt a thrill. He *was* a courier, at least in spirit. He was an anachronism that the dark age had somehow missed when it systematically went about rubbing idealism from the world. Gordon looked straight toward the dark silhouette of the Mayor and silently dared him to shoot.

For several seconds the silence gathered. Then the Mayor began to count.

"One!"

He counted slowly, apparently having made up his mind to go for sadistic effect.

"Two!"

The bluff was certainly lost. Gordon knew he should leave now, at once. Still, his body would not turn.

"Three!"

This is the way the last idealist dies, he thought. The sixteen years of survival were an accident about to be corrected. Hard-won pragmatism had finally given way to . . . to a gesture.

There was movement on the parapet. Someone at the far left was struggling forward.

"Four!"

The guards raised their shotguns. Gordon thought he

saw a few of them move reluctantly. Not that it would do him any good.

The Mayor stretched out the last count, perhaps a bit unnerved by Gordon's stubbornness. Then Gordon saw a shadowy figure raise a hand.

"Excuse me, Mr. Mayor!" a woman's tremulous voice cut in. Her timidity made her words almost inaudible.

"What?" The Mayor's shadow did not turn from Gordon.

"I . . . I'm Grace Horton," the woman said softly.

"What?!" He repeated himself.

"It's my maiden name. I was married the year after the second famine. That was before you and your men arrived . . ."

Gordon sighed. He held up the bundle in his hand and touched his cap with his other.

"Good evening, then, Mizz Horton. Lovely evening, no? Oh by the way, I have a letter here for you, from a Mr. Jim Horton, of Pine View. He gave me this letter twelve days ago . . ."

The people in the crowd all seemed to be talking at once. There were sudden movements and shouts. Gordon had to raise his voice to be heard.

". . . Yes, Ma'am. He seemed to be quite well. I'm afraid that's all I have on this trip. But I'll carry your reply to your brother on my way back. One thing, though. Mr. Horton didn't have enough postage, back in Pine View, so I'm going to have to ask you for ten dollars C.O.D."

The crowd roared. The figure of the Mayor turned left and right, shouting, but nothing he said was heard.

Suddenly the gate swung open and people poured out into the night. They surrounded Gordon. He carefully maintained his composure and walked slowly toward the opening. He smiled and nodded to everyone, especially those who reached out to touch his elbow or the wide curve of his bulging leather bag.

The youngsters looked at him in superstitious awe. On many of the older faces, tears streamed.

Gordon was in the middle of a trembling reaction. He felt a little ashamed, but he struggled to maintain the dignified pose, and told himself, "The hell with it. It's not my fault they want to believe in Santa Claus! I only want what belongs to me! Simpletons."

But he smiled all around as the hands touched and love washed over him. It flowed about him like a rushing stream and carried him, in a wave of desperate, unwanted hope, into the town of Oakridge.

BLOOD MUSIC

by Greg Bear

"Blood Music" was inspired by a 1982 article about "bio-chips" in the U.K. magazine *New Scientist*. The article was an early exploration of some of the possibilities of tiny, protein-based computers. I immediately leaped at the notion of DNA being a kind of biological computer—a pretty broad leap for the time, and even today it's a controversial approach. From there, in a matter of a few minutes, at most, I was thinking about how individual cells could be made to respond in more complex ways to their environment—to become intelligent. (About fifteen years before, Isaac Asimov had published an essay in *TV Guide* responding to such TV shows as *Land of the Giants*, discussing the theoretical limits of intelligence in small creatures. I thought it would be fun to try a new approach to this question.)

At this time, of course, I had heard nothing of nanotechnology, and probably would not have equated it with my story anyway. I was more interested in playing with the themes of distributed intelligence and evolution than with manufacturing and miniaturization.

A few magazines, not too many, rejected the story. Before accepting it, Stanley Schmidt, editor of *Analog*, wanted me to firm up the scientific credibility of the story's basic idea. I did a little math, stretched complexities and scales a bit, and convinced him the story was at least marginally possible. The story was published in *Analog* in 1983.

Even before publication, John Carr and David Brin read "Blood Music" and suggested that it should be expanded into a novel. I began outlining a longer draft shortly thereafter, sold the outline to Beth Meacham at Ace Books, and the novel was well on its way . . .

"Blood Music" won my first Hugo and Nebula awards in 1984.

Sometime in 1984 or 1985 I began hearing about the pioneering work of K. Eric Drexler. The connection with "Blood Music" seemed vague, but some were crediting me with being a jump ahead of the nascent field of nanotechnology. I still don't think that is strictly true—but it does seem obvious now that I was dealing with the mythic side of the issue. Drexler of course was pursuing more practical and revolutionary goals. Later, in a number of novels (particularly *Queen of Angels*) I would address Drexler's challenge directly.

(Coincidentally, Paul Preuss was writing a novel on very similar themes called *Human Error*. The books turned out to be quite complementary, not to mention spookily similar!)

Blood Music over the years has introduced quite a few people to radical notions of biology and intelligence and information. It is not, however, my most popular book—perhaps because some of its themes and descriptions are genuinely disturbing. They don't disturb *me* very much, but then I may be a poor judge of what causes nightmares. I honestly intended *Blood Music* (as a novel, at least) to represent a gentle and relatively nonviolent slide into the next step of evolution.

The short story is more abrupt. As one editor said when rejecting it, "It's talky and morbid." The editor was right about it being talky. As for being morbid, it's no more that than life itself . . . Which in the history of the human race has always, at some point or another, led to morbidity.

Since then, I have taken on evolutionary and biological themes in a more constrained and plausible fashion in *Darwin's Radio* and *Darwin's Children*. These books have been well received in scientific circles, to my delight, and last year I was invited to deliver a paper on my ideas before the American Philosophical Society in Philadelphia. I shared the dais with several of the world's finest virologists—a high honor.

In a real way, this all began, for me, with "Blood Music" and Stan Schmidt's injunction to get the science right.

THERE IS A PRINCIPLE in nature I don't think anyone has pointed out before. Each hour, a myriad of trillions of little live things—bacteria, microbes, "animalcules"—are born and die, not counting for much except in the bulk of their existence and the accumulation of their tiny effects. They do not perceive deeply. They don't suffer much. A hundred billion, dying, would not begin to have the same importance as a single human death.

Within the ranks of magnitude of all creatures, small as microbes or great as humans, there is an equality of "elan," just as the branches of a tall tree, gathered together, equal the bulk of the limbs below, and all the limbs equal the bulk of the trunk.

That, at least, is the principle. I believe Vergil Ulam was the first to violate it.

It had been two years since I'd last seen Vergil. My memory of him hardly matched the tan, smiling, well-dressed gentleman standing before me. We had made a lunch appointment over the phone the day before, and now faced each other in the wide double doors of the employee's cafeteria at the Mount Freedom medical Center.

"Vergil?" I asked. "My God, Vergil!"

"Good to see you, Edward." He shook my hand firmly. He had lost ten or twelve kilos and what remained seemed tighter, better proportioned. At the university, Vergil had been the pudgy, shock-haired, snaggle-toothed whiz kid who hot-wired doorknobs, gave us punch that turned our piss blue, and never got a date except with Eileen Termagent, who shared many of his physical characteristics.

"You look fantastic," I said. "Spend a summer in Cabo San Lucas?"

We stood in line at the counter and chose our food. "The tan," he said, picking out a carton of chocolate milk, "is from spending three months under a sun lamp. My teeth were straightened just after I last saw you. I'll explain the rest, but we need a place to talk where no one will listen close."

I steered him to the smoker's corner, where three die-hard puffers were scattered among six tables.

"Listen, I mean it," I said as we unloaded our trays. "You've changed. You're looking good."

"I've changed more than you know." His tone was motion-picture ominous, and he delivered the line with a theatrical lift of his brows. "How's Gail?"

Gail was doing well, I told him, teaching nursery school. We'd married the year before. His gaze shifted down to his food—pineapple slice and cottage cheese, piece of banana cream pie—and he said, his voice almost cracking, "Notice something else?"

I squinted in concentration. "Uh."

"Look closer."

"I'm not sure. Well, yes, you're not wearing glasses. Contacts?"

"No. I don't need them anymore."

"And you're a snappy dresser. Who's dressing you now? I hope she's as sexy as she is tasteful."

"Candice isn't—wasn't—responsible for the improvements in my clothes," he said. "I just got a better job, more money to throw around. My taste in clothes is better than my taste in food, as it happens." He grinned the old Vergil self-deprecating grin, but ended it with a peculiar leer. "At any rate, she's left me, I've been fired from my job, I'm living on savings."

"Hold it," I said. "That's a bit crowded. Why not do a linear breakdown? You got a job. Where?"

"Genetron Corp.," he said. "Sixteen months ago."

"I haven't heard of them."

"You will. They're putting out common stock in the

next month. It'll shoot off the board. They've broken through with MABs. Medical—"

"I know what MABs are," I interrupted. "At least in theory. Medically Applicable Biochips."

"They have some that work."

"What?" It was my turn to lift my brows.

"Microscopic logic circuits. You inject them into the human body, they set up shop where they're told and troubleshoot. With Dr. Michael Bernard's approval."

That was quite impressive. Bernard's reputation was spotless. Not only was he associated with the genetic engineering biggies, but he had made news at least once a year in his practice as a neurosurgeon before retiring. Covers on *Time, Mega, Rolling Stone.*

"That's supposed to be secret—stock, breakthrough, Bernard, everything." He looked around and lowered his voice. "But you do whatever the hell you want. I'm through with the bastards."

I whistled. "Make me rich, huh?"

"If that's what you want. Or you can spend some time with me before rushing off to your broker."

"Of course." He hadn't touched the cottage cheese or pie. He had, however, eaten the pineapple slice and drunk the chocolate milk. "So tell me more."

"Well, in med school I was training for lab work. Biochemical research. I've always had a bent for computers, too. So I put myself through my last two years—"

"By selling software packages to Westinghouse," I said.

"It's good my friends remember. That's how I got involved with Genetron, just when they were starting out. They had big money backers, all the lab facilities I thought anyone would ever need. They hired me, and I advanced rapidly.

"Four months and I was doing my own work. I made some breakthroughs," he tossed his hand nonchalantly, "then I went off on tangents they thought were premature. I persisted and they took away my lab, handed it over to a certifiable flatworm. I managed to save part of the experiment before they fired me. But I haven't exactly been cautious . . . or judicious. So now it's going on outside the lab.''

I'd always regarded Vergil as ambitious, a trifle cracked, and not terribly sensitive. His relations with authority figures had never been smooth. Science, for him, was like the woman you couldn't possibly have, who suddenly opens her arms to you, long before you're ready for mature love—leaving you afraid you'll forever blow the chance, lose the prize, screw up royally. Apparently, he had. "Outside the lab? I don't get you.''

"Edward, I want you to examine me. Give me a thorough physical. Maybe a cancer diagnostic. Then I'll explain more.''

"You want a five-thousand-dollar exam?''

"Whatever you can do. Ultrasound, NMR, thermogram, everything.''

"I don't know if I can get access to all that equipment. NMR full-scan has only been here a month or two. Hell, you couldn't pick a more expensive way—''

"Then ultrasound. That's all you'll need.

"Vergil, I'm an obstetrician, not a glamour-boy labtech. OB-GYN, butt of all jokes. If you're turning into a woman, maybe I can help you.''

He leaned forward, almost putting his elbow into the pie, but swinging wide at the last instant by scant millimeters. The old Vergil would have hit it square. "Examine me closely and you'll . . .'' He narrowed his eyes and shook his head. "Just examine me.''

"So I make an appointment for ultrasound. Who's going to pay?''

"I'm on Blue Shield.'' He smiled and held up a medical credit card. "I messed with the personnel files at Genetron. Anything up to a hundred thousand dollars medical, they'll never check, never suspect.''

He wanted secrecy, so I made arrangements. I filled out his forms myself. As long as everything was billed properly, most of the examination could take place without official notice. I didn't charge for my services.

After all, Vergil had turned my piss blue. We were friends.

He came in late at night. I wasn't normally on duty then, but I stayed late, waiting for him on the third floor of what the nurses called the Frankenstein wing. I sat on an orange plastic chair. He arrived, looking olive-colored under the fluorescent lights.

He stripped, and I arranged him on the table. I noticed, first off, that his ankles looked swollen. But they weren't puffy. I felt them several times. They seemed healthy, but looked odd. "Hm," I said.

I ran the paddles over him, picking up areas difficult for the big unit to hit, and programmed the data into the imaging system. Then I swung the table around and inserted it into the enameled orifice of the ultrasound diagnostic unit, the hum-hole, so called by the nurses.

I integrated the data from the hum-hole with that from the paddle sweeps and rolled Vergil out, then set up a video frame. The image took a second to integrate, then flowed into a pattern showing Vergil's skeleton.

Three seconds of that—my jaw gaping—and it switched to his thoracic organs, then his musculature, and finally, vascular system and skin.

"How long since the accident?" I asked, trying to take the quiver out of my voice.

"I haven't been in an accident," he said. "It was deliberate."

"Jesus, they beat you, to keep secrets?"

"You don't understand me, Edward. Look at the images again. I'm not damaged."

"Look, there's thickening here," I indicated the ankles, "and your ribs—that crazy zigzag pattern of interlocks. Broken sometime, obviously. And—"

"Look at my spine," he said. I rotated the image in the video frame.

Buckminster Fuller, I thought. It was fantastic. A cage of triangular projections, all interlocking in ways I couldn't begin to follow, much less understand. I reached around and tried to feel his spine with my fingers. He lifted his arms and looked off at the ceiling.

"I can't find it," I said. "It's all smooth back there." I let go of him and looked at his chest, then prodded his ribs. They were sheathed in something rough and flexible. The harder I pressed, the tougher it became. Then I noticed another change.

"Hey," I said. "You don't have any nipples." There were tiny pigment patches, but no nipple formations at all.

"See?" Vergil asked, shrugging on the white robe. "I'm being rebuilt from the inside out."

In my reconstruction of those hours, I fancy myself saying, "So tell me about it." Perhaps mercifully, I don't remember what I actually said.

He explained with his characteristic circumlocutions. Listening was like trying to get to the meat of a newspaper article through a forest of sidebars and graphic embellishments.

I simplify and condense.

Genetron had assigned him to manufacturing prototype biochips, tiny circuits made out of protein molecules. Some were hooked up to silicon chips little more than a micrometer in size, then sent through rat arteries to chemically keyed locations, to make connections with the rat tissue and attempt to monitor and even control lab-induced pathologies.

"*That* was something," he said. "We recovered the most complex microchip by sacrificing the rat, then debriefed it—hooked the silicon portion up to an imaging system. The computer gave us bar graphs, then a diagram of the chemical characteristics of about eleven centimeters of blood vessel . . . then put it all together to make a picture. We zoomed down eleven centimeters of rat artery. You never saw so many scientists jumping up and down, hugging each other, drinking buckets of bug juice." Bug juice was lab ethanol mixed with Dr. Pepper.

Eventually, the silicon elements were eliminated completely in favor of nucleoproteins. He seemed reluctant to explain in detail, but I gathered they found ways to make huge molecules—as large as DNA, and even more complex—into electrochemical computers, using ribosome-like structures as "encoders" and "readers," and RNA as "tape." Vergil was able to mimic reproductive separation and reassembly in his nucleoproteins, incorporating program changes at key points by switching nucleotide pairs. "Genetron wanted me to switch over to supergene engineering, since that was the coming thing everywhere else. Make all kinds of critters, some out of our imagination. But I had different ideas." He twiddled his finger around his ear and made theremin sounds. "Mad scientist time, right?" He laughed, then sobered. "I injected my best nucleoproteins into bacteria to make duplication and compounding easier. Then I started to leave them inside, so the circuits could interact with the cells. They were heuristically programmed; they taught themselves more than I programmed them. The cells fed chemically coded information to the computers, the computers processed it and made decisions, the cells became smart. I mean, smart as planaria, for starters. Imagine an *E. Coli* as smart as a planarian worm!"

I nodded. "I'm imagining."

"Then I really went off on my own. We had the equipment, the techniques; and I knew the molecular language. I could make really dense, really complicated biochips by compounding the nucleoproteins, making them into little brains. I did some research into how far I could go, theoretically. Sticking with bacteria, I could make them a biochip with the computing capacity of a sparrow's brain. Imagine how jazzed I was! Then I saw a way to increase the complexity a thousandfold, by using something we regarded as a nuisance—quantum chitchat between the fixed elements of the circuits. Down that small, even the slightest change could bomb a biochip. But I developed a program that actually predicted and took advantage of electron tunneling. Emphasized the heuristic aspects of the computer, used the chitchat as a method of increasing complexity."

"You're losing me," I said.

"I took advantage of randomness. The circuits could repair themselves, compare memories, and correct faulty elements. The whole schmeer. I gave them basic instructions: Go forth and multiply. Improve. By God, you should have seen some of the cultures a week later! It was amazing. They were evolving all on their own, like little cities. I destroyed them all. I think one of the petri dishes would have grown legs and walked out of the incubator if I'd kept feeding it."

"You're kidding." I looked at him. "You're not kidding."

"Man, they *knew* what it was like to improve! They knew where they had to go, but they were just so limited, being in bacteria bodies, with so few resources."

"How smart were they?"

"I couldn't be sure. They were associating in clusters of a hundred to two hundred cells, each cluster behaving like an autonomous unit. Each cluster might have been as smart as a rhesus monkey. They exchanged information through their pili, passed on bits of memory, and compared notes. Their organization was obviously different from a group of monkeys. Their world was so much simpler, for one thing. With their abilities, they were masters of the petri dishes. I put phages in with them; the phages didn't have a chance. They used every option available to change and grow."

"How is that possible?"

"What?" He seemed surprised I wasn't accepting everything at face value.

"Cramming so much into so little. A rhesus monkey is not your simple little calculator, Vergil."

"I haven't made myself clear," he said, obviously irritated. "I was using nucleoprotein computers. They're like DNA, but all the information can interact. Do you know how many nucleotide pairs there are in the DNA of a single bacteria?"

It had been a long time since my last biochemistry lesson. I shook my head.

"About two million. Add in the modified ribosome structures—fifteen thousand of them, each with a molecular weight of about three million—and consider the combinations and permutations. The RNA is arranged like a continuous loop paper tape, surrounded by ribosomes ticking off instructions and manufacturing protein chains . . ." His eyes were bright and slightly moist. "Besides, I'm not saying every cell was a distinct entity. They cooperated."

"How many bacteria in the dishes you destroyed?"

"Billions. I don't know." He smirked. "You got it, Edward. Whole planetsful of *E. Coli.*"

"But they didn't fire you then?"

"No. They didn't know what was going on, for one thing. I kept compounding the molecules, increasing their size and complexity. When bacteria were too limited, I took blood from myself, separated out white cells, and injected them with the new biochips. I watched them, put them through mazes and little chemical problems. They were whizzes. Time is a lot faster at that level—so little distance for the messages to cross, and the environment is much simpler. Then I forgot to store a file under my secret code in the lab computers. Some managers found it and guessed what I was up to. Everybody panicked. They thought we'd have every social watchdog in the country on our backs because of what I'd done. They started to destroy my work and wipe my programs. Ordered me to sterilize my white cells. Christ." He pulled the white robe off and started to get dressed. "I only had a day or two. I separated out the most complex cells—"

"How complex?"

"They were clustering in hundred-cell groups, like the bacteria. Each group as smart as a ten-year-old kid, maybe." He studied my face for a moment. "Still doubting? Want me to run through how many nucleotide pairs there are in a mammalian cell? I tailored my computers to take advantage of the white cells' capacity. Ten billion nucleotide pairs, Edward. Ten E-f——ing ten. And they don't have a huge body to worry about, taking up most of their thinking time."

"Okay," I said. "I'm convinced. What did you do?"

"I mixed the cells back into the cylinder of whole blood and injected myself with it." He buttoned the top of his shirt and smiled thinly at me. "I'd programmed them with every drive I could, talked as high a level as I could using just enzymes and such. After that, they were on their own."

"You programmed them to go forth and multiply, improve?" I repeated.

"I think they developed some characteristics picked up by the biochips in their *E. coli* phases. The white cells could talk to one another with extruded memories. They almost certainly found ways to ingest other types of cells and alter them without killing them."

"You're crazy."

"You can see the screen! Edward, I haven't been sick since. I used to get colds all the time. I've never felt better."

"They're inside you, finding things, changing them."

"And by now, each cluster is as smart as you or I."

"You're absolutely nuts."

He shrugged. "They fired me. They thought I was going to get revenge for what they did to my work. They ordered me out of the labs, and I haven't had a real chance to see what's been going on inside me until now. Three months."

"So . . ." My mind was racing. "You lost weight because they improved your fat metabolism. Your bones are stronger, your spine has been completely rebuilt—"

"No more backaches even if I sleep on my old mattress."

"Your heart looks different."

"I didn't know about the heart," he said, examining the frame image from a few inches. "About the fat—I was thinking about that. They could increase my brown cells, fix up the metabolism. I haven't been as hungry lately. I haven't changed my eating habits that much—I still want the same old junk—but somehow I get around to eating only what I need. I don't think they know what my brain is yet. Sure, they've got all the glandular stuff—but they don't have the *big* picture, if you see what I mean. They don't know *I'm* in there. But boy, they sure did figure out what my reproductive organs are."

I glanced at the image and shifted my eyes away.

"Oh, they look pretty normal," he said, hefting his scrotum obscenely. He snickered. "But how else do you think I'd land a real looker like Candice? She was just after a one-night stand with a techie. I looked okay then, no tan but trim, with good clothes. She'd never screwed a technie before. Joke time, right? But my little geniuses kept us up half the night. I think they made improvements each time. I felt like I had a goddamned fever."

His smile vanished. "But then one night my skin started to crawl. It really scared me. I thought things were getting out of hand. I wondered what they'd do when they crossed the blood-brain barrier and found out about *me*—about the brain's real function. So I began a campaign to keep them under control. I figured, the reason they wanted to get into the skin was the simplicity of running circuits across a surface. Much easier than trying to maintain chains of communication in and around muscles, organs, vessels. The skin was much more direct. So I bought a quartz lamp." He caught my puzzled expression. "In the lab, we'd break down the protein in biochip cells by exposing them to ultraviolet light. I alternated sun lamp with quartz treatments. Keeps them out of my skin, so far as I can tell, and gives me a nice tan."

"Give you skin cancer, too," I commented.

"They'll probably take care of that. Like police."

"Okay, I've examined you, you've told me a story I still find hard to believe . . . what do you want me to do?"

"I'm not as nonchalant as I act, Edward. I'm worried. I'd like to find some way to control them before they find out about my brain. I mean, think of it, they're in the trillions by now, each one smart. They're cooperating to some extent. I'm probably the smartest thing on the planet, and they haven't even begun to get their act together yet. I don't really want them to take over." He laughed very unpleasantly. "Steal my soul, you know? So think of some treatment to block them. Maybe we can starve the little buggers. Just think on it." He but-

toned his shirt. "Give me a call." He handed me a slip
of paper with his address and phone number. Then he
went to the keyboard and erased the image on the
frame, dumping the memory of the examination. "Just
you," he said. "Nobody else for now. And please . . .
hurry."

It was three o'clock in the morning when Vergil
walked out of the examination room. He'd allowed me
to take blood samples, then shaken my hand—his palm
damp, nervous—and cautioned me against ingesting anything from the specimens.

Before I went home, I put the blood through a series
of tests. The results were ready the next day.

I picked them up during my lunch break in the afternoon, then destroyed all the samples. I did it like a robot.
It took me five days and nearly sleepless nights to accept
what I'd seen. His blood was normal enough, though the
machines diagnosed the patient as having an infection.
High levels of leukocytes—white blood cells— and hista-
mines. On the fifth day, I believed.

Gail was home before I, but it was my turn to fix
dinner. She slipped one of the school's disks into the
home system and showed me video art her nursery kids
had been creating. I watched quietly, ate with her in
silence.

I had two dreams, part of my final acceptance. The
first that evening—which had me up thrashing in my
sheets—I witnessed the destruction of the planet Kryp-
ton, Superman's home world. Billions of superhuman geniuses went screaming off in walls of fire. I related the
destruction to my sterilizing the samples of Vergil's
blood.

The second dream was worse. I dreamed that New
York City was raping a woman. By the end of the dream,
she was giving birth to little embryo cities, all wrapped
up in translucent sacs, soaked with blood from the difficult labor.

I called him on the morning of the sixth day. He answered on the fourth ring. "I have some results," I said.
"Nothing conclusive. But I want to talk with you. In
person."

"Sure," he said. "I'm staying inside for the time being." His voice was strained; he sounded tired.

Vergil's apartment was in a fancy high-rise near the lake shore. I took the elevator up, listening to little advertising jingles and watching dancing holograms display products, empty apartments for rent, the building's hostess discussing social activities for the week.

Vergil opened the door and motioned me in. He wore a checked robe with long sleeves and carpet slippers. He clutched an unlit pipe in one hand, his fingers twisting it back and forth as he walked away from me and sat down, saying nothing.

"You have an infection," I said.

"Oh?"

"That's all the blood analyses tell me. I don't have access to the electron microscopes."

"I don't think it's really an infection," he said. "After all, they're my own cells. Probably something else . . . sign of their presence, of the change. We can't expect to understand everything that's happening."

I removed my coat. "Listen," I said, "you have me worried now." The expression on his face stopped me: a kind of frantic beatitude. He squinted at the ceiling and pursed his lips.

"Are you stoned?" I asked.

He shook his head, then nodded once, very slowly. "Listening," he said.

"To what?"

"I don't know. Not sounds . . . exactly. Like music. The heart, all the blood vessels, friction of blood along the arteries, veins. Activity. Music in the blood." He looked at me plaintively. "Why aren't you at work?"

"My day off. Gail's working."

"Can you stay?"

I shrugged. "I suppose." I sounded suspicious. I was glancing around the apartment, looking for ashtrays, packs of papers.

"I'm not stoned, Edward," he said. "I may be wrong, but I think something big is happening. I think they're finding out who I am."

I sat down across from Vergil, staring at him intently. He didn't seem to notice. Some inner process was involving him. When I asked for a cup of coffee, he motioned to the kitchen. I boiled a pot of water and took a jar of instant from the cabinet. With cup in hand, I returned to my seat. He was twisting his head back and forth, eyes open. "You always knew what you wanted to be, didn't you?" he asked me.

"More or less."

"A gynecologist. Smart moves. Never false moves. I was different. I had goals, but no direction. Like a map without roads, just places to be. I didn't give a shit for anything, anyone but myself. Even science. Just a means. I'm surprised I got so far. I even hated my folks."

He gripped his chair arms.

"Something wrong?" I asked.

"They're talking to me," he said. He shut his eyes.

For an hour he seemed to be asleep. I checked his pulse, which was strong and steady, felt his forehead—slightly cool—and made myself more coffee. I was looking through a magazine, at a loss what to do, when he opened his eyes again. "Hard to figure exactly what time is like for them," he said. "It's taken them maybe three, four days to figure out language, key human concepts. Now they're on to it. On to me. Right now."

"How's that?"

He claimed there were thousands of researchers hooked up to his neurons. He couldn't give details. "They're damned efficient, you know," he said. "They haven't screwed me up yet."

"We should get you into the hospital now."

"What in hell could they do? Did you figure out any way to control them? I mean, they're my own cells."

"I've been thinking. We could starve them. Find out what metabolic differences—"

"I'm not sure I want to be rid of them," Vergil said. "They're not doing any harm."

"How do you know?"

He shook his head and held up one finger. "Wait. They're trying to figure out what space is. That's tough for them. They break distances down into concentrations of chemicals. For them, space is like intensity of taste."

"Vergil—"

"Listen! Think, Edward!" His tone was excited but even. "Observe! Something big is happening inside me. They talk to one another across the fluid, through membranes. They tailor something—viruses?—to carry data stored in nucleic acid chains. I think they're saying 'RNA.' That makes sense. That's one way I programmed them. But plasmid-like structures, too. Maybe that's what your machines think is a sign of infection—all their chattering in my blood, packets of data. Tastes of other individuals. Peers. Superiors. Subordinates."

"Vergil, I'm listening, but I still think you should be in a hospital."

"This is my show, Edward," he said. "I'm their universe. They're amazed by the new scale." He was quiet again for a time. I squatted by his chair and pulled up the sleeve to his robe. His arm was crisscrossed with white lines. I was about to go to the phone and call for an ambulance when he stood and stretched. "Do you realize," he said, "how many blood cells we kill each time we move?"

"I'm going to call for an ambulance," I said.

"No, you aren't." His tone stopped me. "I told you, I'm not sick; this is my show. Do you know what they'd do to me in a hospital? They'd be like cavemen trying to fix a computer the same way they fix a stone ax. It would be a farce."

"Then what the hell am I doing here?" I asked, getting angry. "I can't do anything. I'm one of those cavemen."

"You're a friend," Vergil said, fixing his eyes on me. I had the impression I was being watched by more than just Vergil. "I want you here to keep me company." He laughed. "But I'm not exactly alone."

He walked around the apartment for two hours, fingering things, looking out windows, making himself lunch slowly and methodically. "You know, they can actually feel their own thoughts," he said about noon. "I mean, the cytoplasm seems to have a will of its own, a kind of subconscious life counter to the rationality they've only recently acquired. They hear the chemical 'noise' or whatever of the molecules fitting and unfitting inside."

At two o'clock, I called Gail to tell her I would be late. I was almost sick with tension but I tried to keep my voice level. "Remember Vergil Ulam? I'm talking with him right now."

"Everything okay?" she asked.

Was it? Decidedly not. "Fine," I said.

"Culture!" Vergil said, peering around the kitchen wall at me. I said good-bye and hung up the phone. "They're always swimming in that bath of information. Contributing to it. It's a kind of gestalt thing, whatever. The hierarchy is absolute. They send tailored phages after cells that don't interact properly. Viruses specified to individuals or groups. No escape. One gets pierced by the virus, the cell blebs outward, it explodes and dissolves. But it's not just a dictatorship, I think they effectively have more freedom than in a democracy. I mean, they vary so differently from individual to individual. Does that make sense? They vary in different ways than we do."

"Hold it," I said, gripping his shoulders. "Vergil, you're pushing me close to the edge. I can't take this much longer. I don't understand, I'm not sure I believe—"

"Not even now?"

"Okay, let's say you're giving me the, the right interpretation. Giving it to me straight. The whole thing's true. Have you bothered to figure out all the consequences yet? What all this means, where it might lead?"

He walked into the kitchen and drew a glass of water from the tap, then returned and stood next to me. His expression had changed from childish absorption to sober concern. "I've never been very good at that."

"Aren't you afraid?"

"I was. Now I'm not sure." He fingered the tie of his robe. "Look, I don't want you to think I went around you, over your head or something. But I met with Michael Bernard yesterday. He put me through his private clinic, took specimens. Told me to quit the lamp treatments. He called this morning, just before you did. He says it all checks out. And he asked me not to tell anybody." He paused and his expression became dreamy again. "Cities of cells," he continued. "Edward, they push pili-like tubes through the tissues, spread information—"

"Stop it!" I shouted. "Checks out? What checks out?"

"As Bernard puts it, I have 'severely enlarged macrophages' throughout my system. And he concurs on the anatomical changes. So it's not just our common delusion."

"What does he plan to do?"

"I don't know. I think he'll probably convince Genetron to reopen the lab."

"Is that what you want?"

"It's not just having the lab again. I want to show you. Since I stopped the lamp treatments. I'm still changing." He undid his robe and let it slide to the floor. All over his body, his skin was crisscrossed with white lines. Along his back, the lines were starting to form ridges.

"My God," I said.

"I'm not going to be much good anywhere else but the lab soon. I won't be able to go out in public. Hospitals wouldn't know what to do, as I said."

"You're . . . you can talk to them, tell them to slow down," I said, aware how ridiculous that sounded.

"Yes, indeed I can, but they don't necessarily listen."

"I thought you were their god or something."

"The ones hooked up to my neurons aren't the big wheels. They're researchers, or at least serve the same function. They know I'm here, what I am, but that doesn't mean they've convinced the upper levels of the hierarchy."

"They're disputing?"

"Something like that. It's not all that bad, anyway. If the lab is reopened, I have a home, a place to work." He glanced out the window, as if looking for someone. "I don't have anything left but them. They aren't afraid,

Edward. I've never felt so close to anything before." The beatific smile again. "I'm responsible for them. Mother to them all."

"You have no way of knowing what they're going to do."

He shook his head.

"No, I mean it. You say they're like a civilization—"

"Like a thousand civilizations."

"Yes, and civilizations have been known to screw up. Warfare, the environment—"

I was grasping at straws, trying to restrain a growing panic. I wasn't competent to handle the enormity of what was happening. Neither was Vergil. He was the last person I would have called insightful and wise about large issues.

"But I'm the only one at risk."

"You don't know that. Jesus, Vergil, look what they're *doing* to you!"

"To me, all to me!" he said. "Nobody else."

I shook my head and held up my hands in a gesture of defeat. "Okay, so Bernard gets them to reopen the lab, you move in, become a guinea pig. What then?"

"They treat me right. I'm more than just good old Vergil Ulam now. I'm a goddamned galaxy, a super-mother."

"Super-host, you mean." He conceded the point with a shrug.

I couldn't take any more. I made my exit with a few flimsy excuses, then sat in the lobby of the apartment building, trying to calm down. Somebody had to talk some sense into him. Who would he listen to? He had gone to Bernard . . .

And it sounded as if Bernard was not only convinced, but very interested. People of Bernard's stature didn't coax the Vergil Ulams of the world along, not unless they felt it was to their advantage.

I had a hunch, and I decided to play it. I went to a pay phone, slipped in my credit card, and called Genetron.

"I'd like you to page Dr. Michael Bernard," I told the receptionist.

"Who's calling, please?"

"This is his answering service. We have an emergency call and his beeper doesn't seem to be working."

A few anxious minutes later, Bernard came on the line. "Who the hell is this?" he asked quietly. "I don't have an answering service."

"My name is Edward Milligan. I'm a friend of Vergil Ulam's. I think we have some problems to discuss."

We made an appointment to talk the next morning."

I went home and tried to think of excuses to keep me off the next day's hospital shift. I couldn't concentrate on medicine, couldn't give my patients anywhere near the attention they deserved.

Guilty, anxious, angry, afraid.

That was how Gail found me, I slipped on a mask of calm and we fixed dinner together. After eating, we watched the city lights come on in late twilight through the bayside window, holding on to each other. Odd winter starlings pecked at the yellow lawn in the last few minutes of light, then flew away with a rising wind which made the windows rattle.

"Something's wrong," Gail said softly. "Are you going to tell me, or just act like everything's normal?"

"It's just me," I said. "Nervous. Work at the hospital."

"Oh, lord," she said, sitting up. "You're going to divorce me for that Baker woman." Mrs. Baker weighed three hundred and sixty pounds and hadn't known she was pregnant until her fifth month.

"No," I said, listless.

"Rapturous relief," Gail said, touching my forehead lightly. "You know this kind of introspection drives me crazy."

"Well, it's nothing I can talk about yet, so . . ." I patted her hand.

"That's disgustingly patronizing," she said, getting up. "I'm going to make some tea. Want some?" Now she was miffed, and I was tense with not telling.

Why not just reveal all? I asked myself. An old friend of mine was turning himself into a galaxy.

I cleared away the table instead. That night, unable to sleep, I looked down on Gail in bed from my sitting position, pillow against the wall, and tried to determine what I knew was real, and what wasn't.

I'm a doctor, I told myself. A technical, scientific profession. I'm supposed to be immune to things like future shock.

Vergil Ulam was turning into a galaxy.

How would it feel to be topped off with a trillion Chinese? I grinned in the dark, and almost cried at the same time. What Vergil had inside him was unimaginably stranger than Chinese. Stranger than anything—I—or Vergil—could easily understand. Perhaps ever understand.

But I knew what was real. The bedroom, the city lights faint through gauze curtains. Gail sleeping. Very important. Gail, in bed, sleeping.

The dream came again. This time the city came in through the window and attacked Gail. It was a great, spiky lighted-up prowler and it growled in a language I couldn't understand, made up of auto horns, crowded noises, construction bedlam. I tried to fight it off, but it got to her—and turned into a drift of stars, sprinkling all over the bed, all over everything. I jerked awake and stayed up until dawn, dressed with Gail, kissed her, savored the reality of her human, unviolated lips.

And went to meet with Bernard. He had been loaned a suite in a big downtown hospital; I rode the elevator to the sixth floor, and saw what fame and fortune could mean.

The suite was tastefully furnished, fine serigraphs on wood-paneled walls, chrome and glass furniture, cream-colored carpet, Chinese brass, and wormwood-grain cabinets and tables.

He offered me a cup of coffee, and I accepted. He took as eat in the breakfast nook, and I sat across from him, cradling my cup in moist palms. He was dapper, wearing a gray suit; had graying hair and a sharp profile. He was in his mid-sixties and he looked quite a bit like Leonard Bernstein.

"About our mutual acquaintance," he said. "Mr. Ulam. Brilliant. And, I won't hesitate to say, courageous."

"He's my friend. I'm worried about him."

Bernard held up one finger. "Courageous—and a bloody damned fool. What's happening to him should never have been allowed. He may have done it under duress, but that's no excuse. Still, what's done is done. He's talked to you, I take it."

I nodded. "He wants to return to Genetron."

"Of course. That's where all his equipment is. Where his home probably will be while we sort this out."

"Sort it out—how? What use is it?" I wasn't thinking too clearly. I had a slight headache.

"I can think of a large number of uses for small, super-dense computer elements with a biological base. Can't you? Genetron had already made breakthroughs, but this is something else again."

"What do you envision?"

Bernard smiled. "I'm not really at liberty to say. It'll be revolutionary. We'll have to get him in lab conditions. Animal experiments have to be conducted. We'll have to start from scratch, of course. Vergil's . . . um . . . colonies can't be transferred. They're based on his white blood cells. So we have to develop colonies that won't trigger immune reactions to other animals."

"Like an infection?" I asked.

"I suppose there are comparisons. But Vergil is not infected."

"My tests indicate he is."

"That's probably the bits of data floating around in his blood, don't you think?"

"I don't know."

"Listen, I'd like you to come down to the lab after Vergil is settled in. Your expertise might be useful to us."

Us. He was working with Genetron hand in glove. Could he be objective? "How will you benefit from all this?"

"Edward, I have always been at the forefront of my profession. I see no reason why I shouldn't be helping here. With my knowledge of brain and nerve functions,

and the research I've been conducting in neurophysiol-
ogy—"

"You could help Genetron hold off an investigation
by the government," I said.

"That's being very blunt. Too blunt, and unfair."

"Perhaps. Anyway, yes. I'd like to visit the lab when
Vergil's settled in. If I'm still welcome, bluntness and
all." He looked at me sharply. I wouldn't be playing
on *his* team; for a moment, his thoughts were almost
nakedly apparent.

"Of course," Bernard said, rising with me. He reached
out to shake my hand. His palm was damp. He was as
nervous as I was, even if he didn't look it.

I returned to my apartment and stayed there until
noon, reading, trying to sort things out. Reach a decision.
What was real, what I needed to protect.

There is only so much change anyone can stand. Inno-
vation, yes, but slow application. Don't force. Everyone
has the right to stay the same until they decide otherwise.

The greatest thing in science since . . .

And Bernard would force it. Genetron would force it.
I couldn't handle the thought. "Neo-Luddite," I said to
myself. A filthy accusation.

When I pressed Vergil's number on the building security panel, Vergil answered almost immediately. "Yeah,"
he said. He sounded exhilarated now. "Come on up. I'll
be in the bathroom. Door's unlocked."

I entered his apartment and walked through the hallway to the bathroom. Vergil was in the tub, up to his
neck in pinkish water. He smiled vaguely at me and
splashed his hands. "Looks like I slit my wrists, doesn't
it?" he said softly. "Don't worry. Everything's fine now.
Genetron's going to take me back. Bernard just called."
He pointed to the bathroom phone and intercom.

I sat down on the toilet and noticed the sun lamp
fixture standing unplugged next to the linen cabinets. The
bulbs sat in a row on the edge of the sink counter.
"You're sure that's what you want," I said, my shoulders slumping.

"Yeah, I think so," he said. "They can take better care of me. I'm getting cleaned up, go over there this evening. Bernard's picking me up in his limo. Style. From here on in, everything's style."

The pinkish color in the water didn't look like soap. "Is that bubble bath?" I asked. Some of it came to me in a rush then and I felt a little weaker: what had occurred to me was just one more obvious and necessary insanity.

"No," Vergil said. I knew that already.

"No," he repeated, "it's coming from my skin. They're not telling me everything, but I think they're sending out scouts. Astronauts." He looked at me with an expression that didn't quite equal concern; more like curiosity as to how I'd take it.

The confirmation made my stomach muscles tighten as if waiting for a punch. I had never even considered the possibility until now, perhaps because I had been concentrating on other aspects. "Is this the first time?" I asked.

"Yeah," he said. He laughed. "I've half a mind to let the little buggers down the drain. Let them find out what the world's really about."

"They'd go everywhere," I said.

"Sure enough."

"How . . . how are you feeling?"

"I'm feeling pretty good now. Must be billions of them." More splashing with his hands. "What do you think? Should I let the buggers out?"

Quickly, hardly thinking, I knelt down beside the tub. My fingers went for the cord on the sun lamp and I plugged it in. He had hot-wired doorknobs, turned my piss blue, played a thousand dumb practical jokes and never grown up, never grown mature enough to understand that he was just brilliant enough to really affect the world; he would never learn caution.

He reached for the drain knob. "You know, Edward, I—"

He never finished. I picked up the fixture and dropped it into the tub, jumping back at the flash of steam and sparks. Vergil screamed and thrashed and jerked and then everything was still, except for the low, steady sizzle and the smoke wafting from his hair.

I lifted the toilet and vomited. Then I clenched my nose and went into the living room. My legs went out from under me and I sat abruptly on the couch.

After an hour, I searched through Vergil's kitchen and found bleach, ammonia, and a bottle of Jack Daniel's. I returned to the bathroom, keeping the center of my gaze away from Vergil. I poured first the booze, then the bleach, then the ammonia into the water. Chlorine started bubbling up and I left, closing the door behind me.

The phone was ringing when I got home. I didn't answer. It could have been the hospital. It could have been Bernard. Or the police. I could envision having to explain everything to the police. Genetron would stonewall; Bernard would be unavailable.

I was exhausted, all my muscles knotted with tension and whatever name one can give to the feelings one has after—

Committing genocide?

That certainly didn't seem real. I could not believe I had just murdered a hundred trillion intelligent beings. Snuffed a galaxy. It was laughable. But I didn't laugh.

It was not at all hard to believe I had just killed one human being, a friend. The smoke, the melted lamp rods, the dropping electrical outlet and smoking cord.

Vergil.

I had dunked the lamp into the tub with Vergil.

I felt sick. Dreams, cities raping Gail (and what about his girlfriend, Candice?). Letting the water filled with them out. Galaxies sprinkling over us all. What horror. Then again, what potential beauty—a new kind of life, symbiosis and transformation.

Had I been thorough enough to kill them all? I had a moment of panic. Tomorrow, I thought, I will sterilize his apartment. Somehow. I didn't even think of Bernard.

When Gail came in the door, I was asleep on the couch. I came to, groggy, and she looked down at me.

"You feeling okay?" she asked, perching on the edge of the couch. I nodded.

"What are you planning for dinner?" My mouth wasn't working properly. The words were mushy. She felt my forehead.

"Edward, you have a fever," she said. "A very high fever."

I stumbled into the bathroom and looked in the mirror. Gail was close behind me. "What is it?" she asked.

There were lines under my collar, around my neck. White lines, like freeways. They had already been in me a long time, days.

"Damp palms," I said. So obvious.

I think we nearly died. I struggled at first, but within minutes I was too weak to move. Gail was just as sick within an hour.

I lay on the carpet in the living room, drenched in sweat. Gail lay on the couch, her face the color of talcum, eyes closed, like a corpse in an embalming parlor. For a time I thought she was dead. Sick as I was, I raged— hated, felt tremendous guilt at my weakness, my slowness to understand all the possibilities. Then I no longer cared. I was too weak to blink, so I closed my eyes and waited.

There was a rhythm in my arms, my legs. With each pulse of blood, a kind of sound welled up within me. A sound like an orchestra thousands strong, but not playing in unison; playing whole seasons of symphonies at once. Music in the blood. The sound or whatever became harsher, but mor coordinated, wave-trains finally cancelling into silence, then separating into harmonic beats.

The beats seemed to melt into me, into the sound of my own heart.

First, they subdued our immune responses. The war— and it was a war, on a scale never before known on Earth, with trillions of combatants—lasted perhaps two days.

By the time I regained enough strength to get to the

kitchen faucet, I could feel them working on my brain, trying to crack the code and find the god within the protoplasm. I drank until I was sick, then drank more moderately and took a glass to Gail. She sipped at it. Her lips were cracked, her eyes bloodshot and ringed with yellowish crumbs. There was some color in her skin. Minutes later, we were eating feebly in the kitchen.

"What in hell was *that*?" was the first thing she asked. I didn't have the strength to explain, so I shook my head. I peeled an orange and shared it with her. "We should call a doctor," she said. But I knew we wouldn't. I was already receiving messages; it was becoming apparent that any sensation of freedom we had was illusory.

The messages were simple at first. Memories of commands, rather than the commands themselves, manifested themselves in my thoughts. We were not to leave the apartment—a concept which seemed quite abstract to those in control, even if undesirable—and we were not to have contact with others. We would be allowed to eat certain foods, and drink tap water, for the time being.

With the subsidence of the fevers, the transformations were quick and drastic. Almost simultaneously, Gail and I were immobilized. She was sitting at the table, I was kneeling on the floor. I was able barely to see her in the corner of my eye.

Her arm was developing pronounced ridges.

They had learned inside Vergil; their tactics within the two of us were very different. I itched all over for about two hours—two hours in hell—before they made the breakthrough and found me. The effort of ages on their time scale paid off and they communicated smoothly and directly with this great, clumsy intelligence which had once controlled their universe.

They were not cruel. When the concept of discomfort and its undesirability was made clear, they worked to alleviate it. They worked too effectively. For another hour, I was in a sea of bliss, out of all contact with them.

With dawn the next day, we were allowed freedom to move again; specifically, to go to the bathroom. There were certain waste products they could not deal with. I voided those—my urine was purple—and Gail followed suit. We looked at each other vacantly in the bathroom. Then she managed a slight smile. "Are they talking to you?" she asked. I nodded. "Then I'm not crazy."

For the next twelve hours, control seemed to loosen on some levels. During that time, I managed to pencil the majority of this manuscript. I suspect there was another kind of war going on in me. Gail was capable of our previous limited motion, but no more.

When full control resumed, we were instructed to hold each other. We did not hesitate.

"Eddie . . ." she whispered. My name was the last sound I ever heard from outside.

Standing, we grew together. In hours, our legs expanded and spread out. Then extensions grew to the windows to take in sunlight, and to the kitchen to take water from the sink. Filaments soon reached to all corners of the room, stripping paint and plaster from the walls, fabric and stuffing from the furniture.

By the next dawn, the transformation was complete.

I no longer have any clear view of what we look like. I suspect we resemble cells—large, flat and filamented cells, draped purposefully across most of the apartment. The great shall mimic the small.

I have been asked to carry on recording, but soon that will not be possible. Our intelligence fluctuates daily as we are absorbed into the minds within. Each day, our individuality declines. We are, indeed, great clumsy dinosaurs. Our memories have been taken over by billions of them, and our personalities have been spread through the transformed blood.

Soon there will be no need for centralization.

I am informed that already the plumbing has been invaded. People throughout the building are undergoing transformation.

Within the old time frame of weeks, we will reach the lakes, rivers, and seas in force.

I can barely begin to guess the results. Every square

inch of the planet will teem with thought. Years from now, perhaps much sooner, they will subdue their own individuality—what there is of it.

New creatures will come, then. The immensity of their capacity for thought will be inconceivable.

All my hatred and fear is gone now.

I leave them—us—with only one question.

How many times has this happened, elsewhere? Travelers never came through space to visit the Earth. They had no need.

They had found universes in grains of sand.

BEGGARS IN SPAIN

by Nancy Kress

Novels get written for all kinds of reasons: artistic passion, economic necessity, do-it-yourself therapy, editorial insistence, political ideology. Some books are hard to write; some flow like water. Turning my 1991 novella "Beggars In Spain" into a novel was fairly easy. What was hard was getting the novella version written in the first place.

The first time I created the Sleepless was in a dreadful short story written in 1977, at the very beginning of my career. Sleeplessness was a spontaneous genetic mutation, and the characters were isolated mountaineers. The story was rejected by every editor in the business (Robert Silverberg, who changed editorial positions while I was cycling through the available markets, rejected it twice). Even I, fledgling writer with no ability to objectively evaluate my own stuff, could see that this story was not going to sell. I retired the manuscript.

Five years later I tried again. This time sleeplessness was a deliberate genetic mutation, created by a rogue mad scientist-type who eventually kills himself. Melodrama and nihilism. Again everybody rejected the story.

By 1990 I was ready to try a third time. Now, however, I was finally interested in exploring how science actually works (no more rogue mad scientists working in their basements). After researching various theories about why humans need to sleep at all, I wrote the story in two weeks.

After it was published, I had a nagging feeling that there was much more to say about Leisha and her philosophical struggles. Some of this nagging resulted from having just reread both Ayn Rand and Ursula LeGuin, two writers who stand at opposite ends of the political spectrum. Rand believed that humans owe each other nothing and our economic fate is totally our own responsibility; Le Guin believes that, as a social species, we are inextricably bound up with and responsible for each other. But what did *I* believe? Neither Rand's self-righteous coldness nor Le Guin's embracing communal optimism. But what?

Writing the novel version of *Beggars In Spain,* plus its two sequels, was my attempt to find out. It wasn't an entirely successful attempt. In fact, in a world increasingly fragmented by economic gaps and international terrorism I still ponder Tony's question: "What do the haves owe the have-nots?" The answers may vary, but the question, more than ever, remains worth asking.

With energy and sleepless vigilance go forward and give us victories.

—ABRAHAM LINCOLN, TO
MAJOR GENERAL JOSEPH HOOKER, 1863

THEY SAT STIFFLY on his antique Eames chairs, two people who didn't want to be here, or one person who didn't want to and one who resented the other's reluctance. Dr. Ong had seen this before. Within two minutes he was sure: the woman was the silently furious resister. She would lose. The man would pay for it later, in little ways, for a long time.

"I presume you've performed the necessary credit checks already," Roger Camden said pleasantly, "so let's get right on to details, shall we, doctor?"

"Certainly," Ong said. "Why don't we start by your telling me all the genetic modifications you're interested in for the baby."

The woman shifted suddenly on her chair. She was in

her late twenties—clearly a second wife—but already had a faded look, as if keeping up with Roger Camden was wearing her out. Ong could easily believe that. Mrs. Camden's hair was brown, her eyes were brown, her skin had a brown tinge that might have been pretty if her cheeks had had any color. She wore a brown coat, neither fashionable nor cheap, and shoes that looked vaguely orthopedic. Ong glanced at his records for her name: Elizabeth. He would bet people forgot it often.

Next to her, Roger Camden radiated nervous vitality, a man in late middle age whose bullet-shaped head did not match his careful hair cut and Italian-silk business suit. Ong did not need to consult his file to recall anything about Camden. A caricature of the bullet-shaped head had been the leading graphic of yesterday's on-line edition of the *Wall Street Journal*: Camden had led a major coup in cross-border data-atoll investment. Ong was not sure what cross-border data-atoll investment was.

"A girl," Elizabeth Camden said. Ong hadn't expected her to speak first. Her voice was another surprise: upper-class British. "Blonde. Green eyes. Tall. Slender."

Ong smiled. "Appearance factors are the easiest to achieve, as I'm sure you already know. But all we can do about 'slenderness' is give her a genetic disposition in that direction. How you feed the child will naturally—"

"Yes, yes," Roger Camden said, "that's obvious. Now: intelligence. *High* intelligence. And a sense of daring."

"I'm sorry, Mr. Camden—personality factors are not yet understood well enough to allow genet—"

"Just testing," Camden said, with a smile that Ong thought was probably supposed to be light-hearted.

Elizabeth Camden said, "Musical ability."

"Again, Mrs. Camden, a disposition to be musical is all we can guarantee."

"Good enough," Camden said. "The full array of corrections for any potential gene-linked health problem, of course."

"Of course," Dr. Ong said. Neither client spoke. So far theirs was a fairly modest list, given Camden's money; most clients had to be argued out of contradictory genetic tendencies, alteration overload, or unrealistic expectations. Ong waited. Tension prickled in the room like heat.

"And," Camden said, "no need to sleep."

Elizabeth Camden jerked her head sideways to look out the window.

Ong picked a paper magnet off his desk. He made his voice pleasant. "May I ask how you learned whether that genetic-modification program exists?"

Camden grinned. "You're not denying it exists. I give you full credit for that, Doctor."

Ong held onto his temper. "May I ask how you learned whether the program exists?"

Camden reached into an inner pocket of his suit. The silk crinkled and pulled; body and suit came from different social classes. Camden was, Ong remembered, a Yagaiist, a personal friend of Kenzo Yagai himself. Camden handed Ong hard copy: program specifications.

"Don't bother hunting down the security leak in your data banks, Doctor—you won't find it. But if it's any consolation, neither will anybody else. Now." He leaned suddenly forward. His tone changed. "I know that you've created twenty children so far who don't need to sleep at all. That so far nineteen are healthy, intelligent, and psychologically normal. In fact, better than normal—they're all unusually precocious. The oldest is already four years old and can read in two languages. I know you're thinking of offering this genetic modification on the open market in a few years. All I want is a chance to buy it for my daughter *now*. At whatever price you name."

Ong stood. "I can't possibly discuss this with you unilaterally, Mr. Camden. Neither the theft of our data—"

"Which wasn't a theft—your system developed a spontaneous bubble regurgitation into a public gate, have a hell of a time proving otherwise—"

"—*nor* the offer to purchase this particular genetic modification lies in my sole area of authority. Both have to be discussed with the Institute's Board of Directors."

"By all means, by all means. When can I talk to them, too?"

"You?"

Camden, still seated, looked at him. It occurred to Ong that there were few men who could look so confident eighteen inches below eye level. "Certainly. I'd like the chance to present my offer to whoever has the actual authority to accept it. That's only good business."

"This isn't solely a business transaction, Mr. Camden."

"It isn't solely pure scientific research, either," Camden retorted. "You're a for-profit corporation here. *With* certain tax breaks available only to firms meeting certain fair-practice laws."

For a minute Ong couldn't think what Camden meant. "Fair-practice laws . . ."

". . . are designed to protect minorities who are suppliers. I know, it hasn't ever been tested in the case of customers, except for red-lining in Y-energy installations. But it could be tested, Doctor Ong. Minorities are entitled to the same product offerings as non-minorities. I know the Institute would not welcome a court case, Doctor. None of your twenty genetic beta-test families are either Black or Jewish."

"A court . . . but you're not Black *or* Jewish!"

"I'm a different minority. Polish-American. The name was Kaminsky." Camden finally stood. And smiled warmly. "Look, it is preposterous. You know that, and I know that, and we both know what a grand time journalists would have with it anyway. And you know that I don't want to sue you with a preposterous case, just to use the threat of premature and adverse publicity to get what I want. I don't want to make threats at all, believe me I don't. I just want this marvelous advancement you've come up with for my daughter." His face changed, to an expression Ong wouldn't have believed possible on those particular features: wistfulness. "Doctor—do you know how much more I could have accomplished if I hadn't had to *sleep* all my life?"

Elizabeth Camden said harshly, "You hardly sleep now."

Camden looked down at her as if he had forgotten she was there. "Well, no, my dear, not now. But when I was young . . . college, I might have been able to finish college and still support . . . well. None of that matters now. What matters, Doctor, is that you and I and your board come to an agreement."

"Mr. Camden, please leave my office now."

"You mean before you lose your temper at my presumptuousness? You wouldn't be the first. I'll expect to have a meeting set up by the end of next week, whenever and wherever you say, of course. Just let my personal secretary, Diane Clavers, know the details. Anytime that's best for you."

Ong did not accompany them to the door. Pressure throbbed behind his temples. In the doorway Elizabeth Camden turned. "What happened to the twentieth one?"

"What?"

"The twentieth baby. My husband said nineteen of them are healthy and normal. What happened to the twentieth?"

The pressure grew stronger, hotter. Ong knew that he should not answer; that Camden probably already knew the answer even if his wife didn't; that he, Ong, was going to answer anyway; that he would regret the lack of self-control, bitterly, later.

"The twentieth baby is dead. His parents turned out to be unstable. They separated during the pregnancy, and his mother could not bear the twenty-four-hour crying of a baby who never sleeps."

Elizabeth Camden's eyes widened. "She killed it?"

"By mistake," Camden said shortly. "Shook the little thing too hard." He frowned at Ong. "Nurses, Doctor. In shifts. You should have picked only parents wealthy enough to afford nurses in shifts."

"That's horrible!" Mrs. Camden burst out, and Ong could not tell if she meant the child's death, the lack of nurses, or the Institute's carelessness. Ong closed his eyes.

When they had gone, he took ten milligrams of cyclobenzaprine-III. For his back—it was solely for his back.

The old injury hurting again. Afterward he stood for a long time at the window, still holding the paper magnet, feeling the pressure recede from his temples, feeling himself calm down. Below him Lake Michigan lapped peacefully at the shore; the police had driven away the homeless in another raid just last night, and they hadn't yet had time to return. Only their debris remained, thrown into the bushes of the lakeshore park: tattered blankets, newspapers, plastic bags like pathetic trampled standards. It was illegal to sleep in the park, illegal to enter it without a resident's permit, illegal to be homeless and without a residence. As Ong watched, uniformed park attendants began methodically spearing newspapers and shoveling them into clean self-propelled receptacles.

Ong picked up the phone to call the President of Biotech Institute's Board of Directors.

Four men and three women sat around the polished mahogany table of the conference room. *Doctor, lawyer, Indian chief,* thought Susan Melling, looking from Ong to Sullivan to Camden. She smiled. Ong caught the smile and looked frosty. Pompous ass. Judy Sullivan, the Institute lawyer, turned to speak in a low voice to Camden's lawyer, a thin nervous man with the look of being owned. The owner, Roger Camden, the Indian chief himself, was the happiest-looking person in the room. The lethal little man—what did it take to become that rich, starting from nothing? She, Susan, would certainly never know—radiated excitement. He beamed, he glowed, so unlike the usual parents-to-be that Susan was intrigued. Usually the prospective daddies and mommies—especially the daddies—sat there looking as if they were at a corporate merger. Camden looked as if he were at a birthday party.

Which, of course, he was. Susan grinned at him, and was pleased when he grinned back. Wolfish, but with a sort of delight that could only be called innocent—what would he be like in bed? Ong frowned majestically and rose to speak.

"Ladies and gentlemen, I think we're ready to start.

Perhaps introductions are in order. Mr. Roger Camden,
Mrs. Camden, are of course our clients. Mr. John Jaworski, Mr. Camden's lawyer. Mr. Camden, this is Judith
Sullivan, the Institute's head of Legal; Samuel Krenshaw,
representing Institute Director Dr. Brad Marsteiner, who
unfortunately couldn't be here today; and Dr. Susan
Melling, who developed the genetic modification affect-
ing sleep. A few legal points of interest to both parties—"

"Forget the contracts for a minute," Camden interrupted. "Let's talk about the sleep thing. I'd like to ask
a few questions."

Susan said, "What would you like to know?" Camden's eyes were very blue in his blunt-featured face; he
wasn't what she had expected. Mrs. Camden, who apparently lacked both a first name and a lawyer, since Jaworski had been introduced as her husband's but not hers,
looked either sullen or scared, it was difficult to tell
which.

Ong said sourly, "Then perhaps we should start with
a short presentation by Dr. Melling."

Susan would have preferred a Q&A, to see what Camden would ask. But she had annoyed Ong enough for
one session. Obediently she rose.

"Let me start with a brief description of sleep. Researchers have known for a long time that there are actually three kinds of sleep. One is 'slow-wave sleep,'
characterized on an EEG by delta waves. One is 'rapid-
eye-movement sleep,'" or REM sleep, which is much
lighter sleep and contains most dreaming. Together these
two make up 'core sleep.' The third type of sleep is 'op-
tional sleep,'" so-called because people seem to get along
without it with no ill effects, and some short sleepers
don't do it at all, sleeping naturally only 3 or 4 hours
a night."

"That's me," Camden said. "I trained myself into it.
Couldn't everybody do that?"

Apparently they were going to have a Q&A after all.
"No. The actual sleep mechanism has some flexibility,

but not the same amount for every person. The raphe nuclei on the brain stem—"

Ong said, "I don't think that we need that level of detail, Susan. Let's stick to basics."

Camden said, "The raphe nuclei regulate the balance among neurotransmitters and peptides that lead to a pressure to sleep, don't they?"

Susan couldn't help it; she grinned. Camden, the laser-sharp ruthless financier, sat trying to look solemn, a third-grader waiting to have his homework praised. Ong looked sour. Mrs. Camden looked away, out the window.

"Yes, that's correct, Mr. Camden. You've done your research."

Camden said, "This is my *daughter*," and Susan caught her breath. When was the last time she had heard that note of reverence in anyone's voice? But no one in the room seemed to notice.

"Well, then," Susan said, "you already know that the reason people sleep is because a pressure to sleep builds up in the brain. Over the last twenty years, research has determined that's the *only* reason. Neither slow-wave sleep nor REM sleep serve functions that can't be carried on while the body and brain are awake. A lot goes on during sleep, but it can go on awake just as well, if other hormonal adjustments are made.

"Sleep once served an important evolutionary function. Once Clem Pre-Mammal was done filling his stomach and squirting his sperm around, sleep kept him immobile and away from predators. Sleep was an aid to survival. But now it's a left-over mechanism, like the appendix. It switches on every night, but the need is gone. So we turn off the switch at its source, in the genes."

Ong winced. He hated it when she oversimplified like that. Or maybe it was the light-heartedness he hated. If Marsteiner were making this presentation, there'd be no Clem Pre-Mammal.

Camden said, "What about the need to dream?"

"Not necessary. A left-over bombardment of the cor-

tex to keep it on semi-alert in case a predator attacked
during sleep. Wakefulness does that better."

"Why not have wakefulness instead then? From the
start of the evolution?"

He was testing her. Susan gave him a full, lavish smile,
enjoying his brass. "I told you. Safety from predators.
But when a modern predator attacks—say, a cross-
border data-atoll investor—it's safer to be awake."

Camden shot at her. "What about the high percentage
of REM sleep in fetuses and babies?"

"Still an evolutionary hangover. Cerebrum develops
perfectly well without it."

"What about neural repair during slow-wave sleep?"

"That does go on. But it can go on during wakefulness,
if the DNA is programmed to do so. No loss of neural
efficiency, as far as we know."

"What about the release of human growth enzyme in
such large concentrations during slow-wave sleep?"

Susan looked at him admiringly. "Goes on without the
sleep. Genetic adjustments tie it to other changes in the
pineal gland."

"What about the—"

"The *side effects*?" Mrs. Camden said. Her mouth
turned down. "What about the bloody side effects?"

Susan turned to Elizabeth Camden. She had forgotten
she was there. The younger woman stared at Susan,
mouth turned down at the corners.

"I'm glad you asked that, Mrs. Camden. Because there
are side effects." Susan paused; she was enjoying herself.
"Compared to their age mates, the non-sleep children—
who have *not* had IQ genetic manipulation— are more
intelligent, better at problem-solving, and more joyous."

Camden took out a cigarette. The archaic, filthy habit
surprised Susan. Then she saw that it was deliberate:
Roger Camden drawing attention to an ostentatious display to draw attention away from what he was feeling.
His cigarette lighter was gold, monogrammed, inno-
cently gaudy.

"Let me explain," Susan said. "REM sleep bombards

the cerebral cortex with random neural firings from the brainstem; dreaming occurs because the poor besieged cortex tries so hard to make sense of the activated images and memories. It spends a lot of energy doing that. Without that energy expenditure, non-sleep cerebrums save the wear-and-tear and do better at coordinating real-life input. Thus—greater intelligence and problem-solving.

"Also, doctors have known for sixty years that antidepressants, which lift the mood of depressed patients, also suppress REM sleep entirely. What they have proved in the last ten years is that the reverse is equally true: suppress REM sleep and people don't *get* depressed. The non-sleep kids are cheerful, outgoing . . . *joyous*. There's no other word for it."

"At what cost?" Mrs. Camden said. She held her neck rigid, but the corners of her jaw worked.

"No cost. No negative side effects at all."

"So far," Mrs. Camden shot back.

Susan shrugged. "So far."

"They're only four years old! At the most!"

Ong and Krenshaw were studying her closely. Susan saw the moment the Camden woman realized it; she sank back into her chair, drawing her fur coat around her, her face blank.

Camden did not look at his wife. He blew a cloud of cigarette smoke. "Everything has costs, Dr. Melling."

She liked the way he said her name. "Ordinarily, yes. Especially in genetic modification. But we honestly have not been able to find any here, despite looking." She smiled directly into Camden's eyes. "Is it too much to believe that just once the universe has given us something wholly good, wholly a step forward, wholly beneficial? Without hidden penalties?"

"Not the universe. The intelligence of people like you," Camden said, surprising Susan more than anything else that had gone before. His eyes held hers. She felt her chest tighten.

"I think," Dr. Ong said dryly, "that the philosophy of the universe may be beyond our concerns here. Mr. Camden, if you have no further medical questions, perhaps we can return to the legal points Ms. Sullivan and Mr. Jaworski have raised. Thank you, Dr. Melling.''

Susan nodded. She didn't look again at Camden. But she knew what he said, how he looked, that he was there.

The house was about what she had expected, a huge mock Tudor on Lake Michigan north of Chicago. The land heavily wooded between the gate and the house, open between the house and the surging water. Patches of snow dotted the dormant grass. Biotech had been working with the Camdens for four months, but this was the first time Susan had driven to their home.

As she walked toward the house, another car drove up behind her. No, a truck, continuing around the curved driveway to a service entry at the side of the house. One man rang the service bell; a second began to unload a plastic-wrapped playpen from the back of the truck. White, with pink and yellow bunnies. Susan briefly closed her eyes.

Camden opened the door himself. She could see the effort not to look worried. "You didn't have to drive out, Susan—I'd have come into the city!"

"No, I didn't want you to do that, Roger. Mrs. Camden is here?"

"In the living room." Camden led her into a large room with a stone fireplace. English country-house furniture; prints of dogs or boats, all hung eighteen inches too high: Elizabeth Camden must have done the decorating. She did not rise from her wing chair as Susan entered.

"Let me be concise and fast," Susan said, "I don't want to make this any more drawn-out for you than I have to. We have all the amniocentesis, ultrasound, and Langston test results. The feteus is fine, developing normally for two weeks, no problems with the implant on the uterus wall. But a complication has developed."

"What?" Camden said. He took out a cigarette, looked at his wife, put it back unlit.

Susan said quietly, "Mrs. Camden, by sheer chance both your ovaries released eggs last month. We removed one for the gene surgery. By more sheer chance the second fertilized and implanted. You're carrying two fetuses."

Elizabeth Camden grew still. "Twins?"

"No," Susan said. Then she realized what she had said. "I mean, yes. They're twins, but non-identical. Only one has been genetically altered. The other will be no more similar to her than any two siblings. It's a so-called 'normal' baby. And I know you didn't want a so-called normal baby."

Camden said, "No. I didn't."

Elizabeth Camden said, "I did."

Camden shot her a fierce look that Susan couldn't read. He took out the cigarette again, lit it. His face was in profile to Susan, thinking intently; she doubted he knew the cigarette was there, or that he was lighting it. "Is the baby being affected by the other one's being there?"

"No," Susan said. "No, of course not. They're just . . . co-existing."

"Can you abort it?"

"Not without risk of aborting both of them. Removing the unaltered fetus might cause changes in the uterus lining that could lead to a spontaneous miscarriage of the other." She drew a deep breath. "There's that option, of course. We can start the whole process over again. But as I told you at the time, you were very lucky to have the in vitro fertilization take on only the second try. Some couples take eight or ten tries. If we started all over, the process could be a lengthy one."

Camden said, "Is the presence of this second fetus harming my daughter? Taking away nutrients or anything? Or will it change anything for her later on in the pregnancy?"

"No. Except that there is a chance of premature birth. Two fetuses take up a lot more room in the womb, and if it gets too crowded, birth can be premature. But the—"

"How premature? Enough to threaten survival?"

"Most probably not."

Camden went on smoking. A man appeared at the

door. "Sir, London calling. James Kendall for Mr. Yagai."

"I'll take it." Camden rose. Susan watched him study his wife's face. When he spoke, it was to her. "All right, Elizabeth. All right." He left the room.

For a long moment the two women sat in silence. Susan was aware of disappointment; this was not the Camden she had expected to see. She became aware of Elizabeth Camden watching her with amusement.

"Oh, yes, Doctor. He's like that."

Susan said nothing.

"Completely overbearing. But not this time." She laughed softly, with excitement. "Two. Do you . . . do you know what sex the other one is?"

"Both fetuses are female."

"I wanted a girl, you know. And now I'll have one."

"Then you'll go ahead with the pregnancy."

"Oh, yes. Thank you for coming, Doctor."

She was dismissed. No one saw her out. But as she was getting into her car, Camden rushed out of the house. Coatless. "Susan! I wanted to thank you. For coming all the way out here to tell us yourself."

"You already thanked me."

"Yes. Well. You're sure the second fetus is no threat to my daughter?"

Susan said deliberately, "Nor is the genetically altered fetus a threat to the naturally conceived one."

He smiled. His voice was low and wistful. "And you think that should matter to me just as much. But it doesn't. And why should I fake what I feel? Especially to you?"

Susan opened her car door. She wasn't ready for this, or she had changed her mind, or something. But then Camden leaned over to close the door, and his manner held no trace of flirtatiousness, nor smarmy ingratiation. "I better order a second playpen."

"Yes."

"And a second car seat."

"Yes."

"But not a second night-shift nurse."

"That's up to you."

"And you." Abruptly he leaned over and kissed her, a kiss so polite and respectful that Susan was shocked. Neither lust nor conquest would have shocked her; this did. Camden didn't give her a chance to react; he closed the car door and turned back toward the house. Susan drove toward the gate, her hand shaky on the wheel until amusement replaced shock; It *had* been a deliberately distant, respectful kiss, an engineered enigma. And nothing else could have guaranteed so well that there would have to be another.

She wondered what the Camdens would name their daughters.

Dr. Ong strode the hospital corridor, which had been dimmed to half-light. From the nurse's station in Maternity a nurse stepped forward as if to stop him—it was the middle of the night, long past visiting hours—got a good look at his face, and faded back into her station. Around a corner was the viewing glass to the nursery. To Ong's annoyance, Susan Melling stood pressed against the glass. To his further annoyance, she was crying.

Ong realized that he had never liked the woman. Maybe not any women. Even those with superior minds could not seem to refrain from being made damn fools by their emotions.

"Look," Susan said, laughing a little, swiping at her face. "Doctor—*look*."

Behind the glass Roger Camden, gowned and masked, was holding up a baby in white undershirt and pink blanket. Camden's blue eyes—theatrically blue, a man really should not have such garish eyes—glowed. The baby had a head covered with blond fuzz, wide eyes, pink skin. Camden's eyes above the mask said that no other child had ever had these attributes.

Ong said, "An uncomplicated birth?"

"Yes," Susan Melling sobbed. "Perfectly straightforward. Elizabeth is fine. She's asleep. Isn't she beautiful? He has the most adventurous spirit I've ever known."

She wiped her nose on her sleeve; Ong realized that she was drunk. "Did I ever tell you that I was engaged once? Fifteen years ago, in med school? I broke it off because he grew to seem so ordinary, so boring. Oh, God, I shouldn't be telling you all this I'm sorry I'm sorry."

Ong moved away from her. Behind the glass Roger Camden laid the baby in a small wheeled crib. The name-plate said BABY GIRL CAMDEN #1. 5.9 POUNDS. A night nurse watched indulgently.

Ong did not wait to see Camden emerge from the nursery or to hear Susan Melling say to him whatever she was going to say. Ong went to have the OB paged. Melling's report was not, under the circumstances, to be trusted. A perfect, unprecedented chance to record every detail of gene-alteration with a non-altered control, and Melling was more interested in her own sloppy emotions. Ong would obviously have to do the report himself, after talking to the OB. He was hungry for every detail. And not just about the pink-cheeked baby in Camden's arms. He wanted to know everything about the birth of the child in the other glass-sided crib: BABY GIRL CAM-DEN #2. 5.1 POUNDS. The dark-haired baby with the mottled red features, lying scrunched down in her pink blanket, asleep.

2

Leisha's earliest memory was of flowing lines that were not there. She knew they were not there because when she reached out her fist to touch them, her fist was empty. Later she realized that the flowing lines were light: sunshine slanting in bars between curtains in her room, between the wooden blinds in the dining room, between the criss-cross lattices in the conservatory. The day she realized the golden flow was light she laughed out loud with the sheer joy of discovery, and Daddy turned from putting flowers in pots and smiled at her.

The whole house was full of light. Light bounded off the lake, streamed across the high white ceilings, puddled on the shining wooden floors. She and Alice moved continually through light, and sometimes Leisha would stop and tip back her head and let it flow over her face. She could feel it, like water.

The best light, of course, was in the conservatory. That's where Daddy liked to be when he was home from making money. Daddy potted plants and watered trees, humming, and Leisha and Alice ran between the wooden tables of flowers with their wonderful earthy smells, running from the dark side of the conservatory where the big purple flowers grew to the sunshine side with sprays of yellow flowers, running back and forth, in and out of the light. "Growth," Daddy said to her, "flowers all fulfilling their promise. Alice, be careful! You almost knocked over that orchid!" Alice, obedient, would stop running for a while. Daddy never told Leisha to stop running.

After a while the light would go away. Alice and Leisha would have their baths, and then Alice would get quiet, or cranky. She wouldn't play nice with Leisha, even when Leisha let her choose the game or even have all the best dolls. Then Nanny would take Alice to "bed," and Leisha would talk with Daddy some more until Daddy said he had to work in his study with the papers that made money. Leisha always felt a moment of regret that he had to go do that, but the moment never lasted very long because Mamselle would arrive and start Leisha's lessons, which she liked. Learning things was so interesting! She could already sing twenty songs and write all the letters in the alphabet and count to fifty. And by the time lessons were done, the light had come back, and it was time for breakfast.

Breakfast was the only time Leisha didn't like. Daddy had gone to the office, and Leisha and Alice had breakfast with Mommy in the big dining room. Mommy sat in a red robe, which Leisha liked, and she didn't smell funny or talk funny the way she would later in the day, but still breakfast wasn't fun. Mommy always started with The Question.

"Alice, sweetheart, how did you sleep?"

"Fine, Mommy."

"Did you have any nice dreams?"

For a long time Alice said no. Then one day she said, "I dreamed about a horse. I was riding him." Mommy clapped her hands and kissed Alice and gave her an extra sticky bun. After that Alice always had a dream to tell Mommy.

Once Leisha said, "I had a dream, too. I dreamed light was coming in the window and it wrapped around me like a blanket and then it kissed me on my eyes."

Mommy put down her coffee cup so hard that coffee sloshed out of it. "Don't lie to me, Leisha. You did not have a dream."

"Yes, I did," Leisha said.

"Only children who sleep can have dreams. Don't lie to me. You did not have a dream."

"Yes I did! I did!" Leisha shouted. She could see it, almost: The light streaming in the window and wrapping around her like a golden blanket.

"I will not tolerate a child who is a liar! Do you hear me, Leisha—I won't tolerate it!"

"You're a liar!" Leisha shouted, knowing the words weren't true, hating herself because they weren't true but hating Mommy more and that was wrong, too, and there sat Alice stiff and frozen with her eyes wide, Alice was scared and it was Leisha's fault.

Mommy called sharply, "Nanny! Nanny! Take Leisha to her room at once. She can't sit with civilized people if she can't refrain from telling lies!"

Leisha started to cry. Nanny carried her out of the room. Leisha hadn't even had her breakfast. But she didn't care about that; all she could see while she cried was Alice's eyes, scared like that, reflecting broken bits of light.

But Leisha didn't cry long. Nanny read her a story, and then played Data Jump with her, and then Alice came up and Nanny drove them both into Chicago to the zoo where there were wonderful animals to see, animals Leisha could not have dreamed—nor Alice *either*. And by the time they came back Mommy had gone to her room and Leisha knew that she would stay there with the glasses of funny-smelling stuff the rest of the day and Leisha would not have to see her.

But that night, she went to her mother's room.

"I have to go to the bathroom," she told Mamselle. Mamselle said, "Do you need any help?" maybe because Alice still needed help in the bathroom. But Leisha didn't, and she thanked Mamselle. Then she sat on the toilet for a minute even though nothing came, so that what she had told Mamselle wouldn't be a lie.

Leisha tiptoed down the hall. She went first into Alice's room. A little light in a wall socket burned near the "crib." There was no drib in Leisha's room. Leisha looked at her sister through the bars. Alice lay on her side, with her eyes closed. The lids of the eyes fluttered quickly, like curtains blowing in the wind. Alice's chin and neck looked loose.

Leisha closed the door very carefully and went to her parents' room.

They didn't "sleep" in a crib but in a huge enormous "bed," with enough room between them for more people. Mommy's eyelids weren't fluttering; she lay on her back making a hrrr-hrrr sound through her nose. The funny smell was strong on her. Leisha backed away and tiptoed over to Daddy. He looked like Alice, except that his neck and chin looked even looser, folds of skin collapsed like the tent that had fallen down in the backyard. It scared Leisha to see him like that. Then Daddy's eyes flew open so suddenly that Leisha screamed.

Daddy rolled out of bed and picked her up, looking quickly at Mommy. But she didn't move. Daddy was wearing only his underpants. He carried Leisha out into the hall, where Mamselle came rushing up saying, "Oh, sir, I'm sorry, she just said she was going to the bathroom—"

"It's all right," Daddy said. "I'll take her with me."

"No!" Leisha screamed, because Daddy was only in his underpants and his neck had looked all funny and the room smelled bad because of Mommy. But Daddy carried her into the conservatory, set her down on a bench, wrapped himself in a piece of green plastic that was supposed to cover up plants, and sat down next to her.

"Now, what happened, Leisha? What were you doing?"

Leisha didn't answer.

"You were looking at people sleeping, weren't you?" Daddy said, and because his voice was softer Leisha mumbled, "Yes." She immediately felt better; it felt good not to lie.

"You were looking at people sleeping because you don't sleep and you were curious, weren't you? Like Curious George in your book?"

"Yes," Leisha said. "I thought you said you made money in your study all night!"

Daddy smiled. "Not all night. Some of it. But then I sleep, although not very much." He took Leisha on his lap. "I don't need much sleep, so I get a lot more done at night than most people. Different people need different amounts of sleep. And a few, a very few, are like you. You don't need any."

"Why not?"

"Because you're special. Better than other people. Before you were born, I had some doctors help make you that way."

"Why?"

"So you could do anything you want to and make manifest your own individuality."

Leisha twisted in his arms to stare at him; the words meant nothing. Daddy reached over and touched a single flower growing on a tall potted tree. The flower had thick white petals like the cream he put in coffee, and the center was a light pink.

"See, Leisha—this tree made this flower. Because it *can.* Only this tree can make this kind of wonderful flower. That plant hanging up there can't, and those can't either. Only this tree. Therefore the most important thing in the world for this tree to do is grow this flower. The flower is the tree's individuality—that means just *it,* and nothing else—made manifest. Nothing else matters."

"I don't understand, Daddy."

"You will. Someday."

"But I want to understand *now*," Leisha said, and Daddy laughed with pure delight and hugged her. The hug felt good, but Leisha still wanted to understand.

"When you make money, is that your indiv . . . that thing?"

"Yes," Daddy said happily.

"Then nobody else can make money? Like only that tree can make that flower?"

"Nobody else can make it just the ways I do."

"What do you do with the money?"

"I buy things for you. This house, your dresses, Mamselle to teach you, the car to ride in."

"What does the tree do with the flower?"

"Glories in it," Daddy said, which made no sense. "Excellence is what counts, Leisha. Excellence supported by individual effort. And that's *all* that counts."

"I'm cold, Daddy."

"Then I better bring you back to Mamselle."

Leisha didn't move. She touched the flower with one finger. "I want to sleep, Daddy."

"No, you don't, sweetheart. Sleep is just lost time, wasted life. It's a little death."

"Alice sleeps."

"Alice isn't like you."

"Alice isn't special?"

"No. You are."

"Why didn't you make Alice special, too?"

"Alice made herself. I didn't have a chance to make her special."

The whole thing was too had. Leisha stopped stroking the flower and slipped off Daddy's lap. He smiled at her. "My little questioner. When you grow up, you'll find your own excellence, and it will be a new order, a specialness the world hasn't ever seen before. You might even be like Kenzo Yagai. He made the Yagai generator that powers the world."

"Daddy, you look funny wrapped in the flower plastic." Leisha laughed. Daddy did, too. But then she said,

"When I grow up, I'll make my specialness find a way to make Alice special, too," and Daddy stopped laughing.

He took her back to Mamselle, who taught her to write her name, which was so exciting she forgot about the puzzling talk with Daddy. There were six letters, all different, and together they were *her name.* Leisha wrote it over and over, laughing, and Mamselle laughed too. But later, in the morning, Leisha thought again about the talk with Daddy. She thought of it often, turning the unfamiliar words over and over in her mind like small hard stones, but the part she thought about most wasn't a word. It was the frown on Daddy's face when she told him she would use her specialness to make Alice special, too.

Every week Dr. Melling came to see Leisha and Alice, sometimes alone, sometimes with other people. Leisha and Alice both liked Dr. Melling, who laughed a lot and whose eyes were bright and warm. Often Daddy was there, too. Dr. Melling played games with them, first with Alice and Leisha separately and then together. She took their pictures and weighed them. She made them lie down on a table and stuck little metal things to their temples, which sounded scary but wasn't because there were so many machines to watch, all making interesting noises, while you were lying there. Dr. Melling was as good at answering questions as Daddy. Once Leisha said, "Is Dr. Melling a special person? Like Kenzo Yagai?" And Daddy laughed and glanced at Dr. Melling and said, "Oh, yes, indeed."

When Leisha was five she and Alice started school. Daddy's driver took them every day into Chicago. They were in different rooms, which disappointed Leisha. The kids in Leisha's room were all older. But from the first day she adored school, with its fascinating science equipment and electronic drawers full of math puzzlers and other children to find countries on the map with. In half a year she had been moved to yet a different room, where the kids were still older, but they were nonetheless nice to her. Leisha started to learn Japanese. She loved drawing the beautiful characters on thick white paper. "The Sauley School was a good choice," Daddy said.

But Alice didn't like the Sauley School. She wanted to go to school on the same yellow bus as Cook's daughter. She cried and threw her paints on the floor at the Sauley School. Then Mommy came out of her room— Leisha hadn't seen her for a few weeks, although she knew Alice had—and threw some candlesticks from the mantlepiece on the floor. The candlesticks, which were china, broke. Leisha ran to pick up the pieces while Mommy and Daddy screamed at each other in the hall by the big staircase.

"She's my daughter, too! And I say she can go!"

"You don't have the right to say anything about it! A weepy drunk, the most rotten role model possible for both of them . . . and I thought I was getting a fine English aristocrat!"

"You got what you paid for! Nothing! Not that you ever needed anything from me or anybody else!"

"Stop it!" Leisha cried. "Stop it!" and there was silence in the hall. Leisha cut her fingers on the china; blood streamed onto the rug. Daddy rushed in and picked her up. "Stop it," Leisha sobbed, and didn't understand when Daddy said quietly, "*You* stop it, Leisha. Nothing *they* do should touch you at all. You have to be at least that strong."

Leisha buried her head in Daddy's shoulder. Alice transferred to Carl Sandburg Elementary School, riding there on the yellow school bus with Cook's daughter.

A few weeks later Daddy told them that Mommy was going away for a few weeks to a hospital, to stop drinking so much. When Mommy came out, he said, she was going to live somewhere else for a while. She and Daddy were not happy. Leisha and Alice would stay with Daddy and they would visit Mommy sometimes. He told them this very carefully, finding the right words for truth. Truth was very important, Leisha already knew. Truth was being true to your self, your specialness. Your individuality. An individual respected facts, and so always told the truth.

Mommy, Daddy did not say but Leisha knew, did not respect facts.

"I don't want Mommy to go away," Alice said. She started to cry. Leisha thought Daddy would pick Alice up, but he didn't. He just stood there looking at them both.

Leisha put her arms around Alice. "It's all right, Alice. It's all right! We'll make it all right! I'll play with you all the time we're not in school so you don't miss Mommy!"

Alice clung to Leisha. Leisha turned her head so she didn't have to see Daddy's face.

3

Kenzo Yagai was coming to the United States to lecture. The title of his talk, which he would give in New York, Los Angeles, Chicago, and Washington, with a repeat in Washington as a special address to Congress, was "The Further Political Implications of Inexpensive Power." Leisha Camden, eleven years old, was going to have a private introduction after the Chicago talk, arranged by her father.

She had studied the theory of cold fusion at school, and her Global Studies teacher had traced the changes in the world resulting from Yagai's patented, low-cost applications of what had, until him, been unworkable theory. The rising prosperity of the Third World, the last death throes of the old communist systems, the decline of the oil states, the renewed economic power of the United States. Her study group had written a news script, filmed with the school's professional-quality equipment, about how a 1985 American family lived with expensive energy costs and a belief in tax-supported help, while a 2019 family lived with cheap energy and a belief in the contract as a basis of civilization. Parts of her own research puzzled Leisha.

"Japan thinks Kenzo Yagai was a traitor to his own country," she said to Daddy at supper.

"No," Camden said. "*Some* Japanese think that. Watch

out for generalizations, Leisha. Yagai patented and marketed Y-energy first in the United States because here there were at least the dying embers of individual enterprise. Because of his invention, our entire country has slowly swung back toward an individual meritocracy, and Japan has slowly been forced to follow."

"Your father held that belief all along," Susan said. "Eat your peas, Leisha." Leisha ate her peas. Susan and Daddy had only been married less than a year; it still felt a little strange to have her there. But nice. Daddy said Susan was a valuable addition to their household: intelligent, motivated, and cheerful. Like Leisha herself.

"Remember, Leisha," Camden said, "a man's worth to society and to himself doesn't rest on what he thinks other people should do or be or feel, but on himself. On what he can actually do, and do well. People trade what they do well, and everyone benefits. The basic tool of civilization is the contract. Contracts are voluntary and mutually beneficial. As opposed to coercion, which is wrong."

"The strong have no right to take anything from the weak by force," Susan said. "Alice, eat your peas, too, honey."

"Nor the weak to take anything by force from the strong," Camden said. "That's the basis of what you'll hear Kenzo Yagai discuss tonight, Leisha."

Alice said, "I don't like peas."

Camden said, "Your body does. They're good for you."

Alice smiled. Leisha felt her heart lift; Alice didn't smile much at dinner any more. "My body doesn't have a contract with the peas."

Camden said, a little impatiently, "Yes, it does. Your body benefits from them. Now eat."

Alice's smile vanished. Leisha looked down at her plate. Suddenly she saw a way out. "No, Daddy look— Alice's body benefits, but the peas don't! It's not a mutually beneficial consideration—so there's no contract! Alice is right!"

Camden let out a shout of laughter. To Susan he said,

"Eleven years old . . . *eleven*." Even Alice smiled, and Leisha waved her spoon triumphantly, light glinting off the bowl and dancing silver on the opposite wall.

But even so, Alice did not want to go hear Kenzo Yagai. She was going to sleep over at her friend Julie's house; they were going to curl their hair together. More surprisingly, Susan wasn't coming either. She and Daddy looked at each other a little funny at the front door, Leisha thought, but Leisha was too excited to think about this. She was going to hear *Kenzo Yagai*.

Yagai was a small man, dark and slim. Leisha liked his accent. She liked, too, something about him that took her a while to name. "Daddy," she whispered in the half-darkness of the auditorium, "he's a joyful man."

Daddy hugged her in the darkness.

Yagai spoke about spirituality and economics. "A man's spirituality—which is only his dignity as a man—rests on his own efforts. Dignity and worth are not automatically conferred by aristocratic birth—we have only to look at history to see that. Dignity and worth are not automatically conferred by inherited wealth—a great heir may be a thief, a wastrel, cruel, an exploiter, a person who leaves the world much poorer than he found it. Nor are dignity and worth automatically conferred by existence itself—a mass murderer exists, but is of negative worth to his society and possesses no dignity in his lust to kill.

"No, the only dignity, the only spirituality, rests on what a man can achieve with his own efforts. To rob a man of the chance to achieve, and to trade what he achieves with others, is to rob him of his spiritual dignity as a man. This is why communism has failed in our time. *All* coercion—all force to take from a man his own efforts to achieve—causes spiritual damage and weakens a society. Conscription, theft, fraud, violence, welfare, lack of legislative representation—*all* rob a man of his chance to choose, to achieve on his own, to trade the results of his achievement with others. Coercion is a cheat. It produces nothing new. Only freedom—the freedom to achieve, the freedom to trade freely the results of achievement—creates the environment proper to the dignity and spirituality of man."

Leisha applauded so hard her hands hurt. Going backstage with Daddy, she thought she could hardly breathe. Kenzo Yagai!

But backstage was more crowded than she had expected. There were cameras everywhere. Daddy said, "Mr. Yagai, may I present my daughter Leisha," and the cameras moved in close and fast—on *her*. A Japanese man whispered something in Kenzo Yagai's ear, and he looked more closely at Leisha. "Ah, yes."

"Look over here, Leisha," someone called, and she did. A robot camera zoomed so close to her face that Leisha stepped back, startled. Daddy spoke very sharply to someone, then to someone else. The cameras didn't move. A woman suddenly knelt in front of Leisha and thrust a microphone at her. "What does it feel like to never sleep, Leisha?"

"What?"

Someone laughed. The laugh was not kind. "Breeding geniuses . . ."

Leisha felt a hand on her shoulder. Kenzo Yagai gripped her very firmly, pulled her away from the cameras. Immediately, as if by magic, a line of Japanese men formed behind Yagai, parting only to let Daddy through. Behind the line, the three of them moved into a dressing room, and Kenzo Yagai shut the door.

"You must not let them bother you, Leisha," he said in his wonderful accent. "Not ever. There is an old Oriental proverb: 'The dogs bark but the caravan moves on.' You must never let your individual caravan be slowed by the barking of rude or envious dogs."

"I won't," Leisha breathed, not sure yet what the words really meant, knowing there was time later to sort them out, to talk about them with Daddy. For now she was dazzled by Kenzo Yagai, the actual man himself who was changing the world without force, without guns, with trading his special individual efforts. "We study your philosophy at my school, Mr. Yagai."

Kenzo Yagai looked at Daddy. Daddy said, "A private

school. But Leisha's sister also studies it, although cursorily, in the public system. Slowly, Kenzo, but it comes. It comes." Leisha noticed that he did not say why Alice was not here tonight with them.

Back home, Leisha sat in her room for hours, thinking over everything that had happened. When Alice came home from Julie's the next morning Leisha rushed toward her. But Alice seemed angry about something.

"Alice—what is it?"

"Don't you think I have enough to put up with at school already?" Alice shouted. "Everybody knows, but at least when you stayed quiet it didn't matter too much! They'd stopped teasing me! Why did you have to do it?"

"Do what?" Leisha said, bewildered.

Alice threw something at her: a hard-copy morning paper, on newsprint flimsier than the Camden system used. The paper dropped open at Leisha's feet. She stared at her own picture, three columns wide, with Kenzo Yagai. The headline said YAGAI AND THE FUTURE: ROOM FOR THE REST OF US? Y-ENERGY INVENTOR CONFERS WITH 'SLEEP-FREE' DAUGHTER OF MEGA-FINANCIER ROGER CAMDEN.

Alice kicked the paper. "It was on TV last night too—on *TV*. I work hard not to look stuck-up or creepy, and you go and do this? Now Julie probably won't even invite me to her slumber party next week!" She rushed up the broad curving stairs toward her room.

Leisha looked down at the paper. She heard Kenzo Yagai's voice in her head: "The dogs bark but the caravan moves on." She looked at the empty stairs. Aloud she said, "Alice—your hair looks really pretty curled like that."

4

"I want to meet the rest of them," Leisha said. "Why have you kept them from me this long?"

"I haven't kept them from you at all," Camden said. "Not offering is not the same as denial. Why shouldn't you be the one to do the asking? You're the one who now wants it."

Leisha looked at him. She was 15, in her last year at the Sauley School. "Why didn't you offer?"

"Why should I?"

"I don't know," Leisha said. "But you gave me everything else."

"Including the freedom to ask for what you want."

Leisha looked for the contradiction, and found it. "Most things that you provided for my education I didn't ask for, because I didn't know enough to ask and you, as the adult, did. But you've never offered the opportunity for me to meet any of the other sleepless mutants—"

"Don't use that word," Camden said sharply.

"—so you must either think it was not essential to my education or else you had another motive for not wanting to meet them."

"Wrong," Camden said. "There's a third possibility. That I think meeting them is essential to your education, that I do want you to, but this issue provided a chance to further the education of your self-initiative by waiting for *you* to ask."

"All right," Leisha said, a little defiantly; there seemed to be a lot of defiance between them lately, for no good reason. She squared her shoulders. Her new breasts thrust forward. "I'm asking. How many of the Sleepless are there, who are they, and where are they?"

Camden said, "If you're using that term—'the Sleepless'—you've already done some reading on your own. So you probably know that there are 1,082 of you so far in the United States, a few more in foreign countries, most of them in major metropolitan areas. Seventy-nine are in Chicago, most of them still small children. Only nineteen anywhere are older than you."

Leisha didn't deny reading any of this. Camden leaned forward in his study chair to peer at her. Leisha wondered if he needed glasses. His hair was completely gray now, sparse and stiff, like lonely broomstraws. The *Wall Street Journal* listed him among the hundred richest men in America; *Women's Wear Daily* pointed out that he was the only billionaire in the country who did not move in the society of international parties, charity balls, and personal jets. Camden's jet ferried him to business meetings around the world, to the chairmanship of the Yagai Economics Institute, and to very little else. Over the years he had grown richer, mor reclusive, and more cerebral. Leisha felt a rush of her old affection.

She threw herself sideways into a leather chair, her long slim legs dangling over the arm. Absently she scratched a mosquito bite on her thigh. "Well, then, I'd like to meet Richard Keller." He lived in Chicago and was the beta-test Sleepless closest to her own age. He was 17.

"Why ask me? Why not just go?"

Leisha thought there was a note of impatience in his voice. He liked her to explore things first, then report on them to him later. Both parts were important.

Leisha laughed. "You know what, Daddy? You're predictable."

Camden laughed, too. In the middle of the laugh Susan came in. "He certainly is not. Roger, what about that meeting in Buenos Aires Thursday? Is it on or off?" When he didn't answer, her voice grew shriller. "Roger? I'm talking to you!"

Leisha averted her eyes. Two years ago Susan had finally left genetic research to run Camden's house and schedule; before that she had tried hard to do both. Since she had left Biotech, it seemed to Leisha, Susan had changed. Her voice was tighter. She was more insistent that Cook and the gardener follow her directions exactly, without deviation. Her blonde braids had become stiff sculptured waves of platinum.

"It's on," Roger said.

"Well, thanks for at least answering. Am I going?"

"If you like."

"I like."

Susan left the room. Leisha rose and stretched. Her long legs rose on tiptoe. It felt good to reach, to stretch, to feel sunlight from the wide windows wash over her face. She smiled at her father, and found him watching her with an unexpected expression.

"Leisha—"

"What?"

"See Keller. But be careful."

"Of what?"

But Camden wouldn't answer.

The voice on the phone had been noncommittal. "Leisha Camden? Yes, I know who you are. Three o'clock on Thursday?" The house was modest, a thirty-year-old Colonial on a quiet suburban street where small children on bicycles could be watched from the front window. Few roofs had more than one Y-energy cell. The trees, huge old sugar maples, were beautiful.

"Come in," Richard Keller said.

He was no taller than she, stocky, with a bad case of acne. Probably no genetic alterations except sleep, Leisha guessed. He had thick dark hair, a low forehead, and bushy black brows. Before he closed the door Leisha saw him stare at her car and driver, parked in the driveway next to a rusty ten-speed bike.

"I can't drive yet," she said. "I'm still fifteen."

"It's easy to learn," Keller said. "So, you want to tell me why you're here?"

Leisha liked his directness. "To meet some other Sleepless."

"You mean you never have? Not any of us?"

"You mean the rest of you know each other?" She hadn't expected that.

"Come to my room, Leisha."

She followed him to the back of the house. No one else seemed to be home. His room was large and airy, filled with computers and filing cabinets. A rowing machine sat in one corner. It looked like shabbier version of the room of any bright classmate at the Sauley School, except there was more space without a bed. She walked over to the computer screen.

"Hey—you working on Boesc equations?"

"On an application of them."

"To what?"

"Fish migration patterns."

Leisha smiled. "Yeah—that would work. I never thought of that."

Keller seemed not to know what to do with her smile. He looked at the wall, then at her chin. "You interested in Gaea patterns? In the environment?"

"Well, no," Leisha confessed. "Not particularly. I'm going to study politics at Harvard. Pre-law. But of course we had Gaea patterns at school."

Keller's gaze finally came unstuck from her face. He ran a hand through his dark hair. "Sit down, if you want."

Leisha sat, looking appreciatively at the wall posters, shifting green on blue, like ocean currents. "I like those. Did you program them yourself?"

"You're not at all what I pictured," Keller said.

"How did you picture me?"

He didn't hesitate. "Stuck-up. Superior. Shallow, despite your IQ."

She was more hurt than she had expected to be.

Keller blurted, "You're the only one of the Sleepless who's really rich. But you already know that."

"No, I don't. I've never checked."

He took the chair beside her, stretching his stocky legs straight in front of him, in a slouch that had nothing to do with relaxation. "It makes sense, really. Rich people don't have their children genetically modified to be superior—they think any offspring of theirs is already superior. By their values. And poor people can't afford it. We Sleepless are upper-middle class, no more. Children of professors, scientists, people who value brains and time."

"My father values brains and time," Leisha said. "He's the biggest supporter of Kenzo Yagai."

"Oh, Leisha, do you think I don't already know that? Are you flashing me or what?"

Leisha said with great deliberateness, "I'm *talking* to you." But the next minute she could feel the hurt break through on her face.

"I'm sorry," Keller muttered. He shot off his chair and

paced to the computer, back. "I *am* sorry. But I don't . . . I don't understand what you're doing here."

"I'm lonely," Leisha said, astonished at herself. She looked up at him. "It's true. I'm lonely. I am. I have friends and Daddy and Alice—but no one really knows, really understands—what? I don't know what I'm saying."

Keller smiled. The smile changed his whole face, opened up its dark planes to the light. "I do. Oh, do I. What do you do when they say, 'I had such a dream last night!'?"

"Yes!" Leisha said. "But that's even really minor—it's when *I* say, 'I'll look that up for you tonight; and they get that funny look on their face that means 'She'll do it while I'm asleep.' "

"But that's even really minor," Keller said. "It's when you're playing basketball in the gym after supper and then you go to the diner for food and then you say 'Let's have a walk by the lake' and they say 'I'm really tired. I'm going home to bed now.' "

"But that's really minor," Leisha said, jumping up. "It's when you really are absorbed by the movie and then you get the point and it's so goddamn beautiful you leap up and say 'Yes! Yes!' and Susan says 'Leisha, really—you'd think nobody but you ever enjoyed anything before.' "

"Who's Susan?" Keller said.

The mood was broken. But not really; Leisha could say "My stepmother" without much discomfort over what Susan had promised to be and what she had become. Keller stood inches from her, smiling that joyous smile, understanding, and suddenly relief washed over Leisha so strong that she walked straight into him and put her arms around his neck, only tightening them when she felt his startled jerk. She started to sob—she, Leisha, who never cried.

"Hey," Richard said. "Hey."

"Brilliant," Leisha said, laughing. "Brilliant remark."

She could feel his embarrassed smile. "Wanta see my fish migration curves instead?"

"No," Leisha sobbed, and he went on holding her, patting her back awkwardly, telling her without words that she was home.

Camden waited up for her, although it was past midnight. He had been smoking heavily. Through the blue air he said quietly, "Did you have a good time, Leisha?"

"Yes."

"I'm glad," he said, and put out his last cigarette, and climbed the stairs—slowly, stiffly, he was nearly seventy now—to bed.

They went everywhere together for nearly a year: swimming, dancing, to the museums, the theater, the library. Richard introduced her to the others, a group of twelve kids between fourteen and nineteen, all of them intelligent and eager. All Sleepless.

Leisha learned.

Tony's parents, like her own, had divorced. But Tony, fourteen, lived with his mother, who had not particularly wanted a Sleepless child, while his father, who had, acquired a red hovercar and a young girlfriend who designed ergonomic chairs in Paris. Tony was not allowed to tell anyone—relatives, schoolmates—that he was Sleepless. "They'll think you're a freak," his mother said, eyes averted from her son's face. The one time Tony disobeyed her and told a friend that he never slept, his mother beat him. Then she moved the family to a new neighborhood. He was nine years old.

Jeanine, almost as long-legged and slim as Leisha, was training for the Olympics in ice skating. She practiced twelve hours a day, hours no Sleeper still in high school could ever have. So far the newspapers had not picked up the story. Jeanine was afraid that, if they did, they would somehow not let her compete.

Jack, like Leisha, would start college in September. Unlike Leisha, he had already started his career. The practice of law had to wait for law school; the practice of investment required only money. Jack didn't have much, but his precise financial analyses parlayed $600 saved from summer jobs to $3000 through stock-market investing, then to $10,000, and then he had enough to qualify for information-fund speculation. Jack was fifteen, not old enough to make legal investments; the transactions were all in the name of Kevin Baker, the oldest of the Sleepless, who lived in Austin. Jack told Leisha, "When I hit 84 percent profit over two consecutive quarters, the data analysts logged onto me. They were just sniffing. Well, that's their job, even when the overall amounts are actually small. It's the patterns they care about. If they take the trouble to cross-reference data banks and come up with the fact that Kevin is a Sleepless, will they try to stop us from investing somehow?"

"That's paranoid," Jeanine said. "Leisha, you don't *know*."

"You mean because I've been protected by my father's money and caring," Leisha said. No one grimaced; all of them confronted ideas openly, without shadowy allusions. Without dreams.

"Yes," Jeanine said. "Your father sounds terrific. And he raised you to think that achievement should not be fettered—Jesus Christ, he's a Yagaiist. Well, good. We're glad for you." She said it without sarcasm. Leisha nodded. "But the world isn't always like that. They hate us."

"That's too strong," Carol said. "Not hate."

"Well, maybe," Jeanine said. "But they're different from us. We're better and they naturally resent that."

"I don't see what's natural about it," Tony said. "Why shouldn't it be just as natural to admire what's better? We do. Does any one of us resent Kenzo Yagai for his genius? Or Nelson Wade, the physicist? Or Catherine Raduski?"

"We don't resent them because we *are* better," Richard said. "Q.E.D."

"What we should do is have our own society," Tony said. "Why should we allow their regulations to restrict our natural, honest achievements? Why should Jeanine be barred from skating against them and Jack from investing on their same terms just because we're Sleepless? Some of them are brighter than others of them. Some have greater persistence. Well, we have greater concentration, more biochemical stability, and more time. All men are not created equal."

"Be fair, Jack—no one has been barred from anything yet," Jeanine said.

"But we will be."

"Wait," Leisha said. She was deeply troubled by the conversation. "I mean, yes, in many ways we're better. But you quoted out of context, Tony. The Declaration of Independence doesn't say all men are created equal in ability. It's talking about rights and power—it means that all are created equal *under the law.* We have no more right to a separate society or to being free of society's restrictions than anyone else does. There's no other way to freely trade one's efforts, unless the same contractual rules apply to all."

"Spoken like a true Yagaiist," Richard said, squeezing her hand.

"That's enough intellectual discussion for me," Carol said, laughing. "We've been at this for hours. We're at the beach, for Chrissake. Who wants to swim with me?"

"I do," Jeanine said. "Come on, Jack."

All of them rose, brushing sand off their suits, discarding sunglasses. Richard pulled Leisha to her feet. But just before they ran into the water, Tony put his skinny hand on her arm. "One more question, Leisha. Just to think about. If we achieve better than most other people, and we trade with the Sleepers when it's mutually beneficial, making no distinction there between the strong and the weak—what obligation do we have to those so weak they don't have anything to trade with us? We're already going to give more than we get—do we have to do it when we get nothing at all? Do we have to take care of their deformed and handicapped and sick and lazy and shiftless with the products of our work?"

"Do the Sleepers have to?" Leisha countered.

"Kenzo Yagai would say no. He's a Sleeper."

"He would say they would receive the benefits of contractual trade even if they aren't direct parties to the contract. The whole world is better-fed and healthier because of Y-energy."

"Come on!" Jeanine yelled. "Leisha, they're dunking me! Jack, you stop that! Leisha, help me!"

Leisha laughed. Just before she grabbed for Jeanine, she caught the look on Richard's face, on Tony's: Richard frankly lustful, Tony angry. At her. But why? What had she done, except argue in favor of dignity and trade?

Then Jack threw water on her, and Carol pushed Jack into the warm spray, and Richard was there with his arms around her, laughing.

When she got the water out of her eyes, Tony was gone.

Midnight. "Okay," Carol said. "Who's first?"

The six teenagers in the brambled clearing looked at each other. A Y-lamp, kept on low for atmosphere, cast weird shadows across their faces and over their bare legs. Around the clearing Roger Camden's trees stood thick and dark, a wall between them and the closest of the estate's outbuildings. It was very hot. August air hung heavy, sullen. They had voted against bringing an air-conditioned Y-field because this was a return to the primitive, the dangerous; let it be primitive.

Six pairs of eyes stared at the glass in Carol's hand.

"Come *on*," she said. "Who wants to drink up?" Her voice was jaunty, theatrically hard. "It was difficult enough to get this."

"How *did* you get it?" said Richard, the group member—except for Tony—with the least influential family contacts, the least money. "In a drinkable form like that?"

"My cousin Brian is a pharmaceutical supplier to the Biotech Institute. He's curious." Nods around the circle; except for Leisha, they were Sleepless precisely because they had relatives somehow connected to Biotech. And everyone was curious. The glass held interleukin-1, an immune system booster, one of many substances which as a side effect induced the brain to swift and deep sleep.

Leisha stared at the glass. A warm feeling crept through her lower belly, not unlike the feeling when she and Richard made love.

Tony said, "Give it to me!"

Carol did. "Remember—you only need a little sip."

Tony raised the glass to his mouth, stopped, looked at them over the rim from his fierce eyes. He drank.

Carol took back the glass. They all watched Tony. Within a minute he lay on the rough ground; within two, his eyes closed in sleep.

It wasn't like seeing parents sleep, siblings, friends. It was Tony. They looked away, didn't meet each other's eyes. Leisha felt the warmth between her legs tug and tingle, faintly obscene.

When it was her turn, she drank slowly, then passed the glass to Jeanine. Her head turned heavy, as if it were being stuffed with damp rags. The trees at the edge of the clearing blurred. The portable lamp blurred, too—it wasn't bright and clean anymore but squishy, blobby; if she touched it, it would smear. Then darkness swooped over her brain, taking it away: *Taking away her mind.* "Daddy!" She tried to call, to clutch for him, but then the darkness obliterated her.

Afterward, they all had headaches. Dragging themselves back through the woods in the thin morning light was torture, compounded by an odd shame. They didn't touch each other. Leisha walked as far away from Richard as she could. It was a whole day before the throbbing left the base of her skull, or the nausea her stomach.

There had not even been any dreams.

"I want you to come with me tonight," Leisha said, for the tenth or twelfth time. "We both leave for college in just two days; this is the last chance. I really want you to meet Richard."

Alice lay on her stomach across her bed. Her hair, brown and lusterless, fell around her face. She wore an expensive yellow jumpsuit, silk by Ann Patterson, which rucked up in wrinkles around her knees.

"Why? What do you care if I meet Richard or not?"

"Because you're my sister," Leisha said. She knew better than to say "my twin." Nothing got Alice angry faster.

"I don't want to." The next moment Alice's face changed. "Oh, I'm sorry, Leisha—I didn't mean to sound so snotty. But . . . but I don't want to."

"It won't be all of them. Just Richard. And just for an hour or so. Then you can come back here and pack for Northwestern."

"I'm not going to Northwestern."

Leisha stared at her.

Alice said, "I'm pregnant."

Leisha sat on the bed. Alice rolled onto her back, brushed the hair out of her eyes, and laughed. Leisha's ears closed against the sound. "Look at you," Alice said. "You'd think it was *you* who was pregnant. But you never would be, would you, Leisha? Not until it as the proper time. Not you."

"How?" Leisha said. "We both had our caps put in . . ."

"I had the cap removed," Alice said.

"You wanted to get pregnant?"

"Damn flash I did. And there's not a thing Daddy can do about it. Except, of course, cut off all credit completely, but I don't think he'll do that, do you?" She laughed again. "Even to me?"

"But Alice . . . why? Not just to anger Daddy!"

"No," Alice said. "Although you would think of that, wouldn't you? Because I want something to love. Something of my *own*. Something that has nothing to do with this house."

Leisha thought of her and Alice running through the conservatory, years ago, her and Alice, darting in and out of the sunlight. "It hasn't been so bad growing up in this house."

"Leisha, you're stupid. I don't know how anyone so smart can be so stupid. Get out of my room! Get out!"

"But Alice . . . *a baby* . . ."

"Get out!" Alice shrieked. "Go to Harvard! Go be successful! Just get out!"

Leisha jerked off the bed. "Gladly! You're irrational, Alice! You don't think ahead, you don't plan a *baby* . . ." But she could never sustain anger. It dribbled away, leaving her mind empty. She looked at Alice, who suddenly put out her arms. Leisha went into them.

"You're the baby," Alice said wonderingly. "You *are*. You're so . . . I don't know what. You're a baby."

Leisha said nothing. Alice's arms felt warm, felt whole, felt like two children running in and out of sunlight. "I'll help you, Alice. If Daddy won't."

Alice abruptly pushed her away. "I don't need your help."

Alice stood. Leisha rubbed her empty arms, fingertips scraping across opposite elbows. Alice kicked the empty arms; fingertips scraping across opposite elbows. Alice kicked the empty, open trunk in which she was supposed to pack for Northwestern, and then abruptly smiled, a smile that made Leisha look away. She braced herself for more abuse. But what Alice said, very softly, was, "Have a good time at Harvard."

5

She loved it.

From the first sight of Massachusetts Hall, older than the United States by a half century, Leisha felt something that had been missing in Chicago: Age. Roots. Tradition. She touched the bricks of Widener Library, the glass cases in the Peabody Museum, as if they were the grail. She had never been particularly sensitive to myth or drama; the anguish of Juliet seemed to her artificial, that of Willy Loman merely wasteful. Only King Arthur, struggling to create a better social order, had interested her. But now, walking under the huge autumn trees, she suddenly caught a glimpse of a force that could span generations, fortunes left to endow learning and achievement the benefactors would never see, individual effort spanning and shaping centuries to come. She stopped, and looked at the sky through the leaves, at the buildings solid with purpose. At such moments she thought of Camden, bending the will of an entire genetic research Institute to create her in the image he wanted.

Within a month, she had forgotten all such mega-musings.

The work load was incredible, even for her. The Sauley School had encouraged individual exploration at her own pace; Harvard knew what it wanted from her, at its pace. In the last twenty years, under the academic leadership of a man who in his youth had watched Japanese economic domination with dismay, Harvard had become the controversial leader of a return to hard-edged learning of facts, theories, applications, problem-solving, intellectual efficiency. The school accepted one out of every two hundred applications from around the world. The daughter of England's Prime Minister had flunked out her first year and been sent home.

Leisha had a single room in a new dormitory, the dorm because she had spent so many years isolated in Chicago and was hungry for people, the single so she would not disturb anyone else when she worked all right. Her second day a boy from down the hall sauntered in and perched on the edge of her desk.

"So you're Leisha Camden."

"Yes."

"Sixteen years old."

"Almost seventeen."

"Going to out-perform us all, I understand, without even trying."

Leisha's smile faded. The boy stared at her from under lowered downy brows. He was smiling, his eyes sharp. From Richard and Tony and the others Leisha had learned to recognize the anger that presented itself as contempt.

"Yes," Leisha said coolly, "I am."

"Are you sure? With your pretty little-girl hair and your mutant little-girl brain?"

"Oh, leave her alone, Hannaway," said another voice. A tall blond boy, so thin his ribs looked like ripples in brown sand, stood in jeans and bare feet, drying his wet hair. "Don't you ever get tired of walking around being an asshole?"

"Do you?" Hannaway said. He heaved himself off the desk and started toward the door. The blond moved out of his way. Leisha moved into it.

"The reason I'm going to do better than you," she said evenly, "is because I have certain advantages you don't. Including sleeplessness. And then after I 'outperform' you, I'll be glad to help you study for your tests so that you can pass, too."

The blond, drying his ears, laughed. But Hannaway stood still, and into his eyes came an expression that made Leisha back away. He pushed past her and stormed out.

"Nice going, Camden," the blond said. "He deserved that."

"But I meant it," Leisha said. "I will help him study."

The blond lowered his towel and stared. "You did, didn't you? You meant it."

"Yes! Why does everybody keep questioning that?"

"Well," the boy said, "*I* don't. You can help me if I get into trouble." Suddenly he smiled. "But I won't."

"Why not?"

"Because I'm just as good at anything as you are, Leisha Camden."

She studied him. "You're not one of us. Not Sleepless."

"Don't have to be. I know what I can do. Do, be, create, trade."

She said, delighted. "You're a Yagaiist!"

"Of course." He held out his hand. "Stewart Sutter. How about a fishburger in the Yard?"

"Great," Leisha said. They walked out together, talking excitedly. When people stared at her, she tried not to notice. She was here. At Harvard. With space ahead of her, time to learn, and with people like Stewart Sutter who accepted and challenged her.

All the hours he was awake.

She became totally absorbed in her classwork. Roger Camden drove up once, walking the campus with her, listening, smiling. He was more at home than Leisha would have expected: He knew Stewart Sutter's father, Kate Addams' grandfather. They talked about Harvard, business, Harvard, the Yagai Economics Institute, Harvard. "How's Alice?" Leisha asked once, but Camden said that he didn't know, she had moved out and did not want to see him. He made her an allowance through his attorney. While he said this, his face remained serene.

Leisha went to the Homecoming Ball with Stewart, who was also majoring in pre-law but was two years ahead of Leisha. She took a weekend trip to Paris with Kate Addams and two other girlfriends, taking the Concorde III. She had a fight with Stewart over whether the metaphor of superconductivity could apply to Yagaiism, a stupid fight they both knew was stupid but had anyway, and afterward they became lovers. After the fumbling sexual explorations with Richard, Stewart was deft, experienced, smiling faintly as he taught her how to have an orgasm both by herself and with him. Leisha was dazzled. "It's so *joyful*," she said, and Stewart looked at her with tenderness she knew was part disturbance but didn't know why.

At mid-semester she had the highest grades in the freshman class. She got every answer right on every single question on her mid-terms. She and Stewart went out for a beer to celebrate, and when they came back Leisha's room had been destroyed. The computer was smashed, the data banks wiped, hardcopies and books smoldering in a metal wastebasket. Her clothes were ripped to pieces, her desk and bureau hacked apart. The only thing untouched, pristine, was the bed.

Stewart said, "There's no way this could have been done in silence. Everyone on the floor—hell, on the floor *below*—had to know. Someone will talk to the police." No one did. Leisha sat on the edge of the bed, dazed, and looked at the remnants of her Homecoming gown. The next day Dave Hannaway gave her a long, wide smile.

Camden flew east again, taut with rage. He rented her an apartment in Cambridge with E-lock security and a

bodyguard named Toshio. After he left, Leisha fired the
bodyguard but kept the apartment. It gave her and Stewart more privacy, which they used to endlessly discuss
the situation. It was Leisha who argued that it was an
aberration, an immaturity.

"There have always been haters, Stewart. Hate Jews,
hate Blacks, hate immigrants, hate Yagaiists who have
more initiative and dignity that you do. I'm just the latest
object of hatred. It's not new, it's not remarkable. It
doesn't mean any basic kind of schism between the
Sleepless and Sleepers."

Stewart sat up in bed and reached for the sandwiches
on the night stand. "Doesn't it? Leisha, you're a different
kind of person entirely. More evolutionarily fit, not only
to survive but to prevail. Those other 'objects of hatred'
you cite except Yagaiists—they were all powerless in
their societies. They occupied *inferior* positions. You, on
the other hand—all three Sleepless in Harvard Law are
on the *Law Review*. All of them. Kevin Baker, your oldest, has already founded a successful bio-interface software firm and is making money, a lot of it. Every
Sleepless is making superb grades, none have psychologi-
cal problems, all are healthy—and most of you aren't
even adults yet. How much hatred do you think you're
going to encounter once you hit the big-stakes world
of finance and business and scarce endowed chairs and
national politics?"

"Give me a sandwich," Leisha said. "Here's my evi-
dence you're wrong: You yourself. Kenzo Yagai. Kate
Addams. Professor Lane. My father. Every Sleeper who
inhabits the world of fair trade, mutually beneficial contracts. And that's most of you, or at least most of you
who are worth considering. You believe that competition
among the most capable leads to the most beneficial
trades for everyone, strong and weak. Sleepless are making real and concrete contributions to society, in a lot of
fields. That has to outweigh the discomfort we cause.
We're *valuable* to you. You know that."

Stewart brushed crumbs off the sheets. "Yes. I do.
Yagaiists do."

"Yagaiists run the business and financial and academic worlds. Or they will. In a meritocracy, they *should*. You underestimate the majority of people, Stew. Ethics aren't confined to the ones out front."

"I hope you're right," Stewart said. "Because, you know, I'm in love with you."

Leisha put down her sandwich.

"Joy," Stewart mumbled into her breasts, "you are joy."

When Leisha went home for thanksgiving, she told Richard about Stewart. He listened tight-lipped.

"A Sleeper."

"A *person*," Leisha said. "A good, intelligent, achieving person!"

"Do you know what your good intelligent achieving Sleepers have done, Leisha? Jeanine has been barred from Olympic skating. 'Genetic alteration, analogous to steroid abuse to create an unsportsmanlike advantage.' Chris Devereaux's left Stanford. They trashed his laboratory, destroyed two years' work in memory formation proteins. Kevin Baker's software company is fighting a nasty advertising campaign, all underground of course, about kids using software designed by 'non-human minds.' Corruption, mental slavery, satanic influences: the whole bag of witch-hunt tricks. Wake up, Leisha!"

They both heard his words. Moments dragged by. Richard stood, like a boxer, forward on the balls of his feet, teeth clenched. Finally he said, very quietly, "Do you love him?"

"Yes," Leisha said. "I'm sorry."

"Your choice," Richard said coldly. "What do you do while he's asleep? Watch?"

"You make it sound like a perversion!"

Richard said nothing. Leisha drew a deep breath. She spoke rapidly but calmly, a controlled rush: "While Stewart is asleep I work. The same as you do. Richard—don't do this. I didn't mean to hurt you. And I don't want to lose the group. I believe the Sleepers are the same species as we are—are you going to punish me for that? Are you going to *add* to the hatred? Are you going

to tell me that I can't belong to a wider world that includes all honest, worthwhile people whether they sleep
or not? Are you going to tell me that the most important
division is by genetics and not by economic spirituality?
Are you going to force me into an artificial choice, 'us'
or 'them'?"

Richard picked up a bracelet. Leisha recognized it: She
had given it to him in the summer. His voice was quiet.
"No. It's not a choice." He played with the gold links a
minute, then looked up at her. "Not yet."

By spring break, Camden walked more slowly. He
took medicine for his blood pressure, his heart. He and
Susan, he told Leisha, were getting a divorce. "She
changed, Leisha, after I married her. You saw that. She
was independent and productive and happy, and then
after a few years she stopped all that and became a
shrew. A whining shrew." He shook his head in genuine
bewilderment. "You saw the change."

Leisha had. A memory came to her: Susan leading
her and Alice in "games" that were actually controlled
cerebral-performance tests, Susan's braids dancing around
her sparkling eyes. Alice had loved Susan, then, as much
as Leisha had.

"Dad, I want Alice's address."

"I told you up at Harvard, I don't have it," Camden
said. He shifted in his chair, the impatient gesture of a
body that never expected to wear out. In January Kenzo
Yagai had died of pancreatic cancer; Camden had taken
the news hard. "I make her allowance through an attorney. By her choice."

"Then I want the address of the attorney."

The attorney, however, refused to tell Leisha where
Alice was. "She doesn't want to be found, Ms. Camden.
She wanted a complete break."

"Not from me," Leisha said.

"Yes," the attorney said, and something flickered behind his eyes, something she had last seen in Dave Hannaway's face.

She flew to Austin before returning to Boston, making

her a day late for classes. Kevin Baker saw her instantly, canceling a meeting with IBM. She told him what she needed, and he set his best data-net people on it, without telling them why. Within two hours she had Alice's address from the attorneys' electronic files. It was the first time, she realized, that she had ever turned to one of the Sleepless for help, and it had been given instantly. Without trade.

Alice was in Pennsylvania. The next weekend Leisha rented a hovercar and driver—she had learned to drive, but only groundcars as yet—and went to High Ridge, in the Appalachian Mountains.

It was an isolated hamlet, twenty-five miles from the nearest hospital. Alice lived with a man named Ed, a silent carpenter twenty years older than she, in a cabin in the woods. The cabin had water and electricity but no news net. In the early spring light the earth was raw and bare, slashed with icy gullies. Alice and Ed apparently worked at nothing. Alice was eight months pregnant.

"I didn't want you here," she said to Leisha. "So why are you?"

"Because you're my sister."

"God, look at you. Is that what they're wearing at Harvard? Boots like that? When did you become fashionable, Leisha? You were always too busy being intellectual to care."

"What's this all about, Alice? Why here? What are you doing?"

"Living," Alice said. "Away from dear Daddy, away from Chicago, away from drunken broken Susan—did you know she drinks? Just like Mom. He does that to people. But not to me. I got out. I wonder if you ever will."

"Got out? To *this*?"

"I'm happy," Alice said angrily. "Isn't that what it's supposed to be about? Isn't that the aim of your great Kenzo Yagai—happiness through individual effort?"

Leisha thought of saying that Alice was making no efforts that she could see. She didn't say it. A chicken ran through the yard of the cabin. Behind, the mountains rose in layers of blue haze. Leisha thought what this place must have been like in winter: cut off from the world where people strived towards goals, learned, changed.

"I'm glad you're happy, Alice."

"Are you?"

"Yes."

"Then I'm glad, too," Alice said, almost defiantly. The next moment she abruptly hugged Leisha, fiercely, the huge hard mound of her belly crushed between them. Alice's hair smelled sweet, like fresh grass in sunlight.

"I'll come see you again, Alice."

"Don't," Alice said.

6

SLEEPLESS MUTIE BEGS FOR REVERSAL OF GENE TAMPERING, screamed the headline in the Food Mart. "PLEASE LET ME SLEEP LIKE REAL PEOPLE!" CHILD PLEADS.

Leisha typed in her credit number and pressed the news kiosk for a print-out, although ordinarily she ignored the electronic tabloids. The headline went on circling the kiosk. A Food Mart employee stopped stacking boxes on shelves and watched her. Bruce, Leisha's bodyguard, watched the employee.

She was twenty-two, in her final year at Harvard Law, editor of the *Law Review,* ranked first in her class. The next three were Jonathan Cocchiara, Len Carter, and Martha Wentz. All Sleepless.

In her apartment she skimmed the print-out. Then she accessed the Groupnet run from Austin. The files had more news stories about the child, with comments from other Sleepless, but before she could call them up Kevin Baker came on-line himself, on voice.

"Leisha. I'm glad you called. I was going to call you."

"What's the situation with this Stella Bevington, Kev? Has anybody checked it out?"

"Randy Davies. He's from Chicago but I don't think

you've met him, he's still in high school. He's in Park Ridge, Stella's in Skokie. Her parents wouldn't talk to him—were pretty abusive, in fact—but he got to see Stella face-to-face anyway. It doesn't look like an abuse case, just the usual stupidity: parents wanted a genius child, scrimped and saved, and now they can't handle that she *is* one. They scream at her to sleep, get emotionally abusive when she contradicts them, but so far no violence."

"Is the emotional abuse actionable?"

"I don't think we want to move on it yet. Two of us will keep in close touch with Stella—she does have a modem, and she hasn't told her parents about the net— and Randy will drive out weekly."

Leisha bit her lip. "A tabloid shitpiece said she's seven years old."

"Yes."

"Maybe she shouldn't be left there. I'm an Illinois resident, I can file an abuse grievance from here if Candy's got too much in her briefcase . . ." *Seven years old.*

"No. Let it sit a while. Stella will probably be all right. You know that."

She did. Nearly all of the Sleepless stayed "all right," no matter how much opposition came from the stupid segment of society. And it was only the stupid segment, Leisha argued—a small if vocal minority. Most people could, and would, adjust to the growing presence of the Sleepless, when it became clear that that presence included not only growing power but growing benefits to the country as a whole.

Kevin Baker, now twenty-six, had made a fortune in micro-chips so revolutionary that Artificial Intelligence, once a debated dream, was yearly closer to reality. Carolyn Rizzolo had won the Pulitzer Prize in drama for her play *Morning Light*. She was twenty-four. Jeremy Robinson had done significant work in superconductivity applications while still a graduate student at Stanford. William Thaine, *Law Review* editor when Leisha first came to Harvard, was now in private practice. He had never lost a case. He was twenty-six, and the cases were becoming important. His clients valued his ability more than his age.

But not everyone reacted that way.

Kevin Baker and Richard Keller had started the datanet that bound the Sleepers into a tight group, constantly aware of each other's personal fights. Leisha Camden financed the legal battles, the educational costs of Sleepless whose parents were unable to meet them, the support of children in emotionally bad situations. Rhonda Lavelier got herself licensed as a foster mother in California, and whenever possible the Group maneuvered to have small Sleepless who were removed from their homes assigned to Rhonda. The Group now had three ABA lawyers; within the next year they would gain four more, licensed to practice in five different states.

The one time they had not been able to remove an abused Sleepless child legally, they kidnapped him.

Timmy DeMarzo, four years old. Leisha had been opposed to the action. She had argued the case morally and pragmatically—to her they were the same thing—thus: If they believed in their society, in its fundamental laws and in their ability to belong to it as free-trading productive individuals, they must remain bound by the society's contractual laws. The Sleepless were, for the most part, Yagaiists. They should already know this. And if the FBI caught them, the courts and press would crucify them.

They were not caught.

Timmy DeMarzo—not even old enough to call for help on the datanet, they had learned of the situation through the automatic police-record scan Kevin maintained through his company—was stolen from his own backyard in Wichita. He had lived the last year in an isolated trailer in North Dakota; no place was too isolated for a modem. He was cared for by a legally irreproachable foster mother who had lived there all her life. The foster mother was second cousin to a Sleepless, a broad cheerful woman with a much better brain than her appearance indicated. She was a Yagaiist. No record of the child's existence appeared in any data bank: not the IRS, not any school's, not even the local grocery store's computerized check-out slips. Food specifically for the child was shipped in monthly on a truck owned by a Sleepless in State College, Pennsylvania. Ten of the Group knew about the kidnapping, out of the total 3,428 born in the United States. Of that total, 2,691 were part of the Group via the net. Another 701 were as yet too young to use a modem. Only 36 Sleepless, for whatever reason, were not part of the Group.

The kidnapping had been arranged by Tony Indivino.

"It's Tony I wanted to talk to you about," Kevin said to Leisha. "He's started again. This time he means it. He's buying land."

She folded the tabloid very small and laid it carefully on the table. "Where?"

"Allegheny Mountains. In southern New York State. A lot of land. He's putting in the roads now. In the spring, the first buildings."

"Jennifer Sharifi still financing it?" She was the American-born daughter of an Arab prince who had wanted a Sleepless child. The prince was dead and Jennifer, dark-eyed and multilingual, was richer than Leisha would one day be.

"Yes. He's starting to get a following, Leisha."

"I know."

"Call him."

"I will. Keep me informed about Stella."

She worked until midnight at the *Law Review,* then until four A.M. preparing her classes. From four to five she handled legal matters for the Group. At five A.M. she called Tony, still in Chicago. He had finished high school, done one semester at Northwestern, and at Christmas vacation he had finally exploded at his mother for forcing him to live as a Sleeper. The explosion, its seemed to Leisha, had never ended.

"Tony? Leisha."

"The answer is yes, yes, no, and go to hell."

Leisha gritted her teeth. "Fine. Now tell me the questions."

"Are you really serious about the Sleepless withdrawing into their own self-sufficient society? Is Jennifer Sharifi willing to finance a project the size of building a small city? Don't you think that's a cheat of all that can be accomplished by patient integration of the Group into the mainstream? And what about the contradictions of living in an armed restricted city and still trading with the Outside?"

"I would never tell *you* to go to hell."

"Hooray for you," Tony said. After a moment he added, "I'm sorry. That sounds like one of *them*."

"It's wrong for us, Tony."

"Thanks for not saying I couldn't pull it off."

She wondered if he could. "We're not a separate species, Tony."

"Tell that to the Sleepers."

"You exaggerate. There are haters out there, there are *always* haters, but to give up . . ."

"We're not giving up. Whatever we create can be fiercely traded: software, hardware, novels, information, theories, legal counsel. We can travel in and out. But we'll have a safe place to return *to*. Without the leeches who think we owe them blood because we're better than they are."

"It isn't a matter of owing."

"Really?" Tony said. "Let's have this out, Leisha. All the way. You're a Yagaiist—what do you believe in?"

"Tony . . ."

"Do it," Tony said, and in his voice she heard the fourteen-year-old Richard had introduced her to. Simultaneously, she saw her father's face: not as he was now, since the by-pass, but as he had been when she was a little girl, holding her on his lap to explain that she was special.

"I believe in voluntary trade that is mutually beneficial. That spiritual dignity comes from supporting one's life through one's own efforts, and trading the results of those efforts in mutual cooperation throughout the society. That the symbol of this is the contract. And that we need each other for the fullest, most beneficial trade."

"Fine," Tony bit off. "Now what about the beggars in Spain?"

"The what?"

"You walk down a street in a poor country like Spain and you see a beggar. Do you give him a dollar?"

"Probably."

"Why? He's trading nothing with you. He has nothing to trade."

"I know. Out of kindness. Compassion."

"You see six beggars. Do you give them all a dollar?"

"Probably," Leisha said.

"You would. You see a hundred beggars and you haven't got Leisha Camden's money—do you give them each a dollar?"

"No."

"Why not?"

Leisha reached for patience. Few people could make her want to cut off a comm link; Tony was one of them. "Too draining on my own resources. My life has first claim on the resources I earn."

"All right. Now consider this. At Biotech Institute—where you and I began, dear pseudo-sister—Dr. Melling has just yesterday—"

"Who?"

"Dr. Susan Melling. Oh, God, I completely forgot—she used to be married to your father!"

"I lost track of her," Leisha said. "I didn't realize she'd gone back to research. Alice once said . . . never mind. What's going on at Biotech?"

"Two crucial items, just released. Carla Dutcher has had first-month fetal genetic analysis. Sleeplessness is a dominant gene. The next generation of the Group won't sleep either."

"We all knew that," Leisha said. Carla Dutcher was the world's first pregnant Sleepless. Her husband was a Sleeper. "The whole world expected that."

"But the press will have a windfall with it anyway. Just watch. Muties Breed! New Race Set To Dominate Next Generation of Children!"

Leisha didn't deny it. "And the second item?"

"It's sad, Leisha. We've just had our first death."

Her stomach tightened. "Who?"

"Bernie Kuhn. Seattle." She didn't know him. "A car accident. It looks pretty straightforward—he lost control on a steep curve when his brakes failed. He had only been driving a few months. He was seventeen. But the significance here is that his parents have donated his brain and body to Biotech, in conjunction with the pathology department at the Chicago Medical School. They're going to take him apart to get the first good look at what prolonged sleeplessness does to the body and brain."

"They should," Lesiah said. "That poor kid. But what are you so afraid they'll find?"

"I don't know. I'm not a doctor. But whatever it is, if the haters can use it against us, they will."

"You're paranoid, Tony."

"Impossible. The Sleepless have personalities calmer and more reality-oriented than the norm. Don't you read the literature?"

"Tony—"

"What if you walk down that street in Spain and a hundred beggars each want a dollar and you say no and they have nothing to trade you but they're so rotten with anger about what you have that they knock you down and grab it and then beat you out of sheer envy and despair?"

Leisha didn't answer.

"Are you going to say that's not a human scenario, Leisha? That it never happens?"

"It happens," Leisha said evenly. "but not all that often."

"Bullshit. Read more history. Read more *newspapers*. But the point is: What do you owe the beggars then? What does a good Yagaiist who believes in mutually beneficial contracts do with people who have nothing to trade and can only take?"

"You're not—"

"*What*, Leisha? In the most objective terms you can

manage, what do we owe the grasping and non-productive needy?"

"What I said originally. Kindness. Compassion."

"Even if they don't trade it back? Why?"

"Because . . ." She stopped.

"Why? Why do law-abiding and productive human beings owe anything to those who neither produce very much nor abide by laws? What philosophical or economic or spiritual justification is there for owing them anything? Be as honest as I know you are."

Leisha put her head between her knees. The question gaped beneath her, but she didn't try to evade it. "I don't know. I just know we do."

"Why?"

She didn't answer. After a moment, Tony did. The intellectual challenge was gone from his voice. He said, almost tenderly, "Come down in the spring and see the site for Sanctuary. The buildings will be going up then."

"No," Leisha said.

"I'd like you to."

"No. Armed retreat is not the way."

Tony said, "The beggars are getting nastier, Leisha. As the Sleepless grow richer. And I don't mean in money."

"Tony—" she said, and stopped. She couldn't think what to say.

"Don't walk down too many streets armed with just the memory of Kenzo Yagai."

In March, a bitterly cold March of winds whipping down the Charles River, Richard Keller came to Cambridge. Leisha had not seen him for four years. He didn't send her word on the Groupnet that he was coming. She hurried up the walk to her townhouse, muffled to the eyes in a red wool scarf against the snowy cold, and he stood there blocking the doorway. Behind Leisha, her bodyguard tensed.

"Richard! Bruce, it's all right, this is an old friend.

"Hello, Leisha."

He was heavier, sturdier-looking, with a breadth of shoulder she didn't recognize. But the face was Richard's, older but unchanged: dark brown brows, unruly dark hair. He had grown a beard.

"You look beautiful," he said.

She handed him a cup of coffee. "Are you here on business?" From the Groupnet she knew that he had finished his Master's and had done outstanding work in marine biology in the Caribbean, but had left that a year ago and disappeared from the net.

"No. Pleasure." He smiled suddenly, the old smile that opened up his dark face. "I almost forgot about that for a long time. Contentment, yes, we're all good at the contentment that comes from sustained work, but pleasure? Whim? Caprice? When was the last time you did something silly, Leisha?"

She smiled. "I ate cotton candy in the shower."

"Really? Why?"

"To see if it would dissolve in gooey pink patterns."

"Did it?"

"Yes. Lovely ones."

"And that was your last silly thing? When was it?"

"Last summer," Leisha said, and laughed.

"Well, mine is sooner than that. It's now. I'm in Boston for no other reason than the spontaneous pleasure of seeing you."

Leisha stopped laughing. "That's an intense tone for a spontaneous pleasure, Richard."

"Yup," he said, intensely. She laughed again. He didn't.

"I've been in India, Leisha. And China and Africa. Thinking, mostly. Watching. First I traveled like a Sleeper, attracting no attention. Then I set out to meet the Sleepless in India and China. There are a few, you know, whose parents were willing to come here for the operation. They pretty much are accepted and left alone. I tried to figure out why desperately poor countries— by our standards anyway, over there Y-energy is mostly available only in big cities—don't have any trouble accepting the superiority of Sleepless, whereas Americans, with more prosperity than any time in history, build in resentment more and more."

Leisha said, "Did you figure it out?"

"No. But I figured out something else, watching all those communes and villages and kidnappings. We are too individualistic."

Disappointment swept Leisha. She saw her father's face: *Excellence is what counts, Leisha. Excellence supported by individual effort. . . .* She reached for Richard's cup. "More coffee?"

He caught her wrist and looked up into her face. "Don't misunderstand me, Leisha. I'm not talking about work. We are too much individuals in the rest of our lives. Too emotionally rational. Too much alone. Isolation kills more than the free flow of ideas. It kills joy."

He didn't let go of her wrist. She looked down into his eyes, into depths she hadn't seen before: It was the feeling of looking into a mine shaft, both giddy and frightening, knowing that at the bottom might be gold or darkness. Or both.

Richard said softly, "Stewart?"

"Over long ago. An undergraduate thing." Her voice didn't sound like her own.

"Kevin?"

"No, never—we're just friends."

"I wasn't sure. Anyone?"

"No."

He let go of her wrist. Leisha peered at him timidly. He suddenly laughed. "Joy, Leisha." An echo sounded in her mind, but she couldn't place it and then it was gone and she laughed too, a laugh airy and frothy as pink cotton candy in summer.

"Come home, Leisha. He's had another heart attack."

Susan Melling's voice on the phone was tired. Leisha said, "How bad?"

"The doctors aren't sure. Or say they're not sure. He wants to see you. Can you leave your studies?"

It was May, the last push toward her finals. The *Law Review* proofs were behind schedule. Richard had started a new business, marine consulting to Boston fishermen plagued with sudden inexplicable shifts in ocean currents, and was working twenty hours a day. "I'll come," Leisha said.

Chicago was colder than Boston. The trees were half-budded. On Lake Michigan, filling the huge east windows of her father's house, whitecaps tossed up cold spray. Leisha saw that Susan was living in the house: her brushes on Camden's dresser, her journals on the credenza in the foyer.

"Leisha," Camden said. He looked old. Gray skin, sunken cheeks, the fretful and bewildered look of men who accepted potency like air, indivisible from their lives. In the corner of the room, on a small eighteenth-century slipper chair, sat a short, stocky woman with brown braids.

"Alice."

"Hello, Leisha."

"Alice. I've looked for you. . . ." The wrong thing to say. Leisha had looked, but not very hard, deferred by the knowledge that Alice had not wanted to be found. "How are you?"

"I'm fine," Alice said. She seemed remote, gentle, unlike the angry Alice of six years ago in the raw Pennsylvania hills. Camden moved painfully on the bed. He looked at Leisha with eyes which, she saw, were undimmed in their blue brightness.

"I asked Alice to come. And Susan. Susan came a while ago. I'm dying, Leisha."

No one contradicted him. Leisha, knowing his respect for facts, remained silent. Love hurt her chest.

"John Jaworski has my will. None of you can break it. But I wanted to tell you myself what's in it. The last few years I've been selling, liquidating. Most of my holdings are accessible now. I've left a tenth to Alice, a tenth to Susan, a tenth to Elizabeth, and the rest to you, Leisha, because you're the only one with the individual ability to use the money to its full potential for achievement."

Leisha looked wildly at Alice, who gazed back with her strange remote calm. "Elizabeth? My . . . mother? Is alive?"

"Yes," Camden said.

"You told me she was dead! Years and years ago!"

"Yes. I thought it was better for you that way. She didn't like what you were, was jealous of what you could become. And she had nothing to give you. She would only have caused you emotional harm."

Beggars in Spain . . .

"That was wrong, Dad. You were *wrong*. She's my *mother . . .*" She couldn't finish the sentence.

Camden didn't flinch. "I don't think I was. But you're an adult now. You can see her if you wish."

He went on looking at her from his bright, sunken eyes, while around Leisha the air heaved and snapped. Her father had lied to her. Susan watched her closely, a small smile on her lips. Was she glad to see Camden fall in his daughter's estimation? Had she all along been that jealous of their relationship, of Leisha . . .

She was thinking like Tony.

The thought steadied her a little. But she went on staring at Camden, who went on staring implacably back, unbudged, a man positive even on his death bed that he was right.

Alice's hand was on her elbow, Alice's voice so soft that no one but Leisha could hear. "He's gone now, Leisha. And after a while you'll be all right."

Alice had left her son in California with her husband of two years, Beck Watrous, a building contractor she had met while waitressing in a resort on the Artificial Islands. Beck had adopted Jordan, Alice's son.

"Before Beck there was a real bad time," Alice said in her remote voice. "You know, when I was carrying Jordan I actually used to dream that, and every morning I'd wake up and have morning sickness with a baby that was only going to be a stupid nothing like me. I stayed with Ed—in Pennsylvania, remember? You came to see me there once—for two more years. When he beat me, I was glad. I wished Daddy could see. At least Ed was touching me."

Leisha made a sound in her throat.

"I finally left because I was afraid for Jordan. I went to California, did nothing but eat for a year. I got up to 190 pounds." Alice was, Leisha estimated, five-foot-four. "Then I came home to see Mother."

"You didn't tell me," Leisha said. "You knew she was alive and you didn't tell me."

"She's in a drying-out tank half the time," Alice said, with brutal simplicity. "She wouldn't see you if you wanted to. But she saw me, and she fell slobbering all over me as her 'real' daughter, and she threw up on my dress. And I backed away from her and looked at the dress and knew it *should* be thrown up on, it was so ugly. Deliberately ugly. She started streaming how Dad had ruined her life, ruined mine, all for *you*. And do you know what I did?"

"What?" Leisha said. Her voice was shaky.

"I flew home, burned all my clothes, got a job, started college, lost fifty pounds, and put Jordan in play therapy."

The sisters sat silent. Beyond the window the lake was dark, unlit by moon or stars. It was Leisha who suddenly shook, and Alice who patted her shoulder.

"Tell me . . ." Leisha couldn't think what she wanted to be told, except that she wanted to hear Alice's voice in the gloom, Alice's voice as it was now, gentle and remote, without damage any more from the damaging fact of Leisha's existence. Her very existence as damage. ". . . tell me about Jordan. He's five now? What's he like?"

Alice turned her head to look levelly into Leisha's eyes. "He's a happy, ordinary little boy. Completely ordinary."

Camden died a week later. After the funeral, Leisha tried to see her mother at the Brookfield Drug and Alcohol Abuse Center. Elizabeth Camden, she was told, saw no one except her only child, Alice Camden Watrous.

Susan Melling, dressed in black, drove Leisha to the airport. Susan talked deftly, determinedly, about Leisha's studies, about Harvard, about the *Review*. Leisha answered in monosyllables but Susan persisted, asking questions, quietly insisting on answers: When would Leisha take her bar exams? Where was she interviewing for jobs? Gradually Leisha began to lose the numbness she had felt since her father's casket was lowered into the ground. She realized that Susan's persistent questioning was a kindness.

"He sacrificed a lot of people," Leisha said suddenly.

"Not me," Susan said. She pulled the car into the airport parking lot. "Only for a while there, when I gave up my work to do this. Roger didn't respect sacrifice much."

"Was he wrong?" Leisha said. The question came out with a kind of desperation she hadn't intended.

Susan smiled sadly. "No. He wasn't wrong. I should never have left my research. It took me a long time to come back to myself after that."

He does that to people, Leisha heard inside her head. Susan? Or Alice? She couldn't, for once, remember clearly. She saw her father in the old conservatory, potting and repotting the dramatic exotic flowers he had loved.

She was tired. It was muscle fatigue from stress, she knew; twenty minutes of rest would restore her. Her eyes burned from unaccustomed tears. She leaned her head back against the car seat and closed them.

Susan pulled the car into the airport parking lot and turned off the ignition. "There's something I want to tell you, Leisha."

Leisha opened her eyes. "About the will?"

Susan smiled tightly. "No. You really don't have any problems with how he divided the estate, do you? It seems to you reasonable. But that's not it. The research team from Biotech and Chicago Medical has finished its analysis of Bernie Kuhn's brain."

Leisha turned to face Susan. She was startled by the complexity of Susan's expression. Determination, and satisfaction, and anger, and something else Leisha could not name.

Susan said, "We're going to publish next week, in the *New England Journal of Medicine.* Security has been un-

believably restricted—no leaks to the popular press. But
I want to tell you now, myself, what we found. So you'll
be prepared."

"Go on," Leisha said. Her chest felt tight.

"Do you remember when you and other Sleepless kids
took interleukin-1 to see what sleep was like? When you
were sixteen?"

"How did you know about that?"

"You kids were watched a lot more closely than you
think. Remember the headache you got?"

"Yes." She and Richard and Tony and Carol and
Jeanine . . . after her rejection by the Olympic Committee, Jeanine had never skated again. She was a kinder-
garten teacher in Butte, Montana.

"Interleukin-1 is what I want to talk about. At least
partly. It's one of a whole group of substances that boost
the immune system. They stimulate the production of
antibodies, the activity of white blood cells, and a host
of other immunoenhancements. Normal people have
surges of IL-1 released during the slow-wave phases of
sleep. That means that they—we—are getting boosts to
the immune system during sleep. One of the questions
we researchers asked ourselves twenty-eight years ago
was: Will Sleepless kids who don't get those surges of
IL-1 get sick more often?"

"I've never been sick," Leisha said.

"Yes, you have. Chicken pox and three minor colds
by the end of your fourth year," Susan said precisely.
"But in general you were all a very healthy lot. So we
researchers were left with the alternate theory of sleep-
driven immunoenhancement: That the burst of immune
activity existed as a counterpart to a greater vulnerability
of the body in sleep to disease, probably in some way
connected to the fluctuations in body temperature during
REM sleep. In other words, sleep *caused* the immune
vulnerability that endogenous pyrogens like IL-1 coun-
teract. Sleep was the problem, immune system enhance-
ments were the solution. Without sleep, there would be
no problem. Are you following this?"

"Yes."

"Of course you are. Stupid question." Susan brushed her hair off her face. It was going gray at the temples. There was a tiny brown age spot beneath her right ear.

"Over the years we collected thousands—maybe hundreds of thousands—of Single Photon Emission Tomography scans of you and the other kids' brains, plus endless EEG's, samples of cerebrospinal fluid, and all the rest of it. But we couldn't really see inside your brains, really know what's going on in there. Until Bernie Kuhn hit that embankment."

"Susan," Leisha said, "give it to me straight. Without more build-up."

"You're not going to age."

"What?"

"Oh, cosmetically, yes. Gray hair, wrinkles, sags. But the absence of sleep peptides and all the rest of it affects the immune and tissue-restoration systems in ways we don't understand. Bernie Kuhn had a perfect liver. Perfect lungs, perfect heart, perfect lymph nodes, perfect pancreas, perfect medulla oblongata. Not just healthy, or young—*perfect*. There's a tissue regeneration enhancement that clearly derives from the operation of the immune system but is radically different from anything we ever suspected. Organs show no wear and tear—not even the minimal amount expected in a seventeen-year-old. They just repair themselves, perfectly, on and on . . . and on.

"For how long?" Leisha whispered.

"Who the hell knows? Bernie Kuhn was young—maybe there's some compensatory mechanism that cuts in at some point and you'll all just collapse, like an entire fucking gallery of Dorian Grays. But I don't think so. Neither do I think it can go on forever; no tissue regeneration can do that. But a long, long time."

Leisha stared at the blurred reflections in the car windshield. She saw her father's face against the blue satin of his casket, banked with white roses. His heart, unregenerated, had given out.

Susan said, "The future is all speculative at this point. We know that the peptide structures that build up the pressure to sleep in normal people resemble the components of bacterial cell walls. Maybe there's a connection between sleep and pathogen receptivity. We don't know. But ignorance never stopped the tabloids. I wanted to prepare you because you're going to get called supermen, *homo perfectus,* who-all-knows what. Immortal."

The two women sat in silence. Finally Leisha said, "I'm going to tell the others. On our datanet. Don't worry about the security. Kevin Baker designed Groupnet; nobody knows anything we don't want them to."

"You're that well organized already?"

"Yes."

Susan's mouth worked. She looked away from Leisha. "We better go in. You'll miss your flight."

"Susan . . ."

"What?"

"Thank you."

"You're welcome," Susan said, and in her voice Leisha heard the thing she had seen before in Susan's expression and not been able to name: It was longing.

Tissue regeneration. A long, long time, sang the blood in Leisha's ears on the flight to Boston. *Tissue regeneration.* And, eventually: *Immortal.* No, not that, she told herself severely. Not that. The blood didn't listen.

"You sure smile a lot," said the man next to her in first class, a business traveler who had not recognized Leisha. "You coming from a big party in Chicago?"

"No. From a funeral."

The man looked shocked, then disgusted. Leisha looked out the window at the ground far below. Rivers like micro-circuits, fields like neat index cards. And on the horizon, fluffy white clouds like masses of exotic flowers, blooms in a conservatory filled with light.

The letter was no thicker than any hard-copy mail, but hard-copy mail addressed by hand to either of them was so rare that Richard was nervous. "It might be explosive," Leisha looked at the letter on their hall credenza. MS. LIESHA CAMDEN. Block letters, misspelled.

"It looks like a child's writing," she said.

Richard stood with head lowered, legs braced apart. But his expression was only weary. "Perhaps deliberately like a child's. You'd be more open to a child's writing, they might have figured."

" 'They'? Richard, are we getting that paranoid?"

He didn't flinch from the question. "Yes. For the time being."

A week earlier the *New England Journal of Medicine* had published Susan's careful, sober article. An hour later the broadcast and datanet news had exploded in speculation, drama, outrage, and fear. Leisha and Richard, along with all the Sleepless on the Groupnet, had tracked and charted each of four components, looking for a dominant reaction: speculation ("The Sleepless may live for centuries, and this might lead to the following events . . ."); drama ("If a Sleepless marries only Sleepers, he may have lifetime enough for a dozen brides—and several dozen children, a bewildering blended family . . ."); outrage ("Tampering with the law of nature has only brought among us unnatural so-called people who will live with the unfair advantage of time: time to accumulate more kin, more power, more property than the rest of us could ever know. . . ."); and fear ("How soon before the Super-race takes over?")

"They're all fear, of one kind or another," Carolyn Rizzolo finally said, and the Groupnet stopped their differentiated tracking.

Leisha was taking the final exams of her last year of law school. Each day comments followed her to the campus, along the corridors and in the classroom; each day she forgot them in the grueling exam sessions, all students reduced to the same status of petitioner to the great university. Afterward, temporarily drained, she walked silently back home to Richard and the Groupnet, aware of the looks of people on the street, aware of her bodyguard Bruce striding between her and them.

"It will calm down," Leisha said. Richard didn't answer.

The town of Salt Springs, Texas, passed a local ordinance that no Sleepless could obtain a liquor license, on the grounds that civil rights statutes were built on the "all men were created equal" clause of the Constitution, and Sleepless clearly were not covered. There were no Sleepless within a hundred miles of Salt Springs and no one had applied for a new liquor license there for the past ten years, but the story was picked up by United Press and by Datanet News, and within twenty-four hours heated editorials appeared, on both sides of the issue, across the nation.

More local ordinances appeared. In Pollux, Pennsylvania, the Sleepless could be denied apartment rental on the grounds that their prolonged wakefulness would increase both wear-and-tear on the landlord's property and utility bills. In Cranston Estates, California, Sleepless were barred from operating twenty-four-hour businesses: "unfair competition." Iroquois County, New York, barred them from serving on county juries, arguing that a jury containing Sleepless, with their skewed idea of time, did not constitute "a jury of one's peers."

"All those statues will be thrown out in superior courts," Leisha said. "But God! The waste of money and docket time to do it!" A part of her mind noticed that her tone as she said this was Roger Camden's.

The state of Georgia, in which some sex acts between consenting adults were still a crime, made sex between a Sleepless and a Sleeper a third-degree felony, classing it with bestiality.

Kevin Baker had designed software that scanned the newsnets at high speed, flaggered all stories involving discrimination or attacks on Sleepless, and categorized them by type. The files were available on Groupnet. Leisha read through them, then called Kevin. "Can't you create a parallel program to flag defenses of us? We're getting a skewed picture."

"You're right," Kevin said, a little startled. "I didn't think of it."

"Think of it," Leisha said, grimly. Richard, watching her, said nothing.

She was most upset by the stories about Sleepless children. Shunning at school, verbal abuse by siblings, attacks by neighborhood bullies, confused resentment from parents who had wanted an exceptional child but had not bargained on one who might live centuries. The school board of Cold River, Iowa, voted to bar Sleepless children from conventional classrooms because their rapid learning "created feelings of inadequacy in others, interfering with their education." The board made funds available for Sleepless to have tutors at home. There were no volunteers among the teaching staff. Leisha started spending as much time on Groupnet with the kids, talking to them all night long, as she did studying for her bar exams, scheduled for July.

Stella Bevington stopped using her modem.

Kevin's second program catalogued editorials urging fairness towards Sleepless. The school board of Denver set aside funds for a program in which gifted children, including the Sleepless, could use their talents and build teamwork through tutoring even younger children. Rive Beau, Louisiana, elected Sleepless Danielle du Cherney to the City Council, although Danielle was twenty-two and technically too young to qualify. The prestigious medical research firm of Halley-Hall gave much publicity to their hiring of Christopher Amren, a Sleepless with a Ph.D in cellular physics.

Dora Clarq, a Sleepless in Dallas, opened a letter addressed to her and a plastic explosive blew off her arm.

Leisha and Richard stared at the envelope on the hall credenza. The paper was thick, cream-colored, but not expensive: the kind of paper made of bulky newsprint dyed the shade of vellum. There was no return address. Richard called Liz Bishop, a Sleepless who was majoring in Criminal Justice in Michigan. He had never spoken with her before—neither had Leisha—but she came on Groupnet immediately and told them how to open it, or she could fly up and do it if they preferred. Richard and Leisha followed her directions for remote detonation in the basement of the townhouse. Nothing blew up. When the letter was open, they took it out and read it:

Dear Ms. Camden,

You been pretty good to me and I'm sorry to do this but I quit. They are making it pretty hot for me at the union not officially but you know how it is. If I was you I wouldn't go to the union for another bodyguard I'd try to find one privately. But be careful. Again I'm sorry but I have to live too.

Bruce

"I don't know whether to laugh or cry," Leisha said. "The two of us getting all this equipment, spending hours on this set-up so an explosive won't detonate . . ."

"It's not as if I at least had a whole lot else to do," Richard said. Since the wave of anti-Sleepless sentiment, all but two of his marine-consultant clients, vulnerable to the marketplace and thus to public opinion, had canceled their accounts.

Groupnet, still up on Leisha's terminal, shrilled in emergency override. Leisha got there first. It was Tony.

"Leisha. I'll need your legal help, if you'll give it. They're trying to fight me on Sanctuary. Please fly down here."

Sanctuary was raw brown gashes in the late-spring earth. It was situated in the Allegheny Mountains of southern New York State, old hills rounded by age and covered with pine and hickory. A superb road led from the closest town, Belmont, to Sanctuary. Low, maintenance-free buildings, whose design was plain but graceful, stood in various states of completion. Jennifer Sharifi, looking strained, met Leisha and Richard. "Tony wants to talk to you, but first he asked me to show you both around."

"What's wrong?" Leisha asked quietly. She had never met Jennifer before but no Sleepless looked like that—pinched, spent, *weary*—unless the stress level was enormous.

Jennifer didn't try to evade the question. "Later. First look at Sanctuary. Tony respects your opinion enormously, Leisha; he wants you to see everything."

The dormitories each held fifty, with communal rooms for cooking, dining, relaxing, and bathing, and a warren of separate offices and studios and labs for work. "We're calling them 'dorms' anyway, despite the etymology," Jennifer said, trying to smile. Leisha glanced at Richard. The smile was a failure.

She was impressed, despite herself, with the completeness of Tony's plans for lives that would be both communal and intensely private. There was a gym, a small hospital—"By the end of the next year, we'll have eighteen AMA-certified doctors, you know, and four are thinking of coming here"—a daycare facility, a school, an intensive-crop farm. "Most of our food will come in from the outside, of course. So will most people's jobs, although they'll do as much of them as possible from here, over datanets. We're not cutting ourselves off from the world—only creating a safe place from which to trade with it." Leisha didn't answer.

Apart from the power facilities, self-supported Y-energy, she was most impressed with the human planning. Tony had Sleepless interested from virtually every field they would need both to care for themselves and to deal with the outside world. "Lawyers and accountants come first," Jennifer said. "That's our first line of defense in safeguarding ourselves. Tony recognizes that most modern battles for power are fought in the courtroom and boardroom."

But not all. Last, Jennifer showed them the plans for physical defense. She explained them with a mixture of defiance and pride: Every effort had been made to stop attackers without hurting them. Electronic surveillance completely circled the 150 square miles Jennifer had purchased—some *counties* were smaller than that, Leisha thought, dazed. When breached, a force field a half-mile within the E-gate activated, delivering electric shocks to anyone on foot—"But only on the *outside* of the field. We don't want any of our kids hurt." Unmanned penetration by vehicles or robots was identified by a system that located all moving metal above a certain mass within Sanctuary. Any moving metal that did not carry a special signaling device designed by Donna Pospula, a Sleepless who had patented important electronic components, was suspect.

"Of course, we're not set up for an air attack or an outright army assault," Jennifer said. "But we don't expect that. Only the haters in self-motivated hate." Her voice sagged.

Leisha touched the hard-copy of the security plans with one finger. They troubled her. "If we can't integrate ourselves into the world . . . free trade should imply free movement."

"Yeah. Well," Jennifer said, such an uncharacteristic Sleepless remark—both cynical and inarticulate—that Leisha looked up. "I have something to tell you, Leisha."

"What?"

"Tony isn't here."

"Where is he?"

"In Allegheny County jail. It's true we're having zoning battles about Sanctuary—zoning! In this isolated spot! But this is something else, something that just happened this morning. Tony's been arrested for the kidnapping of Timmy DeMarzo."

The room wavered. "FBI?"

"Yes."

"How . . . how did they find out?"

"Some agent eventually cracked the case. They didn't tell us how. Tony needs a lawyer, Leisha. Dana Monteiro has already agreed, but Tony wants you."

"Jennifer—I don't even take the bar exams until July!"

"He says he'll wait. Dana will act as his lawyer in the meantime. Will you pass the bar?"

"Of course. But I already have a job lined up with Morehouse, Kennedy, & Anderson in New York—" She stopped. Richard was looking at her hard, Jennifer gazing down at the floor. Leisha said quietly, "What will he plead?"

"Guilty," Jennifer said, "with—what is it called legally? Extenuating circumstances."

Leisha nodded. She had been afraid Tony would want to plead not guilty: more lies, subterfuge, ugly politics. Her mind ran swiftly over extenuating circumstances, precedents, tests to precedents. . . . They could use *Clements v. Voy* . . .

"Dana is at the jail now," Jennifer said. "Will you drive in with me?"

"Yes."

In Belmont, the county seat, they were not allowed to see Tony. Dana Monteiro, as his attorney, could go in and out freely. Leisha, not officially an attorney at all, could go nowhere. This was told them by a man in the D.A.'s office whose face stayed immobile while he spoke to them, and who spat on the ground behind their shoes when they turned to leave, even though this left him with a smear of spittle on his courthouse floor.

Richard and Leisha drove their rental car to the airport for the flight back to Boston. On the way Richard told Leisha he was leaving her. He was moving to Sanctuary, now, even before it was functional, to help with the planning and building.

She stayed most of the time in her townhouse, studying ferociously for the bar exams or checking on the Sleepless children through Groupnet. She had not hired another bodyguard to replace Bruce, which made her reluctant to go outside very much; the reluctance in turn made her angry with herself. Once or twice a day she scanned Kevin's electronic news clippings.

There were signs of hope. The *New York Times* ran

an editorial, widely reprinted on the electronic news
services:

PROSPERITY AND HATRED:
A LOGIC CURVE WE'D RATHER NOT SEE

The United States has never been a country that
much values calm, logic, rationality. We have, as a
people, tended to label these things "cold." We have,
as a people, tended to admire feeling and action: We
exalt in our stories and our memorials, not the cre-
ation of the Constitution but its defense at Iwo Jima;
not the intellectual achievements of a Stephen Hawking
but the heroic passion of a Charles Lindbergh; not
the inventors of the monorails and computers that
unite us but the composers of the angry songs of re-
bellion that divide us.

A peculiar aspect of this phenomenon is that it
grows stronger in times of prosperity. The better off
our citizenry, the greater their contempt for the calm
reasoning that got them there, and the more passionate their indulgence in emotion. Consider, in the last
century, the gaudy excesses of the Roaring Twenties
and the anti-establishment contempt of the sixties.
Consider, in our own century, the unprecedented
prosperity brought about by Y-energy—and then consider that Kenzo Yagai, except to his followers, was
seen as a greedy and bloodless logician, while our
national adulation goes to neo-nihilist writer Stephen
Castelli, to "feelie" actress Brenda Foss, and to dare-
devil gravity-well diver Jim Morse Luter.

But most of all, as you ponder this phenomenon in
your Y-energy houses, consider the current out-
pouring of irrational feeling directed at the "Sleepless" since the publication of the joint findings of the
Biotech Institute and the Chicago Medical School
concerning Sleepless tissue regeneration.

Most of the Sleepless are intelligent. Most of them
are calm, if you define that much-maligned word to
mean directing one's energies into solving problems

rather than to emoting about them. (Even Pulitzer Prize winner Carolyn Rizzolo gave us a stunning play of ideas, not of passions run amuck.) All of them show a natural bent toward achievement, a bent given a decided boost by the one-third more time in their days to achieve in. Their achievements lie, for the most part, in logical fields rather than emotional ones: Computers. Law. Finance. Physics. Medical research. They are rational, orderly, calm, intelligent, cheerful, young, and possibly very long-lived.

And, in our United States of unprecedented prosperity, increasingly hated.

Does the hatred that we have seen flower so fully over the last few months really grow, as many claim, from the "unfair advantage" the Sleepless have over the rest of us in securing jobs, promotions, money, success? Is it really envy over the Sleepless' good fortune? Or does it come from something more pernicious, rooted in our tradition of shoot-from-the-hip American action: Hatred of the logical, the calm, the considered? Hatred in fact of the superior mind?

If so, perhaps we should think deeply about the founders of this country: Jefferson, Washington, Paine, Adams—inhabitants of the Age of Reason, all. These men created our orderly and balanced system of laws precisely to protect the property and achievements created by the individual efforts of balanced and rational minds. The Sleepless may be our severest internal test yet of our own sober belief in law and order. No, the Sleepless were *not* "created equal," but our attitudes toward them should be examined with a care equal to our soberest jurisprudence. We may not like what we learn about our own motives, but our credibility as a people may depend on the rationality and intelligence of the examination.

Both have been in short supply in the public reaction to last month's research findings.

Law is not theater. Before we write laws reflecting

gaudy and dramatic feelings, we must be very sure
we understand the difference.

Leisha hugged herself, gazing in delight at the screen,
smiling. She called *The New York Times*: Who had written the editorial? The receptionist, cordial when she answered the phone, grew brusque. The *Times* was not
releasing that information, "prior to internal investigation."

It could not dampen her mood. She whirled around
the apartment, after days of sitting at her desk or screen.
Delight demanded physical action. She washed dishes,
picked up books. There were gaps in the furniture patterns where Richard had taken pieces that belonged to
him; a little quieter now, she moved the furniture to close
the gaps.

Susan Melling called to tell her about the *Times* editorial; they talked warmly for a few minutes. When Susan
hung up, the phone rang again.

"Leisha? Your voice still sounds the same. This is
Stewart Sutter."

"Stewart." She had not seen him for years. Their ro-
mance had lasted two years and then dissolved, not
from any painful issue so much as from the press of
both their studies. Standing by the comm terminal,
hearing his voice, Leisha suddenly felt again his hands
on her breasts in the cramped dormitory bed: All those
years before she had found a good use for a bed. The
phantom hands became Richard's hands, and a sudden
pain pierced her.

"Listen," Stewart said. "I'm calling because there's
some information I think you should know. You take
your bar exams next week, right? And then you have a
tentative job with Morehouse, Kennedy, & Anderson."

"How do you know all that, Stewart?"

"Men's room gossip. Well, not as bad as that. But the
New York legal community—that part of it, anyway—is
smaller than you think. And, you're a pretty visible
figure."

"Yes," Leisha said neutrally.

"Nobody has the slightest doubt you'll be called to the bar. But there is some doubt about the job with Morehouse, Kennedy. You've got two senior partners. Alan Morehouse and Seth Brown, who have changed their minds since this . . . flap. 'Adverse publicity for the firm,' 'turning law into a circus,' blah blah blah. You know the drill. But you've also got two powerful champions, Ann Carlyle and Michael Kennedy, the old man himself. He's quite a mind. Anyway, I wanted you to know all this so you can recognize exactly what the situation is and know whom to count on in the in-fighting."

"Thank you," Leisha said. "Stew . . . why do you care if I get it or not? Why should it matter to you?"

There was a silence on the other end of the phone. Then Stewart said, very low, "We're not all noodleheads out here, Leisha. Justice does still matter to some of us. So does achievement."

Light rose in her, a bubble of buoyant light.

Stewart said, "You have a lot of support here for that stupid zoning fight over Sanctuary, too. You might not realize that, but you do. What the Parks Commission crowd is trying to pull is . . . but they're just being used as fronts. You know that. Anyway, when it gets as far as the courts, you'll have all the help you need."

"Sanctuary isn't my doing. At all."

"No? Well, I meant the plural you."

"Thank you. I mean that. How are you doing?"

"Fine. I'm a daddy now."

"Really! Boy or girl?"

"Girl. A beautiful little bitch, drives me crazy. I'd like you to meet my wife sometime, Leisha."

"I'd like that," Leisha said.

She spent the rest of the night studying for her bar exams. The bubble stayed with her. She recognized exactly what it was: joy.

It was going to be all right. The contract, unwritten, between her and her society—Kenzo Yagai's society, Roger Camden's society—would hold. With dissent and strife and yes, some hatred: She suddenly thought of Tony's beggars in Spain, furious at the strong because they themselves were not. Yes. But it would hold.

She believed that.

She did.

7

Leisha took her bar exams in July. They did not seem hard to her. Afterward three classmates, two men and a woman, made a fakely casual point of talking to Leisha until she had climbed safely into a taxi whose driver obviously did not recognize her, or stop signs. The three were all Sleepers. A pair of undergraduates, clean-shaven blond men with the long faces and pointless arrogance of rich stupidity, eyed Leisha and sneered. Leisha's female classmate sneered back.

Leisha had a flight to Chicago the next morning. Alice was gong to join her there. They had to clean out the big house on the lake, dispose of Roger's personal property, put the house on the market. Leisha had had no time to do it earlier.

She remembered her father in the conservatory, wearing an ancient flat-topped hat he had picked up somewhere, potting orchids and jasmine and passion flowers.

When the doorbell rang she was startled; she almost never had visitors. Eagerly, she turned on the outside camera—maybe it was Jonathan or Martha, back in Boston to surprise her, to celebrate—why hadn't she thought before about some sort of celebration?

Richard stood gazing up at the camera. He had been crying.

She tore open the door. Richard made no move to come in. Leisha saw that what the camera had registered as grief was actually something else: tears of rage.

"Tony's dead."

Leisha put out her hand, blindly. Richard did not take it.

"They killed him in prison. Not the authorities—the

other prisoners. In the recreation yard. Murderers, rapists, looters, scum of the earth—and they thought they had the right to kill *him* because he was different."

Now Richard did grab her arm, so hard that something, some bone, shifted beneath the flesh and pressed on a nerve. "Not just different—*better*. Because he was better, because we all are, we goddamn just don't stand up and shout it out of some misplaced feeling for *their* feelings . . . God!"

Leisha pulled her arm free and rubbed it, numb, staring at Richard's contorted face.

"They beat him to death with a lead pipe. No one even knows how they got a lead pipe. They beat him on the back of the head and they rolled him over and—"

"Don't!" Leisha said. It came out a whimper.

Richard looked at her. Despite his shouting, his violent grip on her arm, Leisha had the confused impression that this was the first time he had actually seen her. She went on rubbing her arm, staring at him in terror.

He said quietly, "I've come to take you to Sanctuary, Leisha. Dan Walcott and Vernon Bulriss are in the car outside. The three of us will carry you out, if necessary. But you're coming. You see that, don't you? You're not safe here, with your high profile and your spectacular looks—you're a natural target if anyone is. Do we have to force you? Or do you finally see for yourself that we have no choice—the bastards have left us no choice—except Sanctuary?"

Leisha closed her eyes. Tony, at fourteen, at the beach. Tony, his eyes ferocious and alight, the first to reach out his hand for the glass of interleukin-1. Beggars in Spain.

"I'll come."

She had never known such anger. It scared her, coming in bouts throughout the long night, receding but always returning again. Richard held her in his arms, sitting with their backs against the wall of her library, and his holding made no difference at all. In the living room Dan and Vernon talked in low voices.

Sometimes the anger erupted in shouting, and Leisha

heard herself and thought *I don't know you.* Sometimes it became crying, sometimes talking about Tony, about all of them. Not the shouting nor the crying nor the talking eased her at all.

Planning did, a little. In a cold dry voice she didn't recognize, Leisha told Richard about the trip to close the house in Chicago. She had to go; Alice was already there. If Richard and Dan and Vernon put Leisha on the plane, and Alice met her at the other end with union bodyguards, she should be safe enough. Then she would change her return ticket from Boston to Belmont and drive with Richard to Sanctuary.

"People are already arriving," Richard said. "Jennifer Sharifi is organizing it, greasing the Sleeper suppliers with so much money they can't resist. What about this townhouse here, Leisha? Your furniture and terminal and clothes?"

Leisha looked around her familiar office. Law books lined the walls, red and green and brown, although most of the same information was on-line. A coffee cup rested on a print-out on the desk. Beside it was the receipt she had requested from the taxi driver this afternoon, a giddy souvenir of the day she had passed her bar exams; she had thought of having it framed. Above the desk was a holographic portrait of Kenzo Yagai.

"Let it rot," Leisha said.

Richard's arm tightened around her.

"I've never seen you like this," Alice said, subdued. "It's more than just clearing out the house, isn't it?"

"Let's get on with it," Leisha said. She yanked a suit from her father's closet. "Do you want any of this stuff for your husband?"

"It wouldn't fit."

"The hats?"

"No," Alice said. "Leisha—what is it?"

"Let's just *do* it!" She yanked all the clothes from Camden's closet, piled them on the floor, scrawled FOR VOLUNTEER AGENCY on a piece of paper and dropped it on top of the pile. Silently, Alice started adding clothes from the dresser, which already bore a taped paper scrawled ESTATE AUCTION.

The curtains were already down throughout the house; Alice had done that yesterday. She had also rolled up the rugs. Sunset glared redly on the bare wooden floors.

"What about your old room?" Leisha said. "What do you want there?"

"I've already tagged it," Alice said. "A mover will come Thursday."

"Fine. What else?"

"The conservatory. Sanderson has been watering everything, but he didn't really know what needed how much, so some of the plants are—"

"Fire Sanderson," Leisha said curtly. "The exotics can die. Or have them sent to a hospital, if you'd rather. Just watch out for the ones that are poisonous. Come on, let's do the library."

Alice sat slowly on a rolled-up rug in the middle of Camden's bedroom. She had cut her hair; Leisha thought it looked ugly, jagged brown spikes around her broad face. She had also gained more weight. She was starting to look like their mother.

Alice said, "Do you remember the night I told you I was pregnant? Just before you left for Harvard?"

"Let's do the library!"

"Do you?" Alice said. "For God's sake, can't you just once listen to someone else, Leisha? Do you have to be so much like Daddy every single minute?"

"I'm not like Daddy!"

"The hell you're not. You're exactly what he made you. But that's not the point. Do you remember that night?"

Leisha walked over the rug and out the door. Alice simply sat. After a minute Leisha walked back in. "I remember."

"You were near tears," Alice said implacably. Her voice was quiet. "I don't even remember exactly why. Maybe because I wasn't going to college afer all. But I put my arms around you, and for the first time in years— years, Leisha—I felt you really were my sister. Despite all of it—the roaming the halls all night and the show-off arguments with Daddy and the special school and the artificially long legs and golden hair—all that crap. You seemed to need me to hold you. You seemed to need me. You seemed to *need*."

"What are you saying?" Leisha demanded. "That you can only be close to someone if they're in trouble, and need you? That you can only be a sister if I was in some kind of pain, open sores running? Is that the bond between you Sleepers? 'Protect me while I'm unconscious, I'm just as crippled as you are'?"

"No," Alice said. "I'm saying that *you* could be a sister only if you were in some kind of pain."

Leisha stared at her. "You're stupid, Alice."

Alice said calmly, "I know that. Compared to you, I am. I know that."

Leisha jerked her head angrily. She felt ashamed of what she had just said, and yet it was true, and they both knew it was true, and anger still lay in her like a dark void, formless and hot. It was the formless part that was the worst. Without shape, there could be no action; without action, the anger went on burning her, choking her.

Alice said, "When I was twelve, Susan gave me a dress for our birthday. You were away somewhere, on one of those overnight field trips your fancy progressive school did all the time. The dress was silk, pale blue, with antique lace—very beautiful. I was thrilled, not only because it was beautiful but because Susan had gotten it for me and gotten software for you. The dress was mine. Was, I thought, *me*." In the gathering gloom Leisha could barely make out her broad, plain features. "The first time I wore it a boy said, 'Stole your sister's dress, Alice? Snitched it while she was *sleeping*?' Then he laughed like crazy, the way they always did.

"I threw the dress away. I didn't even explain to Susan, although I think she would have understood. Whatever was yours was yours, and whatever wasn't yours was yours, too. That's the way Daddy set it up. The way he hard-wired it into our genes."

"You, too?" Leisha said. "You're no different from the other envious beggars?"

Alice stood up from the rug. She did it slowly, leisurely, brushing dust off the back of her wrinkled skirt, smoothing the print fabric. Then she walked over and hit Leisha in the mouth.

"Now do you see me as real?" Alice asked quietly.

Leisha put her hand to her mouth. She felt blood. The phone rang, Camden's unlisted personal line. Alice walked over, picked it up, listened, and held it calmly out to Leisha. "It's for you."

Numb, Leisha took it.

"Leisha? This is Kevin. Listen, something's happened. Stella Bevington called me, on the phone not Groupnet, I think her parents took away her modem. I picked up the phone and she screamed, 'This is Stella! They're hitting me he's drunk—' and then the line went dead. Randy's gone to Sanctuary—hell, they've *all* gone. You're closest to her, she's still in Skokie. You better get there fast. Have you got bodyguards you trust?"

"Yes," Leisha said, although she hadn't. The anger—finally—took form. "I can handle it."

"I don't know how you'll get her out of there," Kevin said. "They'll recognize you, they know she called somebody, they might even have knocked her out . . ."

"I'll handle it," Leisha said.

"Handle what?" Alice said.

Leisha faced her. Even though she knew she shouldn't, she said, "What your people do. To one of ours. A seven-year-old kid who's getting beaten up by her parents because she's Sleepless—because she's *better* than you are—" She ran down the stairs and out to the rental car she had driven from the airport.

Alice ran right down with her. "Not your car, Leisha. They can trace a rental car just like that. My car."

Leisha screamed, "If you think you're—"

Alice yanked open the door of her battered Toyota, a model so old the Y-energy cones weren't even concealed but hung like drooping jowls on either side. She shoved Leisha into the passenger seat, slammed the door, and rammed herself behind the wheel. Her hands were steady. "Where?"

Blackness swooped over Leisha. She put her head down, as far between her knees as the cramped Toyota would allow. Two—no, three—days since she had eaten. Since the night before the bar exams. The faintness receded, swept over her again as soon as she raised her head.

She told Alice the address in Skokie.

"Stay way in the back," Alice said. "And there's a scarf in the glove compartment—put it on. Low, to hide as much of your face as possible."

Alice had stopped the car along Highway 42. Leisha said, "This isn't—"

"It's a union quick-guard place. We have to look like we have some protection, Leisha. We don't need to tell him anything, I'll hurry."

She was out in three minutes with a huge man in a cheap dark suit. He squeezed into the front seat beside Alice and said nothing at all. Alice did not introduce him.

The house was small, a little shabby, with lights on downstairs, none upstairs. The first stars shone in the north, away from Chicago. Alice said to the guard, "Get out of the car and stand here by the car door—no, more in the light—and don't do anything unless I'm attacked in some way." The man nodded. Alice started up the walk. Leisha scrambled out of the back seat and caught her sister two-thirds of the way to the plastic front door.

"Alice, what the hell are you doing? *I* have to—"

"Keep your voice down," Alice said, glancing at the guard. "Leisha, *think*. You'll be recognized. Here, near Chicago, with a Sleepless daughter—these people have looked at your picture in magazines for years. They've watched long-range holovids of you. They know you. They know you're going to be a lawyer. Me they've never seen. I'm nobody."

"Alice—"

"For Chrissake, get back in the car!" Alice hissed, and pounded on the front door.

Leisha drew off the walk, into the shadow of a willow tree. A man opened the door. His face was completely blank.

Alice said, "Child Protection Agency. We got a call from a little girl, this number. Let me in."

"There's no little girl here."

"This is an emergency, priority one," Alice said. "Child Protection Act 186. Let me in!"

The man, still blank-faced, glanced at the huge figure by the car. "You got a search warrant?"

"I don't need one in a priority-one child emergency. If you don't let me in, you're going to have legal snarls like you never bargained for."

Leisha clamped her lips together. No one would believe that, it was legal gobbledygook. . . . Her lip throbbed where Alice had hit her.

The man stood aside to let Alice enter.

The guard started forward. Leisha hesitated, then let him. He entered with Alice.

Leisha waited, alone, in the dark.

In three minutes they were out, the guard carrying a child. Alice's broad face gleamed pale in the porch light. Leisha sprang forward, opened the car door, and helped the guard ease the child inside. The guard was frowning, a slow puzzled frown shot with wariness.

Alice said, "Here. This is an extra hundred dollars. To get back to the city by yourself."

"Hey . . ." the guard said, but he took the money. He stood looking after them as Alice pulled away.

"He'll go straight to the police," Leisha said despairingly. "He has to, or risk his union membership."

"I know," Alice said. "But by that time we'll be out of the car."

"Where?"

"At the hospital," Alice said.

"Alice, we can't—" Leisha didn't finish. She turned to the back seat. "Stella? Are you conscious?"

"Yes," said the small voice.

Leisha groped until her fingers found the rear-seat illuminator. Stella lay stretched out on the back seat, her face distorted with pain. She cradled her left arm in her right. A single bruise colored her face, above the left eye.

"You're Leisha Camden," the child said, and started to cry.

"Her arm's broken," Alice said.

"Honey, can you . . ." Leisha's throat felt thick, she had trouble getting the words out ". . . can you hold on till we get you a doctor?"

"Yes," Stella said. "Just don't take me back there!"

"We won't," Leisha said. "Ever." She glanced at Alice and saw Tony's face.

Alice said, "There's a community hospital about ten miles south of here."

"How do you know that?"

"I was there once. Drug overdose," Alice said briefly. She drove hunched over the wheel, with the face of someone thinking furiously. Leisha thought, too, trying to see a way around the legal charge of kidnapping. They probably couldn't say the child came willingly: Stella would undoubtedly cooperate but at her age and in her condition she was probably *non sui juris,* her word would have no legal weight . . .

"Alice, we can't even get her into the hospital without insurance information. Verifiable on-line."

"Listen," Alice said, not to Leisha but over her shoulder, toward the back seat, "here's what we're going to do, Stella. I'm going to tell them you're my daughter and you fell off a big rock you were climbing while we stopped for a snack at a roadside picnic area. We're driving from California to Philadelphia to see your grandmother. Your name is Jordan Watrous and you're five years old. Got that, honey?"

"I'm seven," Stella said. "Almost eight."

"You're a very large five. Your birthday is March 23. Can you do this, Stella?"

"Yes," the little girl said. Her voice was stronger.

Leisha stared at Alice. "Can *you* do this?"

"Of course I can," Alice said. "I'm Roger Camden's daughter."

Alice half-carried, half-supported Stella into the Emergency Room of the small community hospital. Leisha watched from the car: the short stocky woman, the child's thin body with the twisted arm. Then she drove Alice's car to the farthest corner of the parking lot, under the dubious cover of a skimpy maple, and locked it. She tied the scarf more securely around her face.

Alice's license plate number, and her name, would be in every police and rental-car databank by now. The medical banks were slower; often they uploaded from local precincts only once a day, resenting the governmental interference in what was still, despite a half-century of battle, a private-sector enterprise. Alice and Stella would probably be all right in the hospital. Probably. But Alice could not rent another car.

Leisha could.

But the data file that would flash to rental agencies on Alice Camden Watrous might or might not include that she was Leisha Camden's twin.

Leisha looked at the rows of cars in the lot. A flashy luxury Chrysler, an Ikeda van, a row of middle-class Toyotas and Mercedes, a vintage '99 Cadillac—she could imagine the owner's face if that were missing—ten or twelve cheap runabouts, a hovercar with the uniformed driver asleep at the wheel. And a battered farm truck.

Leisha walked over to the truck. A man sat at the wheel, smoking. She thought of her father.

"Hello," Leisha said.

The man rolled down his window but didn't answer. He had greasy brown hair.

"See that hovercar over there?" Leisha said. She made her voice sound young, high. The man glanced at it indifferently; from this angle you couldn't see that the driver was asleep. "That's my bodyguard. He thinks I'm in the hospital, the way my father told me to, getting this lip looked at." She could feel her mouth swollen from Alice's blow.

"So?"

Leisha stamped her foot. "So I don't want to be inside. He's a shit and so's Daddy. I want *out*. I'll give you 4,000 bank credits for your truck. Cash."

The man's eyes widened. He tossed away his cigarette, looked again at the hovercar. The driver's shoulders were broad, and the car was within easy screaming distance.

"All nice and legal," Leisha said, and tried to smirk. Her knees felt watery.

"Let me see the cash."

Leish backed away from the truck, to where he could not reach her. She took the money from her arm clip. She was used to carrying a lot of cash; there had always been Bruce, or someone like Bruce. There had always been safety.

"Get out of the truck on the other side," Leisha said, "and lock the door behind you. Leave the keys on the seat, where I can see them from here. Then I'll put the money on the roof where you can see it."

The man laughed, a sound like gravel pouring. "Regular little Dabney Engh, aren't you? Is that what they teach you society debs at your fancy schools?"

Leisha had no idea who Dabney Engh was. She waited, watching the man try to think of a way to cheat her, and tried to hide her contempt. She thought of Tony.

"All right," he said, and slid out of the truck.

"Lock the door!"

He grinned, opened the door again, locked it. Leisha put the money on the roof, yanked open the driver's door, clambered in, locked the door, and powered up the window. The man laughed. She put the key into the ignition, started the truck, and drove toward the street. Her hands trembled.

She drove slowly around the block twice. When she came back, the man was gone, and the driver of the hovercar was still asleep. She had wondered if the man would wake him, out of sheer malice, but he had not. She parked the truck and waited.

An hour and a half later Alice and a nurse wheeled Stella out of the Emergency Entrance. Leisha leaped out of the truck and yelled, "Coming, Alice!" waving both her arms. It was too dark to see Alice's expression; Leisha could only hope that Alice showed no dismay at the battered truck, that she had not told the nurse to expect a red car.

Alice said, "This is Julie Bergadon, a friend that I called while you were setting Jordan's arm." The nurse nodded, uninterested. The two women helped Stella into the high truck cab; there was no back seat. Stella had a cast on her arm and looked drugged.

"How?" Alice said as they drove off.

Leisha didn't answer. She was watching a police hovercar land at the other end of the parking lot. Two officers got out and stride purposefully towards Alice's locked car under the skimpy maple.

"My God," Alice said. For the first time, she sounded frightened.

"They won't trace us," Leisha said. "Not to this truck. Count on it."

"Leisha." Alice's voice spiked with fear. "Stella's *asleep.*"

Leisha glanced at the child, slumped against Alice's shoulder. "No, she's not. She's unconscious from painkillers."

"Is that all right? Normal? For . . . her?"

"We can black out. We can even experience substance-induced sleep." Tony and she and Richard and Jeanine in the midnight woods. . . . "Didn't you know that, Alice?"

"No."

"We don't know very much about each other, do we?"

They drove south in silence. Finally Alice said, "Where are we going to take her, Leisha?"

"I don't know. Any one of the Sleepless would be the first place the police would check—"

"You can't risk it. Not the way things are," Alice said. She sounded weary. "But all my friends are in California. I don't think we could drive this rust bucket that far before getting stopped."

"It wouldn't make it anyway."

"What should we do?"

"Let me think."

At an expressway exit stood a pay phone. It wouldn't be data-shielded, as Groupnet was. Would Kevin's open line be tapped? Probably.

There was no doubt the Sanctuary line would be.

Sanctuary. All of them going there or already there, Kevin had said. Holed up, trying to pull the worn Allegheny Mountains around them like a safe little den. Except for the children like Stella, who could not.

Where? With whom?

Leisha closed her eyes. The Sleepless were out; the police would find Stella within hours. Susan Melling? But she had been Alice's all-too-visible stepmother, and was co-beneficiary of Camden's will; they would question her almost immediately. It couldn't be anyone traceable to Alice. It could only be a Sleeper that Leisha knew, and trusted, and why should anyone at all fit that description? Why should she risk so much on anyone who did? She stood a long time in the dark phone kiosk. Then she walked to the truck. Alice was asleep, her head thrown back against the seat. A tiny line of drool ran down her chin. Her face was white and drained in the bad light from the kiosk. Leisha walked back to the phone.

"Stewart? Stewart Sutter?"

"Yes?"

"This is Leisha Camden. Something has happened." She told the story tersely, in bald sentences. Stewart did not interrupt.

"Leisha—" Stewart said, and stopped.

"I need help, Stewart." *'I'll help you, Alice.' 'I don't need your help.'* A wind whistled over the dark field beside the kiosk and Leisha shivered. She heard in the wind the thin keen of a beggar. In the wind, in her own voice.

"All right," Stewart said, "this is what we'll do. I have a cousin in Ripley, New York, just over the state line from Pennsylvania the route you'll be driving east. It has to be in New York, I'm licensed in New York. Take the little girl there. I'll call my cousin and tell her you're coming. She's an elderly woman, was quite an activist in her youth, her name is Janet Patterson. The town is—"

"What makes you so sure she'll get involved? She could go to jail. And so could you."

"She's been in jail so many times you wouldn't believe it. Political protests going all the way back to Vietnam. But no one's going to jail. I'm now your attorney of record, I'm privileged. I'm going to get Stella declared a ward of the state. That shouldn't be too hard with the hospital records you established in Skokie. Then she can be transferred to a foster home in New York, I know just the place, people who are fair and kind. Then Alice—"

"She's resident in Illinois. You can't—"

"Yes, I can. Since those research findings about the Sleepless life span have come out, legislators have been railroaded by stupid constituents scared or jealous or just plain angry. The result is a body of so-called 'law' riddled with contradictions, absurdities, and loopholes. None of it will stand in the long run—or at least I hope not—but in the meantime it can all be exploited. I can use it to create the most goddamn convoluted case for Stella that anybody ever saw, and in meantime she won't be returned home. But that won't work for Alice—she'll need an attorney licensed in Illinois."

"We have one," Leisha said. "Candace Holt."

"No, not a Sleepless. Trust me on this, Leisha. I'll find somebody good. There's a man in—are you crying?"

"No," Leisha said, crying.

"Ah, God," Stewart said. "Bastards. I'm sorry all this happened, Leisha."

"Don't be," Leisha said.

When she had directions to Stewart's cousin, she walked back to the truck. Alice was still asleep, Stella still unconscious. Leisha closed the truck door as quietly as possible. The engine balked and roared, but Alice didn't wake. There was a crowd of people with them in the narrow and darkened cab: Stewart Sutter, Tony Indivino, Susan Melling, Kenzo Yagai, Roger Camden.

To Stewart Sutter she said, You called to inform me about the situation at Morehouse, Kennedy. You are risking your career and your cousin for Stella. And you stand to gain nothing. Like Susan telling me in advance about Bernie Kuhn's brain. Susan, who lost her life to Daddy's dream and regained it by her own strength. A contract without consideration for each side is not a contract: Every first-year student knows that.

To Kenzo Yagai she said, Trade isn't always linear. You missed that. If Stewart gives me something, and I give Stella something, and ten years from now Stella is a different person because of that and gives something to someone else as yet unknown—it's an ecology. An *ecology* of trade, yes, each niche needed, even if they're not contractually bound. Does a horse need a fish? *Yes.*

To Tony she said, Yes, there are beggars in Spain who trade nothing, give nothing, do nothing. But there are *more* than beggars in Spain. Withdraw from the beggars, you withdraw from the whole damn country. And you withdraw from the possibility of the ecology of help. That's what Alice wanted, all those years ago in her bedroom. Pregnant, scared, angry, jealous, she wanted to help *me,* and I wouldn't let her because I didn't need it. But I do now. And she did then. Beggars need to help as well as be helped.

And finally, there was only Daddy left. She could *see* him, bright-eyed, holding thick-leaved exotic flowers in his strong hands. To Camden she said, You were wrong. Alice *is* special. Oh, Daddy—the specialness of Alice! You were *wrong.*

As soon as she thought this, lightness filled her. Not the buoyant bubble of joy, not the hard clarity of examination, but something else: sunshine, soft through the conservatory glass, where two children ran in and out. She suddenly felt light herself, not buoyant but translucent, a medium for the sunshine to pass clear through, on its way to somewhere else.

She drove the sleeping woman and the wounded child through the night, east, toward the state line.

ABOUT THE AUTHORS

Anne McCaffrey has been writing science fiction for nearly half a century and published her first novel, *Restoree,* in 1967. She won acclaim for her third novel, *The Ship Who Sang,* an influential story of human-machine interface written well before the cyberpunk movement, but is renowned for her bestselling Pern novels, introduced in her Hugo Award-winning story "Weyr Search" and Nebula Award-winning story "Dragon Rider" in 1968. The Pern books, which are the chronicle of an Earth colony that is linked symbiotically to a native race of sentient dragons, number more than a dozen, including *The Dragonriders of Pern* trilogy, *The White Dragon* and *The Dolphins of Pern.* They are complemented by a trio of young adult novels—*Dragonsong, Dragonsinger* and *Dragondrums*—set in the same world, as well as the graphic novel rendering, *Dragonflight.* McCaffrey has been praised for her strong female characters, particularly in the Rowan sequence (*The Rowan, Damia, The Tower and the Hive*). She is also the author of *To Tide Pegasus* and *Pegasus in Flight,* a duo concerned with future psychic sleuths, and the Ireta books set on Dinosaur Planet. Her short fiction has been collected in *Get off the Unicorn,* and she has edited the anthology *Alchemy and Academe.* Recently she has co-authored the *Acorna* series, first with Elizabeth Moon, and more recently with Elizabeth Anne Scarborough.

Compared to many other speculative fiction writers, John Varley has produced only a handful of novels, but the breadth and scope of his talent is always impressive, and he shows no fear in taking chances with his characters, plots, or his vision of what the future might look like. His first novel, *The Ophiuchi Hotline,* deals with a planet Earth from which all of the technological advances have been removed by strange alien invaders who want to save the whales and dolphins. The "hotline" is a communication to an unknown being somewhere in the universe that wants humanity to survive and helps by feeding our race vital information when necessary. His next books, *Titan, Wizard,* and *Gaea,* form a trilogy chronicling the adventures of one Cirocco Jones, a female astronaut sent to Saturn, which, it turns out, is a sentient planet, to battle both aliens, and eventually, the "mad goddess" in order to save the alien race inhabiting the ringed world. His more recent works includes *Red Thunder,* about a maverick group of American astronauts' quest to beat the Chinese to Mars, and *Mammoth,* about a billionaire's plan to clone the extinct mammal. The best of his short fiction was recently collected in *The John Varley Reader.*

Orson Scott Card's landmark novels, *Ender's Game* and its sequel, *Speaker for the Dead,* made science fiction history when they became the first books ever to win both the Hugo and Nebula awards in successive years. With *Xenocide* and *Children of the Mind,* they make up one of the most celebrated sagas of modern science fiction, a richly imagined and morally complex inquiry into issues of war, genocide, and human responsibility. Much of Card's fantasy and science fiction interconnects to form inventive extended series, including his *Worthing Chronicle,* a linked group of stories related as the experiences as a messianic leader of a space colony, and his lengthy Hatrick River sequence, a folk history of an alternate United States whose individual chapters include

Seventh Son, Prentice Alvin, and *Heartfire.* Card's eloquent short fiction has been collected in *Maps in a Mirror.* He is also the author of the historical novel *A Woman of Destiny,* the dark fantasy novels *Lost Boys, The Treasure Box,* and *Homebody,* and the Hugo Award-winning guide *How to Write Science Fiction and Fantasy.*

The topics of Greg Bear's science fiction have ranged from nanotechnology run amok in *Blood Music,* to the translation of souls into awesome energy fields in the sf-horror hybrid *Psycholone,* and future evolution in *Darwin's Radio.* He is the author of the Songs of Earth and Power heroic diptych, comprised of *The Infinity Concerto* and *The Serpent Mage,* and two collections of short fiction, *The Wind from a Burning Woman* and *Tangents,* which include his stories "Hardfought" and "Blood Music," each of which won both the Hugo and Nebula Awards. Renowned for his hard science fiction epics, Bear has written the trilogy that includes *Legacy, Eon* and *Eternity,* which features a multiplicity of alternate worlds and timelines accessed through the interior of a hollow asteroid. Novels of equally impressive scope include the alien contact story *The Forge of God* and its sequel, *Anvil of Stars,* the nanotechnology opus *Queen of Angels,* and its follow-up *Slant,* and the Nebula Award-winning *Moving Mars,* which chronicles the fifty-year history of Earth's Mars colony and its revolt against the mother planet. Bear has also written *Dinosaur Summer,* a sequel to Sir Arthur Conan Coyle's *The Lost World,* and *Foundation and Chaos,* which builds on the concepts of Isaac Asimov's *Foundation Series.*

Connie Willis burst onto the science fiction scene in the early 1980s with her powerful short stories featuring all-too-human characters. Her work has won multiple Nebula and Hugo awards. Her first novel, *Lincoln's Dreams,* featured more fantasy in the plot of a woman who shares dreams about the Civil War, showed her assured characterization and deft plotting skills, and hinted of powerful books to come. Her later novels have not disappointed either; they include the impressive *Doomsday Book,* a time-traveling novel featuring a future researcher trapped back in medieval times during the Black Plague, *Uncharted Territory,* about the exploration of an alien planet, and *Remake,* her look at retroactive censorship and a possible version of political correctness in the future. Her short fiction has been collected in *Fire Watch, Distress Call, Daisy, In the Sun,* and *Impossible Things.*

David Brin's groundbreaking Uplift saga spans six novels (*Sundiver, Startide Rising,* and *The Uplift War,* followed by *Brightness Reef, Infinity's Shore,* and *Heaven's Reach*) and postulates a future where mankind has "uplifted" or given sapiency to both chimpanzees and dolphins. The human race is also locked in a struggle with four alien races, known as Patrons, for power and knowledge. His novel *The Postman* is considered a classic of post-apocalyptic fiction with its emphasis on the rebuilding of humanity instead of concentrating on the chaos that would occur afterward. His novel *Earth* deals with our planet in a future that has had practically every conceivable disaster happen, from ecological despoliation to technological overload to societal breakdowns, and postulates what happens next. *Glory Season* set in a matriarchal, society, deals with issues standard to both genders: breeding, sexual relations, the hierarchical classes, and the struggle to find a sense of self and purpose in a larger world. His work has won multiple Hugo and Locus Awards, the Nebula Award, the Balrog Award, and the John W. Campbell, Jr. Memorial Award.

Nancy Kress is the author of twenty-one books: thirteen novels of science fiction or fantasy, one young adult novel, two thrillers, three story collections, and two books on writing. Her books include *Probability Space*—the conclusion of a trilogy that began with *Probability Moon* and *Probability Sun*—and *Crossfire.* The trilogy concerns quantum physics, a space war, and the nature of reality. *Crossfire,* set in a different universe, explores various ways humanity might co-exist with aliens, even though mankind never understands either them or itself very well.

Her short fiction has won three Nebulas: in 1985 for "Out of All Them Bright Stars," in 1991 for the novella version of *Beggars In Spain* (which also won a Hugo), and in 1998 for "The Flowers of Aulit Prison." Her work has been translated into Swedish, French, Italian, German, Spanish, Portuguese, Polish, Croatian, Lithuanian, Romanian, Japanese, and Russian. She is also the monthly "Fiction" columnist for *Writer's Digest Magazine*, and is a regular teacher at Clarion Writer's Workshop.

Tanya Huff

The Finest in Fantasy

SING THE FOUR QUARTERS	0-88677-628-7
FIFTH QUARTER	0-88677-651-1
NO QUARTER	0-88677-698-8
THE QUARTERED SEA	0-88677-839-5

The Keeper's Chronicles

SUMMON THE KEEPER	0-88677-784-4
THE SECOND SUMMONING	0-88677-975-8
LONG HOT SUMMONING	0-7564-0136-4

Omnibus Editions:

WIZARD OF THE GROVE   0-88677-819-0
(Child of the Grove & The Last Wizard)
OF DARKNESS, LIGHT & FIRE   0-7564-0038-4
(Gate of Darkness, Circle of Light & The Fire's Stone)

To Order Call: 1-800-788-6262

DAW 21

TAD
WILLIAMS

TAILCHASER'S SONG

"Williams' fantasy, in the tradion of WATERSHIP DOWN,
captures the nuances and delights of feline behavior in a story
that should appeal to both fantasy and cat lovers. Readers
will lose their hearts to Tailchaser and his companions."
—*Library Journal*

"TAILCHASER'S SONG is more than just an absorbing
adventure, more than just a fanciful tale of cat lore. It is a
story of self-discovery...Fritti faces challenges—responsibility, loyalty, and loss—that are universal. His is the story of
growing up, of accepting change, of coming of age."
—*Seventeen*

"A wonderfully exciting quest fantasy. Fantasy fans are sure
to be enthralled by this remarkable book." —*Booklist*

0-88677-953-7

To Order Call: 1-800-788-6262

TAD WILLIAMS

Memory, Sorrow & Thorn

To Order Call: 1-800-788-6262

DAW 42

Tad Williams

THE WAR OF THE FLOWERS

"A masterpiece of fairytale worldbuilding."
—*Locus*

"Williams's imagination is boundless."
—*Publishers Weekly*
(Starred Review)

"A great introduction to an accomplished
and ambitious fantasist."
—*San Francisco Chronicle*

"An addictive world ... masterfully plays
with the tropes and traditions of
generations of fantasy writers."
—*Salon*

"A very elaborate and fully realized setting
for adventure, intrigue, and more
than an occasional chill."
—*Science Fiction Chronicle*

0-7564-0181-X

To Order Call: 1-800-788-6262

DAW 45